MW01673677

Christianity and Positivism a Series of Lectures to the Times on Natural Theology and Apologetics

Anatiposi

James McCosh

Christianity and Positivism a Series of Lectures to the Times on Natural Theology and Apologetics

Reprint of the original, first published in 1871.

1st Edition 2023 | ISBN: 978-3-38212-620-9

Anatiposi Verlag is an imprint of Outlook Verlagsgesellschaft mbH.

Verlag (Publisher): Outlook Verlag GmbH, Zeilweg 44, 60439 Frankfurt, Deutschland
Vertretungsberechtigt (Authorized to represent): E. Roepke, Zeilweg 44, 60439 Frankfurt, Deutschland
Druck (Print): Books on Demand GmbH, In de Tarpen 42, 22848 Norderstedt, Deutschland

CHRISTIANITY AND POSITIVISM:

A SERIES OF

LECTURES TO THE TIMES

ON

NATURAL THEOLOGY AND APOLOGETICS.

DELIVERED IN NEW YORK, JAN. 16 TO MARCH 20, 1871, ON THE "ELY FOUNDATION" OF THE UNION THEOLOGICAL SEMINARY.

BY

JAMES McCOSH, D.D., LL.D.,
PRESIDENT OF THE COLLEGE OF NEW JERSEY, PRINCETON.

NEW YORK:
ROBERT CARTER AND BROTHERS,
530 BROADWAY.
1871.

PREFACE.

THIS course of Lectures on Christianity and Positivism was delivered, by appointment, as the second course on the foundation established in the Union Theological Seminary by Mr. ZEBULON STILES ELY, of New York, in the following terms:—

"The undersigned gives the sum of ten thousand dollars to the Union Theological Seminary of the city of New York, to found a Lectureship in the same, the title of which shall be 'THE ELIAS P. ELY LECTURES ON THE EVIDENCES OF CHRISTIANITY.'

"The course of Lectures given on this foundation is to comprise any topics that serve to establish the proposition that Christianity is a religion from God, or that it is the perfect and final form of religion for man.

"Among the subjects discussed may be,—

"The Nature and Need of a Revelation;

"The Character and Influence of Christ and his Apostles;

"The Authenticity and Credibility of the Scriptures, Miracles and Prophecy;

"The Diffusion and Benefits of Christianity; and

"The Philosophy of Religion in its Relation to the Christian System.

"Upon one or more of such subjects a course of ten public Lectures shall be given at least once in two or three years. The appointment of the Lecturer is to be by the concurrent action of the directors and faculty of said Seminary and the undersigned; and it shall ordinarily be made two years in advance.

"The interest of the fund is to be devoted to the payment of the Lecturers, and the publication of the Lectures within a year after the delivery of the same. The copyright of the volumes thus published is to be vested in the Seminary.

"In case it should seem more advisable, the directors have it at their discretion at times to use the proceeds of this fund in providing special courses of lectures or instruction, in place of the aforesaid public lectures, for the students of the Seminary on the above-named subjects.

"Should there at any time be a surplus of the fund, the directors are authorized to employ it in the way of prizes for dissertations by students of the Seminary upon any of the above topics, or of prizes for essays thereon, open to public competition.

"ZEBULON STILES ELY.

"NEW YORK, May 8th, 1865."

TABLE OF CONTENTS.

Third Series.

CHRISTIANITY AND HISTORICAL INVESTIGATION.

Appendix.

LECTURES TO THE TIMES

ON

NATURAL THEOLOGY AND APOLOGETICS.

I.

The Argument from Design as affected by Modern Discoveries in Science. — Conservation of Force. — Star Dust. — Protoplasm. — Origin of Life.

MR. J. S. MILL recommends those who would establish the existence of God to stick to the argument from design. As it is lawful to learn wisdom from an opponent, I take his counsel; and I stand by the evidence furnished by the order and adaptation in the universe. The *a priori* proof, so proudly advanced by the rationalists of the age now passing away, is not likely to meet with much acceptance in the time now present, when rationalism is being devoured by sensationalism, and the transcendental philosophy, with its much admired crystals, is melting away, — to give us, may I hope, something better, as much so as the buds and blossoms of spring are superior to the frost-work of winter. The argument from design is that there are evidences everywhere, in heaven and earth, in plant and animal, of natural agents being so fitted to each other, and so combining to produce a beneficent end, as to show that intelligence must have been employed in co-ordinating and arranging them. When unfolded, it comprises a body of facts, and it involves a principle. The principle is that an effect implies a cause. The special consideration and defence of this law may be adjourned to a future lecture, when it will come up in more favorable circumstances to admit of a full discussion. In the first series of lectures in this course, we are invited to contemplate the phenomena and laws of the physical world, so far as they bear marks of being adapted to each other by a designing mind contemplating a good end.

The argument is one which commends itself to all minds, though it is put into shape only by the logician and the expounder of natural theology. The child finds the impression stealing in upon him, as he inspects the curious objects around him, — the fir cone, the flower, the berry, the structure of his favorite animal, or those lights kindled nightly in the heavens, or as he is taught to connect these daily gifts with God the giver. The peasant, the savage, feels it, as he sees the grass and trees springing and growing and bearing seed, as he is led to observe the self-preserving instincts of the brute creatures, as he takes a passing survey of the wondrous provisions for maintaining life in his own frame, or finds himself furnished with food and clothing by very complicated arrangements of Providence. Flowing spontaneously into the minds of all, the conviction will force itself into the innermost heart of the speculative unbeliever. "No one," said David Hume, as he walked home one beautiful evening with a friend, "can look up to that sky without feeling that it must have been put in order by an intelligent being." "But who made all these things ?" was the curt reply of Napoleon Bonaparte, who had been obliged to listen to the wretched sophistries of a set of French atheists, bred in the bloody revolutionary period, — "but who made all these things?" pointing to the heavens.

The argument is one and the same in all ages. "He that formed the eye, shall He not see?" is the way in which the Psalmist expresses it. Socrates is represented, in the "Memorabilia" of Xenophon, as pointing to the traces of purpose in the eye, the ear, and the teeth, and to the care taken of every individual man in the Divine providence. Though the argument is identical, yet it takes different forms in different ages; one reason of which is to be found in the circumstance that the physical facts require to be differently stated as science opens to us new views of the nature of the universe. Balbus the Stoic, the representative of theism in Cicero's treatise "De Natura Deorum," drew a solid enough argument from the order of the heavenly bodies, though he assumed that the sun moved round the earth. Those living since the acceptance of the theory of Copernicus expound the facts in a more scientific manner, but not more conclusively, as bearing on the relation of God to his works. The Scriptures tell us that man cannot number the stars, but it has been found that he can count the stars seen by the naked eye; but the science which enables him to do this has disclosed other stars, so that it is still true that the stars cannot be reckoned for multitude. It is much the same with the argument for the Divine existence: modern investigation modifies old views only to open new and grander ones. The peasant, who notices a watch going and pointing to the hour, is as sure that there is design in it as the mechanic who can trace the relation of all the parts, — the mainspring, the wheels, and the hands. And the same peasant is as sure that there is purpose in the hand as Sir Charles Bell was, when he pointed out the wonderful adaptations of the various bones and joints and muscles and nerves. A theistic writer living in the middle of the seventeenth century, — say Milton in writing "Paradise Lost," or Charnock in delivering his "Discourses on the Attributes," — could not expound the revolutions of the heavenly bodies in the same satisfactory manner as one living in the following century, when Newton had established the law of universal gravitation; but the one might have as reasonable a conviction as the other that "the heavens declare the glory of God."

It is a humiliating but instructive fact that many new discoveries in physical science have, in the first instance, been denounced as atheistic, because they were not conformable to the opinions which religious men had been led to entertain, not of God, but of the phenomena of the world. Even the illustrious Leibnitz charged the system of Newton with having an irreligious tendency, and (as I once heard Humboldt denouncing, in an interview which I had with him a few months before his death) sought to poison the mind of the famous Princess Sophie of Prussia, against him. It is a curious circumstance that the law of gravitation had to be defended on the side of religion, at the beginning of last century, by Maclaurin, in his "Account of the Discoveries of Sir Isaac Newton." In the last age, numbers trained in a narrow theological geology (not found in Scripture, but drawn out of it by wrong inference) opposed the discoveries as to the successive strata and races of animated beings on the earth's surface, and could scarcely be reconciled to them when such men as Buckland and Chalmers, Hitchcock and Hugh Miller, showed that these facts widened indefinitely the horizon of our vision, — added a new province to the universe of God, by disclosing a past history before unknown, — and opened new and grander views of the prescience and preordination of God. And, in our times, there are persons who cannot take in these new doctrines of natural history and comparative language, not because they run counter to any doctrine or precept of religion, but because they conflict with certain historical or scientific preconceptions which have become bound up with their devout beliefs.

All this shows that religious men *qua* religious men are not to be allowed to decide for us the truths of science. Conceive an Ecumenical Council at Rome, or an Assembly of Divines at Westminster, or an Episcopal Convocation at Lambeth, or a Congregational Council at Plymouth, or a Methodist Conference in Connecticut, taking upon it to decide for or against the discoveries of Sir Isaac Newton, or the grand doctrine established in our day of the Conservation of Force and Correlation of all the Physical Forces, on the ground of their being favorable or unfavorable to religion! I have heard fervent preachers denouncing the nebular hypothesis of the heavens and the theories of the origin of organic species in a manner and spirit which was only fitted to damage the religion which they meant to recommend, in the view of every man of science who heard them; and which drew from others of us the wish that they had kept by what they were fit for, proclaiming the gospel to perishing sinners, and illustrating the graces of the Christian character, and left science to men of science. On the other hand, our scientific men are not, as scientific men, qualified to find out and to estimate the theological bearings of the laws which they have discovered. For if there be a religious, there may also be an irreligious bias. There may be some as anxious in their hatred to expel God from his works as there are others resolute in their love to bring him in at times or in ways in which he does not choose to appear. The laws of the physical world are to be determined by scientific men, proceeding in the way of a careful induction of facts; and, so far as they follow their method, I have the most implicit faith in them, and I have the most perfect confidence that the truth which they discover will not run counter to any other truth. But when they pass beyond their own magic circle, they become weak as other men. I do not commit to them — I reserve to myself — the right of interpreting the religious bearings of those laws which they disclose to our wondering eyes.

We proceed to consider the religious aspect of some of the recent discoveries, real or supposed, of physical investigation; which it is all the more necessary to do, because there is a certain school studiously seeking to leave the impression that the argument from design has been set aside by an advanced science. We shall show that, while the proofs drawn by such writers as Paley from the wondrous leverage and curiously formed joints of the animal frame are untouched by recent researches and remain as strong and conclusive as ever, these new views opened of the history of the world disclose evidence which could not have been discovered in earlier ages.

I assume only the one principle already announced, that every effect is caused. Not that every thing has a cause, — for this would make us look for a cause of the uncaused, which is God, — but that every thing which begins to be has a cause. In employing this law, I do not care for the present whether it be regarded as *a priori* or *a posteriori*, as discovered by reason or by experience. It is acknowledged to be presupposed and involved in all scientific research, to be the most universal law of the operations of physical nature, a law with no known exceptions. In our extensive journey through the ages of time we shall discover many things which begin to appear; and we feel justified in arguing that they must have a cause, a cause adequate to produce them.

In conducting our argument, it may be proper to premise two points to avert misapprehension. First, we are not to be precluded from seeking and discovering a final cause, because we have found an efficient cause. Using, as being as good as any other, the illustration which has become associated with the name of Paley, — on seeing a watch, we argue that it has a final cause, a purpose to serve, a contemplated end: this we infer from the fitting of pin, wheel, axle, cylinder, and hands, in order to intimate the time to us who need "to number our days." Yet this little machine has been fashioned, and it continues to go, solely by mechanical power. It is the same with the traces of design we discover in nature: they all spring from the powers and properties of material agencies; but the proof of purpose is derived from the collocation of things, from the disposition of the parts, from the adaptation of property to property, from their being jointed on one to another, from their being dovetailed into each other, from their combining and concurring towards a given end in which order and benevolence are manifested. Our inference is, that these forces, blind and unintelligent in themselves, must be directed by an intelligence which sees and foresees. The rays of light come from the sun ninety-five millions of miles away: they come in vibrations according to mechanical laws. The eye is made up of coats, humors, lenses, nerves, all formed according to chemical and physiological laws. The rays of light emitted from the sun are reflected from objects on the earth, and alighting on the eye are refracted and combined so as to form on the retina an image of the objects from which they have come, and which we see in consequence. The adaptations necessary to accomplish this are many and varied, and some of them of a very delicate and recondite character. To mention only two instances. There is the adjustment of the eyeball to objects at varying distances so as to allow the rays of light to form the image on the retina, and thus furnish distinct vision. Helmholtz has shown that this is done without any will or effort on our part. It is done by the ciliary muscle, which contracts for near objects and relaxes for distant ones. Again, Newton thought that there could not be a refracting telescope of any great power, because of the aberration of the rays of light as they are drawn to a focus. Dollond, in a later age, ingeniously avoided this difficulty by an achromatic apparatus in which the object glass was composed of crown glass and flint glass, and the dispersive power of the one was counteracted by that of the other. But there has been all along, if not an identical, yet an analogous provision in the eye, so that in the healthy organism the image is perfect, having neither penumbra nor prismatic colors. Now the rays of light coming from the sun have not formed the eye, nor has the eye formed the rays of light. The question arises, Whence the correspondence between the two? Proceeding on the principles on which science proceeds, it is as certain as any truth in science that the conformity must have risen from a preordained disposition of the two, brought about by a series of causes evidently contemplated from the beginning. "And he that formed the eye, shall he not see?" When Napoleon asked Laplace why God was not mentioned in his "Méchanique Céleste," he replied, "I have no need of this hypothesis." But, following the principles of reason, there is need of such an hypothesis to account, if not for the agencies, yet for the harmonious combination of agencies in the fitting of every one thing to every other, which we see alike in the stars in their courses, and the structure and movements of the eye, and indeed, if only we carefully inspect it, in every object in the earth and in the heavens.

It is necessary to make such simple and obvious statements as these, because not a few physicists are themselves laboring under the impression, and are conveying it to others, that as soon as we have discovered the physical cause of an occurrence it is no longer necessary to call in a final cause; and, as Laplace expressed it, final causes in "the eyes of philosophers are nothing more than the expression of the ignorance in which we are of the real causes," and "are being pushed away to the bounds of knowledge." But the correct account is, that final cause may best be seen in the concurrence of physical agents to produce a given end; and the advance of knowledge, so far from driving back final cause, only enables us to give a more definite account of its nature, and to specify the powers which are made to combine, to effect the obviously contemplated result. Darwin has shown that certain plants are fertilized by insects, such as bees carrying the pollen from the male to the female; and thus he accounts for the prevalence of certain forms and colors in flowers. Be it so, we are only enabled the better to see in these insects the means of accomplishing a designed end. There is a like error lurking in a favorite principle of Hegel: "That which they call the final cause of a thing is nothing but its inward nature." Now it is doubtless the inward nature of a physical cause to produce its effect; but the purpose or design expressed by the phrase "final cause" is seen in the coincidence and co-operation of independent physical causes, so as to secure an end which no one of them could accomplish by its own inward nature. It is from the collocation of canine teeth, strong claws and muscles, and a flesh-digesting stomach, in carnivorous animals, that we see there has been an end contemplated by the harmony, which could not have been effected by the inward nature of any of the parts.

To correct prevailing misapprehension, it is necessary to announce a second preliminary point: that our argument does not require us to know what are the ultimate powers of nature. These are certainly not known at present, and they may never be known by the science of man. If they be many, there is need of mutual accommodation and reciprocal action, to suit them one to the other, and make them accomplish a good end. If they be few, there is equal need of a nice adjustment, to make them fulfil the infinitely varied purposes which they serve. If the number of elementary bodies in nature be sixty, as chemical science says, provisionally, that they are; and if the number of properties possessed by them — mechanical, chemical, electric, magnetic, vital — be also numerous, there is surely need of a marshalling of these hosts, to keep them from clashing, and working confusion and destruction. Or, if scientific research can succeed in showing that all these may be reduced to a dozen, or half a dozen, an amazing skill must be required to make them produce those infinitely diversified bodies and those wonderfully constructed frames which we see in nature. I have heard Paganini draw exquisite music from one string, wrought upon in all sorts of directions and with all kinds of flexures; and I have listened to strains produced by hundreds of instruments, each with a complexity of strings: but in the one case, as in the other, combination and skill of the highest order were required to create and sustain the melody and the harmony.

Carrying with us these two principles, so obvious, and yet so frequently overlooked, let us now take a glance at some of the recent speculations as to the construction of the universe. We find in the physical world at least two ultimate existences, — Matter and Force. I believe that we know both of these by intuition, and by no process can we get rid of the one or the other. As to Force, it will be expedient to look for a moment at the grandest scientific truth established in our day, — a doctrine worthy of being placed alongside that of universal gravitation, — I mean that of the Conservation of Physical Force; according to which, the sum of Force, actual and potential, in the knowable universe is always one and the same: it cannot be increased, and it cannot be diminished. It has long been known that no human, no terrestrial power can add to or destroy the sum of Matter in the cosmos. You commit a piece of paper to the flames, and it disappears; but it is not lost: one part goes up in smoke, and another goes down in ashes; and it is conceivable that at some future time the two may unite, and once more form paper. "Why may not imagination trace the noble dust of Alexander, till we find it stopping a bung-hole?" "As thus: Alexander died, Alexander was buried, Alexander returneth to dust; the dust is earth; of earth we make loam: and why of that loam, whereto he was converted, might they not stop a beer-barrel?

> "Imperial Cæsar, dead, and turned to clay,
> Might stop a hole to keep the wind away:
> O, that the earth, which kept the world in awe,
> Should patch a wall t' expel the winter's flaw!"

As man cannot create or annihilate matter, so he cannot create or annihilate force. This doctrine has been scientifically established in our day by men like Mayer, Joule, Henry, and others. We now regard it as one and the same force, but under a vast variety of modifications, which warms our houses and our bodily frames, which raises the steam and impels the engine, which effects the different chemical combinations, which flashes in the lightning and lives in the plant.* Man may direct the force, and make it go this way or that way; but he can do so only by means of force under a different form, — by force brought into his frame by his food, obtained directly, or indirectly through the animal, from the plant, which has drawn it from the sun; and as he uses or abuses it, he cannot lessen or augment it. I move my hand; and, in doing so, I move the air, which raises insensibly the temperature of the room, and may lead to chemical changes, and excite electric and magnetic currents, and take the circuit of the universe without being lost or lessened. Now the bearing of this doctrine on religion seems to be twofold. First, it furnishes a more striking manifestation than any thing known before of the One God, with his infinitely varied perfections, — of his power, his knowledge, his wisdom, his love, his mercy; and we should see that one Power blowing in the breeze, smiling in the sunshine, sparkling in the stars, quickening us

* I was prepared, from its first announcement, to receive this truth: for it follows directly from a doctrine laid down by me twenty-one years ago, in my work on "The Method of the Divine Government" (Book II.), that all bodies possess fixed properties, which cannot be increased nor lessened.

as we bound along in the felt enjoyment of health, efflorescing in every form and hue of beauty, and showering down daily gifts upon us. The profoundest minds in our day, and in every day, have been fond of regarding this force, not as something independent of God, but as the very power of God acting in all action; so that "in him we live, and move, and have our being." But, secondly, it shows us that in God's works, as in God himself, there is a diversity with the unity; so that force manifests itself now in gravity, now in molecular attraction and motion, now in chemical affinities among bodies, now in magnetic and diamagnetic properties, now in vital assimilation. And we see that all these forces are correlated: so that the doctrine of the Correlation of all the varied Physical Forces stands alongside of the Conservation of the one Physical Force; and by the action of the whole, and of every part made to combine and harmonize, there arise beauteous forms and harmonious colors; the geometry of crystals; the types of the plant and of every organ of the plant, the branches, the roots, the leaves, the petals, the pistils, the stamens; and the types of the animal, so that every creature is fashioned after its kind, and every limb takes its predetermined form, while there is an adaptation of every one part to every other, of joint to column, and joint to joint, of limb to limb, and of limb to body, of the ear to the vibrating medium, and the nostrils to odors, and the eye to the varied undulations of light.

So much for Force, with its Correlations. But with the Forces we have the Matter of the universe, in which, I believe, the Forces reside. It is maintained that the worlds have been formed out of Star Dust. Now, I have to remark as to this star dust, first of all, that it is at best an hypothesis. No human eye, unassisted, has ever seen it, as it gazed, on the clearest night, into the depths of space. It is doubtful whether the telescope has ever alighted upon it, in its widest sweeps. Lord Rosse's telescope, in its first look into the heavens, resolved what had before been reckoned as star dust into distinctly formed stars. But I am inclined to admit the existence of star dust as an hypothesis. I believe it explains phenomena which require to be explained, and which cannot otherwise be accounted for. I allow it freely, that there is evidence that the planets and moons and sun must have been fashioned out of some such substance, at first incandescent, and then gradually cooling. But, then, it behoves us to look a little more narrowly into the nature of this star dust. Was it ever a mass of unformed matter, without individuality, without properties? Did it contain within itself these sixty elementary substances, with their capacities, their affinities, their attractions, their repulsions? When a meteor comes, as a stranger, within our terrestrial sphere, either out of this original star dust or out of planets which have been reduced to the state of original star dust, it is found to have the same components as bodies on our earth, and these with the same properties and affinities. The spectroscope, which promises to reveal more wonders than the telescope or microscope, shows the same elements — such as hydrogen and sodium — in the sun and stars as in the bodies on the earth's surface. The star dust, then, has already in it these sixty elementary bodies, with all their endowments, — gravitating, mechanical, chemical, magnetic. Whence these elements? Whence their correlations, their attractions, their affinities, their fittings into each other, their joint action? It is by no means the strongest point in my cumulative argument; but it does look as if, even at this stage, there had been a harmonizing power at work, and displaying foresight and intelligence.

As to this material, we must hold one or other of two opinions. One is, that it had from the beginning all the capacities which afterwards appear in the worlds formed out of it. It has not only the mechanical, but the chemical, the electric powers of dead matter; the vital properties of plants and animals, such as assimilation, absorption, contractility; and the attributes of the conscious mind, as of perception by the senses, of memory, imagination, comparison, of the appreciation of beauty, of sorrow, of joy, of hope, of fear, of reason, of conscience, of will. These capabilities may not yet be developed: but they are there in a latent, a dormant state in the incandescent matter; and are ready, on the necessary conditions being supplied, to rise to the instincts of animals, — to the love of a mother for her offspring, — to the sagacity of the dog, the horse, or the elephant, — to the genius of a Moses, a Homer, a Socrates, a Plato, an Aristotle, a Paul, a John, a Shakespeare, a Milton, a Newton, a Leibnitz, or an Edwards. Were all this capacity in the star dust, I would be constrained to seek for a cause of it in a Power possessed of knowledge, wisdom, and beneficence, planting seeds in that soil to come forth in due season. But there is another supposition: that these qualities were not in the original matter, but were added from age to age, — it may be, according to law; and if so, they must have come from a Power out of and beyond the star dust, from a Power possessed of reason and affection. I know not that science can determine absolutely which of these alternatives it should take. But take either; and, on the principle of effect implying cause, the mind must rise to the contemplation of a Being who must himself be possessed of intelligence, in order to impart intelligence.

This star dust has a greater heaviness or thickness of parts in certain places than at others: and, by the attraction of its particles, masses of it begin to rotate, and one planet is set off after another; and the planets cast off satellites, or rings; and the sun settles in the centre, with bodies circulating round him. All this has taken place according to natural law: but we infer that there has been a guardian Intelligence guiding and watching the process; otherwise, the heavy parts causing the rotation might have been in the wrong places in reference to each other, and the circling bodies at the wrong distances; and, as the result, a scene of never-ceasing confusion, in which the elements and powers would have been warring with each other, and rendering it impossible that there should appear any of the higher products of life, intelligence, and love.

The earth is now formed, an oblate spheroid, spinning round its own axis, and round the sun. By the action and counteraction of the inner heat and outer cold, there comes to be a solid land, with a corrugated surface of hill and dale, ocean and atmosphere. There follow rocks, deposited by water or thrown out by fire; and, as these are found to come forth, by aqueous or igneous process, in a state of order and adaptation, and are made to serve a beneficent end towards the living creatures, we argue that they are constructed on a plan.

But as yet there has been no life, vegetable or animal. But the protoplasm now appears. We shall let Professor Huxley describe that now famous substance, which he has taken under his special protection, and by which he works such wonders. It is the material out of which all living forms are made, as pottery is from the clay; it is the elementary life-stuff of all plants and all animals. You may see it as well as anywhere else in the hairs to which the nettle owes its stinging power. "The whole hair consists of a very delicate outer case of wood, closely applied to the inner surface of which is a layer of semi-fluid matter full of innumerable granules of extreme minuteness. This semi-fluid lining is protoplasm, which thus constitutes a kind of bag full of limpid liquid." The protoplasmic layer of the nettle hair is seen to be in a condition of unceasing activity. Local contractions of the whole thickness of its substance pass slowly and gradually from point to point, and give rise to the appearance of progressive waves, just as the bending of the successive stalks of corn by a breeze produces the apparent billows of a cornfield. In addition to these movements, and independently of them, the granules are driven in relatively rapid streams, and there is a general stream up one side and down another. This protoplasm, according to Professor Huxley,* is "the formal basis of all life. It is the clay of the potter; which, bake and paint it as he will, remains clay, separated by artifice, and not by nature, from the commonest brick or sun-dried clod. Thus it becomes clear that living powers are cognate, and that all living forms are fundamentally of one character." He says that "all vital action is the result of the molecular forces of the protoplasm which displays it. And if so, it must be true, in the same sense and to the same extent, that the thoughts to which I am now giving utterance, and your thoughts regarding them, are the expression of molecular changes in that matter of life which is the source of our other vital phenomena."

Now, upon this account of protoplasm I have to remark that the great body of naturalists do not

* Physical Basis of Life.

allow that it is correct. One of the most erudite men of our day, Dr. Stirling,* in a paper read before the Royal College of Physicians of Edinburgh, has shown that the researches of the eminent German physiologists are against him. They do not admit that one and the same protoplasm is the matter of all organisms. It is certain that all protoplasm is not chemically identical. The protoplasm differs in different tissues, is different in the bone from what it is in the muscle, and different in the nerves and brain from what it is in any other part of the frame. Again, it is affirmed that the protoplasm differs in different plants and animals, each of which has its own kind, which is not interchangeable with that of the rest.

But we may let Mr. Huxley's account of it pass. From his description of it, it is evident that this elementary life-stuff is a very complex body, with very peculiar endowments, — quite as likely to work evil as to work good, and requiring to be directed in order to operate beneficently. It is composed chemically of carbon, hydrogen, oxygen, and nitrogen; in one word, of protein. But then protein is not protoplasm: no power known to us can turn protein into protoplasm. Science, at its present advanced stage, cannot change dead matter into living matter. No chemist can do it in his laboratory. The most prying inquiry, by microscope or otherwise, into the laboratory of nature, has not detected her producing living matter in the form of proto-

* As Regards Protoplasm.

plasm, or any other, except by matter already living. No known plant can live upon the uncompounded elements of protoplasm. "A plant," says Mr. Huxley himself, "supplied with pure carbon, hydrogen, oxygen, and nitrogen, phosphorus, sulphur, and the like, would as infallibly die as the animal in his bath of smelling-salts, though it would be surrounded by all the constituents of protoplasm."

Professor Huxley, indeed, tells us that "when carbon, hydrogen, oxygen, and nitrogen are brought together under certain conditions, they give rise to the still more complex body, protoplasm; and this protoplasm exhibits the phenomena of life." Under *certain conditions:* we must not let these words slip in so quietly, as Mr. Huxley would have it. These conditions, be they what they may, constitute the difference between dead protein and living protoplasm. And here I may remark that Mr. Mill has been showing (I think successfully, and I have been aiding him in my own way) that what are usually called conditions are truly parts of the cause, which is the sum of the conditions, — the cause, as I have labored to prove, being dual, plural, complex, always implying more than one agent; and it is only when all are present that the effect is produced. We say the organ produces music on the condition of one playing on it; but surely the man playing is as essential a part of the cause as the organ itself.* By no skill can the chemist turn

* "It is very common to single out one only of the antecedents under the denomination of Cause, calling the others

protein into protoplasm. Professor Huxley thinks it can be done on conditions to him unknown. When he knows what the conditions are, and makes them known to me, I am sure I will be able to discover adaptation and design in them. Herbert Spencer tells us that chemists have shown that many sup-

merely Conditions." "The real cause is the whole of these antecedents; and we have, philosophically speaking, no right to give the name of cause to one of them, exclusive of the others."—*Mill's Logic*, B. III. c. v. § 3. I have shown that in material nature there is always need of the action of two or more agents, in order to an effect. —*Method of Divine Government*, B. II. c. i. § 1. *An Examination of Mr. J. S. Mill's Philosophy*, c. xiii.: "If a ball moves in consequence of another striking it, there is need of the one ball as well as the other; and the cause, properly speaking, consists of the two in a relation to each other. But not only is there a duality or plurality in the cause: there is the same (Mr. Mill has not noticed it) in the effect. The effect consists not merely of the one ball, the ball struck and set in motion, but also of the other ball which struck it, and which has now lost part of its momentum. By carrying out this doctrine, we can determine what is meant by 'condition' and 'occasion,' when the phrases are applied to the operation of causation. When we speak of an agent requiring a 'condition,' an 'occasion,' or 'circumstances,' in order to its action, we refer to the other agent or agents required, that it may produce a particular effect. Thus, that fire may burn, it is necessary to have fuel or a combustible material. In order that my will may move my arm, it is needful to have the concurrence of a healthy motor nerve. So much for the dual or plural agency in the cause. But there is a similar complexity in the effect," &c. To apply this general principle to the case before us: protein, it is said, may become protoplasm under certain conditions. These conditions, whatever they be, constitute the difference between the two; and Mr. H. has thrown no light on the production of protoplasm, till he has shown us what are these conditions, which ought to be represented as forming an essential part of the cause.

posed organic substances are inorganic. Be it so, that men may have made a mistake in the past which they are seeking to rectify in the present. And then, in the usual dogmatic way of a man who may see clearly much truth, but does not see other truths by which it is modified, he assures us that no chemist doubts but he will be able to turn inorganic into organic matter. All I have to say on this is, that when the chemist has done it, and shown the way by which he has done it, I am confident I will be able to point out a curious adaptation in these conditions previously unknown, but now known, by which he has accomplished the feat. If the things composing the conditions were in the star dust, they were there as seeds ready to burst forth in due time. If they have come from without, they have come in so appropriately as to show that they have come of purpose, — whether by natural law or not, we may not be able to tell till the man of science has made them known to us.

And then "protoplasm," says Stirling, "can only be produced by protoplasm, and each of all the innumerable varieties of protoplasm only by its own kind. For the protoplasm of the worm we must go to the worm, and for that of the toadstool to the toadstool. In fact, if all living beings came from protoplasm, it is quite as certain that but for living beings protoplasm would disappear." Where then did we get the first protoplasm and the various kinds of protoplasm, is still the question.

And then it is to be remembered that naturalists

do not admit that protoplasm is all that is necessary to produce the living organism. It has long been known that organized matter, vegetable and animal, is made up of cells. "All the great German histologists still hold by the cell, and can hardly open their mouths without mention of it." "They speak still of cells as self-complete organisms that move and grow, that nourish and reproduce themselves, and that perform specific functions. *Omnis cellula e cellula* is the rubric they work under as much now as ever." Not only so, but it seems that "brain cells only generate brain cells, and bone cells bone cells." If a cell can only be produced from a cell, the question when and whence and how do we get the first cell is still pressed upon us, and requires us to call in a new set of conditions, which I hold must imply a fitting and a purpose.

Nor is this all. Not only do all cells proceed from cells; but all organisms, all plants and animals, proceed from a seed or egg. It is still true as ever, *omne vivum ab ovo*. Not even protoplasm can give us an organized being, even the lowest, without a germ. An attempt was made a few years ago by M. Pouchet to get organized beings, not from unorganized, which he did not try, but from stagnant water containing organized matter without germs. But M. Pasteur, the distinguished naturalist of Paris, came after him and showed that there must have been germs in the water which was employed. He showed first that, if you allowed him to destroy all germs in the matter experimented on by exposing it to a sufficiently high temperature, no living creatures would appear. He showed farther — by experiments conducted in low, marshy places, then on the Jura range, and finally on the high Alps — that living beings did or did not appear just according as there were seeds in the organized matter; that is, that they came forth in greatest numbers in the low, marshy places, in smaller numbers in the higher region of Jura, and that very few appeared in the cold region of the Upper Alps. And in regard to the general question, he has demonstrated that when air is passed through cotton wool, which, acting as a strainer, arrests the germs, no life can be made to appear. And to prove that this was not effected by any occult change produced in the air by cotton wool, he did the same by a bent tube, which allows free passage to the air, but does not allow the germs to pass, as in doing so they would have to mount upward. These experiments were reckoned as decisive at the time, and are referred to by the great body of naturalists in Great Britain and on the Continent as decisive still. Mr. Huxley refers to them in his recent address to the British Association for the Advancement of Science, and says: "They appear to me now, as they did seven years ago, to be models of accurate experimentation and logical reasoning." It is thus shown that not only is there no proof of such a thing as spontaneous generation, — that is, the production of organized out of unorganized matter, — but that there cannot be organisms formed out of organic matter till a seed has been deposited. The question again comes up, Where, when, and whence did we get the first seed or living creature producing seed after its kind? When they show us this, I engage, if they do it while I am alive, to point out some nice adaptations in the production of this before unknown phenomenon.

I am aware that Dr. Bastian has, within the last year, laid before the Royal Society of London a set of experiments, which seem to yield a different result, and to prove that living beings may and do arise, as he expresses it, *de novo*.* Hitherto it has been believed that 100° Centigrade would destroy all organic germs. But he says he "has found organisms in organic fluids, either acid or alkaline, which, whilst enclosed within hermetically sealed and airless flasks, had been submitted not only to such a temperature, but even to one varying 146° C. and 153° C. for four hours." I find that Professor Huxley has no faith in the accuracy of these experiments. "I believe that the organisms which he has got out of his tubes are exactly those which he has put into them. I believe that he has used impure materials, and that what he imagines to have been the gradual development of life and organization in his solutions is the very simple result of the settling together of the solid impurities, which he was not sufficiently careful to see, in their scattered condition, when the solutions were made." But supposing these experiments to have been performed with unimpeachable

* See Nature, July, 1870.

accuracy, what has he established by them? Not that animated beings can be produced without seeds, but merely that certain seeds can bear exposure to a higher temperature than they have hitherto been supposed to be capable of standing. Professor Huxley says that "even if the results of the experiments are trustworthy, it by no means follows that there has been life without a germ. The resistance of living matter to heat is known to vary within considerable limits, and to depend to some extent upon the chemical and physical qualities of the surrounding medium. But if, in the present state of science, the alternative is offered us, either germs can stand a greater heat than has been supposed, or the molecules of dead matter, for no valid or intelligible reason that is assigned, are liable to rearrange themselves into living bodies, exactly such as can be demonstrated to be frequently produced in another way, I cannot understand how choice can be, even for a moment, doubtful." He sums up: "The evidence direct and indirect in favor of Biogenesis [that all life comes from life] must, I think, be admitted to be of great weight." After making this statement so frankly, he thinks he may indulge in a speculation for which he admits he has no proof, and the reasoning involved in which is as illogical as Dr. Bastian's experiments are unscientific: "I think it would be the height of presumption for any man to say that the conditions, under which matter assumes the properties we call 'vital,' may not some day be artificially brought together. All that I feel justified in affirming is, that I see no reason for believing that the feat has been performed yet." But then, "If it were given me to look beyond the abyss of geologically recorded time to the still more remote period when the earth was passing through physical and chemical conditions, which it can no more see again than a man may recall his infancy, I should expect to be a witness of the evolution of living protoplasm from not living matter," he adds, "under forms of great simplicity." I suspect that he has an idea that his favorite protoplasm may be there, and gendering life there. "But I beg you to recollect that I have no right to call my opinion any thing but an act of philosophic faith." May it not be true of this faith, what Mr. Huxley would allow to be true of some religious faiths, that the wish is father to the thought, and that we are inclined to believe what we wish to be true? It may be that in some way, at present inexplicable, lower life did then appear; but over against this faith I set the one which I cherish, on the ground of the whole analogy of nature, that if that way could be explicated we should certainly find there, as we find everywhere, traces of a purpose. But I stand on firmer ground when I maintain that, when known facts are against us, it is utterly unscientific to appeal to what is and must ever be unknown.

We have now protoplasm as the food, and cells to feed upon them, and a germ cell: but we have not, after all, the organized plant or animal; we have not the rose, or the lily, or the oak; we have not even the lichen or the zoöphyte. We have merely the stone and mortar necessary to the erection of the structure. In addition, there must needs be some music, like that which brought together the stones of ancient Thebes, to co-ordinate the materials of which the universe is composed; or, as more reasonable, there must be a builder, who is also an architect, so to arrange them that they may be turned into the form of the pine, the oak, the eagle, or the lion, or that goodly house in which we dwell, and which is "so fearfully and wonderfully made."

Let us suppose that, by constant accretion of powers, we have now the plant: the question is started, How has this risen to the animal? "Notwithstanding," says Professor Huxley, "all the fundamental resemblances which exist between the powers of the protoplasm in plants and animals, they present a striking difference in the fact that plants can manufacture fresh protoplasm out of mineral compounds, whereas animals are obliged to procure it ready made, and hence in the long run depend on plants. Upon what conditions [that convenient word comes in once more] this difference in the powers of the two great divisions of the world of life depends, nothing is at present known." Whether he knows it or not, there must be some cause, or, if he prefers, "condition," of the plant being turned into the animal.

And animals — except, it may be, a few transitional forms at the base of the scale — have Sensation. Whence this sensation, so different from the properties of matter, — this sensation not found in unorganized matter, not even in the plant, and not manifested till the animal appears? Was it in the original matter, — in the incandescent matter out of which our earth was formed? One trembles at the very thought; as, in such scorching heat, the animal must have been in a state of excruciating and intolerable anguish, — we can conceive, seeking extinction, and incapable of finding it. And if the sensation came in at a later date, I ask, Whence? There is surely no power in nature capable of generating sensation out of particles of matter not themselves capable of sensation?

Since the immediately preceding thoughts were written, I find Professor Tyndall following somewhat the same train, in a paper read at the late meeting of the British Association, but avoiding the legitimate conclusion in a very illegitimate way. "The gist of our present inquiry regarding the introduction of life is this: Does it belong to what we call matter? or is it an independent principle inserted into matter at some suitable epoch, — say, when the physical conditions became such as to permit of the development of life?" "There are the strongest grounds for believing that, during a certain period of its history, the earth was not, nor was it fit to be, the theatre of life. Whether this was ever a nebulous period, or merely a molten period, does not much matter; and if we resort to the nebulous condition, it is because the probabilities are really on its side. Our question is this: Did creative energy pause until the nebulous matter had condensed? until the earth had been detached? until the solar fire had so far withdrawn from the earth's vicinity as to permit a crust to gather round the planet? Did it wait until the air was isolated? until the seas were formed? until evaporation, condensation, and the descent of rain had begun? until the sun's rays had become so tempered by distance and by waste as to be chemically fit for the decompositions necessary to vegetable life? Having waited through those æons until the proper conditions had set in, did it send the fiat forth, 'Let life be'? These questions define a hypothesis, not without its difficulties, but the dignity of which was demonstrated by the nobleness of the men whom it sustained. However the convictions of individuals here and there may be influenced, the process must be slow which commends the hypothesis of natural evolution to the public mind. For what are the core and essence of this hypothesis? Strip it naked, and you stand face to face with the notion that not alone the more ignoble forms of animalcular or animal life, not alone the nobler forms of the horse and lion, not alone the exquisite and wonderful mechanism of the human body, but that the human mind itself — emotion, intellect, will, and all these phenomena — were once latent in a fiery cloud. Surely the mere statement of such a notion is more than a refutation." "I do not think that any holder of the evolution hypothesis would say that I overstate or overstrain it in any way. I merely strip it of all vagueness, and bring it before you, unclothed and unvarnished, the notions by which it must stand or fall. Surely these notions represent an absurdity too monstrous to be entertained by any sane mind." The difficulty in the way of carrying out the hypothesis, that all things — mind and body and all their properties — are derived by development from star dust is powerfully put, and should lay an arrest on those who speak so dogmatically of the possibility of accounting for all things by natural law. After having made this strong and apparently satisfactory statement, he tries to lessen the effect of it, by hinting that the difficulties may be lessened, if not removed, by falling back upon a philosophic law, — that of Relativity, which has been adopted by the school to which he belongs; and by hinting that the perplexities may arise from erroneous traditional views about mind and matter.* It will be necessary thoroughly to examine that

* "Why are these notions absurd? and why should sanity reject them? The law of relativity, which plays so important a part in modern philosophy, may find its application here. These evolution notions are absurd, monstrous, and fit only for the intellectual gibbet, in relation to the ideas concerning matter which were drilled into us when young. Spirit and matter have ever been presented to us in the rudest contrast; the one as all noble, the other as all vile. But is this correct?" Speaking of certain supposed enlightened minds, with which he evidently concurs: "They have as little fellowship with the atheist who says there is no God, as with the theist who professes to know the mind of God." This language points to some seemingly very profound truth, which it will be necessary to examine, when it will be found to look so large because of the mist in which we see it.

general doctrine, and the application of it to mind and body, which are alleged to be one and the same; so that, in certain conditions, mind might come out of matter. This will be undertaken in the second series of these Lectures. But, before doing this, we must take up this whole subject of Development, and the Origin of Species, and the Law of Natural Selection, in their relation to the lower animals, to man, and to human history. I am satisfied if in this Lecture I have succeeded in showing that the argument from design is not undermined by modern discoveries; and that, through the process by which the universe has reached its present condition, there runs an evidence of pre-arrangement, skill, and purpose,— quite as much so as in the formation of threads into a web in the loom; as in the types taking their proper places so as to print a volume; as in the dispositions of the soldiers in the campaigns of Hannibal, of Washington, or of Moltke.

II.

Natural Selection. — Origin of Man. — Historical Development. — Christ and the Moral Power.

IN these Lectures, I am considering the argument from design in its application to the subjects discussed in modern science. In the last lecture, I have shown that we have numerous examples of adaptation and purpose in the production of plants and animals. We have seen that no known natural power can produce organized out of unorganized matter, can produce protoplasm out of protein, can generate a cell without a parent cell, or a plant or an animal without a seed or germ, or a sentient animal from insentient matter. But the question has often occurred to me, Is religion essentially bound up with the settlement, one way or other, of these scientific questions?

Suppose it proven that there is such a thing as spontaneous generation: would religion thereby be overthrown, either in its evidences, its doctrines, or its precepts? I have doubts if it would. The great body of thinkers in ancient times — even those most inclined to theism — seem to have believed that lower creatures sprang out of the dust of the earth, without the need of a previous germ. Some of the profoundest theologians and ablest defenders of religion in the early church were believers in the doctrine of spontaneous generation, — which may be consistently held in modern times by believers in natural and revealed religion. The establishment of the need of a germ, in order to the production of life, does not carry us back three centuries. There is really no ground for the fears of the timid, on the one hand, nor, on the other hand, for the arrogant expectation of the atheist, that he will thereby be able to drive God from his works. Spontaneous generation is not to be understood as a generation out of nothing, an event without a cause, an affair of caprice or chance. It is a production out of preexisting materials by means of powers in the materials, — powers very much unknown, working only in certain circumstances, and requiring, in order to their operation, favorable conditions, assorted (so all religious people think) by Divine wisdom. Spontaneous generation, supposing it to exist, cannot be a simple, it must be a very complex process; involving properties possessed by matter, and a concourse of circumstances working to the production of an intended end.

Plants and animals (let me suppose) are now formed out of germs, or, if you can show it to be so, out of wisely endowed and carefully prepared matter. But, How are they propagated? is the next question. By special acts of creation? or by development? I do not know that religion, natural or revealed, has any interest in holding by any particular view on this subject, any more than it has in maintaining any special theory as to the formation of strata of stone on the earth's surface. It is now admitted that Christians may hold, in perfect consistency with religion and Genesis, that certain layers of rock were formed, not at once by a fiat of God, but mediately by water and fire as the agents of God. And are they not at liberty to hold, always if evidence be produced, that higher plants have been developed from lower, and higher brutes from lower, according to certain laws of descent, known or unknown, working in favorable circumstances? There is nothing irreligious in the idea of development, properly understood. We have constant experience of development, — of the development of individual plants and animals from parent plants and animals. And why, if proof be produced, should we not be allowed to believe in the development of a new species from the crossing of two species in favorable circumstances?

Development, if we only carefully inquire into its nature, will not be seen to be so simple an operation as some imagine. The development of an individual plant or animal from its parentage is a very complex process, implying an immense body of agencies, mechanical, chemical, probably electric and magnetic: some would say that it requires, in addition, an independent vital power. But, put the supposition that no distinct vital power is required, — that a certain coincidence of chemical and mechanical and electric agencies will accomplish the whole, — the question would only be started, Whence this combination and co-agency of these diverse forces to accomplish a specific end? What is true of the development of individuals would also hold good of the development of species, if there be such a thing in nature. If man could construct, out of simple mechanical powers, not only a watch telling the hour, but a watch which should produce other watches telling the hour through all time, our admiration of the skill of the artist would not be diminished. In such an instrument, were it possible or conceivable, the maker would require to secure a double end, — not only that the watch would announce the time, but that there should be a second watch and a third watch, on indefinitely, all accomplishing the same purpose. Our wonder would be increased, if the watches thus produced not only produced other watches, but, as they consorted in favorable circumstances, better and yet better watches. So, in vegetable and animal development, there must be adaptation upon adaptation: adaptation of the individual to its mate; adaptation in the growth of the young when yet connected with the parent; adaptation of the birth to external circumstances in the air, food, and clothing supplied for it; adaptation in the instincts of animals, — for example, in the love of offspring, and in the capacity of the creature to grow and strengthen, and, it may be, to produce a progeny better than itself.

The question as to whether there is or is not a

separate vital principle, and whether there may not be a new species developed out of the old, is a question for science to settle. And, whichever way it is settled, there is room for irreligion — I am sorry to say; but there is room also for religion. The assertion that there is a vital principle, capable of originating, unfolding, and perfecting all that is in the organism, may be quite as irreligious as the denial of a separate vital potency. Proceeding on the existence of a vital force, which they suppose, pantheistically or atheistically, to inhere in nature, there are some who imagine that they have thereby explained every thing connected with the development and growth of vegetable and animal organisms. Mr. Huxley can work such wonders by protoplasm, only by imparting to it a life-power such as is ascribed to nature generally by pantheists. I am inclined, on the evidence of science, to believe in a vital power, as different from the chemical as the chemical is from the mechanical; but I do not believe in an independent power called the vegetable or animal life, capable of producing all the beautiful forms and adaptations which we admire in the living creatures. It can be shown, whether we do or do not call in a vital principle, that there is need of a whole series of nice arrangements of part and power before the organism can fulfil its functions, and yield seed after its kind or better than its kind. It is a question to be decided by naturalists, and not by theologians; who, so far as I see, have no authority from the Word of

God to say that every species of tiny moths has been created independent of all species of moths which have gone before. The natural tendency of theologians will be conservative. I go a step farther, and say that it ought to be conservative. It is not for them to run eagerly after every new theory which may be propounded, and live its ephemeral day; and to make religion to lean upon it, only to suffer a fall and a humiliation when it breaks down. "He that believeth will not make haste." Religion can afford to wait till the point is established or dis-established. When a law has been established so as to stand the tests of scientific induction, then theologians may reverently use it, in expounding the traces of design discoverable in the universe.

It is for naturalists to determine the points which have been started by Mr. Darwin. The law with which his name is identified is that of Natural Selection. He has copiously illustrated that law, but has not defined it very clearly. The name, Natural Selection, might lead us to imagine that, somehow or other, the plant or animal has a choice in the matter, or at least some power to improve itself or its position. A plant is liable to be eaten by cattle, and might be the better of spines; and as it needs them, so the need provides them, and they go down to posterity. An animal would be profited by claws to seize its prey; and the wish calls forth rudimentary claws, which go down with improvements from generation to generation. But no such idea is meant to be conveyed by Darwin.

The law is simply, that, where a plant happens to get a thorn, or a beast a claw, it is more likely to live while others perish, and that it transmits its endowment to posterity. It means that, in the struggle for existence, the stronger, or the better adapted to its position, will prevail. Even this presupposes that there are capacities in nature, — the capacity of producing spines and claws in certain circumstances. But there is more than this implied: it is implied that strength, or any useful peculiarity, once acquired, will become hereditary. This last is a very complex law, or rather process, the precise elements of which have not been unfolded. Mr. Darwin says that science has hitherto thrown no light on the nature of heredity. "The laws governing inheritance are quite unknown: no one can say why the same peculiarity in different individuals of the same species, and in individuals of different species, is sometimes inherited and sometimes not so; why it often reverts, in certain characters, to its grandfather or grandmother, or other much more remote ancestor; why a peculiarity is often transmitted from one sex to both sexes, or to one sex alone, more commonly, but not exclusively, to the like sex." * Depend upon it, when the process is explored, there will be found an immense number and variety of adaptations to secure that the peculiarity of the individual, found to be useful, will not perish with the individual, but go down to future ages.

* Origin of Species, chap. i.

As long as such men as Agassiz in this country, and Milne Edwards and his school in France, oppose the theory of Darwin, not only by their authority, but by their facts and arguments, Darwinism cannot be regarded as settled. Sir William Thomson, in a set of papers in the "North British Review" and elsewhere, — papers of which I do not say that they will never be answered, but of which I affirm that they have not hitherto been answered, — shows that the derivation of all animated beings from one original germ cannot be reconciled with astronomy; which declares that the earth was formed at a comparatively late date, whereas the formation of all living creatures by natural selection requires indefinite ages. My opinion on such a subject is of no scientific value; but I am inclined to think that the theory contains a large body of important truths, which we see illustrated in every department of organic nature; but that it does not contain the whole truth, and that it overlooks more than it perceives. Whence this power which raises the plant, which raises the animal, from age to age? Whence, for example, the sensation in animals, their liability to pleasure and pain? Whence the instincts of animals? — of the spider, the bee, the horse, the dog, the elephant? Natural selection might modify them, supposing them to exist; but the question is, How came they to exist? Were they, at least as germs, in the original star dust? Or have they been added? Or, if added, by natural law? or how? To these questions science can give no answer, and should not pretend to be able to give an answer. When it talks, with such seeming profundity and wisdom, of "conditions," let it not imagine that it is giving an explanation, when the conditions are unknown, — the conditions, for example, of the production of the affection of the mother bird or beast for its offspring. But, on this subject, religion can say as little, except that it should trace all things up to God; not being able, however, to determine whether he has been acting by an immediate fiat, or, as he usually does, by secondary causes.

On one point, however, religion has a title to speak out. I do not know that she has any special charge given her of the lower animals, except to see that they are protected and kindly treated. But religion is addressed to man, and she has to see that man's nature is not degraded and reduced to the same level as that of the brutes. There has been a special revelation made as to the origin and destiny of man; and this we must uphold and defend.

There is, account for it as we may, a general correspondence between the record in the Bible and the record in stone. My friend Hugh Miller may not have been able to point out an identity in every minute particular; but he has certainly established a general congruity. There is an order and there is a progression very much the same in both. In both there is light before the sun appears. In Genesis, the fiat goes forth, "Let there be light, and there was light" the first day, and the sun comes forth only the fourth, — in accordance with science, which tells us that the earth was thrown off ages before the sun had become condensed into the centre of the planetary system. In both, the inanimate comes before the animate; in both, the grass and herb and tree, before the animal; in both, fishes and fowls, before creeping things and cattle. In both, we have, as the last of the train, man standing upright, and facing the sky; made of the dust of the ground, and yet filled with the inspiration of God.

As both agree in the history of the past, so both agree as to the future of the world. The Scriptures point, not obscurely, to a day of dissolution. 2 Pet. iii. 5: "This they willingly are ignorant of, that by the word of God the heavens were of old, and the earth standing out of the water and in the water: whereby the world that then was, being overflowed with water, perished. But the heavens and the earth which are now, by the same word are kept in store, reserved unto fire against the day of judgment." All men of science are agreed that, according to the laws now in operation, there is in our system a wasting of energy in the shape of heat, which must, in an indefinite time, bring our cosmos to a state of chillness and death; to be followed, some think, by an accumulation of heat and a conflagration, which will reduce all things to star dust; out of which, by the agglomeration of matter, new worlds will arise. It may be rash in any one to imagine that he sees so far into the future, in which new powers may appear, as they have certainly done in the past; but this, it can be demonstrated, is and must be the issue, according to the powers now working. Such is the correspondence between science and Scripture. You will find no such correspondence between modern discovery and any work of heathen mythology, eastern or western. *Prima facie*, there must be a great truth in that opening chapter of Genesis, which has anticipated geology by three thousand years.

Mr. Darwin has not given to the world his views as to the origin of man.* Mr. Wallace, who, contemporaneously with Darwin, discovered the law of Natural Selection (the publication of a paper by him called forth Darwin's book), has declared, in a work recently published,† that there are insuperable difficulties in applying that law to the derivation of the human race. He declares boldly, "I do not consider that all nature can be explained on the principles of which I am so ardent an advocate;" and he discovers evidence of an "unknown higher law, beyond and independent of all those laws of which we have any knowledge." He conducts an argument to show "the insufficiency of Natural Selection to account for the development of man." There are gaps between the brute and man which

* This was true when this Lecture was delivered. When it is going through the press, "The Descent of Man," Vol. I., has appeared in America. If Vol. II. appears before this volume is issued, I may notice the whole work in the Appendix.

† Wallace on Natural Selection. X.

cannot be filled up. "The brain of the lowest savages, and, as far as we yet know, of the prehistoric races, is little inferior in size to that of the highest types of man, and immensely superior to that of the higher animals." "The collections of Dr. J. B. Davis and Dr. Morton give the following as the average internal capacity of the cranium in the chief races: Teutonic family, ninety-four cubic inches; Esquimaux, ninety-one cubic inches; Negroes, eighty-five cubic inches; Australians and Tasmanians, eighty-two cubic inches; Bushmen, seventy-seven cubic inches. These last numbers, however, are deduced from comparatively few specimens, and may be below the average; just as a small number of Finns and Cossacks give ninety-eight cubic inches, or considerably more than that of the German races. It is evident, therefore, that the absolute bulk of the brain is not necessarily much less in savage than in civilized man; for Esquimaux skulls are known with a capacity of one hundred and thirteen inches, or hardly less than the largest among Europeans. But, what is still more extraordinary, the few remains yet known of prehistoric man do not indicate any material diminution in the size of the brain case. A Swiss skull of the stone age, found in the lake dwelling of Meilen, corresponded exactly to that of a Swiss youth of the present day. The celebrated Neanderthal skull had a larger circumference than the average; and its capacity, indicating actual mass of brain, is estimated to have been not less than seventy-five cubic inches, or nearly the average of existing Australian crania. The Engis skull, perhaps the oldest known, and which, according to Sir John Lubbock, 'there seems no doubt was really contemporary with the mammoth and the cave bear,' is yet, according to Professor Huxley, 'a fair average skull, which might have belonged to a philosopher, or might have contained the thoughtless brains of a savage.'" Let us turn now to the brain of animals. "The adult male orang-utan is quite as bulky as a small-sized man, while the gorilla is considerably above the average size of man, as estimated by bulk and weight: yet the former has a brain of only twenty-eight cubic inches; the latter, one of thirty, or, in the largest specimen yet known, of thirty-four and a half cubic inches. We have seen that the average cranial capacity of the lowest savages is probably not less than five-sixths of that of the highest civilized races, while the brain of the anthropoid apes scarcely amounts to one-third of that of man, in both cases taking the average; or the proportions may be more clearly represented by the following figures: anthropoid apes, ten; savages, twenty-six; civilized man, thirty-two." There is no evidence, then, of a gradual rise, by natural law, from the brute to the lowest form of man. Mr. Wallace emphatically urges that savages have a brain capacity not required by their wants, and which could not have been produced by their wants in the struggle of life.

He dwells on some other capacities, which he says

cannot be accounted for by the theory. "The soft, naked, sensitive skin of man, entirely free from that hairy covering which is so universal among other mammalia, cannot be explained on the theory of natural selection. The habits of savages show that they feel the want of this covering, which is most completely absent in man exactly where it is thickest on other animals. We have no reason whatever to believe that it could have been hurtful, or even useless, to primitive man; and, under these circumstances, its complete abolition, shown by its never reverting in mixed breeds, is a demonstration of the agency of some other power than the law of the survival of the fittest, in the development of man from the lower animals. Other characters show difficulties of a similar kind, though not perhaps in an equal degree. The structure of the human foot and hand seem unnecessarily perfect for the needs of savage man, in whom they are as completely and as humanly developed as in the highest races. The structure of the human larynx, giving the power of speech and of producing musical sounds, and especially its extreme development in the female sex, are shown to be beyond the needs of savages, and from their known habits impossible to have been acquired either by sexual selection or by survival of the fittest." These are difficulties which present themselves to Mr. Wallace as a naturalist. He sees also those which arise from his possession of mental faculties which have no relation to his fellowmen or to his material progress, to his possession of consciousness, his power of conceiving eternity and infinity, and the sense of right and wrong which he finds in uncivilized tribes. After quoting Mr. Huxley, who says that "our thoughts are the expression of molecular changes in that matter of life which is the source of our other vital phenomena," Mr. Wallace remarks that he has not been able to find the clew by which Mr. Huxley "passes from those vital phenomena which consist only, in their last analysis, of movements of particles of matter, to those other phenomena which we term thought, sensation, or consciousness."

Science, it is acknowledged, can produce no direct evidence of man being derived from the brute. The argument against the doctrine must be drawn mainly from his possession of qualities not found in the lower animals. As, most obvious of all, we have organs of speech, and, as more important, the power of using them intelligently.* We have the faculty of reaching abstract and general truth, a faculty which the brute creatures do not possess; when they seem to have it, it arises, as can be shown, merely from the association of ideas. Then there is the capacity of distinguishing between good and evil, and that of free will to choose the good and

* "Although it has been at various times stated that certain savage tribes are entirely without language, none of these accounts appear to be well authenticated, and they are *a priori* extremely improbable. At any rate, even the lowest races of which we have any satisfactory account possess a language, imperfect though it may be, and eked out to a great extent by signs." — Lubbock, *Origin of Civilization*; VIII.

avoid the evil. Crowning them all, is man's power to rise to a knowledge of God, to the contemplation of his perfections, and to acts of worship. These higher attributes of humanity will fall under our consideration, when we come to look at the mind. Science can say nothing as to how all these qualities came to be superinduced. Were they in the star dust when it was incandescent? or did they appear when it began to cool? If so, in what state? If not so, when and where and how did they come in? Science, physiological or paleontological, can throw no light on this subject, and should not decide or dogmatize when it has no data to proceed on. The Book of Genesis, which has so anticipated geology in the account which it has given of the successive appearance of plants and animals, has here gone beyond science, and given an account against which science has and can have nothing to advance.

That account is brief, simple, general, avoiding minute and circumstantial details: Gen. ii. 7, "And the Lord God formed man of the dust of the ground, and breathed into his nostrils the breath of life;" a statement implying first the connection of man with the earth, — with its dust, its flesh, or animal nature, — and at the same time connecting him with heaven by an inspiration, or breath of the Almighty. Such is the very summary account of the physical creation, of the formation of the dust, the flesh, the bodily frame. Does it say how it was done, by natural or supernatural law, by means or without means? Scripture enlarges and dwells only on the higher endowment, the truly human, as distinguished from the animal endowment; as Gen. i. 26, "And God said, Let us make man in our image, after our likeness: and let him have dominion over the fish of the sea, and over the fowl of the air, and over the cattle, and over all the earth, and over every creeping thing that creepeth upon the earth. So God created man in his own image, in the image of God created he him." All this is in accordance with clearly established fact. Man has affinities with the lower animals: this should not be denied. Like them he is formed out of dust and returns to dust. But at the same time he has qualities which assimilate him to God, — a power of looking back into the past and anticipating the future, of tracing effects to causes and anticipating effects from causes, of appreciating the fair and the good, and a free choice to act on his conviction. And is there not need of Divine breath to produce all this, to make this dust a living soul? Is there not need of a Divine decree to make his soul like unto God in knowledge, righteousness, and true holiness? In doing all this, God is only carrying out and completing the plan shadowed forth in the geological ages. These two lectures are only an exposition of what the Apostle says: 1 Cor. xv. 46, "Howbeit, that was not first which is spiritual (πνευματικὸν), but that which is natural (ψυχικὸν); and afterward that which is spiritual."

And so there appear farther evidences of progression, and of a progressive progression. The powers of nature are made by a power above them, to bring forth higher products characterized by wisdom, by skill, and by taste. Your believer in mere Natural Law and Natural Selection has seen only half the truth, or rather he has not seen half the truth. Like one of those insects which he may have been microscopically examining, he has seen only the smallest objects. Mole-like, he has been burrowing a dark and confined tunnel through the underground clay, instead of walking upright like a man, and looking around him on the extended earth, and up into the expanse of heaven. He has used the microscope and seen the infinitely little; but he refuses to look through the telescope, which shows him how the littles are formed into structures of infinite greatness and grandeur. All, no doubt, proceeds from natural laws; but these are made to work out typical forms, geometrically correct and æsthetically beautiful. The cold winter gives us frost-work, and the warm summer yields us flowers; and contemporaneously there appear intellect and taste to measure and appreciate it. The blind forces are made by One who has eyes to evolve ideas, patterns, exemplars, which perceiving minds are constructed to behold and admire. Finally, above the physical, above the intellectual even, there rises the moral, like stars out of the star dust, or rather like stars rising out of these other stars, only brighter, purer, and more enduring. At the point to which we have come, a new progression is opening to us in an endless vista.

Darwin has caught an important fact, when he says that there is a principle of Natural Selection in nature: the strong live and multiply and increase; while the weak die, give way, and disappear. This is certainly a law of the plants and of the lower animals. It looks in the earlier periods of human history as if this law were still the ruling one, as if bodily strength and brute force were to subdue the weak and hold them in subjection. The first empires — the Egyptian, the Assyrian, the Babylonian, the Persian — were very much founded on this principle. And is this to go on for ever, the powerful tyrannizing over the feeble, men making women do all the menial work, and the great body of the people, even in such civilized countries as Greece and Rome, slaves to the few? In the progression of events, there appear clear proofs that the old law is to give way before a higher to which it is subordinated. There are indications that intelligence is to prevail over unreasoning force. Nations of the highest mental power and cultivation, such as the Greeks and Romans, begin to take the lead, and rule by forethought, by counsel, by firm government.

As we advance, we see a new, a still more important law emerging, and urging its claim not only to a place, but a supreme place, declaring that right is above might, that moral good is higher even than intellectual strength. A people with high intelligence may become pleasure-loving, sensual, as the Greeks did in their great commercial cities; may become selfish, cruel, dissolute, as the Romans did in the decline of their empire, — and a hardier and a more moral race comes in like a fresh, cool breeze to fill up the heated and relaxing atmosphere. Not that the law of the prevalence of strength is absolutely set aside, but it is subordinated to a higher law, or rather higher laws, which limit and restrain it, and may be made to direct and to elevate it. The intellectual rises above the physical, and asserts its right to govern it, even as the soul claims to rule over the body. But there is more: the moral rises above the intellectual, and claims that the understanding should be obedient to it, even as the conscience, which is the law in the heart, declares that it should rule over the head, and over the whole man. Nay, the very moral ideas and sentiments make progress by purification and refinement: an earthly morality like that of Jacob is made to flame into the love of John; and the rigid prohibitions of the commandments, written on stone, become the blessings of the discourses of Jesus, meant to be written on the fleshly tables of the heart.

The Law of Natural Selection — that, in the exuberance of seeds and organisms and species, in early nature the stronger should prevail — is in itself a beneficent one. "All changes of form or structure, all increase in the size of an organ or its complexity, all greater specialization or physiological division of labor, can only be brought about, inasmuch as it is for the good of the being so modified." * It

* Wallace on Natural Selection.

allows the weak, after enjoying their brief time of existence, to die and disappear; while the vigorous leave behind a still stronger progeny to rise to a fuller development and intenser enjoyments. But there are stringent limits set to this law. It is, after all, the law of the period of the unconscious plant and irrational brute. It comes to be subordinated to a higher, and this to a still higher. Intellect comes later; but, like the more recent geological formations, it mounts the highest, and overlies and overlooks all the rest. Thought gains, and it retains, the highest positions; the giants disappear, and the civilized peoples take their place; the Canaanites, with their chariots of iron, are conquered by men who carry with them a higher mission; the walls of Jericho fall down before the blowing of trumpets sounding truth to all people. The forests are cut down to let the fields yield corn and wheat, and barley and vines, and figs and olives; and trees are left only for shelter and for lawn ornaments. The creatures with stings and claws and fangs — the foxes, the wolves, the leopards — give way before sheep and horses and kine. There is still a struggle for existence, but the skill which devises means and invents instruments prevails over brute force and fierceness. And this power of understanding is destined to be sublimed into something nobler and more ethereal. Above the dead earth and agitated sea there is to rise an atmosphere in which the living are to breathe and move and fly. The intellectual era seems to culminate in Greece in the days of Pericles, when free thought and art and literature have reached their zenith. But in that very age, a new and a vastly greater power comes into view. Socrates is defeated, and yet Socrates conquers. He drinks the hemlock, and dies; but it is in the hope of an immortality. His body is burned; but the flame by which this was effected, a new correlated force, is never to be extinguished. His persecutors are forgotten, or remembered only to be execrated; but the moral power of Socrates still walks our earth. A new struggle for existence has begun. It was exhibited and symbolized at Thermopylæ, where the power of numbers was met and defeated by the heroism of a devoted few. It was an anticipation of what was to come.

But there were better prefigurations of it among a people specially called and set apart for the purpose; in an enslaved race, trained to become the depositaries of the truth, and in due time the missionaries of the world; in the law delivered first, as if to suit the ages of giant strength, amid thunders and lightnings and tempest, and the voice of the trumpet waxing louder and louder, and then coming forth from the gentle lips of Jesus; first in the strong wind, the earthquake, and the fire, followed by the still, small voice, which is specially the voice of God as heard in the later prophets, and still more sweetly in the discourses of Him who spake as never man spake. In due time the types, the bloody sacrifices, the whole burnt-offerings, culminate in an archetype, in which we see the highest strength coming out of the lowest weakness.

This new struggle, it is so destined, had its grand battle-field on Mount Calvary. You may see it all acted on the cross which is raised high there, that it may draw all eyes towards it. You have there the writhings, the faintings, the cup of gall, the sponge filled with vinegar, the agony closing in death; and you perceive, at the same time, the confidence put in him by suffering and loving hearts, — "Remember me when thou comest into thy kingdom." Yes, that weakest, most forsaken of men is acknowledged as a king and as having a kingdom; and his answer is, To-day thou shalt be with me in this kingdom of paradise. This most defenceless of men, who uses no carnal weapons, who refuses to bring down fire from heaven to destroy his enemies, becomes the greatest conqueror which this world has seen, — greater than the Egyptian, the Babylonian, the Greek, or the Roman, — and subdues under him, not the mere bodies of men, but the loftiest intellects which have adorned our world, and hearts purified and burning with love. He rises out of the grave, to become a victor whose triumphs know no end. Crucified as a slave by a Roman deputy, he conquers the Roman power; and the emperor who fought so long and fiercely against him has to exclaim with his dying breath, "Thou hast conquered me, O Galilean!" By suffering, he has accomplished ends which he could never have gained by prosperity and success. He has become perfect through suffering, and has secured the means of gaining the heart of the sufferer and of elevating the fallen: the fallen man who clings to him; the fallen woman who bathes his feet with her tears, and pours forth the feelings of her heart more precious than the ointment from the alabaster box; the fallen nations, as seen in the once savage tribes of Germany and Britain, who have been raised by Christianity; and of exalting the fallen race of mankind, who have thereby risen from condemnation to justification, from alienation to reconciliation with God. This is a cause for the promotion of which, this is a lesson for the teaching of which, it was worthy of God to become flesh and tabernacle on the earth, and suffer and die. He has thereby shown that there is something greater in him than his almightiness. I have sometimes felt as if God could scarcely be regarded by us as thoroughly perfect, unless he were capable of submitting to suffering. I have felt at times that, if this were denied him, his creatures might reach a perfection which he has not, which he cannot have. I believe that the Word becoming flesh and tabernacling on the earth is an essential part of the plan which we see developing before our eyes; and it seems as if the transaction were placed in the very middle of the ages, as the keystone of the bridge which connects the two compartments of God's works, — the physical, with its force and its struggle for existence, with the moral, with its sufferings and its triumphs. In earthly affairs, there may be a greater glory in suffering and sorrow than in prosperity and dazzling splendor: there may, for example, be a greater glory in the soldier's death than in his life; there was a greater glory in Samson's death than in all the achievements of his life. But speak not of the glory of the soldier bleeding in defence of a nation's rights; speak not of the glory of the patriot toiling and suffering and dying for his country's freedom; speak not of the glory of the martyr calm and rejoicing while tied to the burning stake: these have no glory because of the glory that excelleth, — the glory of Christ's condescension and patience and love, in submitting to shame, to sorrow, and to death.

Now this is the era in which our lot is cast. This is the struggle in which we are required to take our part. It commenced at an early date: "I will put enmity between thee and the woman, and between thy seed and her seed: it shall bruise thy head, and thou shalt bruise his heel." The serpent is seen bruising the heel of the seed of the woman. The good have still to suffer, but in their suffering they show their goodness. We are in a dispensation in which the plant must be bruised before it yields its odors, in which the rose must wither before it yields its undying perfume. A good cause must have its martyrs before it triumphs. John Brown has to be put to death before the manacles are struck from the slave. Your Abraham Lincoln is shot in the midst of the shouts of victory. "Verily, verily, I say unto you, Except a corn of wheat fall into the ground and die, it abideth alone: but if it die, it bringeth forth much fruit. He that loveth his life shall lose it; and he that hateth his life in this world shall keep it unto life eternal."

Let us realize that our lot is cast in such a dispensation. There are strong men, and seemingly wise men, in our day who do not see it. I have set myself all my life against the doctrine taught in the works of Thomas Carlyle (or rather the impression left by them), and the writings of others who ape him, without his strength, and which would lead us to worship heroes and deify force. I repudiate the principle which underlies and runs through the whole of Buckle's "History of Civilization," that intellect has been, is, and ought to be the grand moving power in the world. True, intellect must always, in the end, be the main agent or instrument in helping forward the advancement of the race; but it is only in the sense in which steam is the agent in moving the railway cars. In contemplating the steam-engine, we rise beyond the steam to consider the mind which has constructed and is guiding the whole; so, in weighing the causes which have imparted progress to humanity, we must look beyond the intellectual force to the deeper moral power which has awakened it. Has not intelligence in many countries — as in Switzerland, in Prussia, in Holland, in Scotland, in New England, and in other States of the Union — been called forth by the Reformation, by the Covenanting and

Puritan faith? and nations which lose that faith may find that they have cut down the tree on which the fruit grew, on which fruit they can feed no longer.

Of all acts of cowardice, the meanest is that which leads us to abandon a good cause because it is weak, and join a bad cause because it is strong. The smitten deer is said to be avoided by the herd, — it is the instinct of the brute; but in the higher law which reigns in the breast of mankind and womankind, you never saw the smitten son abandoned by the mother, who may be seen, instead, standing by him at the foot of the cross on which he is suspended, undeservedly or deservedly. I do fear that, in my past life, I have often been tempted to pay obeisance to false gods; but I thank the great God that I have always been kept from that prevalent form of idolatry — found not only in Persia and in the East, but in this Western world — which worships the rising sun. I confess that I might have been enticed to adore him in his setting splendors; that is, in some of those old grandeurs which have had their day, and are now disappearing in a soft radiance which they did not possess in their zenith. I am sure that there is nothing in my past life of which I am entitled to be proud; but if I could take credit for any thing, it would be for the fact, that, — descended from Covenanting forefathers, who, not contented with suffering as the Puritans did, went on to resist oppression on their heather hills, which always look to me as if they had been dyed with their blood, — I have in the great questions of the day, educational and religious, in Scotland and in Ireland, cast in my lot with the minority, which in due season became the majority; and when I left any cause, it was because it had waxed strong, and did not need my poor aid. We have to see to it that, in the struggle of life, we stand by right, and not by might, being sure that in the end the right shall have the might. Should we act otherwise, we shall certainly fall under that law of degradation, which requires that evil, once committed, goes down to the third and fourth generation of them that hate him, when God gives men up to the consequences of their own iniquity, and the curse alights on them: "Curse ye Meroz, curse ye bitterly the inhabitants thereof; because they came not to the help of the Lord, to the help of the Lord against the mighty."

III.

LIMITS TO THE LAW OF NATURAL SELECTION. — THIS WORLD A SCENE OF STRUGGLE. — APPEARANCE OF SPIRITUAL LIFE. — FINAL CAUSE. — NEW LIFE. — UNITY AND GROWTH IN THE WORLD. — HIGHER PRODUCTS COMING FORTH. — SIGNS OF PROGRESS.

THERE are clear indications, in the geological ages, of a progression from the inanimate up to the animate, and from the lower animate to the higher. The mind, ever impelled to seek for causes, asks how all this is produced. The answer, if answer can be had, is to be given by science, and not by religion; which simply insists that we trace all things up to God, whether acting by immediate or by mediate agency. Mr. Darwin would refer it all to the somewhat vaguely enunciated principle of Natural Selection, or the preservation of the creatures best suited to their circumstances, and the success of the strong in the struggle of life. That this principle is exhibited in nature, and working to the advancement of the plants and animals from age to age, I have no doubt. We see it operating before our eyes every spring, when we find the weak plant killed by the frosts of winter, and the strong surviving and producing a progeny strong as itself. But it has not been proven that there is no other principle at work. I am not satisfied that this principle has produced life out of dead matter, that it has produced sentient beings out of insentient, that it has wrought the conscious mind from the unconscious body, that it has generated man from the brute. There is no positive proof that it has so much as produced a new species of animals out of old ones. In regard to this latter point, it seems to account for some of the phenomena, but leaves others unexplained. In particular, there are gaps in the geological ages between the species of one age and those of another age, with no intermediate species to fill it, as being the descendants of the one and the progenitors of the other. There must be other powers and principles at work in nature as well as Natural Selection.

The law of the weak being made to give way before the strong is very apt to be abused, and will certainly be perverted by those who do not take into account the other and higher laws which limit it, and are expected to subordinate it. If they look to it alone, they will understand it as meaning that the poor and the helpless need not be protected or defended, but may be allowed to perish : thus bringing us down to the condition of the South Sea Islanders, who kill their infants; of the Hindoos and Africans, who expose their aged parents, as having become useless. If this doctrine prevails, it will make the shadow on the dial of time go back for ages, and bring us to the age of monster animals, or monster men, like Samson or like Hercules. Persons would look upon it as meaning that the uncivilized races may be allowed to disappear, without an effort being made to raise them; a principle which, in old times, would have required that our German or British or Celtic ancestors, in the days of Julius Cæsar, and as described by him, should have been allowed to die out and to vanish. Nature itself, if only we condescend to discover the final cause in her operations, rebels against this cowardice, and shows us the mother loving with an especial tenderness, not the strong son who can do for himself, but that weak boy who has been the object of her care from his infancy; and she will cherish him, in the hope that he may display softer and finer traits of character to which the healthy youth is a stranger. If the tenet which I am denouncing come to be the prevailing belief in this country, it will issue in the weak races on this continent, the Indian and the Negro, being consigned to a slow but certain dissolution; and ridicule will be poured on the attempts which philanthropic men are at present making to elevate them by schools and colleges, by justice and by kindness. A doctrine this, worse than slave-holding in its worst features, and quite as likely to be entertained by the self-sufficient North as by the conquered South, suffering at present for its sins, but certain to rise in the future, if only it can be induced to aim at raising and improving that race which of late years has, all unknowingly to itself, had so important a place in the providential dealings of God towards this country; and which, as it remains among us, must be for our weal or our woe, according as we hasten to educate them, or allow them to fall into deeper degradation. I admit the tendency of mankind to degenerate; but I believe in a power to restrain and reverse it. It was the power which brought our Lord on that morning from the tomb, and whose function it is to enlighten the ignorant, to strengthen the weak, and raise the fallen; and, as it does so, to put what it attains under the beneficent law of hereditary descent, so that it may go down from father to son, and from one generation to another, through all coming ages.

At this present time, the two theories of man's origin, the earth-born and the heaven-born, are striving for the mastery. According to the earth-born theory, there are essentially inferior races, which are doomed to give way "in the struggle for existence;" and the defenders of it look on the prospect with complacency, provided a few favored races are enabled to advance on "the principle of natural selection." I believe that this tenet is exercising, directly or indirectly, a very injurious influence on public sentiment in this country and in others. This spirit is setting itself determinedly against missionary effort, is scoffing at all alleged good done to the degraded, and undermining that faith among our students which would prompt them to labor for the good of the heathen or the outcast. In the last age the cry was, First civilize, and then Christianize; and it was uttered by men who took no pains either to civilize or to Christianize. The feeling now is, that it is of no use attempting to elevate the inferior races, and that they may be allowed to disappear, provided the higher races (such as the Aryan, and specially the Anglo-Saxon) are made to take their place. It is a fit creed and sentiment for those who wish to make the heathen, or the sunken among whom they dwell, the ministers of their grasping selfishness or of their lusts, without being troubled with any reproaches of conscience. How different in its practical bearing is the faith of the Christian, who holds that God has "made of one blood all nations;" and that all human beings are alike in that they possess souls capable of improvement and destined to live for ever! Catching the spirit of Him who stood by the weak against the strong, who came to seek and save that which was lost, who permitted the woman who was a sinner to approach him, and ever sought to raise the fallen, the disciple of Christ recognizes as brothers and sisters the lowest specimens of humanity, whether found in pagan lands or in the lowest sinks of our cities; and, having experienced the power of truth and grace upon his own heart, he goes forth in the efficacy of the blood of Christ, and in the regenerating power of the Spirit, to elevate them for this world and the next. Need I ask which of these is the genuine philanthropy, most worthy of heaven, and suited to earth and to man's nature? I for one would not like to see all the varieties of mankind disappear, and the whole reduced to one race, though that should be the Anglo-Saxon, any more than I would like to see all the trees of the forest reduced to one species, though that should be the oak. I rejoice in the diversity which I see in all nature, — in sea and land, in hill and vale, in plant and animal; and I should like to see each race of mankind retaining its peculiarities, while all are elevated; so that the song of praise coming from regenerated humanity to the great Creator may not be a mere melody, but a harmony rising from "a great multitude, which no man can number, of all nations, and kindreds, and peoples, and tongues."

We have seen that there are insuperable difficulties, even in a Natural History point of view, in the theory that man is sprung from the brutes. And man appears in a state of things suited to him, and evidently prepared for him, in plants and animals ready to afford him food and clothing and shelter and defence, and also to gratify and to educate his sense of beauty. Often have I heard my lamented friend Hugh Miller fondly dilating on this last subject. "They tell that man's world, with all its griefs and troubles, is more emphatically a world of flowers than any of the creations that preceded it; and that as one great family, the Grasses, were called into existence, in order apparently that he might enter, in favoring circumstances, upon his two earliest avocations, and be in good hope a keeper of herds and a tiller of the ground; and as another family of plants, the Rosaceæ, was created, in order that the gardens, which it would be also one of his vocations to keep and to dress, should have their trees 'good for food and pleasant to the taste:' so flowers in general were properly produced just ere he appeared, to minister to the sense of beauty which distinguishes him from all other creatures, and to which he owes not a few of his most exquisite enjoyments." It does not appear as if the surrounding circumstances could have produced man, or that man could have produced the surrounding circumstances; and in their contemporaneous appearance and mutual adaptation — man loving flowers, and flowers being cared for by him and improved — we may discover traces of design.

When human beings come on the field, a new era commences, even in Natural History. Man modifies Natural Selection, by bringing together which are separated in physical geography. The commission to him was: "Be fruitful, and multiply, and replenish the earth, and subdue it: and have dominion over the fish of the sea, and over the fowl of the air, and over every living thing that moveth upon the earth." Henceforth he acts on natural agents to modify and improve them; causing the earth to wave with grain and with fruits, and substituting sheep and kine and horses for wild and destructive animals.

And as ages roll on, there is doubtless a progression in human nature. The intellectual comes to rule the physical, and the moral claims to subordinate both. It is no longer strength of body that prevails, but strength of mind; while the law of God proclaims itself superior to both. There is still a Law of Natural Selection: but, under the new dispensation, the strong has met with a still stronger; and right, which is the strongest, would regulate both the strong body and the stronger mind. It may still be that the strongest, the fittest, are to prevail; but it is becoming evident that the strongest and the fittest are not physical, or even intellectual strength, but the moral forces supported by the righteous God. But all this is to be accomplished and manifested by a struggle, in which we see that "God hath chosen the foolish things of the world to confound the wise; and God hath chosen the weak things of the world to confound the things which are mighty; and base things of the world, and things which are despised, hath God chosen; yea, and things which are not, to bring to nought things that are."

The champions of Natural Religion, in defending the great doctrines of the Existence and Goodness of God, have often drawn far too fair a picture of the state of our world. Keeping sin and misery entirely out of sight, they argue as if there were nothing but beneficence to be seen. But this world is not now, and, so far as science throws light on the subject, it never has been, in the state in which the sentimental believer in theism represents it, or would wish it to be. Whatever we might expect or desire, our world is not now, and has never been, a scene of perpetual calm and never-ending sunshine, of peace and unmixed happiness, or of unbroken love on the part of every creature to every other. On the contrary, there have been in it, from the beginning, warring elements and raging storms and creatures devouring each other. It is a world in which there are now, and ever have been since life began, pain and suffering, and the struggle of individuals and races for existence and for mastery. Yet, in the midst of these scenes, we see clear proofs of contrivance and wisdom and kindness in the fittings of things into each other, and the evidently beneficent end of every organ of the animal frame, and in good being brought out of evil. The ocean is in many respects an emblem of this world of ours, — often so calm as to reflect heaven upon its bosom, but at times stirred into turbulence and revealing awful depths. There was a struggle in the pre-Adamite ages. There is a struggle in the human ages. The earth yields thorns and thistles, and man has to eat bread in the sweat of his face. Some of us were cherishing the idea that, in consequence of advancing intelligence, wars would very much cease. But this cannot be — perhaps we might go farther, and say it ought not to be — as long as such evils exist in our world; certain it is, it will not be till moral sentiment reaches a higher growth and exercises greater power. In our day, we have had, first in the western continent, and now in the eastern, the two most desolating wars of which the earth has been the theatre; both, it may be, crushing much evil, but both attended with awful suffering, bodily and mental. The world, in its whole structure and administration, shows the goodness of God; but it manifests other qualities, so that as we look at it we "behold the goodness and severity of God." It looks as if, from the beginning until now, our world were meant to be a probation, a battle-field. And is not this the very view the Scriptures give of it, — a contest between the good and the evil, a triumph and then true peace? "The whole creation groaneth and travaileth in pain together until now." Our academic theists were refusing to look at our world under this aspect. Even some of our sentimental Christians were turning away from it. It is a curious circumstance that it is science that has recalled our attention to it. The fool, as he looks at these things, will say in his heart that there is no God; and the proud man will say, "Who is the Lord that we should obey him?" But he who is open to receive the truth, and the whole truth, will discover and acknowledge that we live in a scene in which there is the good, but in which there is also the evil, and in which it is evidently appointed by God that the good is to gain the victory, and "the earnest expectation of the creature waiteth" for it, and "the creature itself also shall be delivered from the bondage of corruption."

But in order to this a new power appears on the earth. And it appears in the person of One who is identified with man, being born of a woman, and bone of our bone and flesh of our flesh, and who yet descends from a higher sphere. The first man, notwithstanding his fall, was a great advance on all that had gone before; but the second man was immeasurably more so. "And so it is written, The first man Adam was made a living soul, the last Adam was made a quickening spirit." He is the representative, as he is the administrator, in fact the life, of this new moral power which came down from heaven. He fits in with all that has gone before. There were predictions of him in nature as well as in the Word, — predictions of him already fulfilled, and many more remaining to be accomplished. "Lo, I come (in the volume of the book it is written of me)." He comes in the fulness of time into a world which was prepared for him, not in the sense of being ready to receive him, but in the sense of needing him. In conformity with the very nature of our world, with all that had gone before he comes to engage in a struggle; he has to fight a battle with evil, and to gain a victory. He has, in accordance with the whole purpose of God in our world, to show his power by contending with the evil, and thereby conquering and subduing it. "Who is this that cometh from Edom, with dyed garments from Bozrah? this that is glorious in his apparel, travelling in the greatness of his strength? I that speak in righteousness, mighty to save. Wherefore art thou red in thine apparel, and thy garments like him that treadeth in wine-fat? I have trodden the wine-press alone, and of the people there was none with me." This, in accordance with the whole past of our world, — a world in which there had ever been the shedding of blood, a world in which there had been sin since man appeared; and here is One, "without father, without mother, without descent," who has come to bear down all opposition and to remove every evil. "Gird thy sword upon thy thigh, O most mighty, with thy glory and thy majesty. And in thy majesty ride prosperously, because of truth and meekness and righteousness; and thy right hand shall teach thee terrible things. Thine arrows are sharp in the heart of the king's enemies; whereby the people fall under thee."

Closely connected with the work of Christ is another work; the one developing out of the other, as in all the operations of God. It was expedient that Jesus should finish his work, and go away, in order that another Agent might appear, and introduce a new life into our world. That life proceeded from Christ's grave, but is sent down by Christ from heaven. The Spirit takes of the things that are Christ's, and shows them unto us. A new life now manifests itself to us; not sprung from the earth, but descending from a higher region. It comes in silently and imperceptibly; so has life always done, — the life of the plant, the life of the animal. "The wind bloweth where it listeth, and thou hearest the sound thereof, but canst not tell whence it cometh, and whither it goeth: so is every one that is born of the Spirit." It is a reality, as every Christian can testify: "One thing I know, that whereas I was blind, now I see." This is an assuring fact to the man himself, and others might do well to ponder it. "But by what he now seeth we know not." We can tell as little of the manner of it, as we can of the natural life within us, which we feel in every organ of our body; as little of its mode of introduction, as the man of science can of the introduction of life, or sensation, or consciousness. But the appearance of this new life is in analogy with all that has gone before, — analogous to the appearance of plant life and animal life and human life; analogous, also, to what has preceded, inasmuch as, while it is something superinduced, it is not independent of what has gone before. The plant contains something higher than dead matter, but gathers up into itself all the properties of inanimate matter; the animal has sensation not in the vegetable, but retains and uses all the qualities of the plant; and man has more than the brute, but retains all the animal endowments. "So is every one that is born of the Spirit." Man has within his compound nature dead matter and living matter and sentient matter, and all his powers of intellect and feeling just as he had before; but he has something higher, controlling, enlivening, and guiding them. It is a new power, yet not separated from the old powers; but grafted upon the old, as the chemical is upon the mechanical, as the vital is upon the chemical, and the mental on the vital. There is no proof that, in historical times, any new species of animal has appeared; but here, in the human period, is a new power, suited to the new era. There were intimations of it in the Old Testament. But it was fully revealed when our Lord "spake of the Spirit which they that believe on Him should receive." We thus see, more clearly than we could before these recent paleontological investigations, that there has been a unity in God's mode of administration on our earth, in all ages. We have new life appearing in the geological ages, and new life in the historical ages. No doubt it all follows laws; that is, order and progression. There was doubtless law in the appearance of species in the geologic ages. There seem to be laws in the operations of the Spirit. It is "like the wind which bloweth where it listeth;" but the wind has laws: so it is with the work of the Spirit in the soul and in the world. But in the case of the appearance of each of these modes of life, we see too little of the arc to be able to describe the whole circle.

We now see clearly the nature of the dispensation under which we live, — the dispensation of the Spirit. There is, as there has been, in our earth, a struggle. But the contest is not between element and element, between the brutes and the elements, or between animal and animal. It is first a contest between man and nature, but it has also become a contest between the spiritual and the natural. It is specially a contest between sin and holiness. We see it in the heart of every man in the contest between the passions raging like the sea and the conscience that would restrain them. We see it in the heart of every believer, in which "the flesh lusteth against the Spirit, and the Spirit against the flesh; and these are contrary the one to the other." We see it in the world, which is a great battle-field, in which the combatants are truth and error, pollution and purity. There are clear indications as to which side is to gain the victory. True, we "see not yet all things put under Him:" and the reason is that we are in the heart of the battle, and have a work to do; and not at the close, to survey calmly what has been done. But there are powers operating, — powers of God which are sure to prevail. "Magna est veritas, et prevalebit." The conscience in the heart claiming supremacy is only a symbol of the good asserting its right to reign, and subdue all things to itself. The believer dies like Samson, midst the glories of his strength, and slays in his death the last of his spiritual enemies. The light has as yet been only partially shed on our earth, but the sun has arisen which is to go round our globe. The work of the Spirit is at present only partial; but we have the assurance that the time is at hand, "when the Spirit of the Lord shall be poured on all flesh."

We have been obliged, in this rapid run through the ages, to step as with seven-leagued boots from mountain-top to mountain-top, without being able to descend into the connections to be found in the interesting valleys lying between. And what have we gathered?

(1.) We have discovered everywhere traces of Ends, or Final Cause. The whole school with which I am arguing are ever seeking to set aside or disparage final cause. Some of them clothe their pride in the garb of humility, and declare that it would be presumptuous in them to discover the purposes of Deity. They are fond of claiming Francis Bacon as countenancing them. It may be of some moment to inquire what was the precise teaching of that far-sighted and sagacious man on this subject He adopts Aristotle's fourfold division of causes: the Material, or the matter out of which a thing is formed; the Efficient, by which it is formed; the Formal, the form which it takes: and the Final, being the end which it is made to serve.* It could be shown, did my subject require or admit, that there is a deeper foundation for this division than later philosophers are disposed to allow. If we want to account for a thing, our inquiry will be, Out of what is it made; by what has it been made; what is the form or nature which it has been made to take; and what purposes is it meant to serve? Bacon sanctions and uses this distinction; and in his division of the sciences he proceeds upon it, and allots Material and Efficient Causes to Physics, and Formal and Final to Metaphysics, which he places above Physics. He condemns those who in Physics would mix up the inquiry into Final with that into Efficient Cause; as if one, who would determine the nature of the clouds, should satisfy

* Aristotle, Metaphysics, B. iii. c. 1.

himself with saying that they are placed in the sky to water the earth with showers. His language on this subject is not so guarded as it ought to be. In physiology, which inquires into the relations of structure in the plant and animal, we look to ends: it was in the very age in which Bacon lived, that Harvey, finding that the valves in the veins opened one way as if to let a liquid pass, but did not open on the other, argued, on the principle of final cause, that the blood must circulate in the frame. Still, Bacon is so far right that it is not expedient to mix the inquiry into physical cause with the inquiry into final. But Bacon takes Final Cause from Physics, simply to carry it up to a higher region and allot it to Metaphysics, which lift us to Theology, to God and Providence, by Formal and Final Causes. In his own graphic way he likens final causes to the vestal virgins, barren of fruit, but consecrated to God.*

Just as there is, and should be, an inquiry into Efficient Cause, so there may be, so should there be, an inquiry into Final Cause. The Final Cause is often more obvious than the Efficient. The end of the eye and of the ear, which is to enable us to see and to hear, presses itself more on our notice than the physical agencies which have produced these complicated organs.

We see now the importance and the application of the two preliminary points laid down in my first lecture. We see that because we have discovered a physical cause, we are not precluded from an

* De Augmentis Scientiarum, iii. 4.

inquiry into final cause. When we discover that a telescope works by the laws of mechanism and of light, we are not to be kept from noticing the design of the instrument, which is to aid the eye in giving us a view of remote objects. Mr. Darwin has thrown out the idea that the eye, as found in the higher animals (such as the eagle), may have been formed on the principle of natural selection, in the course of millions of ages, from the simple apparatus — found in lower creatures — of an optic nerve coated with pigment. Such a theory appears to many to be far-fetched and wire-drawn. He acknowledges that in such a case he cannot point out the transitional grades. But suppose that he could establish his hypothesis, we should still see the necessity of calling in a number of adaptations to account for the wonderful and complicated result. We should first have to presuppose a nerve sensitive to light. On this, all that he has to remark is, "How a nerve comes to be sensitive to light hardly concerns us more than how life itself first originated." * And all I have to remark is, that Mr. Darwin, in accounting for so many phenomena by natural law, does not so much as attempt to account for the origin of life, or of nerve force. And then, secondly, we must see the adaptations which have secured that substances should attach themselves to the nerve till it becomes the beautiful mechanism of the eye of the higher animals and of man. And finally we have not to overlook the

* Origin of Species, chap. vi.

most wonderful fact of all, that this structure enables the animal to see. In like manner, when we have traced the formation of the animal frame to certain powers, mechanical, chemical, and vital, — or because we suppose we have resolved the vital power into the chemical, and the chemical into the mechanical, — this should not prevent us from looking at the obvious purpose served by the eye, the ear, and every organ of the body. So, should it be found that the elevation of species proceeds from the laws of heredity — it may be from the law of selection — this would not even tend to lessen the force of the argument from design. We see, too, the importance of the other preliminary point, that because we are unacquainted with the precise nature of the forces in operation we are not thereby to be precluded from discovering a purpose. The workman may be very imperfectly acquainted with the agencies employed in his factory, but he is sure that there are method and design in the machine which turns out such products. I believe that the most profound physiologist has penetrated but a very little way into the secret machinery of the life of the individual plant and animal, and still less into the agencies which produce one plant or animal from another; and less still into the powers, whatever they be, which made organisms progress from one geologic age to another. But he has only to open his eyes, and allow his intellect to follow its spontaneous course, to discover that in every organ of the animated being, and in the development of the organic being, there is an end to accomplish, and a means to accomplish it.

But it will be necessary, at this place, to answer some of the objections brought by this school against the doctrine of discoverable ends in nature. These objections have no novelty in them. They have been answered, at least in substance, a hundred times; but they require to be answered once more, since they continue to be urged.

There are physiologists who would blunt the edge of the argument, by saying that the organ, which suits the exigencies of the animal so nicely, is only the "condition of the existence" of the animal. I do not object to this language; which is said to have been introduced by Cuvier, so fond of discovering final cause. Our argument is drawn from the very circumstance that so many and such complicated conditions should meet to supply the wants, and promote the comfort, and, it may be, the beauty and utility, of the living creature.

It is asserted that in many cases we cannot see the end contemplated. The reply is not far to seek. In order to discover design in a structure, it is not necessary that we should be able to declare the meaning of every part of it. The soldier may see enough to convince him that there is plan in bringing so many men together to form that powerful army, and skill in conducting that successful campaign, though he be not able to fathom all the intentions of the commander, or discover why this regiment is required to move in this rather than in that direction. We may be able reverently to discover purposes in God's works, without pretending to be able to find out what God doeth from the beginning to the end.

"To the hypothesis of special creations," says Mr. Herbert Spencer,* "a difficulty is presented by the absence of high forms of life during those innumerable epochs of the earth's existence which geology records. But to the hypothesis of evolution this absence is no such obstacle. Suppose evolution, and this question is necessarily excluded. Suppose special creations, and this question (unavoidably raised) can have no satisfactory answer." I am not at present standing up either for or against special creations; but surely the facts referred to have no bearing, real or apparent, in opposition to the doctrine of final cause. Whether it has been by special creation or by evolution, there are plan and purpose visible in the number and variety of animated beings; in all God's creatures, even the lowest, enjoying life; and in the lower creatures rising to the higher.

Mr. Lewes urges that the circumstance that so many of the seeds floating in the air and water never germinate into plants and animals, is an evidence of failure, and is inconsistent with final cause.† But may it not be the very purpose of God, by the superabundance of germs, to secure that there should be living beings everywhere (in every hole and cranny) enjoying life or nourishing life? We know, too, that many of these superfluous (as they

* Prin. of Biol. P. iii. c 3. † Fraser's Magazine, Oct. 1867.

may seem) seeds are the provided nutriment for living creatures. We also know that, in this world of ours, no power is lost; and the seeds which do not rise into animated beings go back into the great ocean of life, out of which other creatures may rise. All analogy leads us to believe that there is not an atom or germ in our world but serves some purpose, whether we are able to discover it or not.

Mr. Wallace maintains that, if the doctrine of final cause holds good, "there ought to be no natural objects which are disagreeable or ungraceful in our eyes. And it is undoubtedly the fact that there are many such. Just as surely as the horse and deer are beautiful and graceful, the elephant, rhinoceros, hippopotamus and camel are the reverse."* To this I reply, in the first place, that, according to the principle of final cause, God is not bound to make every creature beautiful. He has scattered beauty all around us, in earth and sky, in plant and animal, in man and woman; but it is not necessary for our happiness and comfort that he should impart to every object qualities which are fitted to raise excited æsthetic feeling. For, secondly, it is not reckoned the highest taste to have every part of a scene characterized by sublimity or beauty. In historical painting, the grand figures are made to stand out from plain neutral colors. And, once more, God contemplates, in all his works, higher ends than the gratification of æsthetic taste; and we are not to expect him to sacrifice utility to grace

* Natural Selection, viii.

or ornament. To apply these principles to only one of his examples: No one would say that the camel is as beautiful as the horse or the deer; yet no one who has true taste will say that it is ugly. The camel is an object of interest to every thinking mind, and has even a sort of beauty, as it is seen performing its beneficent ends in its native clime. It has been shown that what may seem to be deformities enable it the better to fulfil the good ends of its existence. The enlargement of its feet, with their convex soles, allows it to tread easily on the loose yielding sand of the desert; and the callosities, or pads, upon its legs allow it to lie down and repose on scorching surfaces. And these humps are supplies of superabundant nourishment provided for their long journeys: so that, when deprived of other food, their frames feed on this nutriment; and it has been observed that, at the close of a long journey, their humps have been much diminished in size. Every organ has thus a purpose, though that may not be the production of beauty.

Mr. Spencer appeals to a profounder series of facts, which seem to show that there are provisions in nature which seem to produce evil, instead of good. "Still more marked is this contrast between the two hypotheses, in presence of that vast amount of suffering entailed on all orders of sentient beings by their imperfect adaptations to their conditions of life, and the further vast amount of suffering entailed on them by enemies and by parasites. We saw that, if the organisms were severally designed for their respective places in nature, the inevitable conclusion is, that these thousands of kinds of inferior organisms, which prey upon superior organisms, were intended to inflict all the pain and mortality which results. But the hypothesis of evolution involves us in no such dilemma. Slowly, but surely, evolution brings about an increasing amount of happiness, all evils being incidental." * I acknowledge that Mr. Spencer has here come in sight of a mystery, which our mere academic theists are unwilling to look at, — the profound mystery of the existence of pain and evil in our world. It brings us back to that old contest which, we have seen, has characterized our world from the beginning. Religion cannot dispel that cloud, but it so far irradiates it. These groanings and travailings of the old world seem but an anticipation of the grand battle between ignorance and light, between sin and salvation, in the present era of our earth's history.† We who have risen to a belief in the existence and in the benevolence of God can cherish the reasonable conviction that "what we know not now we shall know hereafter;"

* Principles of Biology, P. iii. 3.

† In answering a like objection brought by Mr. Lewes, I find the thoughtful comparative anatomist of the age, Professor Owen, remarking: "True it is, this is a world of pain as well as of pleasure, wherein I may ask Positivism leave to say, 'God works by means.' Patience, endurance, faith in the end designed, a nature purified as by fire, accepting the trial with thanksgiving, — these be facts visible amongst the higher recognizable phenomena offered to our pondering here below." — *Fraser's Magazine*, Oct. 1867.

that there has been all along goodness in what has occurred; and that the good shall at last utterly destroy the evil. But what can they make of it who believe in no God, and who can see no trace of his goodness in nature? What can they make of those convulsions of nature which have swept away so many animated creatures, so many human beings apparently in the midst of torture, — though, in the case of the lower animals, with less pain than we suppose? What are they to make of pain and sorrows and bereavements when they come upon themselves? Not only can they see no meaning, they have no ground for believing that there is a meaning. They come they know not whence; they tend they know not whither. There is no Father's love in them for the present, and where they may end they cannot tell. Mr. Spencer refers us, as if to comfort us, to the hypothesis of evolution: "Slowly, but surely, evolution brings about an increasing amount of happiness, all evils being incidental." Would this give comfort to the widow grieving over the separation from a husband, to the father deprived of an only son, to the tender woman racked for years with pain? Would it compose their grief to tell them that, fifty millions of years hence, things by rubbing would be so adapted to each other that there might be no more pain or sorrow; being obliged to add, if they told the whole truth, that in fifty millions more the whole race of animated creatures would be, slowly but surely, burnt up in fire? Would they not, as we urged this consolation, say in reply: "Miserable comforters are ye all! — Ye are all physicians of no value"? I do believe that the evolution which we actually see in the world is so beneficently arranged that all the evils are incidental, and that there is an ever-increasing amount of happiness; but it is because it has been arranged by a good God. Without this, evolution might work an ever-increasing amount of misery, and direst evils be the direct consequence. Mr. Spencer is ever telling us, in his usual dogmatic manner and his customary generalizing flights, that the operation of evolution and physical law must be beneficial. But I see no necessity for this: I can find no security for it. If the powers at work be blind forces, they may as readily produce destruction as beneficent construction, and would probably produce now the one and now the other. True, if they be modes of God's action, the issue must be beneficent; for there is intelligence in them and benevolence in them.

It thus appears, as the result of our lengthened induction, that in the midst of the potencies of nature there is a Divine power controlling and guiding them to ends; and bringing order, I do not say out of confusion, for there is no proof that there ever was confusion in God's universe, — chaos is a creation of heathenism, and was never seen in the actual world, — but producing order where there might have been confusion, and making a Cosmos where there might have been a chaos.

(2.) There is the appearance ever and anon of New Agencies. We may allow that there were mechanical, gravitating, and it may be chemical properties in the original star dust. But, superinduced on these, there are new powers. Life appears; plants appear; animals appear; new species of plants and animals appear; and man appears with his high capacities. It is easy for flippant minds to talk of all this being effected by natural forces; but the forces which could accomplish this have not yet been exposed to our view. It may seem profound wisdom to represent all this as produced by development, but development of itself implies a complex process of which we do not know the elements. The chemist cannot produce one of these agents in his laboratory, except out of agents already possessing them; and the widest observation in space and time has not detected nature accomplishing any such feat. The truly scientific man will not dogmatize as to how these agents were introduced, for he has no light from observation to guide him. The religious man, as he has no revelation to instruct him, has no right to say they are the result of a special fiat or of the arrangement of old materials, except indeed in the case of man, whose soul was breathed into him by the inspiration of the Almighty. That there has been law — that is, order — in the appearance of these new agents is very evident; but what were the means, if means there were, is unknown to us. Let us not assert where we have no evidence. But let us declare, for we have evidence, that God is to be seen in these new appearances, whether we trace them to an immediate creation or a preordained arrangement.

(3.) There is proof of Plan in the Organic Unity and Growth of the World. As there is evidence of purpose, not only in every organ of the plant, but in the whole plant; not only in every limb of the animal, but in the whole animal frame, and in the growth of both plant and animal from month to month and year to year: so there are proofs of design, not merely in the individual plant and individual animal, but in the whole structure of the Cosmos and in the manner in which it makes progress from age to age. Every reflecting mind, in tracing the development of the plant or animal, will see a design and a unity of design in it, in the unconscious elements being all made to conspire to a given end, in the frame of the animated being taking a predetermined form; so every one trained in the great truths of advanced science should see a contemplated purpose in the way in which the materials and forces and life of the universe are made to conspire, to secure a progress through indeterminate ages. The persistence of force may be one of the elements conspiring to this end; the law of Natural Selection may be another, or it may only be a modification of the same: all and each work in the midst of a struggle for existence, in which the strong prevail and the weak disappear. But in all this there is a starting point and a terminus, and rails along which the powers run, and an intelligence planning and guiding the whole, and bringing it to its destination freighted with blessings.

The accomplishment of all this implies arrangement and co-agency. There are order and progression, we have seen, in the physical works of God: this is said, in modern nomenclature, to be a law. A law of what? Is it a law in the Divine mind? Yes: it is a law there before it appears as a law in nature. It is a rule of the Divine procedure. But is it not also a law of nature? It certainly is so in the loose acceptation of the word *law* now adopted. But in what sense? Certainly not in the sense of a simple, self-acting property, but in a widely different sense,—in the sense of a generalized fact or co-ordination of facts.* But all such laws are complex: they result from the co-ordination and

* Dr. Chalmers drew the distinction between the Laws of Matter and the Collocations of Matter, and drew the argument from design chiefly from the Collocations of Matter. I have shown that in General Laws collocations, or mutual adaptations, are always implied. "So far from general laws being able, as superficial thinkers imagine, to produce the beautiful adaptations which are so numerous in nature, they are themselves the results of nicely balanced and skilful adjustments. So far from being simple, they are the product of many arrangements; just as the hum which comes from a city, and which may seem a simple sound, is the joint effect of many blended voices; just as the musical note is the effect of numerous vibrations; as the curious circular atoll-reefs met with in the South Seas are the product of millions of insects. So far from being independent principles, they are dependent on many other principles. They are not agencies, but ends contemplated by Him who adjusted the physical agencies which produced them. As such,

adaptation of an immense body of agencies, just as the keeping of time by the chronometer results from an assortment of divers instruments, such as the mainspring and attached machinery. The revolution, for instance, of the earth round the sun is not a property either of the earth or of the sun, but of a combination of a centripetal and centrifugal force, and of the relation of the two bodies to each other. The law followed by the plant when it springs from the seed, grows and bears seed, is still more complex, employing a greater number of powers and adaptations of particles one to another, and of gravitating, chemical, electric, and vital agents. But the law of the progression of all plants and of all animals is a still more complex one, implying adjustment upon adjustment of all the elements and all the powers of nature towards the accomplishment of an evidently contemplated end, in which are displayed the highest wisdom and the most considerate goodness.

(4.) We see Higher and Higher Products appearing, and manifesting higher perfections of God. The blind Forces are made to work out Ideas in the Platonic Sense. The Mundus Sensibilis becomes a Mundus Intelligibilis, taking forms with geometric proportions and of æsthetic beauty, and clothed with melodious and harmonious colors.

they become the rules of God's house, the laws of his kingdom; and wherever we see such laws, there we see the certain traces of a law-giver." — *Method of Divine Government*, B. II. c. i. § 3.

Sensation and feeling now appear; and there is a wonderful structure and adaptation of limb and joint and nerve to furnish means of activity and of enjoyment, which in the whole animal creation become great beyond calculation. We now see that this intelligent is also a benevolent power. Crowning all, we have Mind and the Law written in the heart, and declaring that right is above might; and we have the good advancing in the midst of opposition, and in the face of opposition, asserting that it will at last subdue all to itself, and rule in the name of God. And we now see what God reckons the highest of all, — higher than order, higher than intelligence, higher than sensation; and this is holiness, — a holiness not independent of intelligence, but a holy intelligence; not independent of love, but a holy love. God is the same in all time; but, as the ages roll on, they unfold higher and ever higher perfections. These three — the Power, the Intelligence, the Benevolence — are seen combining to form the pure white light of holy love. "God is a Spirit," "God is Light," and "God is Love." These are the stars which have emerged from the star dust to form One Grand Central Sun of pure and dazzling brightness, which we cannot open our eyes without seeing, but which, as we would gaze upon it, causes them to close in awe and adoration.

(5.) The journey we have taken, and the height we have reached, open glimpses of the Future History of our World. We see everywhere signs of progress. There is progress in agriculture, there is progress in the arts, there is progress in all the sciences; man's dominion over nature is rapidly increasing, and the earth, every succeeding year, is made to yield a greater produce. The fruit of the discoveries of one age contains the germ of the discoveries of the generation following; and the new plant springs alongside of the old one to scatter seed like its progenitor all around. No valuable invention of human genius is ever lost; and most of them become the means of multiplying themselves by a greater than compound proportion, and thus render each generation richer than the one that went before. The wealth of all preceding generations is thus to be poured into the lap of the generations that are to live in the coming ages of our world's history. The struggle for existence still goes on; but there is evidence that the intellectual is to show itself stronger than the physical and the moral, always under the government of God, stronger than either. For the present, we see the serpent biting the heel of the seed of the woman: but the age of serpents, with their crushing force and their cunning, is to pass away; and we see proof that the woman's heaven-born seed is to crush the head of the serpent; and, as Plato forecast it, the good shall be the uppermost, and the evil the undermost, for evermore.

I do not know whether any of my hearers have ever gone up from Riffelberg to Görner Grat, in the

High Alps, to behold the sun rise. Every mountain catches the light according to the height which the upheaving forces that God set in motion have given it. First the point of Monte Rosa is kissed by the morning beams, blushes for a moment, and forthwith stands clear in the light. Then the Breithorn and the dome of Muschabel and the Matterhorn, and twenty other grand mountains, embracing the distant Jung Frau, receive each in its turn the gladdening rays, bask each for a brief space, and then remain bathed in sunlight. Meanwhile, the valleys between lie down dark and dismal as death. But the light which has risen is the light of the morning; and these shadows are even now lessening, and we are sure they will soon altogether vanish. Such is the hopeful view I take of our world. "Darkness covered the earth, and gross darkness the people;" but God's light hath broken forth as the morning, and to them who sat in darkness a great light has arisen. Already I see favored spots illuminated by it: Great Britain and her spreading colonies; and Prussia, extending her influence; and the United States, with her broad territory and her rapidly increasing population,—stand in the light; and I see, not twenty, but a hundred points of light, striking up in our scattered mission stations, — in old continents and secluded isles and barren deserts, according as God's grace and man's heaven-kindled love have favored them. And much as I was enraptured with that grand Alpine scene, and shouted irrepressibly as I surveyed it, I am still more elevated, and I feel as if I could cry aloud for joy, when I hear of the light advancing from point to point, and penetrating deeper and deeper into the darkness which, we are sure, is at last to be dispelled, to allow our earth to stand clear in the light of the Sun of Righteousness.

IV.

PROOF OF THE EXISTENCE OF MIND AND OF ITS POSSESSING THE CAPACITY OF KNOWLEDGE. — DOCTRINES OF NESCIENCE AND RELATIVITY.

THROUGHOUT the previous discussions I have been constantly obliged to employ or to refer to philosophic principles. In the full exposition of the argument, it will be necessary to consider these, as well as the physical facts, that the defence may be complete throughout. But this implies that we take a look at the soul of man. Not that we are to examine the mind in its entirety; not that we are to dissect it metaphysically: we are to view it simply in its relation to God and to religion. Some of the discussions on which I am to enter may seem a little too recondite; but all of them bear upon the prevailing errors of the day. I profess to keep a sharp outlook on the current of opinion all over the world, especially among young men. I am ever asking the watchman, "What of the night?" and, in these Lectures, I take up the topics of the day; but it would be better not to discuss them at all than not discuss them thoroughly. In coming Lectures, I will start from the positions reached in this to examine Positivism and Materialism, — the doctrines likely to flourish for a season among the young men who catch the spirit of the age in its latest fashion.

Those whom I am opposing constitute a school with a diversity of teachers. Though, as a whole, they are men of narrow sympathies and an exclusive temper, and can discern only a small segment of the wide and profound meaning of the universe, — are, in fact, not catholic nor cosmopolitan, but intensely sectarian in their spirit, — yet they cultivate with zeal and ability a number of branches of knowledge. Their physiology is associated with a psychology and a philosophy, and, I may add, a method of history. They have men of eminence in each of these departments; and each in his way joins with others in their way in furthering a common cause and fostering a common belief, or rather unbelief. They have some of the literary and scientific institutions of Great Britain very much in their own hands, and are seeking to find a place in others. They are laboring to lay hold of young men connected with the press, and have been specially successful with two classes: with those who would like to be thought philosophers, but who have no time nor taste for the study of a deeper philosophy; and with those who, in a feeling of disappointment, have been obliged to turn aside from their intended professions in life — most commonly the church — to engage in literary pursuits. They have a body of adherents eager to propagate their system, and ever ready to make an assault on all who would inculcate a philosophy of a higher and more spiritual character.

There is a unity in their system and in their ends. They aim at accounting for the whole of nature by development out of they know not what. They derive man from the brutes, and make him merely an upper brute. They do not deny the existence of the soul; but they identify it with the body. All the higher ideas of man they manufacture, by means of association of ideas, out of impressions got by the senses and an inward sentient experience, and by development from the lower races of humanity and the ancestral animals through millions of ages. History is a mere evolution of natural causes, working without any discoverable meaning or end. The lower animals and the plants come out of the protoplasm, and the protoplasm out of the star dust, and the star dust out of they know not what, — out of what never can be known, and about which, therefore, it is unphilosophical to inquire. They all agree that of the nature and reality of things we know nothing, and can know nothing. All that we know is represented as *Relative;* that is, we can know any one thing merely in relation to some other one thing, itself unknown. They are determinedly agreed that we can discover no indications of first or final causes; that the supernatural, if there be a supernatural, must lie in a region beyond human ken; and that religion has no title to excite a fear or kindle a hope. A young friend of mine, who had to sit from day to day, through a college session, under a distinguished professor belonging to this school, told me that, at the close of every lecture, he had to debate with himself the question : "Have or have I not a soul?" "Am I a reality?" or, "Is there any reality?" As having to withstand the assaults of these men who profess to go down so deep, we must see that our foundations are well laid.

I. AND SO THE QUESTION IS STARTED, WHAT PROOF HAVE WE OF THE EXISTENCE OF MIND? It is necessary to take up such an elementary question as this in our day, to meet the advancing materialism which is springing out of the decay (as they suppose) of all old creeds, philosophical and theological. A materialism, refined, æsthetical, but sensualistic, has been the reigning philosophy (if philosophy it can be called) in France, under that repression of free thought, ever bursting out in secret license, which characterized the *régime* of Louis Napoleon. It has considerable power among physicists in Germany; being the hollow, in this age, on the back of the height which thinkers occupied in the last age (it is, in fact, the bog into which the will-a-wisp Hegelianism has conducted not a few of those who followed it), — my hope is that it will be so far counteracted by the glorious outburst of patriotism which the present war has called forth, and which has been fond of recognizing a providence. It is the issue — whether they see it or no, whether they mean it or no — to which Mill's association theory, and Bain's identification of all our thoughts and feelings with the body, and Mr. Herbert Spencer's development of all things out of an unknowable nothing, and Huxley's physical basis of life and mind in molecular action, are severally and conjointly conducting the young thinkers of Great Britain. The sun rises some hours later in America than in Europe; and doctrines which have sprung up in Deutschland, and come across to England, like a fog from the German Ocean, take some little time to cross the Atlantic; but already we see proof that we are on the eve of a conflict with a physico-philosophy, which would account for all mental action and ideas by molecular motion, or some form of material agency. To meet it, we lay down a few simple positions.

1. *Man has means of knowing the existence of mind as immediate as the means of knowing the existence of matter.* — It is necessary to make this remark, because it is often said that man can know directly only his own bodily frame and the objects falling under his senses, and can arrive at the knowledge of mind — if, indeed, there be a mind, and if he can come to be certain of its existence — only by a circuitous process. It is supposed that he comes first to know the existence of his material organism; and that, proceeding upon this, he concludes that there is or may be a spiritual principle, as it were lying deeper in than the visible and tangible frame. According to this view, our knowl-

edge of the existence of mind is reached by a process of inference, and there are persons who dispute its legitimacy. They tell us that, as physiology is advancing in its researches, mind is retiring farther and farther back; and not a few are cherishing the expectation that, in the course of time, they may be delivered from it altogether; and that they may account for every exercise of thought and feeling by mechanical and chemical processes, by electric and nervous agency. Now, I meet all these objections by denying that it is by any such lengthened or circuitous process that we come to discover the existence of mind. I affirm that we know mind, just as we know matter, directly and immediately.

We can, in a sense, experiment upon the mind, in order to discover its working. We set out from our dwelling into the heart of a pleasant scene of hills and vales, and trees and streams. It is not by a perplexing process of reasoning that we believe this oak and that rock to exist: we have an intuitive and immediate knowledge of them by the senses. While we look at these objects, we are conscious that we do so; we are conscious, intuitively and immediately conscious, of a self different from the scene we are contemplating. While we behold the objects, we are led to form certain judgments regarding them: this hill is higher than this other hill; this tree is a pine and this other a maple; this stream is pure and flowing rapidly. While we thus judge and reason about these objects, we are conscious of a self that is doing so. While we are enjoying the scene, we see a company of children playing on the bank of the river, and they seem so happy that we rejoice in their joy, and are as conscious of our joy as we are of their existence. But, unexpectedly, two of the boys begin to quarrel; and the stronger knocks the other into the water, and the stream is bearing him along, apparently, to destruction. We are forthwith filled with horror and indignation at the deed; we feel ourselves reprobating the conduct of the violent youth; and, feeling pity for the boy who is sinking in the waters, we rush into the stream in the hope of rescuing him. We are as certain that there is a something perceiving the scene, as that there is a scene perceived; that there is a mind comparing the hills, trees, and streams, as that there are hills, trees, and streams to be compared; that there is a soul reprobating the passionate boy, as that there is a boy to be reprobated; that we have not more convincing evidence that there is a boy drowning in the river, than we have of the other fact that we are cherishing compassion towards him; and we are not more assured that the child is in danger, than we are that we have resolved to rescue him. And let us observe, carefully, how much is implied in what we have thus felt as passing through our minds: we are conscious of a self performing a great number and variety of acts, as perceiving, judging, reasoning, distinguishing between good and evil, as under the influence of deep emotion, as willing and fulfilling our determinations. It follows:—

2. *That we have a positive though limited knowledge of mind, even as we have a positive though limited knowledge* of body. There are eminent metaphysicians, among whom we may reckon Kant, who maintain that we can know nothing of matter, except that it exists: matter is described as the unknown something producing the impressions which we feel in our minds. Now, with all deference to the distinguished men who have held this dogma, I believe it to be utterly inconsistent with the intuitive declarations of consciousness. Man is possessed of a power or attribute, by which he knows, I believe, immediately, the objects by which he is surrounded. He knows matter as extended in length, breadth, and depth, and as exercising certain active properties, as moving or striking other objects, or as being repelled. In all this, it is true, he is far from knowing all about matter: matter may have properties which are latent,—latent, inasmuch as we have never seen them exercised; or latent, inasmuch as we may never be able to discover them; but still he has a knowledge, limited, no doubt, but positive and trustworthy so far as it goes. I have referred to this error at the one extreme, only that I may be able the better to expose an error at the other extreme. A living writer says that the only method by which mind can be defined as a substance is, "by taking the realities of which we have experience, and abstracting one property after another, until we have an entity without extension, with-

out resistance, without parts, without divisibility," &c. Now, it appears to me, we might with as much propriety declare that we could not define matter except as an entity, without consciousness, without thought, without will. Just as we define matter by positives as extended, as possessed of attraction and other properties; so we may define mind by positive qualities, all of them known to us, because we have constant experience of them. We may define it as possessing consciousness, intelligence, conscience, emotion, will. The fact is, that, being immediately conscious of mind and its varied actings from hour to hour, and minute to minute, we know more of mind than we know of matter. True, we do not possess a perfect knowledge of man's mental, any more than of his corporeal, nature. We do not know and cannot be expected to know it, as the God who made it knows it: still we have in consciousness a means, and this an immediate means, of knowing so much of its nature and properties, as thinking, feeling, desiring, willing.

3. *As matter cannot be resolved into mind on the one hand, so mind cannot be resolved into matter on the other.* There have been attempts made by ingenious metaphysicians, as by Bishop Berkeley and by Fichte, so to refine matter as to leave little but the name: it is represented either as an idea created by the Divine Mind, to be viewed by the created mind, or as a projection of the human mind itself. There is also a school of physical

speculators in the present day, who are seeking to spiritualize matter by stripping it of some of its distinguishing properties, such as its extension or its occupation of space. With them matter is merely a name for certain powers, mechanical, chemical, or electric, which are supposed to produce all the phenomena falling under the senses. This refined view of body, though supported by names of repute, seems to be inconsistent with that immediate and intuitive knowledge which we possess of it, as not only exercising dynamical powers, but as extended and solid. But while opposing all attempts to resolve matter into mind, I would also set myself against the attempt to resolve mind into matter. By our primitive cognitions, we know matter as extended, solid, divisible, and exercising such qualities as attraction and repulsion; but we also know self as perceiving, judging, reasoning, devising, hating, fearing, loving.

To those who would aver that mind may be merely a modification of matter, I reply, *first*, that the two are made known to us by different organs: we know the one, matter, by the senses; we know the other, mind, by self-consciousness. No man ever saw a thought, touched an emotion, or heard a volition. Nor are we conscious, within the thinking mind, of space occupied, or hardness, or color. We reply, *secondly*, and more particularly, that we know them as possessed of essentially different properties: we know the one as occupying space and exercising certain attractive powers; whereas we know the other as capable of judgment, purpose, and affection. If any one will maintain that, notwithstanding these differences, the two can be reduced to one, the burden of proof lies upon him. And I have never found the materialist advancing any evidence which can stand a sifting scrutiny. He has not demonstrated, and I believe it is impossible for him to demonstrate, that any modification of mere matter — be it electric, nervous, or whatever else — can yield those peculiar phenomena of which we are conscious in the thinking and feeling mind; can give intelligence and choice, and the perception of the distinction between good and evil; or those lofty affections and heroic resolutions which constitute the noblest characteristics of humanity.

I have never found those materialists who profess to explain mental action by material forces so much as having a clear idea of the thing to be explained. The physiologist may, by the study of the nerves and brain, come to know what the nerves and brain are, and has shown that they are soft, pulpy substances, with a certain chemical composition. He has tried to show that electricity will explain all the properties of the nerves, and in this he has hitherto been unsuccessful; for while electricity travels along a tied nerve, the nervous fluid does not. But though he should be successful, he would not thereby enlighten us on the subject of intellect or volition: he might show under what physiological conditions they arise, but would not thereby throw light on the intellect and volition themselves. Let us suppose that an electric force runs along a pulpy substance, the nerve, till it reaches another pulpy substance, the brain, still we have not thereby explained that essentially different phenomenon which we call *thought*, or that other phenomenon which we call *will*. An electric force is one thing, and the ingenious thought of Faraday in speculating on that force is an entirely different thing. An affection of the pulpy substance, the brain, is one thing; and the determination of the mind to resist temptation, the determination of Joseph, for example, when he said, "Can I do this great wickedness and sin against God?" is an entirely different thing. To confound them is to confound things which, so far from being the same, have not even a common point of resemblance. The physiologist can explain, in a curious manner at times, how certain thoughts and feelings arise; but after all he has left the essential point untouched: he has not explained, nay, he has not so much as attempted to explain, thought itself, or volition, or emotion.

In a later Lecture we must subject Materialism to a thorough examination. Meanwhile, I am establishing principles as a preparation for reviewing the prevalent systems of the day. All that I have said has been allowed clearly and unequivocally by Professor Tyndall.* "The passage from the physics of the brain to the corresponding facts of consciousness is unthinkable. Granted that a definite thought and a definite molecular action in the brain occur simultaneously, we do not possess the intel-

* Address before British Association, Aug. 1868.

lectual organ, nor apparently any rudiment of the organ, which would enable us to pass by a process of reasoning from the one phenomenon to the other. They appear together, but we do not know why. Were our minds and senses so expanded, strengthened, and illuminated as to enable us to see and feel the very molecules of the brain; were we capable of following all their motions, all their groupings, all their electric discharges, if such there be, and were we intimately connected with the corresponding states of thought and feeling,—we should probably be as far as ever from the solution of the problem, How are these physical processes connected with the facts of consciousness? The chasm between the two classes of phenomena would still remain intellectually impassable. Let the consciousness of love, for example, be associated with a right-handed spiral motion of the molecules of the brain, and the consciousness of hate with a left-handed spiral motion: we should then know when we love, that the motion is in one direction, and when we hate, the motion is in another direction; but the Why would still remain unanswered." I am not prepared to accept all the phraseology employed in this passage about the phenomena being "associated" and "appearing together," and about the "how" and the "why." We shall show that mind obeys laws of its own very different from those of matter. As to the "how" and the "why," they are in the end referred by this whole school to the region of the unknowable, and they may assert that, though we cannot discover the "how" and the "why," after all thinking may be material. But it is admitted that we are conscious of thought and feeling, of love and hate, and this is enough for my present purpose. The consideration of the more subtle materialism that might be consistent with Mr. Tyndall's statement must be reserved to a future Lecture.

II. THE NEXT QUESTION IS, WHAT DOES THE MIND REVEAL TO US? And, here, in order to settle what realities we have, we must first be rid of certain counterfeits. For we are met at this point by ghosts, which have been walking abroad in the darkness. I have been seeking for years past to scare them away, but have not succeeded, for there are still persons believing in them and frightening us with them; and it is the law of the life of errors, as it is the law of the life of ghosts, that, as long as men believe in them, they will appear: the demand brings the supply; the eye that is looking for them will certainly see them.

I hold, very strenuously, that man is so constituted that he can attain knowledge, that he can know things. I maintain that man's intelligent acts begin with his knowing things. By the senses he knows things: his own bodily frame as affected by all the senses; a solid body by the muscular sense, and a colored surface by the eye. We also know things by self-consciousness, or the inward sense: we know self as thinking, feeling or willing — as at this moment pleased or not pleased with this Lecture. I have studiously chosen my words. In using them, I do not mean that we know simply thinking, feeling, or willing: these have no separate or independent existence, — have no existence apart from self thinking, feeling, or willing, — are in fact mere abstractions. What we know is self thinking, feeling, willing; not self apart from these operations, but self in these operations. This may seem too nice a distinction; but it is the only expression which unfolds the full truth. A man is not conscious of thinking apart from self, any more than he is conscious of self apart from thinking, or some other exercise. It appears, then, that, both by the outward and the inward sense, we begin with knowledge, with the knowledge of things.

But I hear some one asking in astonishment, Do you really mean to say that you know the thing, — the thing in itself? It is said of Scotchmen, whether justly or not I will not take it upon myself to say — for I am not altogether impartial in speaking of Scotchmen — but, truly or falsely, it is alleged of Scotchmen that, when asked a sharp question, they are apt to put a sharp question in return. I am inclined to use the Scotchman's privilege on this occasion, and inquire, What do you mean by a *thing in itself?* The phrase is a German one, the translation of *Ding an sich*, so frequently used by Kant, and with which so many have been conjuring of late years. What a thing means, I know; and I hold that, in every exercise of the senses, we know the thing, this body or that body; and that in every exercise of self-consciousness we know the thing itself, that is, ourselves in a particular state. But what is meant by the *thing in itself* I do not know; and, think it proper not to affect to know. Does it mean that, besides the thing we know, there is something else, — a thing *plus itself?* This *itself*, in addition to the thing, I confess I do not know; and, as knowing nothing of it, I have no faith in its existence, and I do not see any purpose to be served by it. If it mean that the thing is within the thing, I have about as clear a notion of what is signified as I have of the whale that swallowed itself, or of the Kilkenny cats which ate one another all but the tails. Maintaining that we know the thing, I give up the *in itself* to metaphysicians as a ghost to be believed in, or not believed in, just as they please.

But then it is declared, gravely and pompously, by men who look as if they were possessed of all wisdom, that we do not know things, but *phenomena;* that is, appearances. And if, by this, they mean that we can know things only so far as they manifest themselves to us, I admit it: it is a truth; it is a truism. We know things only so far as they appear unto us. A man without eyes cannot see; without hearing, cannot hear. But then it is *the things* which manifest themselves unto us that we know. An appearance without a thing appearing is inconceivable, is an impossibility. Even a cloud appearing has something, is something: it is moisture in a vaporous state; and, were we to enter it, it would leave some of its sprinklings upon us. A shadow, even, is a something: it implies a dense body obstructing light, and keeping it from falling on a defined surface. An image in a mirror is something: it requires glass and quicksilver, and rays of light and an eye. In one of Longfellow's works, there is a dispute as to whether the narcissus, or its shadow reflected in the water, is the reality. The dispute can be settled. Both have a reality: the one in a solid plant, the other in rays of light coming from the plant and thence reflected. I admit that we know phenomena, and only phenomena, but this in the sense of things appearing.

But then it is said, Surely, you do not pretend that you know matter and mind as *substances?* Before replying, I have once more to insist that it be explained what is meant by the phrase. According to Locke, and English metaphysicians, it means something lying under, underneath, or behind the thing known. Locke says, Hamilton says, that this something is unknown and unknowable. Now, I am prepared to give up this substance beneath the thing, even as I gave up the *in itself*, which some place within the thing. This addition is supposed to be a substratum or support. But I am not sure that the thing, say mind or body, needs any such support. I cannot see that this shadowy thing, unknown and unknowable, cloud or abyss, or pit or darkness, is fitted as a substratum to bear up mind and body, which may require nothing else to uphold them as a substratum, beyond the powers with which God has endowed them.

But while I am ready to dispense with this under-support, as an intermeddler which would separate us from things, I maintain very resolutely that mind and body are entitled, not by the aid of any thing else, but of themselves, to be regarded as substances. And if some one pay me back in my own coin, and ask me what I mean by substance, I am prepared to answer. There are three things involved in substance: First, it has being; or, to speak more plainly, the thing exists. Secondly, it has potency; that is, power to act. Thirdly, it has a permanence, or a certain continuance and endurance, — such an abiding nature that it is not created by our looking at it; nor does it cease to exist because we have ceased to contemplate it. Whatever possesses these three qualities, I call a substance. Both mind and matter are known as possessing them. Mind, that is self, is known, first, as having existence or being. We thus know it in every act of self-consciousness. True, we can say little about bare being or existence; but this not because we do not know it, but because it is so simple. About complicated objects we can say a great deal — for instance, about the Roman empire, and modern civilization, and the constitution of the United States — because of their many elements and relations. But we can say little of such things as pain and pleasure and self, not because we do not know them, but because every one knows them, and they cannot be made clearer by a description: they involve no composition, and are not made up of ingredients.

> "Who thinks of asking if the sun is light,
> Observing that it lightens?"

Those who attempt any thing more, and to peer into the object, will find that the light (like that of the sun) darkens as they gaze upon it. "When I burned in desire to question them farther, they made themselves — air, into which they vanished." Again, we know mind as having potency or power; as influencing other things, and being influenced by other things; as exercising power over its own thoughts and over the bodily frame. Once more: I know it as so far permanent and independent that it is not a mere momentary or ephemeral impression or idea; it is not created by my looking at it; it existed prior to my observing it, and it was because it did so, that I was able to observe it; and it does not cease to exist because I have ceased to view it. The mind (like the body) having these three attributes, — being, potency, and permanence, — is to be regarded as a substance.

It is necessary to establish these points; for, ever since the days of David Hume, and especially in these days of revived scepticism, the subtlest form of infidelity proceeds on the denial of them. The denial is defended by metaphysicists, and is eagerly seized by physicists, who are no philosophers, but who are anxious to have a philosophy to serve their purpose. The whole school which I am opposing are defenders of the

DOCTRINE OF NESCIENCE.

It is called Nescience, in so far as it holds that man knows nothing, and can know nothing of the nature of things; and Nihilism, inasmuch as it is averred that there can be nothing known. It is acknowledged that we are cognizant of appearances; but then we do not and never can know whether these correspond to realities. This doctrine is commonly attributed to M. Comte; but the true author of it is my countryman, David Hume. Hume is commonly called the sceptic, and he did not repudiate the name; but the epithet scarcely characterizes him. He did not profess to deny the existence of God, or any thing else. He was evidently painfully affected, when the French Encyclopedists claimed him as an atheist. When the pert Mrs. Mallet came to him, and said: "We deists ought to know one another," he replied sternly (so differently from his usual good-nature): "Who told you that I was a deist?" His professed aim was to show that man can never know any thing of the nature of things, — can never reach philosophic truth, certainly never theological truth. Huxley very properly sets aside Comte as the founder of this school of philosophy. "So far as I am concerned, the most reverend prelate might dialectically hew M. Comte in pieces as a modern Agag, and I would not attempt to stay his hand.

In so far as my study of what specially characterizes the Positive Philosophy has led me, I find therein little or nothing of any scientific value, and a great deal which is thoroughly antagonistic to the very essence of science as any thing in Ultramontane Catholicism." The secret truth is, that the British followers of Comte do not like him; because, feeling that he himself and mankind generally need to have a faith and a worship, he busied himself, in his later days, in constructing a religion of his own, which is certainly sufficiently ludicrous, but is after all a reproach on those who have no religion. Mr. Huxley claims to install Hume as the founder and head of the philosophy which he adopts, and which I am inclined to call Humism. Hume says: "All the perceptions of the human mind resolve themselves into two distinct kinds of impressions and ideas." * He begins with impressions and ideas, — momentary impressions and ideas, — and not with things, and he declares, very properly, that out of these he can draw no realities. I meet this by showing that the mind commences, not with mere impressions and ideas, but with the knowledge of things; and on this primary knowl-

* "The difference betwixt these consists in the degree of force and liveliness with which they strike upon the mind, and make their way into our thought or consciousness. Those perceptions which enter with most force and violence we may name impressions; and under this name I comprehend all our sensations, passions, and emotions, as they make their first appearance in the soul. By ideas, I mean the faint images of these in thinking and reasoning." — Opening of *Treatise of Human Nature*.

edge it builds other and higher. And if I am asked for the proof, I answer that I have the same evidence of it as I have of the existence of impressions and ideas. I never do know an impression, except as an impression of self, the thing impressed; and, in doing so, I know both the impression and the thing impressed. I am never conscious of an idea except as an idea entertained by me. The two ever go together; and if I allow the existence of the one, I must allow the existence of the other: the one is as certain as the other; the one has the same self-evidence as the other. He who builds on any other foundation is building, not on the rock, not even on the sand, but on a surface of waters, or in the fleeting clouds. He who adopts the fundamental principle, that the mind does not start with the knowledge of things, must take all the rest. He must go through with it, even though it should carry and leave him where it left Hume; that is, in inextricable thickets and sinking swamps, in which he must wander on for ever, without coming to a termination: taking now this road, and now that road, to find them all "passages which lead to nothing;" beginning nowhere, and ending nowhere, crossing and recrossing, as the children of Israel did in their wanderings, but with no Canaan remaining for him as a place of rest.

DOCTRINE OF RELATIVITY.

Closely allied to this doctrine of Nescience, springing out of it or leading to it, is that of the Relativity of Knowledge; that is, that the mind does not perceive things, but the relations of things, of things utterly unknown. Grote thinks that this was the doctrine of Protagoras, the old Greek sophist, when he maintained that "man is the measure of all things." Now, I do not reject this doctrine because it was held by the sophists: I reject it because it is sophistic in the expression and defence of it. I reject it as so far untrue. I am not bound to accept it because it has been held by men whom I profoundly revere: such as Sir William Hamilton, of Edinburgh; Dr. Ulrici, of Halle; and Dr. Mansel, of Oxford. On Hamilton's publishing the doctrine in his "Discussions on Philosophy," I examined it in the Appendix to a new edition of my work on the "Divine Government;" and Hamilton meant to reply, but was prevented by infirmities terminating in his death. I labored to show that it was not agreeable to consciousness, and that it would certainly lead to fatal consequences. I was one of the first to protest, which I did in an article in the "North British Review" (Feb. 1859), against Dr. Mansel's application of the doctrine, in his famous Bampton Lectures on the "Limits of Religious Thought," to the defence of Religion, Natural and Revealed. Dr. Mansel thought to employ it to undermine Rationalism; but, in doing so, he undermined as well the ground on which religion stands — some one describes him as going out with a scythe to cut off the legs of others, and succeeding in cutting off his own legs. Mr.

Mill, as we might expect, has accepted the doctrine, only complaining that Hamilton does not carry it out consistently and consecutively. But people did not see the consequences till Herbert Spencer laid his whole system upon it as upon a bottomless abyss. It is a principle adopted by the whole school, and employed by them to undermine all higher truth, philosophic and theological. We have seen that Tyndall, when sore pressed with a difficulty about life and mind coming out of the incandescent star dust, seeks to extricate himself by appealing to "the law of relativity, which plays so important a part in modern philosophy."

The doctrine so designated takes as many shapes as Proteus; and when we would seize it in one form it takes another, and so eludes our grasp. It has, however, a true shape; and, when it takes this, we have only to commend it. There is a sense, or rather there are senses, in which man's knowledge is relative. First, he can know only so far as he has a capacity of knowing. In this sense, man's knowledge is all relative to himself. A man who has no eyes cannot know color; who has no ears cannot know sounds. There is the farther truth that man has the capacity of discovering relations between himself and other things, and between one thing and another. There is a third doctrine which is also true, that man's knowledge is finite: he cannot know all things; he cannot know all about any one thing. This, however, is not a doctrine of relativity: it is the old doctrine of man's knowledge being finite and not infinite, so earnestly inculcated by the Fathers of the Church, and by the profoundest divines and philosophers of modern times. So far we have truths, and truths of some importance, though the phrase Relativity is scarcely the word by which to express them.

But this solid truth is employed as a means of gathering round it other and tenebrous matter,—as the cuttle-fish, when we would catch it, surrounds itself with inky darkness. The doctrine, as interpreted by its defenders, means that we know relations and not things; and, in the case of some, that it is the mind that creates the relations, and that it adds the relation out of its own stores. When it can be made to take and to keep this shape, I seize it at once. This doctrine must issue logically in Nescience. Relations between things unknown can never yield knowledge. But I condemn it, not for its consequences, but because it is untrue, because it is inconsistent with consciousness.

It is inconceivable that we should know relations between things unknown. A relation is the aspect of things towards each other: the Greeks designated it by πρὸς τι. If the things were to cease, there would be no relation; and if the things were unknown, there would be no relations known. Gravitation is a relation of one body to another, say between the sun and the earth; but if there were no sun and no earth, there would be no such relation, and if the sun and earth were unknown to me, I could never know a relation between them.

A relation is a relation of things known, — so far known, — known *qua* that relation. We know that we are related to our fellow-men, because we know what we are, and what our fellow-men are. We know in what relation we stand to God, because we so far know God and know ourselves.

The settlement of these points will be found to have a more direct bearing than might at first appear upon our argument. If man's soul be material, we have really no ground on which to proceed in inferring that there is a spiritual God. The subtlest form of infidelity in our day proceeds on the principle that man knows nothing of the nature or reality of things, or that he can know nothing except relations between things unknown. It no longer takes the form of rationalism, pretending to discover truth which in fact revelation has made known, and in the end setting itself above revelation: it makes human reason proclaim that it cannot discover any truth beyond and above the phenomena of sentient experience. It does not just deny that there is a God, — this, it says, would be unphilosophical, — but it declares that God, if there be a God, is and must be unknown. It does not say that man has not a soul; but it identifies that soul with the body, and thus leaves no evidence that the soul may live after the body dies. It is of course unreasonable to seek after this unknowable God if haply we may find him, or to imagine that we are bound to pay him worship, or that we have any duties to discharge towards him; and as to the other world, if there be another world, we may not draw from it any fears of punishment or hopes of blessedness. In meeting this fundamental scepticism, we need to stand up for the veracity of the human faculties, and to show that the same powers which guide correctly in the business of life and in the pursuits of science are legitimately fitted to conduct to a reasonable belief in One presiding over the works of nature and providentially guiding our lot. This baldest of all the philosophies, which have sprung up in our world, is requiring reason to abnegate one of its indefeasible rights, is cutting the root which supports man's most aspiring hopes, is denying to the soul its highest exercises, is shearing it of its chief glories. It is unlawfully circumscribing that noble view which reason opens, and laboring to keep man gazing for ever on the ground like the beast, when his destiny is to look out on that distant horizon and upward to the glories of heaven.

V.

MENTAL PRINCIPLES INVOLVED IN THE THEISTIC ARGUMENT. — OUR IDEAS LEAD US TO BELIEVE IN GOD AND CLOTHE HIM WITH POWER, PERSONALITY, GOODNESS, AND INFINITY. — GOD SO FAR KNOWN. — CRITICISM OF MR. HERBERT SPENCER. — GOD SO FAR UNKNOWN.

IN these Lectures I have been looking first at the physical world as it is regarded by modern science. But the physical facts do not show that there is a God, unless we take along with them certain general principles. This induced me in my last Lecture to turn to Mental Science, when I showed, first, that the mind exists; and, secondly, that it has the capacity of acquiring knowledge. I am now to show that, in the exercise of this its capacity, it can rise to the knowledge of God and clothe him with infinite perfections.*

Let us understand what I maintain in regard to man's capacity of knowledge. I hold that he has a power of intuition; that is, of looking directly on things without him and things within. But I cer-

* In this Lecture I have used the principles established in my work on the "Intuitions of the Mind," to which I refer those who may wish to see the foundation on which I build more fully discussed.

tainly do not stand sponsor for such innate ideas as Locke exposed till they perished with no one to protect them. Nor do I defend those *a priori* forms which the mind, according to Kant, imposes on things, giving to things what is not in the things, or announcing beforehand what things are, or what they should be. Out of these *a priori* forms, categories, and ideas, able men in Germany constructed in the last age a solemn and ambitious speculative philosophy, which has had its brief season in Britain and America, and may still be seen lingering among us, like venerable gray locks on the heads of men above fifty. But, like the foliage in the fall, it has faded into the "sere and yellow leaf;" and, though still shining in gorgeous colors, its destiny is to die; when, as it contains some elements of truth, it may help, I hope, to form a fruitful soil, — so different from a barren sensationalism, — out of which something better may spring. What I stand up for is a much less proud and pretentious thing: it is not a form to be imposed or superinduced on things, but a power of looking at things. This knowledge is, at first, only of individual things, — of things in the concrete, as they present themselves. But out of this it can draw great abstract and general truths, rising out of great depths and mounting to great heights, constituting a body of philosophy based on the earth, but towering to heaven. It is because we have this original knowledge that we can add to it derived knowledge. Having this acquaintance with individual things, we can rise to general laws about things. Having begun with realities, not with mere impressions, ideas, and phenomena, all that we reach by the abstracting, generalizing process is also real; and this not only a reality in thought, but, thought being rightly conducted, a reality in things.

And, among other things which we thus perceive directly and intuitively, I hold that there is Power; not Power in the abstract, but things exercising Power. This gives the principle of Cause and Effect. I know that I have come to a keenly agitated question. It is acknowledged on all hands that the law of universal causation is sanctioned by an enlarged experience. It is confessed to be the widest law which the mind of man has reached. No exceptions have been found to it. in any part at least of the physical universe, near or far. But some of us maintain that it is more; that it is a conviction of our mental nature, not a conviction above objective things, but a conviction in regard to things. I hold, our consciousness witnessing thereto, that we perceive things, both within and without us, not merely as having existence, but as having potency. We cannot know directly any object without us, except as having power upon us. When we act, we are exercising power. Potency, or property of some kind, is an essential element of things as known to us. When a thing is known to me, I know it, not as an impression, an idea, a bare phenomenon: I know it as exercising power on me or some other thing. Thus knowing power intuitively, we are constrained to connect an effect, a thing effected, with a thing having power to produce it.

But how does all this bear, it may be asked, on the religious question? I answer, Much in every way. Our knowledge of mind is needed, in addition to our knowledge of matter, as a complement to make up our knowledge of God. In particular, the principle of cause and effect supplies the *nexus* which connects God with his works. We have seen in previous Lectures, that everywhere, all throughout the Cosmos and throughout the Æons, there is an adaptation of one thing to another, of every part to every other, of the part to the whole, and of the whole to every part. This shows that there has been a disposition and an arrangement, — in short, a thing effected; and this entitles us, on the principle of cause and effect, to argue that there must have been a cause. It has the guarantee of the observation of external nature, which goes as far as observation can go in establishing a universal law. But it has a higher certitude — the guarantee of a mental principle looking to the very nature of things, and entitling us to argue, not merely within our experience, but beyond it, as to things in general and everywhere, that an effect must have a cause; not only that this watch has had a watch-maker, but that this orderly constructed world has had a world-maker.

If we had not a Spiritual Nature ourselves, we could not rise to the contemplation of God, who is a Spirit. Were we incapacitated for knowledge, we could not mount to the knowledge and contemplation of God. Did we not know ourselves as substances, we never could ascend to the knowledge of God as a substance. But, from the nature of the effects of which we are conscious within ourselves, we ascend to the recognition of a cause adequate to produce them. Having ourselves a spiritual nature, we conceive of God as a spirit. As having a sense, or rather cognition, of power in ourselves, we are led to clothe with power the Being from whom we have sprung. If we believe that the God who made the eye does himself see, we must also believe that he who gave us our knowing powers must himself know.

It is in the same way that we rise to a belief in the Personality of God. Some of those who have been fixed in the grasping vice of the metaphysics of Kant have been sorely troubled with this question; and others, who picture God as unknowable, have taken advantage of their perplexities. We may be "persons," they say; but then it is because we are finite. Personality, they urge, implies limitation. It is not difficult, I think, to solve this puzzle. We have an intuitive knowledge each one of himself as a person distinct from every other person and from the world. Kant, without meaning it, led the whole of German philosophy into a wide waste of pantheism by not allotting to personality a place among the original cognitions of the mind, — as he unfortunately called them "forms of the mind." Having a knowledge of ourselves as persons, we can rise to the contemplation of God as a person, of God as different from his works. It is true that we are limited in our personality as in every thing else: it does not follow that God is limited in his personality or any thing else. True, if we insist on saying that "God is all, and that all is God," we cannot give him personality; but then this is pantheism. And this consciousness which we have of our personality is the truth which undermines pantheism. I am conscious of self as a person different from the universe, different from God; so that God cannot be all, nor can all be God. But God, while he is a person different from his works, may be possessed of power, wisdom, goodness, to which no limits can be set.

But man has higher perceptions than these; and they enable him to clothe the Divine Being with still higher perfections. In looking at the voluntary acts of intelligent beings, he perceives that they may be good or that they may be evil: he sees that gratitude is good, and that cruelty is evil. Let us evolve what is involved in this idea. The good perceived implies that we are under obligation to attend to it; and the evil, that we are under obligation to avoid it. And being under obligation does seem to imply that we are under obligation to a Power, or rather a Being who will call us to account. This seems to point to God as the Moral Governor, and at last to be the Judge of the Universe. This is the only argument for the Divine existence which seemed conclusive to Kant, the great German metaphysician. It is the argument that seemed the strongest to the eloquent Scottish Theologian Chalmers. I am not sure that, taken by itself, it is sufficient to prove the existence of a living Being above the world, its Maker and Preserver. But there is no need of taking it by itself. Combining it with the argument from design, it proves that the God who lives and rules in this world is possessed of moral excellence. We are sure that he who planted the moral sense within us must approve of the good which it would lead us to approve of, and condemn the evil which it would lead us to condemn.

I am quite aware of the process by which persons endeavor to avoid the point of this argument. They would account for these moral feelings of ours by the association of ideas, which exercises some sort of chemical power upon our ideas, and transmutes ideas got from sense into ideas of moral good. Now, in opposition to this, I hold that the laws of association are the mere laws of the succession of our ideas and attached feelings, and can generate no new idea without a special inlet from without or capacity within. Association cannot give a man born blind the least idea of color, and as little can it produce any other idea. By mixing the colors of yellow and blue, the hand could produce green: but give a person the idea of yellow and the idea of blue, and from the two he could not manufacture the idea of green; still less could he, from these sensations or any others, form such ideas as those of moral good and evil. Take the perception of conscience, that deceit is a sin. Take the conviction, that we are not at liberty to tell a lie, when we might be tempted to do so. Take the judgment, that the person who has committed the act is guilty, condemnable, punishable. Take the feeling of remorse which rises when we contemplate ourselves as having told a falsehood. Take the very peculiar and profound ideas denoted by the phrases "obligation," "ought," "blameworthy." We have here a series of mental phenomena quite as real, and quite as worthy of being looked at, as our very sensations or ideas of pleasure and pain.

Give us mere sensations, say of sounds or colors or forms, or of pleasure and pain, and they will never be any thing else, in the reproduction of them, than the ideas of sounds, colors, forms, pleasures, or pains; unless, indeed, there be some new power introduced, and this new element, in itself or in conjunction with the sensations, be fitted to produce a new idea, and that very idea. The process by which some affect to generate our moral beliefs is like that of the old alchemists, who, when they put earth into the retort, never could get any thing but earth, and who could get gold only by surreptitiously introducing some substance containing gold. The philosopher's stone of this psychology is of the same character as that employed in mediæval physics. If they put in sensations only, as some do, they never have any thing but sensations; and a "dirt philosophy," as it has been called, is the product. If gold is got, it can only be because it has been quietly introduced by the person who exhibits it. Provided we had the ideas, the laws of association might show how they could be brought up again; and how, in the reproduction, certain parts might sink into shadow and neglect, while others came forth into light and prominence; and how the whole feeling, by the confluence of different ideas, might be wrought into a glow of intensity: but the difficulty of generating the ideas, such ideas, ideas so full of meaning, is not thereby surmounted. The idea I have of pain is one thing, and the idea I have of deceit — that it is morally evil, condemnable, deserving of pain — is an entirely different thing, our consciousness being witness. On the supposition that there is a chemical power, as is alleged, in association to create such ideas as those of duty and merit, sin and demerit, this chemical power would be a native moral power; not the product of sensations, but a power above them, and fitted to transmute them from the baser into the golden substance, and would entitle us to clothe that Being, who had given us such power, with the moral qualities with which he has endowed us.

But then it is urged that all that you have said does not prove that this Being, whom you have thus clothed with power and goodness, is the Infinite God. I admit this at once. No one ever said that it does. The physical works of God in the earth and heavens can never furnish proof of any thing more than the large, the immense, the indefinite, — not the infinite. To argue otherwise would be placing in the conclusion what is not in the premises. If we would clothe God with infinity, we must look within to our perceptions and belief as to infinity.

I feel that I am approaching a profound subject. It is not easy to sound its depths. It was long before I was able to attain any thing like clear ideas on the subject. I have pondered for many successive hours on it, only to find it shrouding itself in deeper mystery. On the one hand, I found the more profound philosophers of the continent of Europe giving this idea of the Infinite a high place, indeed the highest place, in their systems. In coming back from flights in company with the German metaphysicians, to inquire of British philosophers what they make of this idea, I found their views meagre and unsatisfactory; for the idea of the infinite, according to them, is a mere negation, a mere impotency. But if we can entertain no such idea, how do all men speak of it? If it be a mere impotency, how do we come to clothe the Divine Being with Infinity?

Feeling as if I needed somewhere to find it, I proceed in the truly British or Baconian method to inquire, How does such an idea or belief in the infinite, as the mind actually has, rise within us, and what is its precise nature? The imagination can add and add: so far, we have the immense, the indefinite. Thus, in respect of time, it can add millions of years or ages to millions of years and ages. In respect of extension, it can add millions and billions and trillions of leagues to millions and billions and trillions of leagues, and then multiply the results by each other, millions of billions of trillions of times. But when it has finished this process, it has not infinity: it has merely immensity. If, when we had gone thus far, time and space ceased, we should still have the finite, — a very wide finite, no doubt, but not the infinite. But it is a law of the mind that, when we have gone thus far, we are necessitated to believe that existence does not stop there, — nay, to believe that, to whatever other point we might go, there must be a something beyond. Suppose we were carried to such a point, would we not stretch out our hand, confidently believing that there is a space beyond, or that, if our hand be stayed, it must be by body occupying space? We are necessitated to believe that, after we have gone thus far, we are not at the outer edge of the universe of being, — nay, though we were to multiply this distance by itself, and this by itself ten thousand millions of times, till the imagination felt itself dizzy, still, after we have reached this point, we are constrained to believe that there must be something beyond. This seems to me to be the very law of the mind in reference to infinity: not only can it not set limits to existence, it is constrained to believe that there are no limits. "If the mind," says John Foster, "were to arrive at the solemn ridge of mountains which we may fancy to bound creation, it would eagerly ask, Why no farther? what is beyond?"

But this is only one side of this idea and conviction: the mind has another and a more important. We apprehend, and are constrained to believe, in regard to objects which we look upon as infinite, that they are incapable of increase or diminution. We represent to ourselves the Divine Being with certain attributes, — say, as wise or good, — and our belief as to Him and these attributes is, that he cannot be wiser or better. This aspect may be appropriately designated as the Perfect. This is the conviction of the Perfect of which so many profound philosophers make so much; but not more, as I think, than they are entitled to do. We think of God as having all his attributes such that no addition could be made, and we call such attributes his perfections. In regard to the moral attributes of Deity, it is this significant word Perfect, rather than infinite, which expresses the conviction we are led to entertain in regard, for example, to the wisdom, or benevolence, or righteousness of God. Join these two aspects, and we have such an idea as the finite mind of man can form of the infinite. The first of these views tends to humble us, as showing how far our creature impotency is below Creator Power. The other has rather a tendency to elevate us by showing a perfect exemplar. The Perfect shines above us like the sun in the heavens, distant and unapproachable, dazzling and blinding us as we would gaze upon it; but still our eye ever tends to turn up towards it, and we feel that it is a blessed thing that there is such a light, and that we are permitted to walk in it and rejoice in it.

This seems to be a necessary perception: we cannot be made to believe, to think otherwise. Not only so: it is in a sense a universal belief. No doubt the widest image formed by many human beings, as by children and savages, must be very narrow; but, whether narrow or wide, they always believe that there must be something beyond, and that this is incapable of augmentation. Pursue any line sufficiently far, and we shall find it going out into infinity. So true is it that

> The feeling of the boundless bounds
> All feeling as the welkin doth the world.

But the infinite in which the mind is led intuitively to believe is not an abstract infinite. It is a belief in something infinite. When the visible things of God declare that there is an intelligent Being, the Author of all the order and adaptation in the universe, we are impelled to believe that this Being is and must be infinite; and we clothe him with eternal power and godhead. The intuition is gratified to the full in the contemplation of a God Eternal, Omnipresent, All Mighty, and All Perfect.

Thus it is that I construct the argument for the existence of God; and the same considerations which prove that he is, prove that he has certain perfections. I do not stand up for a God-consciousness as a simple and single instinct gazing directly on God. I maintain that there are a number and variety of native principles, each of which, being favored by external circumstances, would lead us up to God. Every deeper principle which guides us in the practical affairs of life, and in the pursuit of science, and in our obligations towards our fellow-men, prompts us to look upward to a Being to whom we stand in the closest relationship. The law of cause and effect, the law of moral good, the striving after the idea of the infinite, these with the circumstances in which we are placed, with the traces of purpose and providence and retribution, with a generated sense of dependence, all, each in its own way, and all together would draw or drive our thoughts above nature to a supernatural power. All the living streams in our world, if we ascend them, conduct to the fountain. All the scattered rays show us the luminary. I find the materials of the argument in every work of God, and the strings that bind them in the laws or principles of knowledge, belief, and judgment. It gets its nutriment from objects, and it has its roots in the mind itself.

The conviction springs up spontaneously in all minds. At the same time it may be repressed or it may be perverted, — by ignorance, by sinful stupidity, by lusts, by worldly engrossments; by pride, indisposing us to submit to restraints; by our shrinking instinctively from condemnation. We can thus account for two things conjoined in the whole religious history of mankind. We have in all ages, in all countries and states of society, a tendency to believe in some sort of supernatural or divine power. There is no nation, in fact no individual, without some rudiment of religion. Some, indeed, have declared that they have found not only persons, but tribes, without religion. And this is true when by religion they mean a belief that would be accepted by civilized men, and involving a conception of a spiritual God. But more careful observers, able to search the depths of the heart, have always found some vague apprehension of a being or a power supposed to be different from the natural elements, and fitted to raise up fear or hope.* But along with

* In that curious conglomerate, Sir John Lubbock's book, "On the Origin of Civilization and Primitive Condition of Man," there is a heterogeneous collection of statements by travellers, historians, and missionaries, as to the religion and morality of savage nations. Some of the authors quoted are not fitted to penetrate the depths of the human heart; yet there is a general concurrence as to some sort of religious faith or fear being found among the lowest tribes. The Australians "possess certain vague ideas as to the existence of evil spirits and a general dread of witchcraft." The Backapins, a Kaffir tribe, have no outward worship, but "they believe in sorcery and the efficacy of amulets." The Indians of California had "certain sorcerers whom they believed to possess power over diseases, to bring small-pox, famine, &c., and of whom, therefore, they were in much fear." The Hottentots have very vague ideas about a good spirit, but "have much clearer notions about an evil spirit, whom they fear, believing him to be the occasion of sickness, death, thunder, and every calamity that befalls them." On Williams placing a Fijian before a mirror, he stood delighted, and said softly, "Now I can see into a world of spirits." Sir John says that "certain phenomena, as, for instance, sleep and dreams, pain, disease, and death, have naturally created in the savage mind a belief in the existence of mysterious and invisible Beings." This general tendency, I add, must have a common cause in the nature of man.

this there is about as universal a disposition to pervert and degrade the divine nature and character. Some, from ignorance and narrowness of view and heart, see God in only a small part of his workmanship; some only in certain of his gifts, as in rain and harvest; some, with a secret consciousness of sin, only in his judgments. The misconception of his character varies with the mind, disposition, and sympathies of the individual or of the nation. The light is shining all around, and each soul has so far a capacity to receive it: but each receives only so much, and rejects the rest; hence the meagre, the ridiculous, the caricatured shapes and colors in which God is made to appear. Persons low in the scale of intelligence make him a mere Fetich, probably identifying him with certain objects or powers which we know to lie within the domain of nature. Communities, with a low moral standard, will love to have a God who patronizes thieving or robbery or murder. We see the same disposition working even in civilized countries. The lover of fine sentiment clothes him in robes of beauty, but takes no cognizance of his justice; and the academic moralist, declining to recognize the existence of sin in our world, paints him as a being of pure benevolence; while the conscience-stricken array him in colors of blood. The course of religious history in our world, under the influence of these two opposite forces, is thus a devious and inconsistent one, — an inclination to believe in God and an inclination to misrepresent him; a tendency to turn towards him, and a tendency to turn away from him; a disposition to receive him, but a disposition to receive only so much as may suit or gratify.

In these Lectures I have traversed two worlds, that of mind and that of matter, — in too rapid a manner I acknowledge. My object is gained, if I have in any measure succeeded in showing that every part of creation in the past and in the present, without us and within us, speaks in its own way, in loud or in low accents, in behalf of its great Creator. The argument is cumulative, derived partly from without, and partly from within, — partly from the external world, and partly from the principles of the mind. The evidence is not so much a melody as a harmony produced by the union of many melodies. The voice is like the voice of many waters; some soft as the sighing of the gentle stream, others loud as the roar of ocean sent forth by ten thousand waves. It is like the song which ascends in heaven from a people gathered out of every tongue and nation, each chanting in his own strain, but all uniting in one melodious and harmonious song. In particular we are constrained to believe that the true, the lovely, and the holy, all meet as in a focus of surpassing brilliancy in the character of God. Wherever these are to be found in his creatures, they are emanations from him. Thus our discussions, beginning with the creature, have ended with the Creator; beginning with the finite have ended with the Infinite; beginning with the imperfect have ended with the Perfect, — and lead us to Him in whom all excellence meets and centres.

Having thus built up the structure, it will be necessary to meet those who assail it. You see that I set myself entirely against that prevailing style of talk in our day which represents God as unknown and unknowable. It was introduced, unfortunately, by Sir William Hamilton, who would make the Apostle Paul favor it because he starts in his argument from an altar which he had seen dedicated to the unknown God. But Paul said expressly to the men of Athens, to whom he was speaking, "Whom therefore ye ignorantly worship, him declare I (*καταγγέλω*) unto you." And in writing to the Romans, he says, "The invisible things of God from the creation of the world are clearly seen" — not seen by the eye, but by the mind; "being understood" (*νοούμενα*, comprehended by the higher mind) "from the things that are made." Herbert Spencer has turned Hamilton's rash expression to a purpose never intended. Mr. Spencer observes, very justly and sensibly, that "it is rigorously impossible to conceive that our knowledge is a knowledge of appearances only, without at the same time conceiving a reality of which they are appearances; for appearance without reality is unthinkable." * This is a

* "First Principles," 2d ed., p. 88. In the Appendix to this volume will be found A Critical Note on Mr. Herbert Spencer's Speculations.

very important admission, of which I mean to take advantage. But then he maintains that this reality beyond the appearances must ever remain unknown to man. It is at this point I meet him. He reckons it the province of science to master the known appearances; and he allots to religion, the sphere of unknown realities, that unascertained something which phenomena and their relations imply. This is the "fundamental verity" common to all religions, the ultimate religious truth of the highest possible certainty, "that the power which the universe manifests to us is utterly unscrutable." * I do not know what religious profit Mr. Spencer may derive from meditating on this Unknown, whether he feels that he should pay IT (we cannot say HIM) any worship, or render it any service, or feel under any obligation of duty to it; or whether it tends to draw him to what is good or drive him from what is evil. But of this I am sure, that if people generally should be led to embrace his creed, it would come to mean that men need not trouble themselves about religion, in the darkness of which no object can be seen to revere or to love. I am sure that if we banish religion to this Siberia, it will be to make it perish in the cold. To consign it thus is to bury it in the grave from which it will not send forth even a ghost to trouble any one.

I meet Mr. Spencer on his own ground. I proceed on his own admission. He comes down to a "fundamental verity." He does so on the ground

* First Principles, p. 46.

of his being necessitated to assume it. He is constrained to believe that there is something beyond the visible appearances, and that this is a reality; for he says that "appearance without reality is unthinkable." Now I, too, rest on a "fundamental verity." I, too, believe that there is a something beyond what falls under the senses; and that this something is real. But on the same ground on which Mr. Spencer proceeds, in arguing a reality beyond our sensible experience, I proceed in maintaining that we know that reality, so far know it. If the one is a fundamental verity, so also is the other. If we are necessitated to believe the one, we are equally necessitated to believe the other. Or, rather, the "fundamental verity" is, that we are constrained to believe, not in an unknown reality, but in a known reality. The truth is, we know this something to exist, because we so far know it.

I have my doubts whether this "fundamental verity," as Mr. Spencer puts it, can stand a sifting examination. It embraces three clauses: (1) that there is a something beyond, (2) that it is a reality, and (3) that it is unknown and unknowable. He is powerful in dogmatic assertion, and there are dependent minds that will at once bend under his authority; but there are persons as independent as he, who will ask themselves, and ask him, whether he is entitled, on his principles, to assume that, beyond what appears, there is a something which is a reality. Might not the belief have sprung up without a cause? Or, if Mr. Spencer admit the principle that every effect has a cause, he must seek for other causes, which, as they are brought in, may destroy the whole symmetry of his system, and turn this unknown into a known cause. Or, might not this belief have been produced by hereditary descent from some instinct of our ancestors among the lower animals? And what proof is there, or can there be, that this unknown something is a reality, — is any thing more than a belief? Of this I am sure, that Mr. Spencer's followers will care nothing for this something beyond, for this unknown something. They will say that, if we know and can know nothing of its nature, it is a matter of no moment whether it exists or not; that the admission can carry with it no practical consequences for instruction, for comfort, or for admonition. If this be so, then this region which Mr. Spencer has so kindly allotted to religion, and in which all religions may meet — in the dark — vanishes; and mankind will not miss it, there being extremely little difference to us between absolute nothing, and the absolutely unknowable. But Mr. Spencer is completely mistaken, consciousness being witness, as to the nature and character of this fundamental verity, which, when properly interpreted, is, that we know things appearing; and on principles which can be specified and defended, as, for instance, on the principle of causation, we argue that these things appearing, being real, imply other things also real, though not appearing to the senses.

The school against which I am arguing do not profess to deny the existence of God: this, they say, would be unphilosophical; it would be as unphilosophical to deny as to affirm any thing as to a *terra incognita*. What they hold is, that if he exist, he must be unknown. But, towards an absolutely unknown being we can cherish no affection; and we do not feel as if he could have any claim upon us for service or obedience. To look on this object is merely to gaze upon the darkness without a point of light to cheer us. It can supply no high ideal after which to mould our character. From such a God, if he deserve the name, we can draw no sympathy in our sorrows, no help in our weakness. From him we can derive no hopes to cheer, though I can conceive that he might raise some fears of evil, to come we know not when or how.

Now, I meet all this by showing that we are capable of knowing, and that what we know is a reality. From what we know directly, we can rise to the knowledge of other things. We cannot look immediately into the souls of our neighbors; but we infer that they exist, and can learn much of their character from what we see them do. We may not have been in India or China ourselves; but we know much about these countries, from the reports brought us by travellers. I allow that we are not directly conscious of God, any more than we are of our fellow-men; but we legitimately infer his character from the works of creation and providence, and the revelation he has made of himself in his Word. We cannot know the world to come by visiting it; but we know what it must be from the character of God, and the moral laws by which he governs the universe.

A thing, I hold, can be known by its effects. Most of the things we know are known to us simply by what they do. We know the sun and stars; we know that distant house and hill; not directly, but as reflecting rays of light which reach our eyes. There is a man we have never seen: but we know him to be eloquent from his speeches which we have read; to be benevolent, from his deeds of charity; to be truthful, from his continuing in the path of integrity when he might have been tempted to swerve from it. In like manner, we can come to know God from his works: know him to be powerful, from the traces of power everywhere visible; to be good, from the provision made for the happiness of his creatures; and to be just, from his mode of government. The real effects in nature carry us up to a real cause above nature. We recognize him, not as the unknown cause, but as the known cause of known effects. We clothe him with varied attributes, so as to make him capable of producing the varied effects we discover. The evidences of design argue an adequate cause in an intelligent designer; the traces of beneficent contrivance show that he is animated by love; and the nature of the moral power in man, and of the moral government of the world, is a proof of the existence of a Moral Governor.

We know all created things better, from the very circumstance that we know God as their author. Aristotle uttered a profound truth when he said we know things in their causes.* The truth is, we can scarcely be said to have a full knowledge of a thing till we know its causes. I hold that we have a very imperfect knowledge of the works of nature till we view them as works of God, — not only as works of mechanism, but works of intelligence; not only as under laws, but under a law-giver, wise and good.

True, we do not know all about God. We know, after all, only a part; but, "we know in part," and what we know is truth, so far as it goes. "Clouds and darkness are round about him; righteousness and judgment are the habitation of his throne." The truth is, there is no object with which we have such ample means of becoming acquainted. We cannot open our eyes without discovering his workmanship. We cannot inspect any part of nature without contemplating in the very act his ways of procedure. We are ever, whether we acknowledge it or not, recipients of his bounty. There is no being, excepting ourselves, with whom we come into more immediate and frequent contact. We know only in part, because of his infinity and our finity; but to know a very little of him is to know much. As Paul told the men of Athens, "He giveth to all life and breath, and all things,"

* Τότε γὰρ εἰδέναι φαμὲν ἕκαστον, ὅταν τὴν πρώτην αἰτίαν οἰώμεθα γνωρίζειν. — *Metaphysics*, B. I. c. iii.

and he is "not far from every one of us: for in him we live, and move, and have our being, as certain also of your own poets have said, For we are also his offspring." We know enough to gain our faith; to inspire our confidence; to kindle our love; to awe us in the time of prosperity when we might be tempted to become vain, proud, and presumptuous; and to sustain us in all the critical positions of life and the dark dispensations of providence.

It requires to be added that as most errors contain some truth, as all prevalent errors contain a sufficient amount of truth to make them plausible, so we may discover some truth even in the meagre fundamental principle of Spencer. I must ever hold that we can come to know God: still he is to a great extent unknown. "Canst thou by searching find out God? canst thou find out the Almighty unto perfection? It is as high as heaven; what canst thou do? deeper than hell; what canst thou know?" We can so far apprehend him; but, to use an old distinction, we cannot comprehend him. We know him as we know the ocean when we stand upon its shores: what we see is the ocean, but not the whole ocean, which stretches beyond our ken. This arises mainly from our limited capacity; but partly, also, it may be, because of our pollution, as not capable of reflecting the full brightness of God. It is clear that God has attributes like ours; for, by the powers with which he has endowed us, we can produce effects like those we see produced by him in nature. We have been formed in his likeness, and can thus understand those qualities in Him which are like those he hath been pleased to communicate to us. But, even as to these, the attributes which are limited in us are infinite in him, and cannot be grasped by us who are finite. But there is more than this involved in our ignorance. There is another and deeper sense in which God is unknown. We discover effects in nature which we must refer to a sovereign power that must ever remain a mystery to us in this world. God seems to possess perfections differing not only in degree but in kind from any thing possessed by man. The blind man cannot form the most distant idea of colors, nor the deaf man of music; so there may be attributes of God of which we cannot form the dimmest conception, differing as much from any thing we have experienced, as colors do from sounds, as mind does from body. It is in this high region that we place the mysteries of the decrees of God, of the origin of evil, and such doctrines as that of the Trinity. Is not this the very view that is given in Scripture where he is described as known and yet unknown? "The invisible things are clearly seen, being understood from the things that are made." "Yet verily thou art a God that hidest thyself." All this is suited to our nature, to its strength and to its weakness. If God were all darkness, we could look upon him only with an ignorant terror: if he were all light, he might dazzle us by excess of brightness. As it is, we are led at once to revere and to love him. We instinctively avoid the open, uninteresting plain, with the long, straight road leading through it, from which we see at once all we ever can see; and we prefer the country with hill and dale, with open lawn and forest, with light and shade, where we ever get glimpses of new objects and see them in distant perspective. It is from a like principle that we delight to lose ourselves in the contemplation of the mysteries of the divine nature, in which there is the brightest light, and yet enough of darkness to awe us into reverence, and subdue us into a sense of dependence. God may truly be described as the Being of whom we know the most, inasmuch as we cannot open our eyes without looking on the operations of his hands, and we see more of his works and ways than of the works and ways of any other; and yet He is the Being of whom we know the least, as we know comparatively less of his whole nature than we do of ourselves, or of our fellow-men, or of any object falling under our notice in this world. They who know most of him in earth or heaven know that they know little after all; but they know that they may know more and more of him throughout eternal ages.

VI.

Progress of Free Thought in America.—Rationalism. —Boston Theology.—Positivism.

I KEEP it before me throughout these Lectures, that I am addressing young men who have been thrown into the current of the times; who must swim with it, or resist it, or, better still, seek to guide it. I presume that you look, from time to time, into the literary organs of the day, and that you have heard of, and may have to take your part —by act, vote, or speech—in, the questions discussed. You wish to be able to form a sound judgment, each for himself, and then take your position, and act your part intelligently, charitably, wisely, courageously, in the eventful and critical era in which your lot has been cast.

In the Lectures already delivered, I have laid down what I believe to be the right positions, and defended them to the best of my ability, and as fully as my limited space allowed. I feel that I must now apply them, in the good old way of Puritan preaching, to the circumstances in which the students in this Seminary are placed. I cannot forget what are your surroundings, as you are pursuing your education in this country in an age in which old thought is being thoroughly sifted. I have now to survey the history and the state of opinion in America: this I would do in no harsh or narrow manner, but in order to estimate with candor the influences under which you may have to form your opinions and decide on your line of conduct.

In doing so, it will be necessary to take a look at the nature and progress of the new opinions which have been opposing or seeking to undermine the old. But, in order to this, you must take an excursion with me into New England, and pay a visit to Boston, which has exercised such an influence on the literature and theology of America, — on literature altogether for good; and on theology, whether for good or for evil, we must now seek to determine. We must, in particular, follow the progress of what has been called the Boston Theology; for there is a Boston Theology, just as there has been a Genevan Theology, a Wesleyan Theology, and an Oxford Theology.

I feel as if I were familiar with the Boston Theology. It is known not only here, but has a name in Europe. There were anticipations of it in Old England, and all over New England; but it was Dr. Channing who first brought it under the notice of the world. Of the illustrious man now named, no one should allow himself to speak except with profound reverence. His style — with a little too much of glitter and of rhetoric at times — is worthy of being compared with that of Macaulay. His essay on the character of Napoleon has a higher tone than any thing Macaulay ever wrote, and is one of the noblest specimens of moral criticism which we have in the English language. His firm and consistent opposition to slavery is a continued rebuke of the conduct of many chicken-hearted or time-serving Evangelicals, who are loud enough now in their denunciations, but could keep wonderfully quiet an age ago, and ever said hush, when the troublesome subject was started. To his credit, so I reckon it, he stuck by the inspiration of Scripture, as I understand it, and has left us defences of the Word of God as true as they are eloquent. But everybody sees that he has failed to prove that Socinianism or Unitarianism is in the Bible, in the letter or in the spirit of it. Whatever may be found in the Word of God, it is clear that rationalism is not there. Paul is certainly no rationalist, when he proclaims that Jesus held it no robbery to be equal with God; that a man is justified by faith; and that Jesus died for sinners, — the just for the unjust. John is certainly no rationalist when he declares that the Logos, which was with God and was God, became flesh, and shows us a way by which we may rise through him to fellowship with God; and, "truly, our fellowship is with the Father, and with his Son Jesus Christ." And, surely, Jesus is no rationalist, when he, the meekest and the most truly humble of all men that have appeared on earth, could say so calmly, "I and my Father are one," and when the Jews were proclaiming, "No one can forgive sin but

7*

God only," could command, "Thy sins be forgiven thee." The Old Testament shadow going before the substance, and telling of its approach dimly and yet clearly, is certainly not rationalism. So opinion could not stay at the place to which Channing conducted it. Those who in these times keep his position are made to feel that they are left high and dry upon a sandy beach, to which he had floated them, but from which they are not likely to be delivered by any subsequent wave rising to their relief.

So a bolder and more out-spoken thinker appeared: a man somewhat too self-dependent and self-conscious, but courageous and ever ready to defend the weak against the strong, and to run to the rescue of suffering humanity. He does not affect to derive what doctrine he held from the Bible; and all men felt that he was right there. His creed is not to be found in the Old Testament with its sacrificial types; or in the New Testament with a bloody cross on its title-page; in the unworldly discourses of Jesus recommending meekness, self-denial, the casting away of our own righteousness, and trust in God; or the elaborate exposition of an atonement in the epistles of Paul. His mother, living in the declining age of Puritanism, — when its life had withered and only its bare stalks were left, like stubble after the grain had been cut down, — recommended: "In my earliest boyhood I was taught to respect the instinctive promptings of conscience, regarding it as the voice of God in the soul of man, which must always be obeyed; to speak the truth without evasion or concealment; to love justice and conform to it; to reverence merit in all men, and that regardless of their rank or reputation; and, above all things, I was taught to love and trust the dear God." All good, we say, only this conscience needs to be quickened, enlightened by the revealed word of God, and strengthened in its contest with sin in the heart by the God who planted it there. This ardent man was not satisfied with the creed of his party, so like a winter day, cold, colorless, so soon setting in freezing night. "Their cry was ever 'duty, duty, work, work;' but they failed to address with equal power the soul, and did not also shout 'joy, joy! delight, delight!'" "Their water was all laboriously pumped up from deep wells. It did not gush out leaping from the great spring. That is indeed on the surface of the sloping ground, feeding the little streams that run among the hills, and both quenching the wild asses' thirst, and watering also the meadows, newly mown, but which yet comes from the Rock of Ages, and is pressed out by the cloud-compelling mountains that rest thereon: yes, by the gravitation of the earth itself; yes, by the gravitation of the earth itself." "I thought they lacked the deep internal feeling of piety which alone could make feeling lasting. Certainly they had not that most joyous of all delights. This fact seemed clear in their sermons, their prayers, and even in the hymns they made, borrowed, or adopted." "It is a dismal fault in a religious party this lack of piety, and dismally have the Unitarians answered it!" "Their creed was only a denial always trembling before the Orthodox." This did not suit the strong, impulsive nature of the man; and so he must construct a religion for himself. It was what he called an Absolute Religion, which belongs to man's nature. He rejected the sensationalism, so earthly, of the old Unitarian school, and betook himself to intuitions, which seem to carry him up to the heavens, and actually took him up to the clouds. He drew his system (1) from the instinctive intuition of the Divine, the consciousness that there is a God; (2) The instinctive intuition of the just and right, a consciousness that there is a moral law, independent of our will, which we ought to keep; (3) The instinctive intuition of the immortal, a consciousness that the essential element of man, the principle of individuality, never dies. He got the inspiration which led to all this from the works of Carlyle and Coleridge, reprinted in America, and reviews and translations of Cousin, and longed earnestly to get aid from the destructive Biblical criticism and the constructive *a priori* philosophy of Germany, which aid he never got; for the Germans thought his religion very irreligious, and his rationalism very irrational. But when they heard these utterances, the young men of Boston — that is, men who were young thirty or forty years ago — shouted, and flung up their hats in the air, and said, Channing is setting as the sun on a winter day, but Theodore Parker is rising like the sun on a spring morning.

The icy, the frigid, and rigid rationalism of the winter now came to be dissolved in the heat of a warmer season, and your fathers had a time of wading deep in melting matter. It is now acknowledged that the logical processes of definition and reasoning can do little in religion: and those who in the previous age would have appealed to these now called in something livelier,—Feeling, Belief, Inspiration; in one word, Intuition. In the age then passing away, "excelsior" youths were like to be starved in cold; in the age which succeeded, they are in greater danger of having the seeds of wasting disease fostered by lukewarm damps and gilded vapors. The appeal was to faith, feeling, intuition. But what were men to believe in? Did any two men agree in their feelings? Are we quite certain when we have intuition and when we have not intuition? The arbiter was too vague in its utterances to teach certainty, to secure assurance, or even to gain general consent. A dreamer appeared as the representative of this period, getting the material of his dreams from Goethe and Thomas Carlyle, but ever colored with the hues of his own peculiar genius. He is thus introduced by Theodore Parker: "The brilliant genius of Emerson rose in the winter night and hung over Boston, drawing the eyes of ingenuous young people to look to that great new star, and a beauty and a mystery which charmed for the moment, while it gave also perennial instruction, as it led them forward along new paths and towards new hopes. America has seen no such sight before." "A beauty and a mystery," I admit, "which charms for the moment." If I were inclined to believe in dreams of any kind, I would as readily believe in Emerson's as in any others. The visions seen by De Quincey, the opium-eater, are not more beautiful. Coming from such a soul they must contain truth, some of it welling up from the deepest intuitions of the mind as from a fresh, clear fountain. Some are the unconscious reflection of the light shining from the Word of God in a Christian land. Others are to be read, like dreams, by contraries. The oracles which he utters are often capable of a double meaning: and men will interpret them to suit their purpose. And what, after all, am I to think and believe about God and the soul and the world to come, and of the way of rising to communion with God and the enjoyments of heaven? is the question which is often put to me by young men, after reading Emerson's papers; and I have to tell them that Mr. Emerson must answer them, for I cannot.

About thirty years ago, when men now fifty years of age were boys at college, they believed that something great and good and stable was to come out of a showy Intuitionalism, as I call it, which drew all truth out of the depths of the soul. Men like Goethe and Coleridge and Carlyle, and their admirers in Great Britain and America, looked so profound and threw out such mysterious utterances of their being able — if only they chose — to divulge something very profound, that earnest and confiding youths believed in them. But somehow or other they never chose: some of us think, because they had nothing to utter. Though often pressed to expound their secret, they have always shunned doing so; and people begin to suspect that there is nothing in it. There was an expectation, long entertained by many, that something better than the old Christianity of the Bible, literally interpreted, might come out of the great German philosophic systems of Kant, Fichte, Schelling, Hegel, and Schleiermacher; but these hopes have been doomed to acknowledged disappointment. Coleridge has played out his tune, sweet and irregular as the harp of Æolus; and all men perceive that he never had any thing to meet the deeper wants of humanity, except what he drew from the songs of Zion. It has long been clear in regard to Goethe, and is now being seen in regard to Carlyle, that neither of them ever had any thing positive to furnish in religion, and that all they had to utter was blankly negative; and I rather think that the last hope of deriving any thing soul-satisfying from such quarters has vanished from the minds of those who have been impressed with their genius.

The spirit is still lingering in certain circles of America, and it clothes itself at times in such beautiful forms that I am inclined to admire it, as I do the clouds in the evening sky, convinced though I be, all the while, that they are mere vapors, and soon to fade into dulness and gloom. As to the intuitionalism, which rose out of rationalism as fogs rise out of the melted ice, it is acknowledged that it is not rational. No man can draw Parker's creed — a creed noble in so many respects — out of human reason, any more than he could derive Channing's creed out of the Scriptures. One-half of all that is noble was drawn through a noble mother out of the Bible, is in fact the reflection of the light which is diffused all throughout the atmosphere in a Christian country while the sun is shining, but without persons being conscious of the source from which it comes. The other half has come from a heart with noble instincts, but cannot stand the sifting examination of the reason. There is no arbiter provided to decide what we should accept, and what we should reject. In constructing a rational theology, these men, to use an expression of Lessing's, have constructed an irrational philosophy. The stratum which promised to be so auriferous is becoming thin, and is ready to crop out to the surface, and terminate its existence, or at least the hopes which men entertained regarding it.

To what is the appeal to lie? The old and cold reason of the antiquated Unitarians? None so ready as the men of the new school to denounce the heartless natural theology of the old rational school. Every one sees how flickering a light the reason, in the sense of the logical understanding and the reasoning process, can throw on the grand problems of religion, which the heart insists upon having solved. "Sufficient," as Bacon says, "to convince of atheism, but not to inform religion."

To what then is the appeal to be? To science, say some. To what science? To physical science? Physical science has its own grand domain, wide as the telescope or spectroscope can penetrate; but among all its atoms, earths, and stars, it discovers nothing to throw light on the great questions started as to the relation in which man stands to God, and the existence of the soul after death. All our wiser expounders of science confess this. And the scientific school, which is specially guiding these men, is ever taking pains to show that science should avoid such questions, as having no light to shed upon them. A Lecturer in Boston allows that, at present, science cannot answer the question as to the immortality of the soul, but "from the future, not the past, must the light come;" and he seems to indicate that it must be "untold years" before it can come to this. Verily, it is poor consolation to the mother, mourning over her boy removed by death, to assure her that, some millions of years hence, science will settle the question as to whether she may ever expect to meet her son in another world; and science will have to add that all things are approaching nearer to that cold in which all life is to perish, to be followed by a conflict and conflagration in which all things are to be absorbed.

But the same lecturer hints, and another lecturer states plainly, that what physical science cannot establish, what the alleged resurrection of Jesus cannot prove, may be founded on certain moral ideas, on a sense of virtue and moral obligation, by the faculties which distinguish between right and wrong. But, meanwhile, they are aware that the school which can generate life, and plants, and animals, and man, out of star dust, can develop these ideas, by natural law, out of sensations and impressions. I believe that we are entitled to appeal to these ideas in constructing a reasonable religious conviction. I am sure that the arguments employed by Mr. Mill and Mr. Bain to undermine these ideas can be answered, just as the arguments against final cause can be answered. Along with the traces of design in the universe, and other first or fundamental truths, such as that of cause and effect, these ideas do conduct us to a belief in God. I am truly glad to find the most advanced of the Boston school still cleaving to these grand moral principles. Finding in these ideas ground on which they feel that they can stand and stay, they may be allured to look back and retrace their steps. I do hope this of some of them who are evidently dissatisfied with their position, and afraid of the termination of the path on which they have entered. But when these moral ideas are adopted, they must be consistently followed out. And when they are carried out logically, when the intimations of conscience and the sense of sin are carefully looked at and weighed, they give a very different view of God from that which is taken in the new theology, and tend to bring them back, and settle them upon the old foundations.

But in the mean time the appeal of these men is to the faith, to the feelings. But if there be no truth set before the faith, it may become the weakest credulity; and as to the feelings, they may change quicker than the phases of the fickle moon which lovers worship, quicker than the winds which are an emblem of human wishes and passions. If I dream one way and you dream another, which of them is a third party to follow? Some are inclined to believe their own dreams, but few are disposed to believe the dreams of their neighbors. And so, in the end, every one will be found to take the way which his impulse or his fancy or his self-interest may lead him.

And, as the result of the whole, the party is, at present, in a state of unrest, discontented with their position, and quarrelling with one another. An age ago the old rationalistic party were very self-sufficient, feeling that if they had not the Bible, they had natural religion to fall back upon. Now they are made to realize that they cannot be so sure of their foundation. Men of a devout spirit in the party of progress, corresponding to the *ἄνδρες σεβόμενοι* mentioned so often in the Book of Acts, are becoming alarmed. The piety which Theodore Parker did not find in the old Unitarian body has not appeared in the new body. There are fathers shuddering at the thought of bringing up their sons to such a creed, or, rather, negation of creed: they have fears that its gossamer threads will not restrain the youth when flesh and blood are strong and temptations are in the way. Mothers are not sure that the faith expounded will stay and support their daughters, and keep them from rushing into and running round the giddy whirls of pleasure, in which they are certain to become dizzy and fall. For many such I have strong hopes that they will be prepared to move back to the old foundations. And whether they come up to the full faith which I cherish or no, my whole soul will be with them in their struggle, and my prayer is that they may gain the victory.

But meanwhile the party of Free Thought is moving on. They are sliding down a steep slope, catching at times at lumps of yielding earth or brittle branches, only to find, as they give way, that their fall is hastened. It writes beautiful papers with noble thoughts and elevated sentiments, which I much admire, in the pages of some of our magazines, but with no settled doctrine or logical consistency. It has a literature, and it has lectures, and men go to hear them who have no faith, and who do not wish to have any, and who would relieve the dulness of a Sabbath in a city in which Puritanism has still its influence by listening to fine sentiment and ingenious speculation, which are more pleasing to them than preaching about these weary subjects, sin and salvation. But with all its literary ability, it has not been able to secure a church organization or church fellowship: it has not even a rope of sand; it has only a ribbon of cloud to bind its members. It has discourses, but no united prayers. It has certainly no God who can or will hear prayer.

I am speaking what I know; for there are men and women, young men and maidens, who have so far opened their hearts to me. And God forbid that I should look on them with a sulky enmity or a supercilious pride, as if I had a title to say to them, "Stand by, for I am holier than thou." Some of them are feeling as if the foundations are giving way; they are too proud to go back, too timid to go forward, and yet are conscious that they have no ground to stand on. Most of them know not what to give up and what to hold, or what they have left. To my knowledge, there are young hearts wrung with anguish, till feelings, more bitter than tears, have been pressed from them without bringing any relief. With some their voice is a cry like that of the child coming into the world; like that of Goethe, when he left the world, demanding "more light." With some it is a wail of disappointment, like that which came from the Hebrews when they looked into the Ark of the Covenant and saw it empty, the tables of the law, the pot of manna, and the budding rod all gone. With some it is a bitterness against what has deceived the world and deceived themselves; and it would vent itself in a curse, if they knew of a God or a devil against whom to direct it. With some it is a feeling of wanton levity, as if they rejoiced at being delivered from all their fears, and were able to say, "I have got rid of thee, O mine enemy!"

Fortunately or unfortunately, it is the last of its race; and, like certain doomed Indian tribes, it feels itself to be so. It is "the last rose of summer left blooming alone;" but it must go, for the winter is coming. Its doom is to be eaten up by a spectral figure which you may see approaching with firm and steady step, but with lean and haggard form, spreading like death a shivering feeling wherever it goes. I am sorry to be obliged to show to these fair forms which move so gaily what is the doom awaiting after they have danced a little time longer.

> An immense solitary spectre waits:
> It has no shape, it has no sound; it has
> No place, it has no time; it is, and was,
> And will be; it is never more nor less,
> Nor glad nor sad. Its name is Nothingness.
> Power walketh high; and misery doth crawl;
> And the clepsydron drips; and the sands fall
> Down in the hour-glass; and the shadows sweep
> Around the dial; and men wake and sleep,
> Live, strive, regret, forget, and love, and hate,
> And know it. This spectre saith, I wait,
> And at the last it beckons and they pass;
> And still the red sands fall within the glass,
> And still the shades around the dial sweep;
> And still the water-clock doth drip and weep.
> And this is all.

This is *Positivism*. I suppose Diodorus, surnamed Chronos, the Slow, must have written about it in ancient times; for it is recorded of him that he wrote a treatise on the Awful Nothing and died in despair. As his work has not come down to us, I will be obliged to describe it, even though I should expose myself to the sarcasm of the Scythian traveller, *Vae Quantum Nihili*.

POSITIVISM.

I take as representatives of it, M. Comte, Mr. Mill, and Mr. Herbert Spencer. They have auxiliaries in Mr. Grote, Mr. Lewes, Mr. Buckle, Professor Bain, Professor Huxley, and others powerful in particular departments; but these three may be held as the ablest defenders of their peculiar principles. All agree in this, that man can know nothing of the nature of things; that he can know merely phenomena, or relations of things unknown; and that all he can do with these is to generalize them into laws. All agree farther, that it is impossible for us to rise to the knowledge of first or final causes, and they exert their whole energy in denouncing the attempt to find what they call occult causes. So far they agree. On other and not unimportant points they differ. Comte says that all our knowledge comes through the senses, and that the study of the mind must be a study of the brain. Mill says we have other ideas, or rather he would call them feelings, besides those got through the senses; and both he and Herbert Spencer argue that we can study the mind through self-consciousness. Mill generates all our ideas from sensation, and feelings springing up in an unknown way by means of association of ideas, which is capable of turning them into the varied shapes which they take. Spencer gets them by development through long ages, first in the brutes and then in the human races. Comte, who was largely an impetuous intellectual steam-engine, — he would have said brain-engine, — takes little or no notice of our ideas of beauty and morality. Mill derives them from association, giving to association an indefinitely large power. Spencer ascribes them to development, but not unfolding what are the powers involved in the development. Comte is an open and rabid atheist. Mr. Mill evidently feels that he has no argument left, on his system, to prove the existence of God, utters no profession of his faith, and believes that an atheist may be a man of high piety. Herbert Spencer argues that beyond known phenomena there is, and must be, a great unknown; and he allots this region to religion, where there may, or there may not be, an unknown God. Comte is the most original thinker; but is, throughout, narrow, one-sided, dogmatic, moving on in one line like the blindered horse, or the steam locomotive, seeing nothing on either side of him. Mill has the widest sympathies, and is the most appreciative of the views of others, though often he is narrow and exclusive, and is not able to follow out his views consistently. Spencer is the most vigorous speculator of them all; and, like the giants of old, he would heap Pelion and Pindus, and presumptuously reach the greatest heights without passing through the intermediate steps.

M. Comte provided a religion and a worship for his followers. He had no God, but he had a "Grand Etre," in Collective Humanity, or "the continuous resultant of all the forces capable of voluntarily concurring in the universal perfectioning of the world," being in fact a deification of his system of science and sociology. In the worship he enjoined, he has nine sacraments, and a priesthood, and public honors to be paid to the Collective Humanity; with no public liberty of conscience or of education in sacred, or, indeed, in any subjects. The religious observances were to occupy two hours every day. Mr. Mill tells us, "Private adoration is to be addressed to Collective Humanity in the persons of worthy individual representatives, who may be either living or dead, but must in all cases be women; for women, being the *sexe aimant*, represent the best attribute of humanity, that which ought to regulate all human life, nor can humanity possibly be symbolized in any form but that of a woman. The objects of private adoration are the mother, the wife, and the daughter, representing severally the past, the present, and the future, and calling into active exercise the three social sentiments,—veneration, attachment, and kindness. We are to regard them, whether dead or alive, as our guardian angels, 'les vrais anges gardiens.' If the last two have never existed; or if, in the particular case, any of the three types is too faulty for the office assigned it,—their place may be supplied by some other type of womanly excellence, even by one merely historical." * The Christian religion surely does not suffer by being placed alongside of

* Comte and Positivism, p. 150.

this system, which is one of the two new religions which this century has produced, the other being Mormonism. The author clung more and more fondly to this faith and ceremonial as he advanced in years. His English followers are ashamed of it, and ascribe it to his lunacy; as if he had not been tinged with madness (as his poor wife knew) all his life, and as if his whole system were not the product of a powerful, but of a constitutionally diseased, intellect.

He denounces his English followers because they did not adopt his moral and social system; he characterizes the conversion of those who have adopted his positivity and rejected his religion as an abortion; and declares that it must proceed from impotence of intellect, or insufficiency of heart, commonly from both! * There is a basis of wisdom in this complaint. All history shows that man is a religious, quite as certainly as he is a feeling and a rational, being. But what has the British school provided to meet man's religious wants? As yet they have furnished nothing. But Mr. Mill, who always weighs his words, and who is too skilful a dialectician to say more than he means, evidently points to something which is being hatched, and may some day burst forth. While he has the strongest objection to the system of politics and morals set forth in the "Politique Positive," he thinks "it has superabundantly shown the possibility of giving to the service of humanity, even without the belief in a Providence, both the psychological power and the

* Politique Positive, Tome I. Pref. p. xv., III. p. 24.

ocial efficacy of a religion; making it take hold f human life, and color all thought, feeling, and ction in a manner of which the greatest ascendancy ver exercised by any religion may be but a type nd foretaste." * More specifically in a late work Ir. Mill says, that "though conscious of being an xtremely small minority," — a circumstance which s sure to catch those "individualists" who are bent n appearing original, — "we venture to think that a eligion may exist without belief in a God, and that religion without a God may be, even to Christians, n instructive and profitable object of contempla-ion." † He tells us that, in order to constitute a eligion, there must be "a creed or conviction," "a elief or set of beliefs," "a sentiment connected vith this creed," and a "*cultus*." I confess I should ke excessively to see this new religion with its reed and its *cultus* fully developed. It would match he theologies, with their ceremonial observances, rojected by *doctrinaires* in the heat of the first 'rench Revolution. There is no risk of the Brit-sh school setting up a religion and a worship so uperbly ridiculous as that of M. Comte; but I enture to predict that when it comes, it will be so cientifically cold, and so emotionally blank, as to e incapable of gathering any interest around it, of ccomplishing any good, or, I may add, inflicting ny evil.

The world will soon be in a position fairly to stimate M. Comte, who has often been under-

* Utilitarianism, p. 48. † Comte and Positivism, p. 133.

estimated, and as often over-estimated. At first lit tle appreciated by the mass, even of thinkers, h secured at an early stage the admiration of a selec few, who discerned the vigor of his intellect an saw the partial truth which his system contained or who were subdued by his dogmatic spirit an power of assertion: these men spoke of him i exaggerated terms, and compared him to Baco and to Leibnitz. His direct influence has all alon been very small, being confined to those who ha the courage to read through his ponderous volumes in which most had to confess with Mr. Huxley: " found the veins of ore few and far between, and th rock so apt to run to mud, that one incurred th risk of being intellectually smothered in the work ing." But his indirect influence, through eminen men who followed his method and caught his spirit has been very great. However, the time of reac tion against him and his exclusive pretensions seem to have come. Sir John Herschel showed, twent years ago, that he was guilty of mathematical blun ders which would have disgraced any student seek ing for honors in Cambridge. And now his friend are turning out to be his bitterest foes. Mr. Mil cannot express in too strong language his abhor rence of his system of social organization, whicl admits of no liberty of action, or even of thought an conscience. Mr. Spencer has criticised severel his much lauded generalization of the progress o knowledge, which is said to be first theological, the metaphysical, then positive, showing that it is ful of error and confusion. And now Professor Huxley tells us: "That part of M. Comte's writings which deals with the philosophy of physical science appeared to me to possess singularly little value, and to show that he had but the most superficial, and merely second-hand, knowledge of most branches of what is usually understood by science. I do not mean by this merely that Comte was behind our present knowledge, or that he was unacquainted with the details of the science of his own day. No one could justly make such defects cause of complaint in a philosophical writer of the past generation. What struck me was his want of apprehension of the great features of science, his strange mistakes as to the merits of his scientific contemporaries, and his ludicrously erroneous notions about the part which some of the scientific doctrines, current in his time, were destined to play in the future." * Every man, after being buffeted about — it may be — in this world, will at last find his level. These men are placing M. Comte somewhat lower than I do. But it is a question for them to settle. These criticisms show that the day of M. Comte is fast declining.

* "Lay Sermons," p. 164. Mr. Huxley thinks that there is some value in "the chapters on speculative and practical sociology." But this is not just the department in which Mr. Huxley is an authority. I am reminded of a story told by Hugh Miller of a company of *savans* who were discussing the merits of the "Vestiges of Creation," then newly published. The naturalist was sure that it was full of bad natural history, but believed that the astronomy was good; while the natural philosopher had heard that the geology was good, but knew that the astronomy was incorrect, &c.

But will the other members of the school have a longer day, or even so long? So far as they have advanced any branch of natural science, of history, or of political economy, their names will live, and go down with their discoveries to future generations. But it is the mistake of these men, that because they are eminent in some one or two branches of science, say natural history or geology, they are therefore fitted to speculate on all the sciences, on the whole history and destiny of mankind, and to settle or unsettle for ever all the questions bearing on the relations of the universe to its Maker. For this work, some of them seem to me to have no aptitude and no calling. I am sure that, in the wide fields of theology and philosophy, they are as ignorant as Comte was in the domains of mathematics and experimental science. Their generalizations here have a rashness which would not be tolerated for one instant in the special fields of science in which they have made discoveries. The time is not far off when they, too, will come to their level, which will be considerably lower than their present eminence.

In my early Lectures in this series, I met their fundamental principles. It is possible that some have felt that in these I dwelt too much on certain abstract points about knowledge and existence. But I did it of design. I had powerful antagonists to meet, and I had to prepare my weapons with care. I labored to show that the mind begins its intelligent acts with knowledge, a knowledge of things. I have no objection to call it a knowledge of phenomena; but, by phenomena in that case, I mean not phenomena apart from things, which is a mere abstraction, but things as appearing. The mind knows relations, but not relations between things unknown, which is impossible, but relations between things known so far known. Beginning with knowledge, what it reaches by generalization is also knowledge, and a knowledge of realities. Beginning with intuitive knowledge, it adds to it by logical processes; and what it gains is also knowledge. Its intuitive power is confined within very stringent limits. In particular, it has no *a priori* forms to impose on things. It does not override experience. It simply gives us a certain knowledge of things. Its main office is to enable us to gain experience, and to assure us that the knowledge we thus gain is of real things. Mr. Mill, proceeding on a different theory, declares — and his theory requires him to do so — that there may be worlds in which two and two make five, in which parallel lines meet, in which a straight line may return upon itself and enclose a space, and in which there may be effects without a cause. In all this he is consistent: it is the logical consequence of his theory. And you can meet him only by undermining his theory. This is what I endeavored to do in previous Lectures. On his principles, you cannot prove the existence of God, just as you cannot prove that two and two make four in the planet Jupiter, or that a straight line may not enclose a space in the constellation Orion. For aught that this theory can say to the contrary, it may be an accepted axiom in the universities of the Dog Star that parallel lines may and must meet if prolonged sufficiently far, and not coming in the way of a little planet called Earth — seen by a telescope of monster power — where a small mortal called man says, in his ignorance, that parallel lines cannot meet. I admit that if we cannot prove that two and two make four everywhere, we may also be unable to prove that every effect has a cause, or that this world has had a cause. But if, as Aristotle says, a man's mind is organized to discover truth, and truth be not beyond his reach, then I hold that we are entitled to say that in all times and in every place two and two make four, and a thing effected implies a power effecting it, and that the existence of benevolent affections in man implies benevolence in Him who planted them there, and that the Moral Law in the heart implies a Moral Governor. The spectroscope directed to that star, which takes a hundred thousand years to send its light to the earth, tells us that these effects could not be produced on the instrument, unless there were hydrogen and sodium in that star; and I am constrained to believe, on the principle of cause and effect, that it speaks the truth. And when I discover that beautiful adjustment in the eye which enables it to receive light from that distant star, I am as sure that there has been a designing mind constructing it, as I am that there has been an intelligence planning and making that spectroscope. These same principles that entitle us to argue that there s a God authorize us to say that we so far know that God, — the adequate cause of the effects we perceive, the source of that power we feel in ourselves and see exhibited on the earth, the fountain of that benevolence from which our affections flow as petty rills, the authority from which the moral power in us derives its authority.

Having examined the theory, I believe fairly and logically, we may now look for a moment at its consequences, speculative, moral, and practical. What have we left according to this new philosophy? We have a series of feelings aware of itself and permanent, or rather prolonged; and we have an association of sensations, and perceived resemblances and possibilities of sensations. Truth can be nothing more than an accordance of our ideas with sensations and laws of the association of sensations; which sensations come we know not whence, and are associated by resemblances existing we know not how; or more frequently by contiguity, with no relation of reason, with no connection in the nature of things, and being very possibly altogether fortuitous or absolutely fatalistic. The sensations and associations of sensation generate ideas and beliefs which do not, however, either in themselves or their mode of formation, generate any reality. This is the consequence on Mr. Mill's theory; and on Mr. Spencer's it is development out of a thing unknown, according to an absolute fatalism. And is this the sum of what has been gained by the highest science of the nineteenth century? Can this satisfy the wants of the soul seeking truth, yearning for reality, seeking for light as plants do in the dark cellar, and striving towards it, being sure that it exists and is to be found? Does it not undermine every belief in goodness, in affection, in beauty, and in truth, to which men have ever clung? Does it not leave the soul as the moon is supposed to be left, and as some think the earth will be ultimately left, with its rocks, its extinct volcanoes, but without atmosphere, without water, without life? Diodorus the Slow, after writing his profound treatise on the Awful Nothing, died in despair; and, deprived of all their deepest instincts and highest hopes, I feel as if there was nothing left for those who accept this theory of nescience but to do the same.

This, then, is the gulf to which we have come. It is as well that young men entering on the path should know what is the swamp in which it terminates. Some who have gone so far will draw back. But they will not fall back upon the icy crystals constructed by Channing, or the melted snow of Parker and Emerson. Yet they cannot stand where they now do. If they do not draw back, they must go forward; and they will find that, beneath this deep, there is a lower deep still. This deep is Materialism, which I mean to examine in my next Lecture.

VII.

Materialism. — Circumstances favoring it. — Parts of the Body most intimately connected with Mental Action. — Grosser and more Refined Forms of Materialism. — Büchner, Maudesley, Bain, Huxley, Tyndall, Spencer. — Objections to Materialism. — Mind not one of the Correlated Physical Forces.

IN my last Lecture I gave a sketch of the progress of Free Thought in this country, and showed that it is tending to sink towards Positivism. But this negative philosophy cannot last any great length of time. Persons cannot live long, for they cannot breathe, in a vacuum. A terrible wind will rush in to fill up the void when it begins to be felt. If men's heads do not discover the fallacy, their hearts will turn away from the emptiness. But, meanwhile, the movement has its course to run; and, as it does so, it will freeze, by its coldness, much blood at the heart, which would otherwise be felt vitally in every member of the frame and go forth in practical activity; nay, as it is dragged along, it may crush much life under its Juggernaut wheels. Before it closes its course it must assume another form: it will become a prevailing Materialism.

A number of concurring circumstances favor this tendency. Thus our young thinkers have come to see the utter futility of the whole *a priori* philosophy of the age now passing away, and are prepared for a reaction, in which the ebb will be as strong as the previous tide. It has ever been the great error and sin of the speculative rational philosophy that it has been expending its strength in building up in one age ingenious theories which the next age proceeds to take down. This has produced the sentiment first expressed by Lessing, and so extensively adopted in the present day: "It is not truth which makes man worthy, but the striving after truth. If God in his right hand held every truth, and in his left hand the one inward impulse after truth, although with the condition that I should err for ever, and bade me choose, I would humbly incline to his left, saying, O Father, give me that: pure Faith is for thee alone." There is a wide-spread idea, favored very much by the way in which the department has been taught, that philosophy is at best a mere gymnastic, exercising the faculties, but not capable of revealing truth; and people say that whatever may have been the need and the use of such Indian clubs and parallel bars in the Middle Ages, we do not require them now, when we have such pleasant open-air exercise in the natural sciences, which do reveal truth. Will men continue to search after truth when it has been discovered, and is allowed, that truth cannot be found? The father, in the fable, got his sons to dig in the field in the hope of finding a treasure: but they would not have done this, had they thought there was no treasure; and I am sure they would not have been led by like motives to dig a second field. Such dialectic activity wastes the energy, without increasing the strength. He who thus fights is like one beating the air; and his exertion ends not in bracing and exhilaration, but in weariness and restlessness. The bird which has been buffeting the wind on the wild waste of the ocean will alight on the first bare rock or mast-top it falls in with. Persons who have been cheated by those who promised to give them every thing, but really gave them nothing, will be ready to trust the first man who bestows on them ever so small a boon. So there are youths in our day, who, feeling as if metaphysics could give them nothing, are occupying themselves exclusively with the baldest physics.

Then, there is the exclusive study of the material sciences in so many of our educational institutions. I say *exclusive*, not extensive; for I rejoice in the extensive study of natural science, and believe that every settled branch of knowledge should have a place in every academic institution. But if we would not produce a one-sided — that is, a malformed — set of minds, we must have other studies mingled with them. In this country, a Bachelor's Degree, which used to mean that the youth was a scholar with varied accomplishments in literature, and in mental as well as natural science, can now be had with little or no knowledge of mind or its laws. I rejoice in the establishment of medical schools, and the multiplication of scientific schools; but steps should be taken to secure that in these there also be instruction in branches fitted to cultivate and refine the taste, and that our young men be reminded that they have souls, which they are very apt to forget when their attention is engrossed with the motions of stars or the motions of molecules, with the flesh, the bones, the brain. The cry of the times is for what they call *practical* studies to prepare young men for life; but fathers may find that their sons, after all, are not just prepared for life with its temptations, when they have no instruction in the duties they owe to their own souls and to God.

The result of all this is the creation of a certain spirit. For there is such a thing as the spirit of the age, — such a thing as the spirit of a college, more powerful than the influence of all teachers. There are susceptible youths who catch the spirit of the times, as lake waters take the hue of the sky above, or as worms take the dye of the herbage they feed on. Just as there was a great run two ages ago towards rationalism, and an age ago towards intuitionalism, so there is a corresponding set of youths in our day who will become Comtists, or Millites, or Spencerites, or even Huxleyites: the demand will create the supply; and they will find able men to lead them on over the dreary plain strewn with the skeletons of those who have there wandered and perished.

Any observant man may see the tide sweeping along. Materialism was a prevailing creed in France during the whole period of the repression of thought under the *régime* of Louis Napoleon, and was very agreeable to the *demi-monde* which ruled the manners and morals of Paris, and prepared the way for the present humiliation of that country. "Vive la Matérialisme" has been shouted from a number of their schools of medicine at their openings and public exhibitions. In Germany, theology is becoming orthodox in the theological Faculties, and a high philosophy has still a place in some of the universities; but, for a number of years, materialism has had a considerable acceptance among a set of able physiologists, among medical men and schoolmasters. In England, there are a thousand influences opposing it in the religion of the country, in the moral tone long sustained among the people, and become hereditary: but there is an active school of philosophy exercising a power over the young men, soon to become the influential men of the country; and this is strongly set in current towards sensationalism and positivism, which are certain to end in materialism. There are like agencies resisting the entrance and the progress of the materialistic school in this country, and the higher Unitarians heartily unite at this point with the Evangelicals; but still there are underground rumblings, which show that an earthquake is at hand, in the predilections of some of our physical inquirers and medical schools, sure to be favored by and to find acceptance with the votaries of pleasure, increasing among us with our wealth, and more rapidly than our wealth.

This materialism will require to be met. In meeting it, it will be proper to begin with admitting that there is a close and intimate connection in this present state of things between mind and body. This has been all along seen and allowed by the most determined spiritualists. Man does not consist of mind alone: he consists of soul and body. This is all that modern physiology has established, throwing a little, and only a little, light upon it; no, not on the connection between soul and body, but on the bodily organs most intimately connected with mental action.

It is shown that in the animal body there is an Automatic System, consisting of ganglia with reticulated nerves, some fibres of which conduct towards the centre, others outwards from the ganglia to muscles: an impression made upon the former, the afferent fibres, conducted inward to the centre, is followed by an action outward through afferent nerves, resulting in motion. Thus, on pricking the leg of a frog, there is an action from the periphery to the centre of the ganglion, and again an action outwards, and the leg is drawn in. These ganglia serve most important purposes in the lower animals, as in bees and articulated animals generally, where they carry on the motions of the creature. But they are found also in man. They run along the spinal cord, and there is no scientific proof — though some allege that there is — that their action is accompanied with sensation or with will. It has always appeared to me that we may justifiably discover final cause in this complicated arrangement for enabling the lower creatures, and even human beings, to perform certain needful motions, without the effort and the labor of the reason and the will. All this is evidently a mere organic apparatus, and we do not discover in it any manifestation of mental action.

It is shown that there is a Sensori-Motor apparatus. Here we have no will, but we have sensation. Thus, in sneezing and coughing, the act is not voluntary; but we feel it. We have examples of the same kind in the quick withdrawal of the hand when it is touched with a hot iron; in the cry which excessive pain calls forth; in the distortion of the face on account of an offensive taste or smell; in the closing of the eyes when a strong light falls on them; and in the start produced by a loud sound. Under the same head may be placed the marvellous adjustment of the human eye to the distance of objects, effected by a change in the convexity of the lens or cornea, together with an alteration in the direction of the axes of the eyes. This, too, is a beautiful provision for the convenience and comfort of the creature, whereby many necessary acts are performed without any labor of the will. Except in regard to the sensation felt,—in the *thalami optici*, as some think,—there is no special mental action or affection.

But in the higher animals there is a farther provision. Above the automatic process in the spinal cord, above the sensory centre, at the base of the brain are the two Cerebral Hemispheres. These brain hemispheres have no sensation: they can be pared off without any pain being felt. They cannot produce motion directly: they can do so only by acting directly, or indirectly, through the motor nerves upon the muscular system. We are now in the close proximity of proper mental action. We have come to the seat of memory, of intellect, and of will. The brain is composed of a gray matter and a white matter. Of these the gray substance is most intimately connected with mental action. That gray matter may be seen upon the surface of the two hemispheres of the brain, and exists in the shape of minute cells. It may be allowed that the operations of the intellect are intimately connected with the minute cells of the cortical layers. Without the concurrence of those cells, or rather perhaps of the forces operating in them, and which they direct, there can be no healthy intellectual action. They supply something which, as a concause, is necessary to mental action. When they are deranged, the operations of the mind are apt to be deranged. It may be farther allowed that there is a general, though by no means an invariable, correspondence between the size of the hemispheres, and still more the convolution of the hemispheres, and the intellectual strength. So far physiology can carry us. This is the form which the old expression of the connection between mind and body should take in our day, — a dependence of intellect and will on the cortical layers and contained cells and forces of the brain hemispheres. But physiology can go no farther. "So exquisitely delicate, however," says Dr. Maudesley, "are the organic processes of mental development which take place in the minute cells of the cortical layers, that they are certainly, so far as our present means of investigation reach, quite impenetrable to the senses: the mysteries of their secret operations cannot be unravelled." *

So the question remains where it was before. All this amounts to nothing more than the old statement that in the present order of things mind is so far dependent on the bodily organism. Professor Tyndall is candidly confessing the truth, when he says, "The problem of the connection of soul and body is as insoluble in its modern form as it was in the pre-scientific ages." It may be maintained, with great show of reason, that the brain-case is the mere instrument of the mind to enable it to perform its function, even as the automatic system is an apparatus to enable the animal to move, and the sensori-motor system is a process to warn it of danger. From all this it does not follow that the cell, or cell-power, constitutes thought. It does not tend to show that the physical power which circulates in the cell becomes in the cell an idea, or recollection, or feeling, or moral approbation, or will. It may be, after all, the mere organ by which the mind communicates with the body, and through the body with the external world. No one is entitled to say that the brain, or the forces in it, generate

* Phys. & Path. of Mind, p. 124.

mind. It might be nearer the truth to affirm that mental action forms the gray substance, and forms it to suit its purposes. Certain it is, that intellectual exercise enlarges the brain and makes it more convoluted, and gives it greater capacity and aptitude.

I must endeavor to furnish a sketch of the forms which Materialism has assumed of late years. First, I must refer to its grosser shapes. They are scarcely worthy of being noticed before such an audience as this, for their enormous fallacies will at once be seen. Still, it is necessary to state them, and so far expose them; for these are, after all, the forms in which the doctrine is held by the great body of materialists. It is thus that it is presented to our young men, to medical students, and others. And this is the common sewer into which the finer forms, which may amuse refined minds for a time, must ultimately flow. They are expressed in the brief sentence of Cabanis, that "the brain secretes thought as the liver secretes bile." Coming to our day, we find Vogt adopting this statement: "Thought stands in the same relation to the brain as bile to the liver." Moleschott says that "thought is a motion of matter." We may take, as representative of this school, Büchner, whose work, "Force and Matter," has been translated into English, and circulated widely in Great Britain and America. No doubt his work is very superficial, but it is relished all the more by multitudes who do not wish to be troubled with deep philosophical discussions.

And then he is clear and outspoken and dogmatic, uttering his dicta as if they could not be disputed. "The soul is the product of a peculiar combination of matter."—"In the same manner as the steam engine produces motion, so does the organic complication of force-endowed materials produce, in the animal body, a sum of effects so interwoven as to become a unit, and is then by us called spirit."—"As there is no bile without liver, so there is no thought without brain." But he thinks that this comparison gives a greater permanence to mind than it is entitled to. "The secretion of the liver and kidneys proceeds imperceptibly, and produces a tangible substance." It is different with thought as the product of the brain. "Mental activity is a function of the cerebral substance."—"It is emitted by the brain as sounds are by the mouth, as music is by the organ," and so has no such permanence as the bile has. It is a breath which exists as long as the lungs act, but which vanishes when they cease to play. Of this doctrine it may be said that it does not require any stretch of mind to understand it. The organ plays and produces music, the music of Mozart and Beethoven; the brain plays and produces the thought, the thoughts of Shakspeare and Newton. This settles every thing, and avoids all troublesome questions. And, as the brain does not play after death, so there is no proof that there is any mind existing after the dissolution of the body.

"To sleep! perchance to dream; —ay, there's the rub."

But this "rub" is polished off, for when the brain is dissolved in dust the power of dreaming is gone; and the most wicked, the most fleshly materialist, who has seduced one fair virgin after another, need not be troubled with any fear as to the second death, or the worm that never dies, for there is no worm but the worm that feeds on the body, and it dies when it has fed on the body and reduced it to corruption. Büchner quotes, with a feeling of profound admiration, the saying of the dissolute Mirabeau: "Death is an eternal sleep."

I defer to a later part of my Lecture the arguments against Materialism in every form. But I cannot avoid the exposure of this weak theory when it is before us. We can comprehend how the liver produces bile out of itself and the matter with which it comes in contact: the bile is the result of the liver and the matter brought to the liver, and, no doubt, partakes of the nature of both, — is, in fact, the old agents in a new form. The liver has acted on the matter, and bile is the result. But when the soft, pulpy substance, the brain, is supposed to produce thought, there is surely a process of a different kind. There is something in the effect which is not in the cause, nor in any of the constituents of the brain, nor in all the constituents put together. "Without phosphorus, no thought," is one of the axioms of the school. Later and more careful inquiry seems to show that phosphorus is not so intimately connected with thought as physiologists have been accustomed to say; but if phosphorus could produce thought, — say the rapt visions of Isaiah or Milton, — it would be a cause producing an effect not in itself, altogether unlike itself.

The other illustration, that from the organ producing music, is more plausible for Büchner's purpose, as it might seem as if the music were so unlike the instrument from which it comes. But we have only to determine precisely what it is that the organ produces, to find the loose analogy entirely to fail. What the organ produces is simply an orderly motion. The vibrations in the tubes, excited by the performer, produce a certain motion in the air which comes to our ear. This is really all that is done by the organ: it is a vibration in the instrument, producing a vibration in the external air. As to what follows — the pleasant sensation in the ear, and the swelling emotions in the mind, of sympathy, sorrow, joy, or admiration, — these are the product, not of the organ, but of a highly organized ear, and a finely strung mind. The motion in the organ, producing motion in the air, is certainly no evidence that the brain can generate thought.

I now turn to a much more refined writer. Dr. Maudesley has evidently considerable literary ability: he has read and he appreciates Goethe, and poets generally, specially those of the more sensuous school. He has been resident physician of the Manchester Royal Lunatic Hospital, and has studied the causes of insanity. He believes that mental insanity arises from pathological disturbances, — in short, from bodily causes; and he has evidently searched these with care, and has brought under our notice, in his "Physiology and Pathology of Mind," a curious set of phenomena, illustrating the influence of a diseased brain upon the operations of the mind. But he has been guilty of the inexcusable blunder of supposing that when he has stated these things, commonly without offering any explanation of them, he has explained the whole phenomena of the mind. He is like one who would speculate on the whole constitution of Great Britain or the United States, after having made himself acquainted with the cases that come before a police court. In his "Body and Mind," being Lectures delivered before the Royal College of Physicians, he studiously leaves on the minds of his medical hearers the impression that because he can explain certain morbid affections of the mind by bodily causes, especially at the critical periods of life, therefore he can account, by physiological processes, for the production of all our ideas, sentiments, beliefs, and judgments.

He is for ever denouncing the old metaphysics, and all who would study the mind by self-consciousness, or internal observation. "Psychology cannot, in fact, be truly inductive, unless it is studied objectively;" that is, physiologically, in the brain and nervous system. He acknowledges, "No one pretends that physiology can, for many years to come, furnish the complete data of a positive mental science: all that it can at present do is to overthrow the data of a false psychology." I agree with him that physiology has not been able to construct a mental science; and I believe it will never be able to do so, — though it may, and I believe will, greatly aid those who examine the mind by self-consciousness. But he thinks it has undermined the views entertained by those attached to the old psychology. In particular, he thinks that he can show that self-consciousness deceives. This is a bold attempt, and has seldom been made by any philosopher. David Hume himself was too shrewd to try to cast doubts on the veracity of consciousness. Dr. Maudesley's charges of falsity against self-consciousness proceed on an entire misapprehension of the nature of the testimony which it gives. He makes the witness lie, only by perverting his declarations and making him say what he never said. "Consciousness can never be a valid and unprejudiced witness; for although it testifies to the existence of a particular mental modification, yet, when that modification has any thing of a morbid character, consciousness is affected by the taint and is morbid also. Accordingly, the lunatic appeals to the evidence of his own consciousness for the truth of his hallucination or delusion, and insists that he has as sure evidence of its reality as he has of the argument of any one who may try to convince him of his error; and is he not right from a subjective stand-point? To one who has vertigo the world turns round." — "Is it not supremely ridiculous that, while we cannot trust consciousness, as to whether we are hot or cold, we should be content to rely entirely on its evidence in the complex phenomena of our highest mental activity?"* This whole statement proceeds on so entire a misapprehension of the testimony given by self-consciousness, that the student of philosophy who would fall into it in any of our American colleges would infallibly be rejected at an examination. Self-consciousness does not profess to reveal what is passing without us, but what is passing within; it tells us when we feel cold that we do feel cold; but certainly does not say at what point the thermometer stands. It testifies, and this truly, that the lunatic imagines that he sees a figure, but does not say whether this figure is a reality or a spectre. In trying to prove that consciousness deceives, Dr. Maudesley has only shown that he has been deceived himself, and is seeking to deceive us, by an entire misapprehension of what consciousness says.

He has thus failed, utterly and palpably, in showing that consciousness is a liar. The greatest sceptics have allowed that we must trust consciousness. And so we will trust it, notwithstanding Dr. Maudesley's allegations against it. And there is one point on which consciousness speaks, and speaks authoritatively, and will allow no man to think or believe otherwise. It declares clearly and unequivocally that man is *a person*, a distinct person, — distinct from all other persons and all other objects, — distinct from the nerves and cells of the brain. It declares, too, — with the aid of memory, — that there

* Physiology and Pathology of Mind, p. 25.

is a unity and identity of person, that I am the same to-day as I was yesterday,—the same now as I was as far back as memory can go. It asserts of itself, amid all shiftings of surrounding circumstances, amid all changes in the body or in the brain, that it is one and the same. Whatever else is true, this is and must be true; and we cannot be made to believe or think otherwise.

Dr. Maudesley sets himself determinedly against the doctrine of the unity of the soul. It is a unity only as a house is one, as a tree is one. A house is one only by the collocation of its several parts,—timbers, nails, and slates: a tree is one only by the co-operation of its component elements and members. So the soul is one only by the combination and co-operation of the brain-cells, and is in fact composed of essentially different elements, or parts, which shift from year to year,—in fact, from moment to moment; and its whole unity may be dissolved by the dissolution of the brain-cells, which are its constituents. It is vain to expect an immortality for such a soul when the parts are separated by the death of the body; in fact, any unity which it has in this life is altogether fictitious and delusive. Now, in all this, Dr. Maudesley is opposing an intuitive conviction of the mind as to the unity and personality of self, which is far more certain than any truth he has been able to establish by physiological investigation. This conviction at once sets aside — I do not say any physiological fact — but the perversely wrong inferences which he has drawn from his facts, by refusing to combine the evidence of self-consciousness with the evidence got from the senses.

Dr. Maudesley identifies the brain-cells, and the forces operating in them, with mental operations. Somehow or other (he is at no pains to tell us how) the action produced in the body by external objects — say by a rose or lily before us — goes up into the brain-case with its cells, and there becomes thoughts, fancies, feelings. Then he has a theory about these ideas and feelings leaving behind them certain *residua*, which become organized in the nervous centres. These *residua* play, with him, a very important part; in fact, come to constitute the Ego, to constitute what is permanent in mind. The whole process of manufacturing ideas in this brain work-shop becomes, with him, a very simple one. See how easily they appear, — as easily as sheets from a paper mill: "As in reflex action of the spinal cord, the residual force, which was over and above what passed directly outwards in the reaction, travelled upwards to the *sensorium commune* and excited sensation; and as in sensori-motor action the residual force, which was over and above what passed outwards in the reaction, travelled up to the cortical cells, and gave rise to an idea: so in ideational action [that is, the formation of ideas] the force which does not pass, or the residual force which may be over and above what does pass immediately outwards in the reaction, abides in action in the cortical centres, and passes therein from cell to cell."

Thus he makes "the formation of an idea an organic process." It is strange that so accomplished a man does not see what unfilled-up gaps there are in this theoretical process. A man has before him the grave of Washington. There is a mound of earth with grass upon it: rays of light come from it, and form an image on the retina of the eye, which raises an action in the optic nerve. This is all the length that the physiologist can trace it. But Dr. Maudesley can carry it up to the brain-cells, and turn it into an idea of the mound of earth and grass; can make it declare that this is a grave, and Washington's grave; and then become a thought of his calm, unerring judgment, and his disinterested patriotism, —all by a current which, while it travels on, finds that it is stayed, and, as it is stayed, finds that what "does not pass, or the residual force which may be over and above," becomes an idea of Washington's grave, and Washington himself, and his military and administrative skill, with an admiration of his unselfish character and high aims. When sheets of paper come out of the paper-mill, we have only what was potentially in the rags, with the water and the other matters employed to purify them; but here we have rays of light, that is, vibrations of air reaching the eye, and these come out the approbation of duty and of goodness. Verily, this beats the most astonishing trick ever performed by necromancer, when he turns a rod into a serpent; or by juggler, when he puts in a piece of cloth into a bag and it becomes an egg, or puts in an egg and brings out a fowl. People trained in a rigid, inductive logic will insist that there must be steps in this process which he has kept out of sight; that there is a wide interval between a residual physical force left in cells, and the idea of consistency of character, and singleness of purpose, and beneficence of intention. Yet this is the cool way in which he forms our ideas, even the highest: "The cells of the central ganglia do in reality idealize [that is, form ideas out of] the sensory perceptions, grasping what is essential in them, and suppressing or rejecting the unessential: they mould them by their plastic faculty into the organic unity of an idea, in accordance with fundamental laws." I would like to know how brain-cells should know what is "essential" in Washington's character, and reject the "unessential." It all takes place "in accordance with fundamental laws;" but these laws are of a very different kind from those of ganglia and cells: they are, in fact, mental and not material laws. He might do well to attend to the more scientific statement of Professor Tyndall: "I do not think that the materialist is entitled to say that his molecular grouping and his molecular motions explain every thing. In reality, they explain nothing. The utmost he can affirm is the association of the two classes of phenomena, of whose real bond of union he is in absolute ignorance. The problem of the connection of soul and body is as insoluble in its modern form as it was in the prescientific ages."

We now turn to a higher school of materialists,

who will not, for various reasons, let themselves be called materialists, not only from the unhappy associations of the name, but from profounder reasons. Some of them will not allow themselves to be so denominated because they do not take the gross views of matter which are generally entertained. We have found Professor Tyndall referring to this when he finds a difficulty in getting mind out of star dust. Matter, say the whole of the school I am now referring to, is something vastly higher in itself than what it is supposed to be in the popular apprehensions gendered by religious prejudices, which represent the body and matter as altogether inert and vile and despicable. Matter, they show, has high qualities: it has immense, indeed immeasurable, activity, and lofty powers of attraction and repulsion and assimilation; and they hint, if they do not assert, that it may have the power of fashioning ideas and pronouncing judgments, moral and intellectual. Now I admit freely that matter is not that inert substance which it has often been represented as being. Matter has essential activities: its atoms and its worlds are in a state of continural motion. The earth, sun, and moon, and stars are all flying through space with incredible velocity; and within every piece of earth, stone, and wood, there is as constant a motion of the particles as there is of the planets in their orbits, or of bees in the hive. Every change of heat in the temperature of a room makes a change in the internal structure of every object in it. I give up the idea of matter being passive. And

I repudiate the idea that our bodies are only the sources of evil, and to be despised. This notion came from certain Eastern theosophists, and was adopted by certain Christian mystics, and sanctioned by the Church in the ages when monasticism prevailed; but is not countenanced in Scripture, which represents the body as one of the constituents of man, which gives Christ a body, and unites soul and body at the resurrection, in order to enjoy full fruition. I do not seek to lower or disparage the capacities of body. I believe it has properties many and various. But there is no proof that thinking is one of these properties. We have seen in Lecture IV., *first*, that we know body and mind by different organs: we know body by the senses; we know mind by self-consciousness. We cannot perceive mind, or thought, or moral sentiment, by the eye, the ear, the touch, or any of the senses. And then, *secondly*, we know them as possessing different properties. We know body as extended in three dimensions, and resisting our energy and the entrance of another body into the same space. But we do not know mind as having length, breadth, and thickness, and as either penetrable or impenetrable. Again, we know mind as perceiving, judging, reasoning, desiring, willing, and we do not know matter as exercising these qualities. As knowing them thus by different organs, and as different in themselves, if there are any who hold them to be the same, the burden of proof must lie on them. And they cannot prove this by so spiritualizing matter as to make it discharge the functions of mind. However etherealized, matter is still matter, still occupies space, still resists our energy, has bulk and shape, can be weighed and measured; and there is no proof that it can form ideas, — say the ideas of the true, the beautiful, and the good.

In fact, those who profess thus to spiritualize matter so as to make it capable of performing mental operations, so as to make it capable of constructing the poetry of Homer and Dante, and the sciences of astronomy and mathematics, are found in the end to confine its powers within the very narrowest limits; in fact, making it possess merely the power of molecular motion under forces which are, after all, merely the sum of the motion, real or potential. "All vital action," says Professor Huxley, "is the result of the molecular forces of the protoplasm which displays it." He adds, "And, if so, it must be true, in the same sense and to the same extent, that the thoughts to which I am giving utterance, and your thoughts regarding them, are the expression of molecular changes in that matter of life, which is the source of our other vital phenomena;" and he says that "even those manifestations of intellect, of feeling, and of will, which we rightly name the higher faculties," are known, "to every one but the subject of them," only as "transitory changes in the relative positions of the part of the body." Upon this I say that the subject of them knows them to be different; and, as knowing them to be different in himself, he knows them to be something higher in others than "mere changes in the relative positions of the body." But I quote the language to show what is to be the end scientifically of all this pretended spiritualizing of the body: it ends in making thought molecular change, and mind — like heat — a mode of motion. This is the issue scientifically; and the end practically will be to make man to see and argue, that he has no evidence of the immortality of the soul; and believing that, he is a mere throb in the pulse of life, a mere bubble on the ever-moving stream of time: he will feel as if all he had to do was to dance along as gayly as possible, and get as many of the enjoyments of this world as he can, using as his motto and practical maxim, "Let us eat and drink, for to-morrow we die."

But Professor Huxley says he is no materialist.* "I, individually, am no materialist; but, on the contrary, believe materialism to involve grave philosophic error." This brings me to the second ground on which these men decline to be called materialists: it is because they believe neither in mind nor matter as substances. "For, after all, what do we know of this terrible 'matter,' except as a name for the unknown and hypothetical cause of states of our own consciousness? And what do we know of that 'spirit' over whose threatened extinction by matter a great lamentation is arising, like that which was heard at the death of Pan, — except that it is also a name for an unknown and hypothetical cause or condition of

* Physical Basis of Life.

the states of consciousness?" You will see now more fully the object I had in view in discussing the subject of Nescience in Lecture IV. of this course, and the importance of showing that we know both mind and matter as having real existence and power and permanence. Mr. Huxley, in a Lecture on Descartes, of whose profound philosophy he has a very superficial appreciation, tells us: "Nor is our knowledge of any thing we know or feel more or less than a knowledge of states of consciousness." "Strictly speaking the existence of a 'self' and of a 'not self' are hypotheses by which we account for the facts of consciousness." I have labored to show, by an appeal to consciousness, that we have quite as direct and immediate and certain knowledge of "self" as we have of the "states of self." We never do know a state of consciousness, except as a state of self. On the ground on which we deny the one, we may deny the other. If we affirm the one, we ought also to affirm the other. Some persons have been put into a state of high ecstasy because Mr. Huxley has so decidedly declared that he is no materialist. But he is no materialist simply in this sense: that, as he frankly acknowledges, he is a Humist, believing neither in matter nor spirit, except as "hypothetical assumptions of the highest practical value." But then, unlike Hume, he uses, as he confesses, a "materialistic terminology," which will be understood, as it has in fact been understood, by his readers in a materialistic sense, which will leave its practical impression. He is no materialist, he proclaims; but let all men observe that he falls back on a "physical basis" of life and of mind. I do not see that, logically and consistently, he has a right to call in any sort of basis. But men's instincts are stronger than their speculative opinions; and he has fallen back on a basis, and makes this basis not spiritual, as spiritualists do, but physical. What he has done scientifically, the mob of sensual men will do practically, and will believe in nothing but what has a physical basis, but what can be seen and felt. The office of the positive philosophy will turn out in the end to be to sanction, in the name of a philosophy, what is not a philosophy, but wishes to call itself a philosophy. This materialism, whether it calls itself materialism or not, will be more or less refined according to the character of the minds that adopt it, — more artistic and dilettante among the refined, coarse and licentious among the vulgar.

The materialists of the higher sort all admit that there is such a thing as thought, or mind, and that the properties of mind are different from those of ordinary matter. But, in one way or other, they identify thought with material agency. The conclusion to which Professor Bain comes, after a historical survey of opinions, is: "The arguments for the two substances have, we believe, now entirely lost their force: they are no longer compatible with ascertained science and clear thinking. The one substance, with two sets of properties, two sides, — the physical side and the mental side, a double-faced unity, — would appear to comply with all the exigencies of the case." * "Two sides" is, at best, a metaphorical phrase, and is altogether materialistic. It is not easy to see how benevolence, or the idea of goodness, can be one side of a substance, while the other side may be heat or figure. Mr. Bain is fond of introducing anatomical descriptions in the midst of psychological investigations, and in doing so leaves the impression that he has accounted for intellectual or emotional operations by organic affections. But there is ever a wide and an unfilled-up gap between the bones, muscles, and nerves, which he describes from books of anatomy, and the comparisons, emotions, and resolutions of the mind. Even when he is successful in showing that a sensation originates in an organic affection, he fails to mark the difference between the organic action and sensation, and he utterly fails in showing how our ideas — how our higher ideas, such as those of duty and charity — can arise out of, or be identified with, cell-force, or brain-force. His division of the Faculties of the Mind is into the Senses and the Intellect, the Emotions and the Will. His division is, in my opinion, a defective one. It allots no separate place to the Moral Faculty, and it embraces under Feeling two such diverse phenomena as sensations of pleasure and pain, and the mental emotions of fear, hope, and love. But such as it is, it is a division formed by contemplation of the workings of the conscious mind, and not by the

* Fortnightly Review, May, 1866.

observation of the nerves, the cells, or brain, which can tell of no such distinctions. No one acquainted with later physiology will maintain that he has discovered one part of the brain, or one set of agencies in the brain, devoted to the Intellect, another to Feeling, a third to Will. He narrows very much the functions of the Intellect: he admits that the mind has the power of perceiving resemblances and differences; but he has not shown that such comparison, — the comparison, for instance, which groups nature into a grand system, — is the product, or even the concomitant, of a group of cells, or of co-ordinated nerve currents.

I am unwilling to look upon Professor Tyndall as a materialist, especially after his defence of the existence — he does not say the separate existence — of mind. His language is guarded: he speaks of the phenomena of mind being ever "associated" with those of matter, and of their "appearing together." "In affirming that the growth of the body is mechanical, and that thought, as exercised by us, has its correlative in the physics of the brain, I think the position of the materialist is stated as far as that position is a tenable one. I think the materialist will be able finally to maintain this position against all attacks." And he argues, in behalf of "the extreme probability of the hypothesis, that for every fact of consciousness, whether in the domain of sense, of thought, or of emotion, a certain definite molecular condition is set up in the brain; that this relation of physics to consciousness is invariable, so that, given the state of the brain, the corresponding thought or feeling might be inferred, or, given the thought or feeling, the corresponding state of the brain might be inferred." * Some of these statements seem to me to go beyond what has been determined either by physiology or psychology. When the poor man refuses the bribe proffered him in his hour of need; when the patriot resolves to die for his country, which he is thus able to save; when the Christian cherishes the hope of heaven in the most trying circumstances, — I have no proof that any one could discover all this by simply looking at the state of the brain. In the interests of science, as well as of philosophy and religion, the rash statements of these men must be corrected.

All attempts to localize the different faculties in different parts of the brain, or connect them with special nerves, cells, or currents, have utterly failed. Some have held that the anterior lobes of the brain are the seat of the higher faculties, and the upper and posterior lobes the seat of the emotions; but no scientific man in our day will venture to say that this has been scientifically established; and even if it were established, it would merely prove that intellect is more intimately connected with one part of the brain, and emotion with another. Of late years, M. Broca has endeavored to show "that the third frontal convolution of the left hemisphere of the brain is the seat of language;" but others dispute this, and urge facts which appear to be incon-

* Address before British Association.

sistent with it. "On the whole," says Dr. Maudesley, "it must be confessed that, so far, we have not any certain and definite knowledge of the functions of the different parts of the cerebral convolutions. The anatomists cannot even agree on any convolution as peculiar to man: all that they can surely say is, that his convolutions are more complex and less symmetrical than those of the monkey." *

After this critical survey, I am prepared to lay down a few positions fitted to meet Materialism, whether of the grosser or more refined form.

(1) There is the consciousness of the Personality and the Unity of the Mind. I have no such conviction in regard to any material object. I cannot open my eyes without seeing the objects before me, — that hill and that tree; and I know them to exist, but I do not regard them as having a specific personality. I can easily believe that the particles that compose them may be constantly changing, and that they may be broken up and become other things, mud or mould. But I believe, and must ever believe, myself to have an individuality different not only from that hill and that tree, but from that changing body of mine, from those nerves and cells and brain currents. I can believe, on evidence being produced, that these parts of the body are intimately connected with mental action; I can believe that every particle of my body may be changed in seven years; but meanwhile I am as assured as ever that I who think am different from that organ

* Physiology and Pathology of Mind, p. 125.

which I think about, and that I have a personality such as is not possessed by the cells or vesicles of the brain.

(2) The mind follows laws of its own, which are not laws of matter. The laws of body are such as these: that matter attracts other matter; that the elements combine in certain definite proportions; that organized bodies exercise such functions as assimilation and absorption. But there are laws of mind quite as clearly and certainly established as those of matter. In the very act of knowing matter, mind is exercising a property very different from any property of the matter observed by it. In the exercise of the senses, the perception of the figure of a body is very different from the figure. Then the soul in all its actings has a consciousness of an abiding self which it can never get rid of. In memory, it looks back upon the past, and recognizes objects and events not now before it. In imagination, it can picture new and fairer scenes than any reality, and rise in the contemplation towards the good and the perfect. Even in association of ideas, there is more than bodily laws; as, for instance, when like suggests like, when a scene before us suggests a far distant one. In every judgment there is comparison, — a comparison of two things, one of which may not be present, neither of which may be present; and in our higher judgments we may connect things by very refined analogies. The nature of reasoning has been known since the time of Aristotle; and, with a few

slight differences, there is a wonderful agreement among logicians as to the law which regulates it. The principle underlying the whole is, that whatever may be predicated of a class may be predicated of all that is contained in that class. Or take the laws of the moral faculties: as when the soul contemplates an immoral act, — say the murder of a father, — and condemns it, and proclaims that right is supreme, and that every thing should give way before it. The laws of the emotions are as well established as those of the material universe; as, for instance, the law that feeling depends on a previous idea or conception of good or evil. The consciousness of free-will, the feeling of obligation and of responsibility, these may be dependent, in an inferior sense, on a concurrent organism, but they rise to an infinitely higher region. These are laws as certainly and definitely established as the law of gravitation or of chemical affinity or vital assimilation. But these are not laws of body, of motion, or of molecules, or electricity, or magnetism, or vital absorption, but differ from them as widely as we can conceive one thing to differ from another.

(3) Mind cannot be shown to be one of the correlated physical forces. I have already noticed the grand truth established in our day, that the sum of physical force in the universe is always one and the same; and that all the varied forces, mechanical, chemical, and electric, and probably the vital, are modifications of that one force. This can be shown

as to each of the forces by weighing it. Mr. Joule, of Manchester, showed that 772 pounds falling through one foot produces sufficient heat to raise one pound of water 1° F.; and they speak of the mechanical equivalent of heat as being 772 foot pounds. Now some have insinuated, and some have asserted, that mind is merely one of the correlated physical forces. But *prima facie* there is one grand difficulty in the way of establishing this doctrine, in the fact that, even if it were true, we have no means of proving it,—certainly no such means as we have of proving that heat is one of the correlated forces. Scientific men can measure heat and the other physical forces—we can measure the degrees of heat produced by the fall of a pound so many feet; but we cannot weigh or measure thought or feeling or will. This is a fact which shows at once the essential difference between the two, between body and mind. The barometer has not yet been constructed which will measure the weight of a thought,—say the thought of Sir Isaac Newton when he got the first glimpse of the law of gravitation. We have yet to find a thermometer which will measure the intensity of love on the part of a mother for her boy when he is being torn from her to go to a distant land, or expiring before her eyes; or the love of a Christian,—say the Apostle John—for his Saviour.

Mr. Herbert Spencer tells us,* "That no idea or feeling arises, save as a result of some physical

* First Principles, p. 217.

force expended in producing it, is fast becoming a common-place of science; and whoever only weighs the evidence will see, that nothing but an overwhelming bias in favor of a pre-conceived theory can explain its non-acceptance." This is by no means a correct expression of the facts. Let us carefully observe what actually takes place. A mother receives a letter intimating the death of a son. The paper with the black strokes on it is all that falls under the senses; but the mind at once apprehends the meaning, and the idea of the loss so affects the mother that, after violent outbursts of grief, she is left thoroughly exhausted. Now there is no evidence that all this anxious thought and sorrowful feeling is the "result of some physical force expended." What follows the simple perception by the senses is a mental operation, an idea of the loss of a beloved son arising according to psychical and not physical laws. This is seen more clearly when the affection is produced solely by internal contemplation, without any external occasion; as when on reflecting on our past conduct we feel that we have done wrong, and experience the qualms of conscience. True, these mental states exercise an influence on the brain, whereby brain force is expended and physical prostration is the result. But the grief of the mother, the condemnation of the conscience, is not the result of a physical force expended. The expenditure of the physical force laid up in the brain is rather the result of the strong mental affection which has risen up according to the laws of mind.

An American chemist has made an attempt to prove that mental force is one of the correlated forces.* The facts on which he proceeds are said to be these: There are states of mental torpor in which the galvanic needle applied to the brain may remain stationary for hours. "But let a person knock on the door outside the room, or speak a single word, even though the experimenter remained absolutely passive, and the reception of the intelligence caused the needle to swing through twenty degrees." Dr. Barker has not seen what is involved in this fact. The person was passive in respect of bodily action; but, upon the knock or the word reaching him, the mind was startled into action. Now here we have, first, a thought produced by the knock, or, rather, by the apprehension in the mind of the knock. This thought was not the product of physical laws, but of mental laws, — an idea awakened by an intimation of the senses, coming suddenly and unexpectedly. The idea, or thought, was not the conversion of a physical force; but the idea in the mind probably increased the circulation of the brain, and with this its animal heat, and hence the needle moved. Dr. Barker is entirely wrong in his interpretation of the fact, when he says, "The heat evolved during the reception of an idea is energy which has escaped conversion

* "The Correlation of Vital and Physical Forces," by Professor Geo. F. Barker, M.D., Yale College.

into thought." In the actual process, there has been a thought in the mind, produced by mental laws, prior to the evolution of heat, which in fact follows in consequence of the action of thinking and emotion on the brain. Dr. Barker tells us, farther, that "experiments have shown that ideas which affect the emotions produce most heat in their reception;" "a few minutes' recitation to one's self of emotional poetry producing more effect than several hours of deep thought." This is what we might anticipate, according to mental laws, that emotional thoughts, such as poetical images, would excite the mind more than calm thoughts, and thereby use and expend more physical force. Surely Dr. Barker does not mean that the physical forces, that the heat of the brain, could distinguish between emotional poetry and deep thought? All this does not go to prove that poetical images, such as those of Shakspeare, are the conversion of physical energy. The correct statement is, that the emotions produced by mental action use and waste the brain energy. Again, we are told that "Dr. Lombard's experiments have shown that the amount of heat developed by the recitation to one's self of emotional poetry was, in every case, less when that recitation was oral." I can readily believe this; for when the recitation was oral, the force which would have affected the needle was used in connection with the muscular contraction necessary to articulation. Thus, too, we can explain the well-known fact that, when emotion is allowed its natural outlet and expression in bodily action, it is moderated. Not that the emotion is converted into muscular energy, but that the physical energy in the brain becoming less, the emotion is restrained, and lassitude follows. I do not require, then, to dispute any of Dr. Barker's statements as to facts. I simply dispute his interpretation of the facts, especially his rash inference in the assertion that thoughts and emotions are merely the conversion of physical energy; of which there is not a particle of evidence. The change in the state of the brain does not produce the thought, — say the thought of duty or the thought of danger, — but follows it. The ideas — whether the being startled by a sound, or the calm meditation of a philosopher or mathematician, or the emotional image of the poet, or the same thoughts recited alone or to others — all arise according to mental laws, which can be very definitely expressed; and the liberated heat and electricity are the accompaniment of the action of thought upon the brain.

When physical force disappears in one form, we can find it in another. When it vanishes as heat, we may detect it in the mechanical power of the steam-engine. We know, too, where the power in plants and animals goes. When they die, it descends into the earth to increase the organic substance in the soil. But, surely, in mind we must have, if it be a physical force, a higher concentration of power than in any of these. But where has mind-force gone on the dissolution of the body?

Can the man of science detect it in air or earth? Can he weigh it or turn it to any use, as he can turn mechanical power or decaying vegetable and animal matter? It is said that there is as much electricity in a rain-drop as might produce, when emitted, a thunder charge. How much larger must have been the force in the brain of Shakspeare! But, when Shakspeare died, was there any evidence of the conversion of that force into any correlated force, chemical, mechanical, or vital?

Altogether, the special operations of the mind,—the recognition of an event as past by the memory, the remembrance of a mother long since ascended into glory, the tracing of an effect through a long process to a remote cause, the discovery of a new planet by mathematical ratiocination before the telescope had alighted upon it, the brilliant fancies and wide imaginings of the poet, the fondness of a mother for her son, the refusal to tell a lie when strongly tempted, the resolution of the sailor to cast himself into the sea to preserve the life of a fellow-creature at the risk of his own, the abhorrence of sin on the part of a sanctified mind, the idea of God and of holiness, the constant aim to reach the purity of heaven,—these, considered simply as phenomena, belong to an entirely different order from heat, or mechanical power, or an electric current, or chemical affinity: we feel that there is an incongruity in the very proposal to weigh or measure them, and there is no proof that they can be converted into a physical force, or that a physical force can be converted into them.

The following is a hypothesis which seems to combine a number of the facts established by recent science. Mind does not seem to me to be connected with rude matter, with the molecules of matter; but with the forces in matter, with the correlated forces. There is need of a concurrence of force in the brain in order to mental action. This is supplied by the alimentary and digestive organs, which may send it to the brain in the form of blood. They get it in the shape of food from vegetables or animals, which again get it, as every man of science knows, from the sun. The power which radiates from the sun enters the plant, which is eaten by the ox, which is eaten by us; and the organs of the body send it on to the brain, where it is laid up like water in a reservoir. One main function of the brain, especially of the gray matter, is to receive and distribute it. The brain is provided for this purpose; is partly formed, I believe, by this very force accumulating there from day to day and year to year. Here, then, we have force of some kind, and a brain to hold it, to direct it, and enable the mind to use it. But all this is not thinking, is not knowing or feeling or willing; in all this there is no discernment, no hope or fear or desire, or appreciation of the beautiful, or of good and evil. A current of nerve force running through the cortical cells of the brain is one thing, the thought of Mayer in arguing out the doctrine of the correlation of the physical forces is an entirely different thing.

I am inclined to admit that God has so constituted our present compound nature, that, without physical force distributed in the brain, the mind will not work, — just as a water-mill will not work if it has no water. And when the mind works, it uses and changes this power, which takes a new form. It is not thereby either increased or diminished : it merely gets a new distribution ; runs down, in fact, to the lower parts of the frame, and goes out in dregs, and is no longer available to the mind, which will act healthily only so far as it has a supply of this physical force. When this force is exhausted, the mind feels helpless for the time — the mill stops. If, by a disturbance in the brain, the force is improperly directed, there may be that most melancholy of all sights, a derangement in the mental operations. On the needful force being supplied, the mind is ready to work, and in doing so obeys its own laws — the mill obeys the laws of its own machinery : the mind thinks according to logical laws, feels according to the laws of feeling, appreciates beauty according to the laws of æsthetics. If the force is supplied in proper measure, and in the proper channels, the mind acts freely and healthily. If not supplied in due order, the mind is arrested, disturbed, agitated, and its proper action interfered with ; and gloomy thoughts and perverted feelings may arise. But all this, while the physical force is one thing, and mental action is another thing,—just as the mill machinery is one thing, and the water which it needs another thing. And though the one were to cease, it does not follow that the other must also cease. The water would flow on whether there be a mill or no. The mill might go by some other power,—say steam,—supplying the needful conditions. As man is at present constituted, the mind needs the physical force and the brain-case to hold that force and direct it; but this does not show that in another state of things the mind might not without the body,—and on other conditions being supplied,—think and feel and act as it did before. When a blacksmith's stroke is stayed by striking on the anvil, we know where the power has gone: it has gone into the molecular motion or heat of the body struck. When the body of the animal dies, we know where the power has gone: it has gone into the soil to enrich it. When Newton died, where did the intellectual force go? I know where: it went not down into the earth with the body, but up to God in heaven. When the Christian dies, where has his love gone? Not into the grave for worms to feed on it, but up to the bosom of the Saviour from which it has flowed. Yes: it is a universal law of nature and of grace that nothing dies, though every thing changes. "The dust shall return to the earth as it was, and the spirit shall return unto God who gave it."

VIII.

Our Lord's Life a Reality and not a Romance. — Criticism of Renan's Life of Jesus.

THE points which I have been discussing in the previous lectures have a bearing both upon Natural and Revealed Religion. If we cannot know any thing except what passes under our sentient experience, we have no evidence of those great verities to which faith looks; and if the soul of man be material, it is not easy to see how we can rise to the conception of an immaterial God, or be justified in holding by the immortality of the soul. And it is to be borne in mind, that the Scriptures do not set about proving that there is a God: they assume that he exists, and claim to be a revelation of his will. There have been persons who sought to undermine our belief in natural religion, in order to shut us up into revealed religion, — a very perilous undertaking, inasmuch as in pulling down the platform on which their opponents are placed, they pull down that on which they themselves stand. I can join heartily with all those who would establish in a logical manner the great truths of Natural Theology; and I confidently expect help at this point from the best Unitarians and Rationalists of America. It must now be clear to them that, if these foundations are destroyed by the rising Positive or Materialist schools, they have no religion left: and I am cherishing the hope that they will employ the literary and philosophical abilities which God has given them, in defending the great truths of the existence of God, the immortality of the soul, and the indelible distinction between good and evil; and in doing so, my hope is that they may be led into a higher religious position than that which they at present occupy. Standing on these fundamental truths, they will feel that what they know impels them to desire to know more. For the question will press itself upon them, How do I stand in relation to that God in whose existence I believe? to that holy God who hates sin? to that God to whom I must give an account? That law in the heart condemns the possessor of it: how am I to be reconciled to the Lawgiver? These questions carry us beyond natural to revealed religion.

With a special object before me in these Lectures,—that is, to meet the wants of the times,—I am not to enter on the whole wide subject of the Evidences of Christianity. It is now felt on all hands that the question turns round the Life, the Character, and the Works of Jesus. This is the stronghold which has often been assailed and never been taken. With it secured, we can defend the whole territory,—Old Testament and New Testament, doctrine, history, and morality. An ingenious attempt has been made in our day to seize this citadel; and this I seek to meet.

There are two, and only two, ways in which an attack can be made on the reality of our Lord's life. It may be urged, first, that the gospel history is a fable, in which it is vain to seek for any truth; or that it is such a mixture of fact and fable, that it is impossible to distinguish the one from the other. It is after this manner that Grote proceeds in dealing with the siege of Troy. He says, we have no account of the siege except in books of poetry, which do not profess to be history, and which were composed ages after the alleged occurrence; and so we cannot be quite sure that there ever was such an event: or, on the supposition that there may have been a basis of fact, we cannot separate the actual from the traditional and legendary. There have been assailants who took this ground in seeking to undermine our confidence in the gospel history. It is now acknowledged that the attempt was a complete and a miserable failure. Our Lord lived not in fabulous, but in historical, times, in which Grecian culture and literature were widely diffused, and in which the Roman government had introduced settled law and means of communication. And these four Gospels are, on the very face of them, not poems or legends or myths, but historical narratives, professedly by eye-witnesses, or persons who received their information from eye-witnesses. In their structure and spirit they are simple and artless, life-like and truth-like. Satisfactory evidence can be produced that they existed very much as we now have them in the age immediately succeeding the crucifixion of Jesus, — three of them in less than forty, and the other in about sixty, years from that event. If we maintain that the life of our Lord is not an historical event, we are landed in hopeless difficulties: in consistency, we shall have to give up all ancient history, deny that there ever was such a person as Alexander of Macedon, or that there was such an event as the assassination of Julius Cæsar. M. Renan has seen this, and has followed another method. He allows that the four Gospels are in substance historical books, and that Jesus spoke and acted very much as he is represented as doing in these narratives; but then he claims to take so much, and rejects the rest. He has thus avoided some of the difficulties in which infidels have involved themselves, but he is caught in others quite as formidable. He has drawn out from these four Gospels a superficially connected and plausible biography which he chooses to call a fifth Gospel; but in doing so he has violated all the laws of historical investigation, proceeded on caprice and prejudice, drawn a character inconsistent with itself, and given us a history utterly incongruous and incredible.

It is one of the disadvantages under which we labor in contending with the sceptic, that he objects to every weapon which we may bring with us. It is fortunately possible in the argument with this critic of our Lord's life, that we can fight him with his own weapons. M. Renan receives a large portion of the gospel history, but he will not accept the whole. Now I meet him by showing that he is acting capriciously in taking so large a part and rejecting the remainder, and that the same historical reasons which lead him to adopt so much should in consistency constrain him to go farther and hold by the rest. Suppose some one were to affirm that Shakspeare had written all those plays which deal with war and stirring incident, but that he could not have conceived or depicted the reflective and moralizing Hamlet; or to maintain that while Milton had composed the dignified and magnificent "Paradise Lost" he had not written the livelier "Comus," or the duller "Paradise Regained," which, it is alleged, must have been produced by an imitator of inferior genius: how would you meet such a preposterous hypothesis? You would prove that we have as good historical proof of the one work, as of the other, proceeding from the authors whose names they bear; and you might show, farther, that the works themselves bear traces in style and manner, in thought and sentiment, of proceeding from the same writers. It is in this way that I am to proceed in reviewing the French critic. I am to show that when he has gone so far, he cannot in consistency stop where he does, but must advance considerably farther.

I am to assume nothing which he does not allow in his candor or in his ingenuity. What, then, does he admit? He allows that Matthew wrote a Gospel; that Matthew was an eye-witness and an ear-witness of what he records, or had very direct means of knowing the truth of it. He concedes all this on the internal credibility of the narrative, and on the authority of Papias, who wrote early in the second century, and of a chain of succeeding writers, who quote or refer to the Gospel. He is specially fond of insisting that Matthew preserved the Discourses of our Lord, — "he deserves, evidently, a confidence without limit for the discourses;" * and, in particular, he grants that the parables, as being one narrative, could not be altered, and that we have them as our Lord delivered them. He allows farther that there was a Gospel by Mark; that Mark was a disciple and an eye-witness, and to be trusted as to the facts which he relates; that he was a relative of Peter, who may be supposed to have given his sanction to Mark's Gospel; and that Peter was originally an illiterate fisherman, and the impulsive, impetuous, open, and honest man which he is described as being in the Gospels. He admits that Matthew and Mark were not men of genius or invention; that neither was capable of writing the discourses put into the mouth of our Lord, of imagining the wonders which he is represented as performing, or of conceiving the finer and loftier features of his character. He grants farther that these two Gospels must have been written about the time of the siege of Jerusalem; that is, between thirty and forty years after our Lord's crucifixion.

So far all seems satisfactory to the Christian.

* Introd. p. xxxvii (in 13th ed. p. lxxxi.).

But, to enable our critic to dispense with any passages that displease him, he alleges that the two Gospels underwent a change. He thinks that when a person happened to have either of the Gospels, in order to have a complete text, he would write on the margin passages from the other Gospel. It was in this way, he supposes, that the two Gospels were fashioned into the shape in which we now have them. The theory may seem an ingenious one; but it is a crazy fabric, which, as it tumbles down, only injures the man who built it. For, by such a process, we should have had, not two Gospels, but a hundred or a thousand. The disciple at Jerusalem with a copy of Matthew would make additions in one way; and the Christian at Antioch with a copy of Mark would supplement in a different way; while readers at Alexandria, at Ephesus, at Corinth, and at Rome would amend in still different ways: and thus we should have had innumerable variations and discrepancies ever multiplying and becoming more exaggerated; whereas, as is admitted by all, we have, from a very old date, certainly from the beginning of the second century — I believe earlier — these two Gospels in their present form, and soon after we have them fixed for ever, by their being translated into other tongues.

M. Renan does not look with so favorable an eye on Luke's Gospel. He evidently does not like the account given in the first two chapters of our Lord's supernatural descent. But he makes important admissions as to this Gospel. It is allowed that it was written by Luke, and that Luke also wrote the Book of Acts; that Luke was a disciple of our Lord, and had means of knowing about his sayings and acts; that, as he claims, he "had perfect understanding of all things from the first," and got information "from them that were eye-witnesses and ministers of the Word;" that he was the companion of Paul, and must have had the countenance of that Apostle to his Gospel. He will not allow that Luke published his Gospel before the destruction of Jerusalem; for this would imply that our Lord gave a most minute prediction of that event (chap. xxi.): but he is sure it must have been given to the world soon after; that is, within forty years of our Lord's death. He qualifies all this by alleging that Luke admitted legends and adopted traditions. Here again our critic involves himself in perplexities from which there is no honest outlet. For in these forty years there was not time for the gathering of traditions or the formation of myths. We have unfounded traditions and legends of occurrences which happened centuries ago, but not of the lives of John Quincy Adams, Henry Clay, and General Jackson. At the time when Luke wrote, a large body of eye-witnesses and of actors in the scenes, Galilean and Jewish, such as apostles, disciples, priests, scribes, and rulers, — friendly and unfriendly, — must have been alive, and many of them ready to expose any erroneous statement put forth by the friend of so well known an apostle as Paul. If it be alleged that additions may have been made by others to this

Gospel, we are involved in the same difficulties as we have shown Renan is in regard to the first two Gospels; that is, instead of one settled Gospel, we should have a hundred Gospels according to Luke, each differing from the others according to the kind of legends adopted.

M. Renan does not know very well what to make of John's Gospel. He is sure it must have been the same person who wrote the Gospel and the three epistles that bear the name of John: the style is sufficient to prove this. He reckons it quite established by historical evidence that this Gospel was published before the end of the century; that is, less than seventy years after our Lord's ascension. He is certain that the author must have been John, or an immediate disciple of John, and thinks it highly probable that it must have been written by John: in fact, he thinks, we may consider John as the author. He allows that John was an apostle very intimate with our Lord, and constantly with him, and that he wrote later than the other evangelists, and with the view of furnishing a connected chronological account of our Lord's life, and of reporting discourses and detailing incidents which had not appeared in the other Gospels. He concedes that this John was originally an illiterate fisherman, son of Zebedee the fisherman, on the lake of Galilee; and that he could not have conceived or written certain of the discourses in the Gospel, such as that sublime prayer which Jesus is represented (chap. xvii.) as putting up in behalf of his disciples. But to counteract these concessions, he would have it that parts of chap. xxi. are an addition made by one who was nearly a contemporary. He insinuates that good faith was not always John's rule in writing his Gospel.* But observe into what a mess of difficulties our author has plunged himself by these admissions and denials. Chap. xxi. has all the peculiarities of style which have convinced Renan that the other parts of the Gospel and the Epistles are by the same writer. That writer opens his First Epistle: "That which was from the beginning, which we have heard, which we have seen with our eyes, which we have looked upon and our hands have handled of the Word of Life; for the Life was manifested, and we have seen it and bear witness." M. Renan is evidently right when he finds the same author saying in the same style (John xix. 35), "And he that saw it bare record, and his record is true, and he knoweth that he saith true that ye might believe." But surely it must be the same who says in the rejected chapter xxi. 24, "This is the disciple which testifieth of these things, and wrote these things, and we know that his testimony is true." I believe the testimony thus solemnly given. To refuse this is to make a liar and a hypocrite of the beloved disciple of our Lord, the apostle who has recorded the most heavenly and loving of his discourses, and who, according to history, lived a long and consistent life, bearing persecution and exile, because of

* Page 159.

his belief in what he has attested, and ever with the words of purity and truth upon his lips.

Such was the view taken of John's Gospel in the first twelve editions of his work. In the thirteenth he modifies his previous opinions. He is now inclined to think that the Apostle John is not the author of the fourth Gospel. But he argues still that it has a real connection with the Apostle John, and that it was written towards the end of the first century. He insists that this Gospel possesses at bottom a value parallel to that of the Synoptics, and in fact superior to them at times.* But by these changes he has not improved his position. He acknowledges that the author of the fourth Gospel wishes to pass for the Apostle John.† He farther allows that it contains some references (*renseignments*) infinitely superior to those of the Synoptics.‡ He appreciates the beauty and propriety of the discourses of our Lord closing with the sublime prayer, recorded from chap. xiii.–xvii.; and insists that there must be truth in these circumstantial and characteristic narratives of the transactions towards the close of our Lord's life. What then are we to make of these? Were the discourses and the prayer uttered by Jesus? Then they carry with them the whole incidents of which they formed a part, and out of which they arose.

* Pref. de la Treiz. Ed., p. xii. In Lecture IX. will be found some remarks on the apparent discrepancies between John and the Synoptics; and in Lecture X. on John's Gospel.

† Introd., p. lxv. ‡ App., p. 514.

Renan acknowledges that the parables in the Synoptics could not have been composed by the disciples who scarcely understood them, who were not capable of inventing them, and could not have altered them without entirely destroying their unity. And it will at once be admitted that they were quite as incapable of fashioning the discourses and the prayer of our Lord on the night he was betrayed. Nor can it be reasonably maintained that, with a basis of fact, they may have had additions made to them by legendary traditions, for in that case they would have lost all consistency. And so M. Renan alleges that the fourth Gospel was written by some member of the schools of Asia which attached themselves to John. But to this I reply, first, that no mystic of Asia Minor, or of any other country, ever produced any thing worthy of being compared with these chapters. And, secondly, this is to suppose that there were two persons in that century, one of whom could deliver the Sermon on the Mount, and the other the addresses and the petition for the church — so radiant with heavenly light — recorded in the close of John's Gospel. It is to suppose, farther, that these breathings of the heart were composed by one guilty all the while of the deceit implied in wishing to pass himself off as the Apostle John. M. Renan evidently felt himself in difficulties in his old position, but in shifting his ground he has only got into new perplexities.

It is out of these four Gospels that the critic composes what he calls a Fifth Gospel. I have occupied myself many laborious hours in ascertaining how much of the four Gospels is acknowledged in the fifth. I have marked by pencil in a copy of the New Testament the passages employed in the construction of the "Life of Jesus," and which are sanctioned by quotation or by reference at the foot of the page, and have thus made out the Gospel history acknowledged by this unbeliever. The portion of my Testament occupied by the Gospels is quite black with the strokes I have drawn. There is not a single chapter of the four evangelists in which we have not more or less acknowledged. The author has accepted whole chapters as written by Matthew or Mark or Luke or John, and as containing the real discourses of Jesus, or narrating the deeds performed by him. I find that there are about 971 verses in Matthew's Gospel, and Renan refers to no fewer than 791 of these as giving an accurate account of the sayings or doings of our Lord; and he quotes other 73 as being in the Gospel by Matthew, but not allowed by him to state the facts correctly. In Mark's Gospel there are about 678 verses; and our author uses 384 to draw up his own account of our Lord's life; and ascribes other 82 to Mark, who, however, in these does not please the critic. Of the 1151 verses in Luke, 606 are employed for his own history by Renan, and 136 more are attributed to Luke without the statements being sanctioned. I have not summed up John's Gospel so carefully because he speaks so indecisively about it; but a like calculation would give us very much the same result.

And here it is of the utmost moment to have it settled what the critic admits to be true in our Lord's life. He allows that Jesus was the son of Mary, who was married to Joseph the carpenter; that he had brothers and sisters, and was the oldest of the family; that he was brought up at Nazareth; that he went up to Jerusalem at the age of twelve and conversed with the doctors; that he could read, but did not know any foreign literature; that he preached at Nazareth, and was in danger of being thrown over the brow of a hill (which M. Renan can point out), and was driven out of Nazareth; that he had transactions in Cana of Galilee, and went to Capernaum on the lake; that he was much in the houses of Zebedee and Peter; that he gathered round him a body of disciples, and that the twelve named in the Gospels were his apostles; that he visited in his labors of love the cities and villages lying round the north-west of the lake; that he was believed to cure diseases and work miracles, and allowed the people to think that he did so; that he delivered discourses from a ship on the lake and from a mountain in the neighborhood; that these discourses, and especially his Sermon on the Mount and his parables, have been handed down to us as he delivered them; that he was a relative of John the Baptist, and had intercourse with him, and was much influenced by him, receiving messages from him and sending messages to him, and that John was a genuine though a stern man: that he took occasional excursions into other regions, such as the coasts of Tyre and Sidon, and to Cesarea Philippi and the Peræa, and Jericho and Ephraim; and that he went up regularly to Jerusalem at the religious feasts, and there delivered discourses and purified the Temple, and was supposed to do wonderful works, — all this as detailed in the four Gospels. In particular Renan gives a full account of our Lord's last visit to Jerusalem and of his death. He tells us that Jesus was intimate with Martha and Mary and the family at Bethany, that he often spent the night there, that he brought Lazarus out of the tomb there, and that ointment was poured on his body there in anticipation of his burial; that he went into Jerusalem during the day, and M. Renan can point out his favorite resorts and places of promenade; that at the passover he ate the last supper with his disciples; that the priests and rulers plotted against him, and that Judas betrayed him; that he often went into the garden of Gethsemane, and that the officers seized him there; that he was brought before Caiaphas the high priest, and Annas, who (it is acknowledged by Renan in striking consonance with the Gospel narrative) ruled the high priest; that his trial, as reported by the evangelists, is in remarkable accordance both with the Roman law and with the Jewish customs as given in the Jewish Talmud; that the disciples fled, that Peter stood afar off and denied him, and that John and the women went to the foot of the cross; that Pilate was unwilling to condemn him and proposed to let him go, but yielded to the clamors of the Jews, who insisted that Barabbas should be released instead; that he was scourged and buffeted, and led to crucifixion through the streets of Jerusalem; that, being exhausted, they laid his cross on a young man from the country; that he was crucified between two thieves, and that, after being some hours upon the cross, there was a bursting of a vessel of the heart; that his side was pierced, and that a fluid substance came out of it; that Joseph of Arimathea begged the body, and was joined by Nicodemus in preparing it for the sepulture; that Pilate, after exacting precautions from the centurion, allowed this; that he was buried in the tomb, and a great stone rolled upon it, and a guard set to watch it. Here Renan closed his Life, and promised to take up the resurrection in a future volume. It is a suitable close. The Fifth Gospel gives us a death, but gives no resurrection. In the Christian Church, as at the creation of the world, the evening and the morning constitute the day: in this new religion, which is to supersede the Christian, the night cometh, but there is no morning.

We do wonder, when all this is allowed, that the other parts of the gospel narrative should be denied. But Renan cannot admit that our Lord possessed supernatural power; and so he is obliged to devise a theory to account for our Lord's character, influence, and alleged wonderful deeds, without allowing him to be a divine messenger or teacher. He finds three periods in our Lord's life. In the *first* period, he sets out as a moralist and gentle reformer: he begins to preach and gather round him a company of disciples, and to travel from village to village in Galilee. In the *second* period, he comes into closer communion with the stern and gloomy Baptist: he imagines himself, or allows himself to be thought, the son of David and the Messiah of the prophets; and seeks to establish a kingdom of a romantic or ideal character, in which civil government and private property were to cease, and in which the rich were to be degraded and the poor exalted. Failing in this, there comes a *third* period, in which he becomes disappointed and embittered; nay, is tempted to use artifice, and is hurried on to death in a troubled manner and spirit, expecting some undefined world-revolution to come. This is the new theory of the life of Jesus, stript of some of the paint with which the artist has daubed it. It is one of the most baseless historical theories ever formed by perverted ingenuity. In order to confute it, I am to use no other materials than those which the author of it has sanctioned. The passages which I quote (except when notice is given) are all employed by the critic in constructing his theory, and may therefore be legitimately employed in overturning it.

First Period. At this stage Jesus is placed before us in what is meant to be a very engaging light. There never was so lovely a person as he. Of a ravishing form, of a genial and loving spirit, he drew towards him the hearts of all the men, but especially of all the women, with whom he came in contact. Somehow — our author cannot tell us how — the youth had risen to a high morality, far above that of degraded Galilee or bigoted Judæa. He had come to feel that God was his Father, and the Father of all mankind. This was all his theology; he knew no more: but this idea penetrated and filled his soul. With no sense of individuality, he could not distinguish himself from God. In a happy hour, — so our author expresses it, — he begins to be a reformer and the preacher of a new morality. Drawn by his charming person, and the evidences of his love, a number of men and women gather round him. Putting himself at their head, he rides about the country. "He thus traverses Galilee in the midst of a perpetual *fête*. He rode upon a mule, an animal in the East well adapted for riding, sure-footed, and with a dark eye shadowed with long lashes and full of mildness. His disciples sometimes gave vent to their enthusiasm by attempting a sort of rustic triumph. Their garments took the place of drapery: they cast them upon the mule that bore him; they spread them upon the ground where he had to tread. Wherever he dismounted, his arrival was held to be a joy and a blessing to that house. He stayed chiefly in the villages and at the large farms, where he met with an eager welcome"!! The picture is a very pretty one, and resembles the pilgrimages which I have seen in Austria of men and women to favorite shrines. Our author at this place gives a very enchanting picture of the scenery of Galilee, of its lake and mountains, its trees and shrubs, its grass and lilies, which he supposes the carpenter's son and his attendant fishermen to admire, in much the same way as the boy poets of this century, who have caught the spirit of Rousseau, Scott, and Chateaubriand, rave about natural scenery. Full of ideal dreams and pastoral visions, our Lord is represented as delivering his Sermon on the Mount, acknowledged to be perfect, and also the most beautiful and instructive of his parables.

This is Renan's picture of the First Period. As to some points in this description, it is clear that they are pure romance. It is instructive to find that no evangelist, no early Christian, says a word about the beauty of Christ's person. I rather think that Renan here draws from the Roman Catholic painters. As to his riding on a mule, we read of his once riding into Jerusalem on an ass, as a symbol of his being a king, but a lowly king; but at all other times he walked it on weary foot over burning plain and rugged mountain. As to his admiration of natural scenery, it is obvious that he did love and appreciate his Father's workmanship, that grass and these lilies, and the fowls of the air, but it was with a far loftier feeling than the Frenchman gives him credit for; and there is really no reason to believe that Peter and Andrew, Philip and Thomas, did ever break forth into ecstasies about flowers, like boarding-school girls of the nineteenth century, or were any thing more than plain, earnest fishermen, striving to earn an honest livelihood on their lake, and seeking withal to know what is true about God and right in duty. And then that sermon, acknowledged to be so perfect that none but Jesus could have uttered it, how did it come that a Galilean peasant could utter it? Whence that morality, pure, it is acknowledged, beyond all displayed to us before or since? I believe that he who expounded it must have been taught of God.

That morality is not only pure and ethereal, as Renan allows: it is profound, penetrating, and soul-searching, in a way which our smart critic cannot estimate. It is certainly very different from the light, airy sentiment which is painted and recommended in our modern romances, French and British. It is different in its whole spirit from the narrow, self-righteous ceremonial of the Pharisees, who busied themselves with laying down regulations as to the tithing of mint, anise, and cummin, and as to the washing of pots and vessels. It is equally removed by its spirit of love and self-sacrifice above that of the proud old pagan philosophers of Greece or Rome, or that of the modern, self-sufficient rationalist. It presupposes that man is a sinner; it sets before him a high ideal of purity and love, and points out a way of reaching it by grace; and it recommends the graces of faith in God, repentance, humility, and charity.

It can be farther shown, that, while he was from the beginning a moralist, he was from the first more than a moralist. It was not in the progress of events that the idea occurred to him of setting up a kingdom: he intended all along to do so. It was not as he met with keen opposition at Jerusalem that he contemplated persecution: he foresaw it from the commencement of his public ministry. All this can be established by passages sanctioned by Renan as belonging to the earliest part of our Lord's ministry.

In proving this, I will not insist on the intimation of Jesus, contemplating a great work, at the age of twelve, "I must be about my Father's business" (Luke ii. 49); for the critic, while he quotes the passage, is not sure about our Lord's younger years. Neither will I dwell on his being consecrated to his work by baptism, as our author is not very willing to give his adhesion to all that is said about John baptizing Jesus; for he sees it implies the supernatural, — the heavens opened, the dove descending, and the Father approving. But I ask, What meaneth the temptation which preceded our Lord's preaching and ministry? Recorded by the first three evangelists; reported by Mark, who is said to be so accurate as to facts, — Renan acknowledges that there must be reality in it. And mark that it comes in, not at the close of his ministry, when his spirit was supposed to be chafed by opposition; but at the commencement, showing that there was already a cloud over his spirit, and denoting that thunders would speedily burst. Then, let us listen to our Lord's first sermon. It is not of that light, romantic character which we might expect from Renan's theory. The subject of it is given, Mat. iv. 17, "Repent: for the kingdom of heaven is at hand," in which two great truths are brought out: one, that there was a kingdom at hand; and the other, that men were to enter it by repentance. The account is fuller in Mark i. 14, 15: "Jesus came into Galilee preaching the gospel of the kingdom of God, and saying the time is fulfilled, and the kingdom of God is at hand; repent ye and believe the gospel;" where it should be marked that our Lord connects the kingdom he was to set up with the predictions of the prophets, the fulfilment of which is said to be at hand; that the coming kingdom is twice mentioned; that the gospel is said to be about that kingdom; and that repentance is the proper preparation for it.

Let us turn now to the Sermon on the Mount so much lauded. The first beatitude is one suited to sinners (Mat. v. 3): "Blessed are the poor in spirit." The second implies that men are sinners, v. 4: "Blessed are they that mourn." There is a distinct apprehension of persecution coming, and an admonition to prepare for it, v. 11, 12: "Blessed are ye, when men shall revile you and persecute you, and shall say all manner of evil against you falsely. Rejoice, and be exceeding glad; for great is your reward in heaven: for so persecuted they the prophets that were before you." A kingdom is everywhere kept before our view, and the disciples were taught to pray, "Thy kingdom come." Those who use the Lord's prayer are assumed to be sinners, to be weak and liable to temptation, and exposed to the assaults of the Evil One, vi. 12: "And forgive us our debts, as we forgive our debtors; and lead us not into temptation, but deliver us from the Evil One." The difficulties of the Christian course are clearly announced, vii. 14: "Strait is the gate, and narrow is the way, which leadeth to life, and few there be that find it." I quote these utterances (and others to the same effect might be added), because it is acknowledged that they were delivered in the First Period, when it is supposed that he was so light and hopeful, and his whole prospect gladdened with sunshine. It should be frankly admitted that Jesus developed his plans gradually, as they had been ordained in the counsels of heaven, and according as men were able to bear them. But he had in him all along what he afterwards became, just as the tree is in the seed, as the oak is in the acorn. His course was one from first to last, along one road to one goal; beginning with his baptism and temptation, and ending with his crucifixion, resurrection, and ascension.

SECOND PERIOD. In this period, Jesus comes into closer connection with John, is seized with a revolutionary ardor, and purposes to set up a kingdom. Though not descended from David, he allows it to be thought that he is. He never goes so far as to make himself equal with God; but he identifies himself with God, and reckons himself the Messiah. The kingdom which he contemplates is not to be a political one established by a rebellion against the Roman government. It is an ideal, that is a visionary, one, with no magistrate and no private property, and is to appear immediately. In order to bring it in, he ordains apostles and sends them out to preach and proclaim the new reign. Meanwhile he allows his ardent followers and the superstitious multitude to imagine that he heals diseases by a miraculous power, which he does not possess. Such was his aim and his work during the middle portion of his ministry, in which, according to our author, we have his enthusiasm kindled into a nobler flame, and his contemplated end enlarged; but in which also we have the commencement of deflections from the pure morality of his early career, and of that accommodation to circumstances which led to positive artifice in the Third Period. If Jesus had died before this stage of his existence, he would not have been heard of beyond a small district of Galilee or after his own age; but he would have been purer and more faultless.

It is easy, from the materials which the critic allows, to scatter this vision. We have seen that from the very first our Lord meant to set up a kingdom. As his public ministry advances, the plan is developed more fully; but it is, in the end, merely the filling in of what had been described in outline from the beginning. The kingdom is obviously a spiritual one. But there was never a purpose to set aside the temporal power. He refused to interfere in matters of civil government, saying, when he was called to decide in a legal dispute (Luke xii. 14), "Who made me a judge or a divider over you?" He wrought a miracle, in order to pay tribute, and laid down the important principle (Mat. xxii. 21), "Render unto Cæsar the things which are Cæsar's, and unto God the things that are God's." Here we have a clear and admirable enunciation of his doctrine, both as to the kingdoms of this world and his own kingdom, subsisting together and alongside, each having a place and a sphere: namely, that in temporal things tribute, honor, and obeisance are to be rendered to Cæsar, the civil governor; while in spiritual things the heart, conscience, and worship are to be reserved for God. Our Lord clearly announces that his kingdom is to be a spiritual one. And here I will not insist on John iii. 3, where he says, we must be born again, in order to enter the kingdom; for Renan is not sure about this passage, though it is consonant with the whole teaching of our Lord. The critic acknowledges that Matthew may be implicitly trusted as to our Lord's discourses. Let us turn, then, to Mat. xiii., where we find a full account, by Jesus, of the nature of his kingdom. We see how the kingdom is to be established and men brought into it, v. 3, by the scattering of the seed of the Word; and we should observe how it is declared that a large body of mankind are not prepared to receive that seed, because their hearts are impenetrable as the beaten wayside, or thin as gravelly places, or choked up as with thorns. Again, this kingdom is to be the result of a long process and of growth, and is to be so far a mixed kingdom; for, v. 24, it is likened to a man sowing good seed, while the enemy sows tares, and both grow together till the harvest. In v. 47, it is represented as a net which gathers all kinds of fishes, which shows that our Lord saw that in the visible church the evil was to come in with the good, and that his views and expectations were never of that ideal, Utopian character which the Frenchman supposes them to have been. The same lesson is taught by the comparison of the kingdom, v. 31, to a grain of mustard-seed and, v. 33, to leaven. Fortunately our author acknowledges the parables to be genuine: the disciples had not genius to fashion them, and they are too consistent to be made up of legends. The whole of Luke xv. is sanctioned by our sceptic, and we see from it who were to be members of Christ's kingdom: v. 5, the lost sheep brought back on the shoulders of the shepherd; v. 8, the lost piece of money saved from the dust; v. 11, the lost son brought back by the remembrance of a father's love to the father's house. The kingdom was to be a reign of God in men's hearts (Luke xvii. 21): "Neither shall they say, lo here! or, lo there! for, behold, the kingdom of God is within you." The whole object of our Lord's mission is described (Luke xix. 10.): "The son of man is come to seek and save that which was lost." Renan quotes twice Mat. xviii. 3, where the necessity of a spiritual change is clearly pointed out: "Verily, I say unto you, Except ye be converted, and become as little children, ye shall not enter into the kingdom of heaven."

THIRD PERIOD. We approach the view given of this period with aversion: it so grates upon our feelings. We would shrink from the examination of it if we could; but there is no help for it: the charges have been brought, and we must face them. Jesus has been filled with an idea which makes him dizzy.* His idea he finds is not to be realized; and so bitterness and reproach affect his heart more and more every day,† and he gives way to feelings of disappointment and sourness, and in the end he hurries on to his death as a sacrifice which he cannot avoid. In order to set up his kingdom, he must leave Galilee and go up to Jerusalem. But there the scenery is so sterile and horrid in Judæa, when compared with the smiling northern province, that his spirits become oppressed! The Jewish doctors cannot appreciate his fine morality or his lofty visions, and the people are too indifferent to take any notice of him. He must do something to make himself known. What is this to be? He must either renounce his mission, or become a worker of miracles.‡ And here we have excuses offered for the conduct of Jesus which grate upon our moral sense, and to which we indignantly refuse to listen. Jesus has now to use less pure means: § he has to yield to opinion and satisfy the ideas of the time:‖ at first the *artifice* (oh! we shrink from the

* p. 318. † p. 324. ‡ p. 257. § p. 92. ‖ pp. 160, 360.

word as applied to Jesus) is innocent;* he allows himself to be thought a worker of miracles against his will.† There lives on the back of the Mount of Olives, where it begins to slope from the summit, a reputable and loving family, the members of which have become attached to Jesus. They are anxious to further his views and promote his cause. We shrink from the thought of giving the account which follows, as we would from repeating a scandal against a brother or sister, a father or mother. But the calumny has been uttered, and we must repel it. Martha and Mary devise a plan of putting their brother Lazarus, while yet living, into the tomb, and Jesus consents to come to the grave and call him forth. When we read this, we feel that we must reject with scorn all the compliments which Renan has been paying to our Lord throughout the volume, when he lauds him as so great and pure, as "the individual who has approached nearest the Divine," and as "the creator of the eternal religion of morality."

But let us pursue the development of the romance, which has now become so unnatural. The miracle does call the attention of many: but it only irritates the Jewish rulers, and they conspire to put Jesus to death. He has seen, for a considerable time, that he cannot establish his kingdom. He becomes bitter in his expressions and fierce in his denunciations. He feels that he must prepare for leaving this world. He might have avoided death; but love carries him on,‡ and he makes the sacrifice, expecting some

* p. 162. † p. 268. ‡ p. 370.

speedy renovation of the world to be brought about he knows not how.

Need I enter upon any elaborate statement to show how false the picture, if there be any consistency in character, any reality in the gospel narratives? It can be established, in the first place, that our Lord did not begin to work miracles at this time, that he habitually performed them from the commencement of his public ministry: we have as good evidence of this as of any other incident in his history, as we have of his reputed miracle at Bethany. The same John tells us (chap. ii.) that he began his miracles three years before at Cana of Galilee; and Matthew gives detailed accounts of many miraculous cures, such as of the centurion's servant (viii. 5–13), and of the man with the palsy (ix. 2–6). Mark, so commended for the accuracy of his narrative of facts, tells us (iii. 15) that when he ordained the Twelve, he gave them power to "heal sicknesses."

And as to Jesus being engaged in the alleged transaction at Bethany, our better nature sensitively recoils from it. He has here felt himself in difficulties. If he entirely omit the incident, his whole version of our Lord's life loses its credibility; for we have an account of the transaction — minute, circumstantial, and consistent — by John, a professed spectator. And so our author gives the event; and, as he cannot admit it to be miraculous, he makes it a deception. But in making it an artifice, he has made it an inconsistency, an improbability; indeed, a moral impossibility. Renan's version of it is before us, and we have to examine it. If Jesus was what the author describes him, the purest, loftiest, and most truthful of men, he could not have done the deed. If he did the deed, he could not have had that lofty consciousness and those high moral aims which he is represented as setting continually before him. This critic is here in a dilemma; and we leave him exposed, on the horn he may prefer, to the scorn of all truth-seeking historical investigators. The cunning artist has here outwitted himself, and has been led to do so by his false theory. He makes one, represented by him as entitled to be called "divine," act as if he were a vulgar juggler or a wandering professor of mesmerism. If such an incongruity were exhibited on the stage, it would be hissed off it; as it is, we must hiss it off the stage of history. That one who, it is acknowledged, did such deeds of holiness, endured such self-sacrificing sufferings, and delivered such lofty discourses, should have descended to so low a deception, is monstrous, is utterly incredible. I would as soon believe that there was not a single honorable merchant or trustworthy tradesman in our country, or a single honest man or virtuous woman in our world; I would sooner believe that my father never cared for me, that my mother never loved me, as that one so truthful and sincere and loving should have done so hypocritical an act.

So far I wrote at the time when the work was published.* I think it proper that what I then said

* Good Words, 1864.

should appear in these Lectures, directed against the errors of our day. For the charge brought by M. Renan is allowed to remain in the editions issued at present in the book-stores of America, and in the English translation, even in the impressions bearing the date of 1870. But it requires to be stated that, after allowing the allegation to run through twelve editions, he withdrew it in the thirteenth edition, published in 1867. He was driven from his first position by the remonstrances of scholars and the indignation of the public, who feel that his insinuations are unjust. For his first theory he has substituted a second, which is as weak as the other is unworthy. He still continues to insist that there were transactions in which Jesus consented to play a part; and, with pointed reference to the event at Bethany, that "there never was a great religious creation which did not imply a little of that which people call fraud." * But he softens his language, and represents the supposed miracle as proceeding from a misunderstanding. The friends of Jesus thought it needful that some wonder should be performed to impress the minds of the hostile inhabitants of Jerusalem. In particular, the pious sisters were sure that it would melt the hearts of the impenitent, were one to rise from the dead. "No," said Jesus, "they will not believe, though one should rise from the dead." Then they recalled to him a history with which he was familiar, that of the poor good Lazarus covered over with sores, who died and was carried into Abraham's bosom; but he as-

* Treiz. Ed., App., p. 510.

sured them that, "if Lazarus should return, they would not believe on him." In time misunderstandings collected around this subject. "The hypothesis was changed into a fact.* They spoke of Lazarus as resuscitated, and of the unpardonable obstinacy which could resist such testimony." It was impossible that a report of this should not reach Jerusalem, where it only exasperated the enmity of the rulers and brought disastrous consequences to Jesus. This is certainly a very slender basis on which to rear such a structure. M. Renan argues that there is need of some such foundation. He refuses to take refuge in the allegorical or mythical theory of Strauss and the rational theologians, which he is sure is not applicable to the characteristic incidents and accurate details, as to our Lord's life, found in the account of his latter days in John's gospel.† And I admit to him that popular legends may collect in nebulous matter round a very small nucleus. But not such a history and moral traits as are indissolubly intertwined with the resurrection of Lazarus. In the earlier editions, he fixed on a foundation utterly inconsistent with the acknowledged character of our Lord. In later editions, he has nothing left on which to rear such tender incidents as the sympathy of Jesus, the conduct of the sisters, and the grand truth evolved: "I am the resurrection and the life: he that believeth in me, though he were dead, yet shall he live; and whosoever liveth and believeth in me shall never die." M. Renan declares that the narrative of the resurrection of Lazarus is

* pp. 372, 373. † App., p. 508.

bound up with the last transactions in the life of Jesus by such strict ties, that if we reject it as imaginary the whole edifice, so solid, of the last weeks of the life of Jesus, is crushed by the same blow.

It can be shown that, in this third period, Jesus is unfolding as pure a morality as in the first. Matthew, who reports the discourses so faithfully, represents him as at this time summing up the law in love, in love to God and love to man (chap. xxii. 37–40). It is clear that he is developing the plan of his work which had been all along before his mind. He is still contemplating the establishment of a kingdom, and the very same kingdom. This is brought out in the parable reported by Matthew (xxv. 14–30), in which the master distributes talents among his servants, and departs with the assurance that he will return. The new kingdom is to be established in consequence of the death of the Son (Mat. xxi. 33; Mark xii. 1–12). He had been announcing his death for a considerable time (Mark ix. 31), "For he taught his disciples and said unto them, The Son of Man is delivered into the hands of men, and they shall kill him, and after that he is killed, he shall rise the third day." He brings out clearly that it is through his death that life is to be imparted to the church (John xii. 24): "Verily, verily, I say unto you, Except a corn of wheat fall into the ground and die, it abideth alone; but if it die, it bringeth forth much fruit." The death is an atonement for sin, for when he takes the cup he says (Mat. xxvi. 28): "For this is my blood of the New Testament, which is shed for many for the remission of sins." He gives instructions as to the discipline, communion, and prayer to be instituted and kept up in the church when he should have departed (Mat. xviii. 20): "For where two or three are gathered together in my name, there am I in the midst of them." It is clear that it is the same kingdom which was to be entered by repentance and regeneration that is to be continued by worship and holy fellowship.

It may be allowed that Jesus becomes more faithful in his warnings, first to the Galileans, and then to the Jews at Jerusalem, as he draws near the close of his pilgrimage. But there is no trace of bitterness or disappointment. The darkness, no doubt, is becoming denser; but the eclipse had begun at the commencement of his atoning work: we see it in the temptation immediately following the baptism. And he continues as loving, as tender, as full of sympathy, as he ever was. Nay, have we not all felt as if the prospect of his death and of his parting with his disciples imparted an additional pathos to these heart utterances of our Lord? That sun looks larger, and glows upon us with a greater splendor as he sets. The plant sends forth a greater richness of odor by being crushed. The fragrance is poured forth in richer effusion from the alabaster box when it is broken. Certain it is, that some of the tenderest incidents in our Lord's life occur towards its close. It was at the period when he is supposed to have been soured; it was when he had left Galilee for the last time, and was setting his face steadfastly towards Jerusalem, — that he rebuked the disciples, when they were for calling down fire from heaven (Luke ix. 55). It was at this time that he took little children in his arms, when the disciples would have driven them away, saying, "Of such is the kingdom of heaven" (Mat. xix. 14). It was in one of his last visits to Jerusalem that he looked so complacently upon the poor widow casting her mite into the treasury (Mark xii. 42). It was as he hung upon the cross that, turning to Mary, he said, "Woman, behold thy son;" and, turning to John, he said, "Behold thy mother." I know that our critic has cast doubts on this incident, but very fruitlessly. A great living historian has argued that certain letters must be genuine; for, on the supposition that they are fictitious, they must have been written by a Shakspeare. The argument is not altogether conclusive, for they might have been written by one with a genius like that of our great poet. Now we here argue in the same way: but our argument is conclusive, for none but the highest poet could have conceived such an incident: and the evangelists, however highly elevated spiritually, had not the skill of our unmatched dramatist. The same may be said of the comfortable assurances given by our Lord to the thief on the cross, "To-day thou shalt be with me in Paradise;" and of his dying prayer, "Father, forgive them; for they know not what they do." This petition, and the confiding expression, "Into thy hands I commend my spirit," were the fitting close of a life devoted to the redemption of man and the manifestation of the Divine glory.

IX.

UNITY OF OUR LORD'S LIFE, — IN THE ACCOUNTS GIVEN OF HIM, — IN HIS METHOD OF TEACHING, — IN HIS PERSON, — AND IN HIS WORK.

IN this Lecture I am to show that the life, the character, and mission of our Lord are one in idea, in purpose, in accomplishment, and result. In doing this I have two ends in view. One is to furnish evidence of the genuineness of the whole. M. Renan argues that we have the Sermon on the Mount and the Parables very much as Jesus delivered them; for the evangelists were incapable of conceiving them, and if they had attempted to add or to alter they would have spoiled them. It is the same with our Lord's life. It is a conception which no Galilean, Jew, Greek, Oriental, or Roman could have formed, and which could not have grown into such beauty and consistency out of popular tradition. Another purpose may also be accomplished; and that is, to show that in accepting Christ's life we must accept it entire, — doctrine, miracles, and precepts. Our Lord's life is woven throughout and without seam, and cannot be divided: we must either take all or get none.

(1) *We have four Gospels, and yet the account*

which they give is one. There is a beautiful unity and consistency in the character and acts of our Lord as exhibited by the whole four.

But then it is said that there are discrepancies and contradictions in their narratives when compared one with another. And there certainly is not in these biographies that labored consistency which we always find in a *trumped-up* story, and which so prejudices all who are in the way of shrewdly estimating testimony. The writers are artless in every thing; but they are specially so in this, that, conscious of speaking the truth, they are not careful to reconcile what they say in one place with what they or others may say in another place. I admit that we have such differences as are always to be found in the reports of independent witnesses; but I deny that there are contradictions. Commentators may differ, and are at liberty to do so, as to the explanations which they offer of the apparent discrepancies. All meanwhile may agree in declaring that the difficulties arise solely from our not knowing more than the evangelists have told us, and that they would vanish if we knew all the circumstances. To illustrate what I mean in a very familiar way: One day, when passing along the streets of the city in which I lived at the time, I saw that there was a house on fire about half a mile off; and as I happened to have an official interest in a dwelling in that quarter, used for a philanthropic purpose, I proceeded towards the spot. Meeting a person who seemed to be coming from the fire, I asked him where it was, and he told me it was in a certain street. Passing on towards that street, I asked another person where the fire was, and he gave me the name of a different street. I asked a third witness about the fire: he told me he had been there, and it was nearly extinguished. I met a fourth individual a little way farther on, and he informed me that it was blazing with greater fury than ever. Had I stopped here, I might have been tempted to say, What a bundle of contradictions! — one says the fire is in one street, and another that it is in a different street: one says that the flames are nearly extinguished and another says they are increasing; and had I stopped it might have been impossible for me to reconcile the inconsistencies. But I had reason to be concerned about that fire, and so I went on, and found that all the witnesses had spoken the truth. The house was a corner one, between the two streets which had been named: the flames had been kept down for a time, but afterwards burst forth with greater fury than ever. Nowhere in these Gospels do we meet with such violent discrepancies as I had in the statements of these four men. But I have a deep interest in the depositions of the evangelical biographers. For there is a fire burning in the earth, a fire burning in my bosom, and I am supremely concerned to know how it may be extinguished, as I hope it may be by Him of whom these witnesses testify; and I go on to combine their declarations, and to inquire whether, after all, there be any real contradictions. I take up those passages dwelt upon by the infidel.

Luke tells us, ii. 1: "And it came to pass in those days, that there went out a decree from Cesar Augustus, that all the world should be taxed;" *ἀπογράφεσθαι πᾶσαν τὴν οἰκουμένην*: that the whole Roman world should be enrolled. "(And this taxing [or census] was first made when Cyrenius was governor of Syria.) And all went to be taxed [or enrolled], every one into his own city. And Joseph also went." Now it so happens that Josephus, usually a correct historian as to his own times, tells us that Cyrenius, or Quirinius, took charge of a taxation in Judea, but at a considerably later date. Proceeding on this, the infidel tells us that Luke must be wrong here; and Renan argues that the whole account of our Lord's being born in Bethlehem must be a later legend, inserted to make our Lord's birth correspond to the prophecy of Micah. I remember that when I was a student of theology we were greatly perplexed with this; for the key to unlock the mystery had not then been found. But later German scholarship has very much cleared up this subject. It is shown first that the two Roman historians, Tacitus and Suetonius, represent Augustus as issuing about this time an edict, that throughout the empire and the allied States there should be accounts taken of the number of the inhabitants, of the property, and its liability to taxation,—this, years before the taxation mentioned by Josephus. Then, secondly, a

German scholar, Zumpt, has shown that in the roll of the successive Syrian proconsuls there occurs a blank at that time, and reasons can be given for filling up the blank with the name of Quirinius, who appears to have been governor of Syria from about A. U. C. 750 to 753. Thus it turns out that both Luke and Josephus are right: there was first a census in the time of Augustus, and then a taxing at a later date; and Quirinius had to do with both. And it is a circumstance worthy of being mentioned, that Luke, wiser than his critics, seems to have known of both; and as he mentions the one in his Gospel, so he refers to the other in his second work, Acts v. 37, where he speaks of Judas of Galilee rising up in the days of the taxing.

This discovery helps us to clear up another difficulty. Roman law, says M. Renan, did not require Joseph and Mary to leave Nazareth, the place where they dwelt, and go up to Bethlehem, in order to have their names enrolled. All true, as regards Roman law. But when Jesus was born (two years after it would have been different), Herod, an ally of Augustus, was king of Judea, which was governed by Jewish and not by Roman law; and, according to Jewish law, the place to which they had to go in order to be enrolled was Bethlehem, as they were both of the house and lineage of David, and had legal claims there, according to the Jewish law of inheritance. Thus the objection turns against him who urges it, and shows a beautiful correspondence, of the nature of an undesigned coincidence, between the Jewish law and customs and the narrative of the evangelist. Luke, by simply speaking the truth, has avoided a blunder into which his critic, with all his learning, would have fallen, had he constructed, as he has endeavored to construct, a gospel. We see how men who simply speak what they know will always be justified in the end, while those who would construct artificial narratives will be exposed, sooner or later.

As to the apparent discrepancies between the evangelists, there is often room for difference of opinion as to the proper reconciliation; and a candid man may often find it proper to say, I believe both accounts, and I am sure they could be reconciled if we knew the whole facts. Sometimes the difficulty is to be removed by supposing that the two evangelists are not recording the same events, but different incidents so far alike. It is clear that our Lord proceeded on a system or method in the deeds he performed, and was in the way of performing very much the same sort of deeds at different times and places. Thus we have him multiplying loaves and fishes on two several occasions. Matthew tells us (xv. 32–39; see also Mark viii. 1–9) that Jesus fed four thousand, but he had previously told us that he had fed five thousand; and if he had not done so, the infidel might have urged that Matthew (xv. 32–39) was contradicted by John (vi. 5–16), where we are told that five thousand were fed. It is clear that there were two such transactions; that Mark records the one and John the other, while

Matthew details both. It appears then that we may remove some of the seeming inconsistencies by help of the principle, that our Lord having certain specific ends in view, to be accomplished by certain kinds of works, does often repeat himself, even as God the Creator repeats himself by like organs and members and plants and animals and earths and moons and suns running through all creation. More frequently we are to account for the seeming discrepancy by the very simple and intelligible fact, that one witness gives one feature, and another supplies a different feature, and that we are to combine the two, if we would have the whole figure before us. As an example of the first, I may refer to the healing of the nobleman's son (John iv. 46–54), when our Lord was at a distance, which is not the same as the healing of the centurion's servant (Matt. viii. 5–13): for though the two incidents resemble each other, both being after the type of our Lord's miracles, yet they are not the same; for, in the one case, the person cured was a son, in the other he was a servant. As an example of the second, — that is, of the two recorded incidents being the same, — I quote Matt. viii. 5–13, where the occurrence is the same as that of the centurion's servant (Luke vii. 1–10), though the two narrators give different details of one and the same transaction.

There is a palpable discrepancy between the genealogy of our Lord as given by Matthew and by Luke. In saying so, I do not refer merely to the circumstance that the one goes back only to

Abraham, whereas the other ascends to Adam; but to real differences in the account. The number of ancestors in the two rolls is not the same, nor are the individual names identical. Matthew's division into three fourteens gives forty-two ancestors from Jesus to Abraham, whereas Luke reckons fifty-six. Matthew (i. 6) makes the descent from David through Solomon; whereas Luke (iii. 31) makes it from David through Nathan, "which was the son of Nathan, which was the son of David." Some have tried to explain this by supposing that Matthew gives the genealogy through the Virgin Mary (i. 16): "Joseph the husband of Mary, of whom was born Jesus, who is called Christ;" whereas Luke's is confessedly the genealogy through Joseph (iii. 23), "being, as was supposed, the son of Joseph, which was the son of Heli." Now there is no doubt that Joseph and Mary were both of the tribe of Judah, and the family of David: it is probable that Mary, the mother of Jesus, was the daughter of Jacob, and first cousin to Joseph, her husband. But this very circumstance renders it impossible for us to reconcile the differences, for it would make the lineage one backward from the grandfather of Joseph and Mary, whereas they are different throughout. The subject has been taken up and discussed with great care and a large amount of success, by Lord Arthur Hervey, in an elaborate volume.* Matthew's genealogy, he argues, is meant to show that Jesus was legal successor to the

* Genealogies of our Lord.

throne of David; and therefore his descent is traced through the line of kings,—through Solomon, Rehoboam, Abia, and Asa, and Jehosaphat, and Jehoram, and so forth. Luke, on the other hand, gives his private, his natural, his family genealogy, which he traces back to David through Nathan. Matthew shows that he was legally the heir of the throne of David, through the monarchs of Judah and their legal descendants. Luke brings out the real progenitors, who were not kings, though descended from David. You may understand what I mean, if you consider that a man might be the legal heir of a property which was not possessed by his father or grandfather, or actual progenitors for generations immediately past. In such a case he might have two genealogies, one through the persons possessing the property, the other of his proper, natural progenitors. By this simple principle the author brings the two accounts into harmony. To give only one example: The two genealogies coincide in the name of Matthan, or Matthat, (Matt. i. 15, and Luke iii. 24), "to whom two different sons, Jacob and Heli, are assigned but one and the same grandson and heir, Joseph the husband of Mary." The simple and obvious explanation is, "that Joseph was descended from Joseph, a younger son of Abiud (the Juda of Luke iii. 26), and that, on the failure of the line of Abiud's eldest son in Eleazar, Joseph's grandfather Matthan became the heir; that Matthan had two sons, Jacob and Heli; that Jacob had no son, and consequently that Joseph, the son of his younger brother Heli, became heir to his uncle and to the throne of David. Thus, the simple principle that one evangelist exhibits that genealogy which contained the successive heirs to David and Solomon's throne, while the other exhibits the paternal stem of him who was the heir, explains all the anomalies of the two pedigrees, — their agreements as well as their discrepancies, and the circumstance of their being two at all."

As to how it comes that there should be such a resemblance between the first three Gospels and yet such diversities, there is room for difference of opinion among those who may speculate on the subject. The following seems to me the most probable theory, — it is sanctioned by some profound German scholars: The particular incidents of Gospel history had been so repeatedly narrated by the apostles in their interviews one with another, and in their addresses to the church, that a certain type of narrative had formed itself. "The particular points, especially in sayings of Christ, were always reproduced: unusual expressions were the more firmly retained, since, when they were uttered, they had more strongly attracted the attention of the disciples. Sermons and sayings were naturally retained with more care, and reported with more uniformity, than incidents; although even in the latter, in the same degree that the incident was surprising and peculiar, a fixed type of narration had involuntarily formed itself." It is thus we have found the members of a family, who have often had occasion to talk to one another and to others of the virtues of a deceased parent, coming to repeat the same incidents in much the same language. In some such way as this we are to account for the curious sameness of event and phrase in the account given. As to the differences, they are easily explained by each writer so far following an independent course, as a witness and narrator, and having a special end in view. Matthew wrote specially to the Hebrews; and, as he declares (i. 1), he sets before us Jesus as the son of David and the son of Abraham, the Messiah promised by the prophets. Mark exhibits Jesus (see i. 1) as the Son of God, and dwells forcibly on his deeds of power. Luke, the companion of Paul, the apostle to the Gentiles, shows, as he professes (iii. 38), how Jesus "was the son of Adam, which was the son of God."

As to the obvious circumstance that John's Gospel differs so much from the others, not only in the narrative, but in the sort of discourses put into our Lord's mouth, I have never thought that it raises any very formidable difficulty. John tells us at the close of his Gospel, "And there are also many other things which Jesus did, the which, if they should be written every one, I suppose that even the world itself could not contain the books that should be written." Of the things which he did, of the words which he spake, we have only a few recorded. The first three evangelists give us so much: they give us what had been inscribed most deeply on the hearts and memories of the apostles at Jerusalem, each, however, writing independently of the others. John wrote his Gospel at a later date, and he studiously brings out other incidents of our Lord's life, and new features of his character. I believe that each writer presents our Lord under the aspect which most impressed him. Every scholar knows that we have something very much parallel in Grecian history. We have two separate and independent accounts of the great Greek teacher, who, of all heathens, most resembles our Lord in his life, in his teaching, and in his death, though in all respects falling infinitely beneath the perfect model. One of these is by Xenophon, a soldier, a man of the world, and trained in the business of life: he has given us a plain narrative of the acts and common conversation of Socrates, bringing out fully to view his earnestness, his shrewdness, his high moral aims, and his exalted views of the providence of God. The other is by Plato, the lofty speculator, the skilful dialectician, and the writer of such prose as only a poet of the highest order could compose. In the Socrates, of the Platonic dialogues, we have the subtle analyst, the acute cross-questioner, the exposer of pretension, the master of the most delicate irony, and the profound lover of wisdom, who can penetrate into the greatest depths to bring forth gold, and mount like Franklin's kite into the heavens to draw down lightning. Whence the difference of the two representations? Some have at once and peremptorily declared that, while the one is a true picture, the other is an ideal figure drawn in the rich colors of Plato's own mind. I have pondered much on this subject; and I am convinced that both are correct portraits, and of the same individual, but in different attitudes and when in different humors. I allow freely that Plato does at times use Socrates merely as a vehicle for expressing his own ideal speculations, and puts his own sentiments and language into the mouth of his master. But I am firmly convinced that Plato, after all, gives a true picture of one side of Socrates's character, and brings out lofty characteristics which Xenophon was not capable of comprehending, or at least of appreciating. I argue this from the circumstance that in the plainer narrative of Xenophon we have thoughts here and there ascribed to Socrates which carry us up towards that empyrean in which Plato makes him habitually dwell;* while Plato, ever and anon,

* Thus, in Xenophon's Memorabilia, B. IV. c. IV., we have a dialogue with Hippias of Elis concerning Justice, very much in the spirit of the dialogues of Plato. "*Hippias.* I think that I have certainly something to say now which neither you nor any other person can refute. *Socrates.* By Juno, it is a great good you say you have discovered; since the judges will now cease from giving contradictory sentences, the citizens will cease from disputing about what is just, from going to law and from quarrelling, and communities will cease from contending about their rights and going to war; and I know not how I can part with you till I have learned so important a benefit from its discoverer. *Hippias.* You shall not hear it, by Jupiter, until you yourself declare what you think justice to be; for it is enough that you laugh at others, questioning and confuting everybody, while you yourself are unwilling to give a reason to anybody, or to declare your opinion on any subject. *Socrates.* What, then, have you not perceived that I never cease declaring my opinions as to what I conceive to be just," &c. — *Watson's Translation.*

brings him down to the earth and makes him utter practical maxims quite in the spirit of the conversations detailed by the other biographer.

It is much the same with the two accounts which we have of the life of our Lord, that in the Synoptical Gospels on the one hand, and that in John's Gospel on the other. Both are true, and both are delineations of the same lofty character standing on the earth, but with his head in the sunshine of heaven. I argue so from the fact that in Matthew, Mark, and Luke, we have here and there sayings of our Lord quite in the spirit of those recorded by John; and that in John there are plain familiar statements quite in the manner of the first three evangelists. Thus the address of Jesus, in Matt. xi. 25, reads as if it were recorded by John: "At that time Jesus answered and said, I thank thee, O Father, Lord of heaven and earth, because thou hast hid these things from the wise and prudent, and hast revealed them unto babes. Even so, Father, for so it seemed good in thy sight. All things are delivered unto me of my Father; and no man knoweth the Son, but the Father; neither knoweth any man the Father, save the Son, and he to whomsoever the Son will reveal him." On the other hand, certain narratives in John read as if they had been written by Matthew or Luke, as (v. 8): "And a certain man was there, which had an infirmity thirty and eight years." "Jesus saith unto him, Rise, take up thy bed, and walk. And immediately the man was made whole, and took up his bed, and walked:

and on the same day was the Sabbath," &c. It is the same person; but the two portraits, though both correct likenesses, are different, in that one brings one set of attitudes or expressions into prominence, and another a different set. In the one we have certain qualities which all the disciples comprehended and relished, and we have specially his human side brought fully into view; whereas the apostle who leaned on his bosom, and evidently looked into that bosom, and was warmed by it, has brought out perfections of our Lord founded in the depths of his divine nature. From that day to this the great body of Christians have always turned first to the Synoptic Gospels; while there have always been a select few who have felt that the disciple of love carries them closer to the inner nature, to the heart of Jesus. We should thank God for providing both, that all and each may find something to attract the eye and gain the confidence of the heart.

The light which comes from the sun is one and the same; but how different are the colors as reflected from different objects! The same rays fall on every part of that plant, but from the leaves are reflected the soft and lively green, and from the flowers the deeper purple or the brighter red or yellow. So it is with Him who is expressively called the sun of righteousness and the light of the world: he shone on all the evangelists alike, but each reflects the hue that most impressed him. I am tempted once more to use a familiar illustration from my own history. My father died when I was a boy, and I have a dimmer recollection of him than I could wish. In order to get a clearer idea of him, I have applied to different persons. I have applied to neighbors; I have applied to elder sisters; I have applied to a nearer still, to his widow and my mother. The accounts given by them were substantially one; but they differed in some points, and the most endearing of all was by the dearest friend. I believe that the disciple whom Jesus loved was able to enter into and reciprocate some of the deepest and yet the most delicate of the characteristics of our Lord. As being himself struck with them, he has recorded the incidents and preserved the discourses in which they were exhibited. It is in John's Gospel that it is so pressed upon us (chap. iii.) that there must be a spiritual change before we can enter the kingdom of God: and (in chap. vi.) that we must feed by faith on the body and blood of Jesus if we would have life in us. It is in this same Gospel that we have so tender a view of the sympathy of Jesus as he wept over the grave of Lazarus (chap. xi.); such gracious promises of the outpouring of the Spirit (xiv. and xvi.); and of the intimate relation between the Father and the Son (x. 30), — "I and my Father are one;" and of the followship between the Father and the Son (in chap. xvii.), — "O righteous Father, the world hath not known thee: but I have known thee, and these have known that thou hast sent me. And I have declared unto them thy name, and will declare it:

that the love wherewith thou hast loved me may be in them, and I in them."

May I not go a step farther? May we not without presumption believe that Jesus unfolded his doctrine as his listeners were able to bear it? If I address Sabbath-school children, I speak in one way; if I preach to a congregation on the Sabbath, I have to speak in a different manner; if I lecture to a class in college, I have to speak in yet a third way. I am ashamed to refer to myself in such a connection. But if man with imperfect knowledge and small resources has to do this, may we not suppose that He in whom dwelt all wisdom was ready to pour it out in the measure which his hearers could receive it? I am inclined to think that, while all received much, John took in most, and so has been able to give out most, of the profundity of our Lord's doctrine and the tenderness of his sentiment. However we may account for it, there is certainly a glow rich and pure and yet somewhat mystic, as if it required to be dulled before we could gaze upon it, round our Lord's person, as we gaze upon him in the light in which he is presented in the pages of the beloved apostle.

And as to the apostle's own style in his Gospel and in his three Epistles being so like that of our Lord, we are to account for it as we explain the sameness of style in prose, poetry, and painting, on the part of pupils and the masters whom they admire. I believe it is to be traced to the circumstance that John, as he leant upon the bosom of his Master, had drunk into his spirit, and moulded himself in style as in character upon the great Exemplar.

(2) *There is a unity in our Lord's method of teaching.* Every one sees and feels at once that there is something peculiar in his manner of imparting instruction. It originates with himself: it is fresh and novel. It differed equally from the two modes employed by the eminent teachers of his time, from the Rabbinical method of the Jewish doctors and the Dialectic method of the Greek and Roman philosophers.

It differed from the Rabbinical method, which appeared soon after the Babylonish captivity, which became permanently embodied in the Mishna and Talmud, written some ages after the time of our Lord, and has been continued by the Jewish doctors to this day. Those who look into the Jewish works see a considerable amount of acuteness and ingenuity running to waste, and may find precious grains of wheat here and there in bushels of chaff. The Rabbinical teachers professed to be expounders of the Old Testament Law, but they paid no regard to its spirit and its moral lessons. The passage was studied with the view of drawing from it formal restrictions and ingenious conceits. Passing by the obvious meaning, they discovered a deep signification in certain words and phrases, and drew inferences from particles and the position of particles. In doing this they indulged in ingenious fancies, and laboriously employed themselves in constructing silly legends, dealing, as Paul says (1 Tim. i. 4), in fables and genealogies. These were handed down from father to son, and in the course of ages so accumulated that they overloaded the simple truth, and buried it in dust as effectively as the ashes from Vesuvius buried Pompeii and Herculaneum. All the commandments were interpreted in a narrow spirit, and minute regulations laid down as to the outward conduct and smaller duties, — the tithing of mint, anise, and cummin, — while the weightier matters of the law were neglected. Not only so, but by the additions which they made, they often perverted the whole meaning and spirit of the law. Thus in regard to the fifth commandment: "Ye say, Whosoever shall say to his father or his mother it is a gift, by whatsoever thou mightest be profited by me, and honor not his father or his mother, he shall be free. Thus have ye made the commandment of God of none effect by your traditions." It was thus, too, that they perverted the seventh commandment, by giving, under one pretext or other, unrestricted liberty of divorce. In such interpretations they differed as widely from each other as they did from Scripture; and this gave rise to numerous schools, which contended with each other, and all in the same spirit, thus gendering, as Paul expresses it (1 Tim. vi. 4), "questions and strifes of words."

Our Lord must have been familiar with this mode of instruction; and the people knew what it was, as they listened to the teaching in the synagogue from Sabbath to Sabbath. Jesus proceeds in an entirely different manner, and the people at once discover it. It is said of him, after delivering the Sermon on the Mount: "It came to pass when Jesus had ended these sayings, the people were astonished at his doctrine. For he taught them as one having authority, and not as the Scribes." Going beneath the outward conduct, he seeks to reach and to sway the motives, and requires and enforces a change of heart, saying, "Except ye be converted, and become as little children, ye shall not enter into the kingdom of heaven." "Out of the heart proceed evil thoughts, murders, adulteries, fornications, thefts, false witness, blasphemies: these are the things that defile a man: but to eat with unwashen hands defileth not a man." Our Lord takes great pains in his Sermon on the Mount to correct these perversions of the Jewish doctors, to remove the rubbish of traditions, and to bring back his hearers to the true interpretation of the spirit of the law, — showing how the sixth commandment, in forbidding murder, condemns all the malignant passions which lead to it; how the seventh, in forbidding adultery, condemns all the thoughts and lusts which might end in the outward act. In dealing with mankind, he seeks first to gain their faith and confidence; he encourages them by forgiving their sins and curing their maladies, if they have any, and then brings them under the law of love. "Thou shalt love the Lord thy God with all thy heart, and with all thy soul, and with all thy mind. This is the first and great commandment. And the second is like unto it, Thou shalt love thy neighbor as thyself." His hearers felt that they were listening to a very different teacher from any they had ever heard before; "who taught them as one having authority, and not as the Scribes." But his method differed as essentially from the other employed in his day; from —

The *Dialectic Method*, or the method of the heathen philosophers. The Apostle Paul knew both. Bred at the feet of Gamaliel, one of the most famous of the Jewish doctors, he knew the Rabbinical Method, and would evidently have been inclined to follow it, had he not been taught by a higher Master, who cast down his pride on the road to Damascus, and made him receive instruction as a little child, and drink in a new spirit. And he also knew the other method from his acquaintance with the schools of Greek Philosophy, acquired at Tarsus, a city of no mean reputation for Greek learning. He refers to it once and again, calling it "the wisdom of words," "the wisdom of this world." "The Jews," he says, "require a sign: the Greeks seek after wisdom." I call it the Dialectic Method. The phrase was applied first to the Eleatic School, which indulged in subtle distinctions as to the nature of being; and the method was used more or less by all the Greek and Roman speculative thinkers, and in many cases degenerated into mere quibbling, into sophistic or eristic. Do not understand me as speaking against the study of the ancient philosophy, so much superior to that to which some of our colleges would turn the mind of our youth in the present day, — the wretched and debasing systems of positivism or materialism. The "Memorabilia" of Xenophon, with its lessons of Socrates; the "Dialogues of Plato;" the logical and metaphysical works of Aristotle; and the moral maxims of the Stoics, particularly the "Meditations" of Marcus Aurelius, — are about the highest products of human intellect in ancient times, and are worthy of the eager study of any educated man. But how different from the discourses of Jesus, both in their subjects, and manner of treating them! First, the Greek philosophies treat chiefly of speculative questions, of the nature of substance, the origin of worlds, the elements out of which all things are produced; and they do not investigate them in the Method of Induction introduced by Bacon, — that is, by the careful collation of facts, — but by subtle analysis, by discussion, by arguments on the one side or other; and some of them, such as Plato and the Academic sect, scarcely profess to reach any settled or satisfactory results. None of them professes to speak with authority; and most of them leave the great religious and moral questions, — as, for instance, in regard to the nature of God and the immortality of the soul, — in a state of doubt and uncertainty. Where mankind have no other light, when there is no light shining upon them from heaven, men may usefully resort to such tapers to help them to grope their way in the darkness. But Christ can speak, and does speak, in a very different manner. He resorts to no sophistic distinctions, or lengthened ratiocinations difficult to follow, liable to be disputed, and in which subtle error may lurk; but he speaks as one having authority. He claims such authority, — authority to speak the truth concerning God and the world to come; authority to lay down and explain the law, and to point out the way by which man may rise to eternal fellowship with God. And as he speaks, we feel that he has authority to do so. He tells us much which we could never have discovered of ourselves; but when he announces it, there is something in us which responds to it. All history shows that mankind are not able of themselves to discover the unity of God and his holy and spiritual nature; but when Christ proclaims it in the Word, we see that it is, that it must be, true. Unaided reason has never arisen to a pure conception of the moral law; but when it is proclaimed in the Sermon on the Mount, there is found to be a law in the heart which approves of it. Jesus speaks as having authority, and there is a conscience in us which declares that we ought to bow before it. We might not yield to the Scribes: there is nothing in their formal rules and endless restrictions to gain our better nature. We may refuse to give in to the acute arguments of the Greeks: we might rather be tempted to square arms and fight them, and to raise objections and start theories of our own. But when Christ speaks, and tells us of "God who is a Spirit," and of the temper which we ought to cherish, and the duties devolving on us, we feel that we cannot, that we should not, resist, that we ought at once to bow before him in implicit faith and willing obedience.

We recall many able reasoners, many eloquent orators, in ancient and modern times, in ancient Greece and Rome, in modern Europe and America; but here is one who is different from them all, and who speaks as never man spake. The truth is so perspicuous and so profound, that we are sure it is uttered from the clear depths of heaven; and yet, as it comes to us and penetrates us, we feel that it has come through one who is on the earth, who knows what is in man, who knoweth our frame and remembereth that we are dust; we feel that it is addressed to us by a fellow-man, by a brother, — it so touches and melts and moves our hearts. The discourses of men of profound thought have commonly tended to drive away little children; but the words of Jesus, as it were, say, "Suffer the little children to come unto me, and forbid them not." Plato and the Greek philosophers spoke and wrote only for the educated, and never thought of addressing the great mass of the people, who were in fact despised by them. But the prediction regarding Christ was, not only that he would open the eyes of the blind, but that by him the poor were to have the gospel preached to them; and it was found in fact that "the common people heard him gladly." This constituted a new era in the history of the world, as it was the means of raising the great mass of the people. While a child, a savage, can understand and appreciate our Lord's discourses, the profoundest thinkers are made to feel that there are depths here, deeper than hell, which they cannot fathom; heights higher than heaven which they cannot gauge. We feel as we do when we gaze into the expanse of heaven on a clear night, and see every star shining so distinctly, and yet are made to realize that there are depths there far beyond our vision. When officers were sent out by the Jewish council to apprehend Jesus, they were induced to listen; and, as they did so, they were awed, and felt themselves incapable of fulfilling their purpose, and returned to say so to those who commissioned them. And not a few who have begun to read his words, with the view of finding fault and getting matter to condemn him, have been obliged to say, "Never man spake like this man."

(3) *There is a unity in the account given of the Person of our Lord.* Everywhere Christ is spoken of and acts as man, fully and altogether man. Thus is he foretold in the prophecies, thus he appears on the earth. Of the race of Adam, the seed of the woman, the seed of Abraham, the son of David, born of the Virgin Mary, — he has all the sinless characteristics, bodily and mental, of our nature, liable to weakness, acquainted with grief, full of the milk of human kindness and of compassion. The biographers speak of him as born; as growing in wisdom and stature; as wearied, athirst, hungry; as rejoicing, sorrowing, in pain; bleeding, dying, and being buried. The language of John is as express

on this subject as that of the other three evangelists. For he tells us that the Word became flesh and dwelt among us; and some of the most human incidents of his life are recorded by this evangelist, such as his close intimacy with the two sisters, Martha and Mary, and their brother Lazarus. When speaking of himself, he takes the name of the Son of Man, — the representative man, the model man. He shows us what man would have been had he not sinned; and yet shows what man had never been had he not sinned, and produced suffering to call forth sympathy. He shows us what man purified is to become in heaven; and yet what man will not be in heaven, for in heaven there will be no sin nor suffering to call forth forgiveness and pity such as Christ exhibited on earth. Thus is he man, but unique as man, flowing pure as a river through the midst of pollution, which calls forth the deepest commiseration, and which he would sweep away without himself being stained by it.

But while he is man, very man, it is clear that he is something more. This appears everywhere on the surface; and as we dig down, we see how deep it goes, and we find that it is ever casting up. It has often been noticed that the inspired writers seldom take the trouble of asserting that God exists: they no more think it needful to do so than to assert their own existence. They assume that God exists, and they presume that men believe in his existence, and proceed to give a revelation of his will. In like manner they are not in the way of asserting that

Christ is a divine person, but they proceed upon the doctrine as allowed by the Church. The doctrine is very prominent in John's Gospel, where Jesus is represented as the Word who was "in the beginning," "who was with God," — an expression which shows that he was somehow different from the Father, and yet "was God" and the Maker of all things. But the same truth is constantly implied in the other Gospels, and is expressly stated ever and anon. If there is any doctrine more forcibly taught than another in Scripture, it is that there is only one God, and that he will not allow worship to be paid to any other. When Peter went into the house of Cornelius, the centurion would have fallen down and worshipped him; but the apostle hastened to raise him up, saying, "Stand up: I myself also am a man." When Paul and Barnabas performed a notable miracle at Lystra, the ignorant heathens mistook them for the gods come down to earth, and would have done sacrifice with the people; but Paul and Barnabas were shocked at the proposal, and ran in among them and cried, "Why do ye these things? We also are men of like passions with you." But once and again divine honors are paid to Jesus, and he accepts them: Matt. viii. 2, a leper came and worshipped him; ix. 18, a ruler worshipped him; xiv. 33, they that were in the ship worshipped him; xv. 25, the woman of Canaan came and worshipped him, — and he receives the homage, not as if he were vain of it, but as if it were his due. It is in the close of Matthew, written specially to the Hebrews, who stood up so resolutely for the unity of God, that our Lord is represented as requiring all his followers to be baptized in the name of three persons: Matt. xxviii. 19, "Go and teach all nations, baptizing them in the name of the Father, and of the Son, and of the Holy Ghost."

But, with two such natures, he is, after all, one, — quite as much so as the plant composed of animate and inanimate matter is one; quite as much so as the animal composed of a bodily and a sentient part is one; quite as much so as man composed of body and mind is one. How there should be such a union we are unable to say, just as we are not able to tell how our soul and body are united, and work so harmoniously. To separate the divine and human natures in Christ, we feel to be like separating soul and body in man, — the destruction and death of the whole.

A living English writer has tried to give us one of these aspects of our Lord without the other. I refer to Professor Seeley, of London University College, who, in "Ecce Homo," has exhibited some very interesting and attractive views of our Lord's character. I have known some young men, whose faith was being undermined, being profited by the study of the work: and the pictures which he presents are so pure and lovely that I have known none who have been injured by it. Those who go heartily with him, and as far as he goes, will feel that they cannot stay there; that in consistency they must go farther, and take a profounder view of One represented as so enlightened and spiritual, but who, to do what he is represented as doing, must have been more than man, who as he claimed to be God must really be divine. The features which he has portrayed so gracefully are those which we may conceive to have struck a young Church of England man, of cultured taste, who has been trained in the criticism of the age, and at a university where the highest refinement is imparted, and where all old religious opinions are being unsettled, but who feels that, whatever he may give up, he cannot give up Christ. He shows clearly that Christ from the beginning proposed to set up a kingdom of a spiritual character, and with high social aims, such as English churchmen delighted to picture and expected to realize when established churches were in no danger. But he has not seen, after all, the true nature of Christ's kingdom, which is to be entered by the strait gate of conversion, and to be composed of men born again of the Spirit. "Marvel not that I said unto you that ye must be born again." Marvel not: it cannot be otherwise. Our nature requires it; and the kingdom is such that it requires a radical change before men can enter it.

(4) *There is a unity in his Work and in the End which he seeks to accomplish.* His mission was one throughout, — that of one sent from the Father, sent into the world for mercy and not for judgment; travelling ever with a heavy load upon him, having for the fulfilling of his purposes to suffer and to die. The load of responsibility is

seen to be lying upon him at the age of twelve. "I must be about my Father's business;" showing that, while he was subject to Joseph and Mary, he had another Father, and a work to do of which they had no idea. He keeps the same aim before him through all his pilgrimage, in all his discourses, and in all his deeds.

Fortunately I am not called in these Lectures to enter on the wide subject of miracles, which I have discussed elsewhere.* The school which I am opposing, admitting no *a priori* truth, cannot in consistency urge any *a priori* objections against surpernatural occurrences. Mr. Mill in particular has argued that it is possible to prove a miracle.† I am in these Lectures to show that there is evidence that Jesus performed deeds beyond the capacity of man and the laws of nature.

We cannot take the discourses of our Lord and reject his deeds. We cannot accept his words and repel his miracles. His discourses are among the greatest of his miracles. They would have been a miracle coming from any man, from a Greek in the farthest advanced stage of his nation's culture: they are, *a fortiori*, a miracle, as uttered by a workman from Galilee. We have evidence, it is conceded, to prove that his natural life must have been such as is detailed in the four Gospels; and that he delivered his discourses very much as they have been reported. But it is impossible to separate be-

* The Supernatural in relation to the Natural.

† Logic, B. III. c. XXV.

tween his ordinary acts and discourses on the one hand, and his miracles on the other: they are woven through and through each other as weft and woof. They could be separated only by tearing the garment to pieces. Let us notice that supernatural acts are mixed up with every part of our Lord's life; in particular how they mingle with his discourses, so that some of his profoundest sayings arose out of his miracles. We have a detailed account in the Gospels of between thirty and forty miracles, besides such general references as, "Now when the sun was setting, all they that had any sick with divers diseases brought them unto him: and he laid his hands on every one of them, and healed them (Luke iv. 40, cf. Matt. viii. 16, Mark i. 32); and again in his message to the Baptist (Matt. xi. 5), "The blind receive their sight, and the lame walk, the lepers are cleansed, and the deaf hear, the dead are raised up."

Let us look at some of these miracles, that we may see how they are mixed up indissolubly with some of the first and most peculiar features of his character, and with some of the deepest of his sayings. His miracle of turning water into wine is associated with his sanctioning of marriage and the marriage feast, and his delicate way of promoting the social joys of the poor (John ii. 1–11). At his first public appearance at Jerusalem, after the commencement of his ministry, he performs such miracles that Nicodemus comes to him and says, "No man can do these miracles that thou doest, except

God be with him;" and at the interview our Lord tells him that a man enters the kingdom of God by a spiritual change. The miraculous draught of fishes (Luke v. 1–11) is associated with the characteristic trait of Peter falling down at Jesus' knees, saying, "Depart from me; for I am a sinful man, O Lord;" and our Lord's giving so special a mission to his disciples, "Fear not: from henceforth thou shalt catch men." The fear of the apostles when the storm arose to such a pitch on the Sea of Galilee, our Lord's being asleep, and then rising and rebuking the winds and the sea, is felt to be beautifully symbolic and prophetic of his whole mission (Matt. viii. 23–27; Mark iv. 35–41; Luke viii. 22–25). The raising of Jairus' daughter, and of the widow's son at a later date, both illustrate his sympathy with parents grieving over the death of beloved children. The healing of the woman with the issue of blood brings out some very interesting features of the suppliant: she was unwilling to be seen, and had such faith that she was sure that if she "but touched the hem of his garment she would be made whole;" and when she was brought forth, she came trembling, and he said, "Go in peace, and be whole of thy plague." The healing of the paralytic (Matt. ix. 1–8) leads him to assume the power of forgiving sins, and to connect his healing with his forgiving power: "But that ye may know that the Son of man hath power on earth to forgive sins (then saith he to the sick of the palsy), Arise, take up thy bed." The cleansing of the leper brings out very beautifully the nature of faith, and the way in which Jesus responds: "Lord, if thou wilt, thou canst make me clean," to which the answer is, "I will; be thou clean" (Matt. viii. 2, 3). The healing of the heathen centurion's servant (Matt. viii. 5–13; and Luke vii. 1–10) gives us glimpses of the ingathering of the Gentiles into the kingdom of God: "I say unto you, I have not found so great faith, no, not in Israel."—"Many shall come from the east and from the west, and shall sit down with Abraham and Isaac and Jacob in the kingdom of heaven." The healing of the impotent man at the pool of Bethesda, followed by our Lord's bidding him take up his bed, and walk, on the Sabbath, leads him to the condemnation of the Pharisaic view of the Sabbath, and the profound saying, "My Father worketh hitherto, and I work" (John v. 17). The feeding of the five thousand gives rise to that discourse so full of spiritual meaning, in which our Lord expounds his doctrine as to his body being meat indeed, and his blood being drink indeed (John vi. 27 to end). His walking on the sea, and inviting Peter to come to him, led to the declaration, "Be of good cheer; it is I; be not afraid" (Matt. xiv. 22–23). The opening of the eyes of one born blind originates all those deeply interesting and instructive discourses in John ix., and to the man being cast out of the synagogue. The restoring of the man with the withered hand leads to his gracious declaration, "But if ye had known what this meaneth, I will have mercy, and not sacrifice, ye would not have condemned the guiltless," and to the true doctrine of the Sabbath (Matt. xii. 7–13). The cleansing of the ten lepers brings out the instructive incident so characteristic of human nature, that only nine returned to give thanks (Luke xvii. 11–19). The healing of the daughter of the Syrophenician woman unfolds the importunateness of faith and the certainty of its bringing a blessing. It is the finding of the coin in the fish's mouth which leads him to enforce the duty of paying tribute. The raising of Lazarus discloses to our view nearly every tender feature in our Lord's character: "Jesus wept." — "I am the resurrection, and the life; he that believeth in me, though he were dead, yet shall he live: and whosoever liveth, and believeth in me, shall never die." The healing of Malchus' ear (Luke xxii. 49–51), besides being a proof of our Lord's tenderness in very trying circumstances, taught the disciples the nature of the instruments by which they were to propagate the truth; that is, not by the sword, but by spiritual weapons. The resurrection of our Lord is the very keystone of the believer's hopes. And what a rich fragrance gathers round the incidents of our Lord's life after his resurrection, from his rising from the grave to his ascending into heaven! M. Renan allows that Jesus himself did not distinguish between the natural and the supernatural. I am sure that our Lord did not deceive himself here. The supernatural was to him as easy as the natural; the supernatural was as it were natural to him; and the two so mingle in every part of his public life that it is vain to seek to separate them, and to take the one without also taking the other.

Our Lord's miracles are a piece with his discourses, with his whole life, mission, and kingdom. It has been asserted or insinuated that, though Jesus may be supposed to have lived and to have spoken very much as he is described, his miracles may have been inserted by a later hand. But it is utterly inconceivable that miracles thus added should have so fitted into all the rest, — in design, spirit, and moral and spiritual lessons. Who added these miracles entirely in consonance with the whole purport of our Lord's life? Certainly not Matthew or Mark, acknowledged to be men of no genius or invention. If it be said that they rose up as popular stories, the answer is at hand: They would in this case have been incongruous, blundering, inconsistent, as all legends are. We know what was the character of some of the legends which sprang up about this time, — as, for example, the miracles ascribed to Simon Magus by his followers. He is represented as flying through the air, as transforming himself into a serpent or goat, as putting on two faces, as rolling himself unhurt upon burning coals, as making statues to talk, and dogs of brass or stone to bark.* Depend upon it, this would have been the sort of miracles ascribed to our Lord, had they sprung from the wonder-loving spirit of the times. I know a famous hall

* Trench's Notes on the Miracles, c. ii.

in a European city, left all but complete by the architect when he died: he left only the stair and one or two minor parts unfinished, but no living man could carry out his grand conception: and all the portions added by others are acknowledged to be failures. I hold that if Jesus had left any part of his work unfinished, no man could have added to it without the addition being seen to be an inconsistency and an encumbrance.

Our Lord's miracles were all essential parts of his one consistent life. They were wrought as evidences not only of his power, but of his mercy. They were throughout moral in their character, and spiritual in the ends contemplated by them. They were in fact embodiments of his whole character, exemplars of his whole teaching, emblems of his whole mission. They consisted almost exclusively in the remedying of evils, in renovations and regenerations. There were some exceptions no doubt, but these too were moral. There were, in particular, two miracles of judgment to exhibit the justice of God; but it is remarkable that one of these was wrought on an unconscious fig-tree, and the other on the lower animals, as if He who came to save men's lives were unwilling to smite them. Both were directed against hypocrisy and inconsistency: in the one he smote the fig-tree, which should in these regions have brought forth first fruit and then leaves, but had produced leaves and no fruit,—like too many professors of religion; by the other he punished the Gadarenes, who kept swine contrary to the law of Moses, which they professed to reverence. But, with these instructive exceptions, all his other miracles were miracles of restoring, of reviving, of saving; and so were symbols of the works of Him who came to seek and to save that which was lost. The parables of the lost sheep brought back, of the lost money found, of the lost son in his father's embrace, have all their counterparts in the diseased being made whole, in the lame walking, and the dead restored to life. His grand redeeming and saving mission is seen quite as clearly in his miracles as in his discourses.

Every one must have observed that a large number of the miracles of our Lord consist in the healing of diseases. There was evidently a moral meaning, a spiritual lesson, in this. Disease is to the body what sin is to the soul: the one, like the other, is a disorder, a derangement. The cure of the one is a type of the healing of the other. He who removed the one showed that it was his mission to remove the other likewise. He who cured the paralytic showed that he had power on earth to forgive sins: "But that ye may know that the Son of man hath power on earth to forgive sins (then saith he to the sick of the palsy), Arise, take up thy bed, and walk. And he arose, and departed to his house" (Matt. ix. 6). These two go together: "Who forgiveth all thine iniquities; who healeth all thy diseases" (Ps. ciii. 3). Disease of the body is an expressive and awful representation of the evil of sin. And I have often thought that particular diseases may be taken as furnishing affecting pictures of particular sins, — in their power, or their secrecy and subtlety, or their rapidity, or their weakening and prostrating effect, or their loathsomeness, or fatal issue. I believe that He who when on earth healed all manner of disease demonstrated thereby that he can cure all kinds of soul maladies. He who opened the eyes of the blind meant thereby to show that he is able to open the eyes of our understandings to discern the beauty of spiritual things. He who unstopped the ears of the deaf does still open the ear of faith, so that it attends to the intimation of God's will, given in his Word and by his Spirit. He who allayed the burning fever does still assuage the fierce burnings of wrath and malice. He who stopped the issue of blood is powerful to stanch the outbursts of lust and temper. He who restored to soundness the encrusted and loathsome leper can make the selfish man generous, and the licentious man pure. He who made the lame to walk can rouse the disabled and impotent from their lethargy, and make them walk and run in the way of God's commandments. He who restored the withered hand does still impart life to our palsied faculties. He who calmed the demoniac, that could not be bound by cords or chains, can bring down and subdue the man of raging passion, and make him "sit at his feet clothed, and in his right mind." Other miracles teach the same lessons, all in unison with his discourses. He who walked on the sea and calmed the agitated waters, is above all the powers of nature, and can still the troubles that rage around us, so that there is a great calm. He who fed the multitudes gives to his people "bread to eat of which the world knoweth not." He who raised the dead does still quicken the spiritually dead, and restore them to newness of life.

As he draws near the close of his earthly pilgrimage, he explains more fully the nature of his mission, and the way in which he was to accomplish it, by suffering and dying. "The Son of man came to seek and to save that which was lost." He refers in mysterious language to the terrible conflict by which this was to be effected: "I have a baptism to be baptized with; and how am I straitened till it be accomplished." He shows his disciples (Matt. xvi. 21), "that he must go unto Jerusalem, and suffer many things of the elders, and chief priests, and Scribes, and be killed, and be raised again the third day." John xii. 27: "Now is my soul troubled; and what shall I say? Father, save me from this hour." In instituting the most significant and solemn rite of our religion, he points to his death as a sacrifice and an atonement for sin: "This cup is the New Testament in my blood, shed for many for the remission of sins." In the garden he is "in agony," and in the struggle prays that the cup may pass from him, adding, "Nevertheless, not my will, but thine, be done." On the cross he had to say: "My God, my God, why hast thou forsaken me?"

When this question is put, no answer is given. To that forsaken son the Father deigns no reply. Let us come to the foot of the cross, and answer, "He was wounded for our transgressions, he was bruised for our iniquities."

Science seems to be joining with our felt experience to show that our world has within deranging as well as arranging powers. Later research has taught no lesson so specially and effectively as this, that there has been a contest in our world from the beginning, a war of elements, a struggle of races. It is seen in the geological ages, as an anticipation of the deeper struggle in the historic ages, when human beings appear on the scene; and it becomes a contest between man and man, between sin and holiness. And is this to go on for ever, deepening, widening, as higher forces appear on the field, and weapons of a more terrible power come to be employed in the fight? With a God looking down from above, we are sure that this is not to be so. But what is there in our world to stop this contest, and insure the victory on the right side? There is no sufficiency in the physical agencies to do it. The power which knowledge gives may only place new weapons in the hands of evil. Nor is there any security that mental agencies will certainly accomplish it. For in this field passion excites passion, fire kindles fire, war breeds war, — as wave meets wave the gurgitation is increased. Yet we are sure that, under the government of a good God, the evil will at last be put under. And in Him who was sent forth in the fulness of time we see how all this is to be accomplished. It is done by reaching the root of the evil. It is done, first, by the Son glorifying God. It is done in the work of the appointed Reconciler, by whom the law was magnified and made honorable, and divine justice satisfied, while room was opened up for the fullest manifestation of mercy. It is done in the name and nature of those who had so dishonored God; so that as by man God has been dishonored, so by man God is now glorified. All this is done in the very scene in which the wickedness of man had been so great; so that as on the earth God had been so dishonored, on earth God is now glorified. This is accomplished, secondly, by making provision through pardon and reconciliation to gain the heart of the sinner, and by his spirit to subdue the love and dominion of sin, and set men forth on a course of new obedience. And in accomplishing all this he stirs up intelligence, which lessens the physical evils in our world, diminishes the virulence of disease, and lengthens the average life of mankind. The inspired writers had foretold all this, probably without seeing the full meaning of the language they employed. For from the beginning they spoke of seed of the woman who was to crush the head of the Evil One; of a seed of Abraham, in whom all the nations of the earth were to be blessed. And Paul opens to us glimpses of a yet wider reconciliation, in which all the warring elements are to be embraced: "And having made peace through the blood of his cross, by him to reconcile all things to himself; by him, I say, whether they be things in earth, or things in heaven."

The old question is still pertinent: "Whence hath this man this wisdom and these mighty works? Is not this the carpenter's son? Is not his mother called Mary? And his brethren James, and Joses, and Simon, and Judas? And his sisters, are they not all with us? Whence, then, hath this man all these things?" There can be but one satisfactory answer: He brought them with him from heaven.

X.

The Planting of the Christian Church. — Legendary and Mythic Theories. — Accordance of the Book of Acts with Geography and History. — Coincidences between Acts and Paul's Epistles. — Present Position of Christianity.

THERE is, let me suppose, an intelligent, well educated youth, — say a Hindoo of the Brahminical caste, — with no prepossession for or against Christianity, but anxious to know whether it has the sanction of God. He knows what it is now as exhibited in the Books of the Bible, and the beliefs and lives of Christians; but he wishes to ascertain what is its origin, — from earth or from heaven? For this purpose he goes back to a point when there is no dispute about its being in existence, about its being firmly rooted and having become a power in the world. He takes his stand at the beginning of the second century, or about seventy, or between that and one hundred years after the death of Christ. He searches the history of the times, and finds a number of points established by evidence, which can be set aside only on principles that would undermine all history. First, he finds that Christianity was then widely spread, had numerous adherents in the principal Greek cities, in Rome, and in nearly every province of the Roman Empire; and that the members exhibited certain marked characters, in particular holding firmly by their convictions, and submitting in consequence to the bitterest persecutions. He will find, too, that they claimed Jesus as the founder of their faith, and that it was allowed by all that this Jesus was crucified at Jerusalem when Tiberius was Emperor of Rome and Pontius Pilate was governor of Judea. Tacitus writing about seventy years after the crucifixion, and speaking of the fire which consumed a large portion of the city of Rome in the reign of Nero, — that is, a little more than thirty years after our Lord's death, — tells us that, in order to do away with the imputation under which he lay of ordering the city to be set on fire, he threw the blame on the Christians. "To put an end to the report, he laid the guilt, and inflicted the most cruel punishments, upon a set of people who were abhorred for their crimes, and called Christians by the people The founder of that name was Christ, who suffered death in the reign of Tiberius, under his procurator, Pontius Pilate. This hurtful superstition, thus checked for a time, broke out again, and spread not only over Judea, where the evil originated, but through Rome also, to which every thing bad finds its way, and in which it is practised. Some who confessed that they belonged to the sect were first seized; and afterwards, on their information, a vast multitude were apprehended and convicted, not so much of the crime of burning Rome as of hatred to mankind. Their sufferings at their execution were aggravated by insult and mockery; for some were disguised in the skins of wild beasts and worried to death by dogs, some were crucified, others were wrapt in pitch and set on fire when the day closed, that they might serve to illumine the night. Nero lent his gardens for these exhibitions, and exhibited at the same time a mock Circensian entertainment, and was a spectator of the whole in the dress of a charioteer, sometimes mingling with the crowd on foot, and sometimes viewing the spectacle from his car. This conduct made the sufferers pitied; and though they were criminals, and deserving the severest punishment, yet they were regarded as sacrificed, not for the public good, but to gratify the cruelty of one man." Suetonius, who lived at the same time with Tacitus, refers to them in the same way: "The Christians, a set of men of a new and evil superstition, were punished." But the most remarkable testimony in their behalf is given by Pliny the Younger, a very thoughtful and elegant writer, in what may be regarded as an official letter to Trajan, his master, the emperor. In the year A.D. 112 he is governor of Pontus and Bithynia, and he thus writes of the Christians, that they were "many of every age, and of both sexes. Nor has the contagion prevailed among cities only, but among villages and country districts." He tells us that "accusations, trials, examinations, were and had been going on against them in the provinces over which he presided; that schedules were delivered by anonymous informers, containing the names of persons who were suspected of holding or favoring the religion; that in consequence of these informations many had been apprehended, of whom some boldly avowed their profession and died in the cause." About the same time contemptuous allusions were made to their sufferings and their fortitude or obstinate attachment to their belief by the popular satirists, Juvenal and Martial, and at a somewhat later date by the philosophic Marcus Aurelius.*

These are testimonies by heathen writers, who lived altogether out of the circle of the new religion, who did not profess to understand it, and who despised it in their ignorance, but whose declarations prove that it arose at a particular time and in a particular way, and was extensively known by the end of the first century. It can be proven by indubitable evidence, and is admitted on all hands, that by that time the gospel, coming from Judea only sixty or seventy years before, had been preached for a witness in nearly every country of the wide Roman Empire, and in some regions beyond. It was known in the palace of the Cæsars, and had been proclaimed to Greeks and barbarians, bond and free. It had attained a firm footing in the great cities, the centres of power and enlightenment, — in Rome, in Corinth, in Ephesus, in Antioch, in Alexandria. It had planted stations in various parts of North Africa between Egypt and Carthage. In the West it had a hold in Spain, in Gaul, and perhaps as far as Britain. In

* Tacitus, Ann: xv. 44. Suetonius, Nero c. 16. Juvenal, Sat. I. 155.

the East it was known in Arabia, in Parthia, some think as far as India. It had defied the edicts of emperors, stood firm amidst the tumults of the people, and come forth purified by the fires of persecution. Everywhere it had exerted a moral influence, so that a learned apologist, writing a little later, could say: "We, who formerly delighted in vicious excesses, are now temperate and chaste; we, who once practised magical arts, have consecrated ourselves to the good and unbegotten; we, who once prized gain above all things, give even what we have to the common use, and share it with such as are in need; we, who once hated and murdered one another, who, on account of difference of customs, could have no common hearth with strangers, now, since the appearance of Christ, live together with them. We pray for our enemies; we seek to persuade those who hate us without cause to live conformably to the goodly precepts of Christ, that they may become partakers with us of the joyful hope of blessings from God, the Lord of all." *

But in addition to this we have a whole series of writings. We have, very much as we now have them, the Four Gospels, with the connected history of the life of Jesus, of his parables and other discourses, and of his wonderful acts of love. It is admitted on all hands that between A.D. 150 and A.D. 200, the present Four Gospels were universally acknowledged by the church as written by the authors whose names they bear, and as of divine

* Justin Martyr. See Killen's "Ancient Church," p. 276.

authority; and that they were translated into Latin and Syriac. But their general acceptance at that time over all the scattered churches implies a long previous existence. The First Gospel has been universally regarded as written by Matthew, and addressed specially to the Hebrews. Papias, who was Bishop of Hierapolis, in Phrygia, the beginning of the second century, is quoted by Eusebius (Hist. Eccl. iii. 36) as referring to the Gospel by Matthew; and from that date downward there is a chain of witnesses in its behalf. We have like evidence in favor of Mark's Gospel. Eusebius (iii. 39) quotes from Papias the testimony of John the Presbyter, that Mark, as the interpreter of Peter, gave an account of the deeds of Jesus. It is admitted on all hands that it was the same author who wrote the Third Gospel and the Book of Acts; and both must have been published long before the end of the first century. Attempts have been made to throw the composition of John's Gospel down to the middle of the second century; but these have utterly failed. Irenæus, who was the scholar of Polycarp, the disciple of John himself, ascribes the Gospel to John. "John, the disciple of our Lord, who leaned upon his bosom, did himself publish a Gospel while dwelling at Ephesus, in Asia" (Contra Hær. iii. 1). All this has been confirmed in our day by the recovery of the long-lost Philosophoumenon of Hippolytus, who was Bishop of Pontus in the first half of the third century. In this work Hippolytus quotes Basilides, who lived in the reign of Adrian, A.D. 111–138, and makes use of St. John and St. Luke. He quotes John i. 9: "That was the true Light, which lighteth every man that cometh into the world;" and John ii. 4, "Mine hour is not yet come."

Then we have the Epistles of Paul. I believe that by this time we have the whole of them known more or less throughout the church. It is acknowledged on all hands that we have some of them, and these for doctrinal and historical purposes the most important of any, at least thirty years before the close of the century. These have stood unshaken all the destructive assaults of modern German criticism. Baur allows that the Epistle to the Romans, the two Epistles to the Corinthians, the Epistle to the Galatians, are genuine, and were written by Paul not long after the middle of the first century. M. Renan argues that the two Epistles to the Thessalonians and the Epistle to the Philippians are the works of the apostle, and that it is probable that he also wrote the Epistle to the Colossians, and the characteristic letter to Philemon.* I believe that the very same arguments, — the sameness in doctrine, in style of writing, and in the personal characteristics of the apostle, — would prove that the Epistle to the Ephesians and the Epistles to Timothy were written by Paul. There are the same deep truths underlying them all, the same doctrines of predestination, election, redemption by blood, salvation by grace, the necessity

* Saint Paul. Introd.

of regeneration, faith, and holiness, and the same ardor of spirit, and the same impetuosity and abruptness of style. But it is not needful for my purpose to defend the whole of this ground. It is enough for me that the letter to the metropolis of the world, with its salutations to Christians there; that two letters to the chief commercial city of Greece; that letters to another Grecian city, to a Macedonian city, and to a scattered Celtic people in the province of Galatia, are allowed to have been written by Paul within less than an age of the death of Christ,—within a shorter time after the death of Christ than has elapsed since most of those now before me began to interest themselves in public events. In these Epistles we have all the essential truths of Christianity set forth,—the doctrines of the sinfulness of man, of justification by faith, of the divinity of our Lord, of purification by the Spirit; we have glimpses of the mode of worship followed by the early Christians, of their churches "in the house," of their prayers, and the observance of the Lord's Supper; of the difficulties which the Gentiles experienced in eating things offered to idols, and which the Jews felt in reconciling their reverence for the law with their devotion to the gospel; we have notices of the disputes that were springing up, of the predictions of a coming apostasy; while we have everywhere moral precepts, pure as the atmosphere of heaven, and suited to the life we have to lead on earth: as Rom. xii. 1: "I beseech you therefore, brethren, by the mercies of God, that ye present your bodies a living sacrifice, holy, acceptable unto God, which is your reasonable service. And be not conformed to this world; but be ye transformed by the renewing of your mind;" and 1 Cor. xiii. 4: "Charity suffereth long, and is kind; charity envieth not; charity vaunteth not itself, is not puffed up, doth not behave itself unseemly, seeketh not her own, is not easily provoked, thinketh no evil; rejoiceth not in iniquity, but rejoiceth in the truth; beareth all things, believeth all things, hopeth all things, endureth all things."

Besides these, we have a very important history, professedly by the same who wrote the Third Gospel, by one who travelled with the apostle, who introduces himself to us simply by changing *he* or *they* into *we*, when he is with Paul, as Acts xvi. 10: "And after *he* had seen the vision, immediately *we* endeavored to go into Macedonia, assuredly gathering, that the Lord had called us for to preach the gospel unto them. Therefore loosing from Troas, *we* came with a straight course to Samothracia," &c.; and it has been remarked that when he uses the *we*, the narrative is always fuller and more minute. This Book of Acts, M. Renan shows, must have been published at least by the year 80 of our Lord.* I believe it was written earlier, as, if it had not been written before that time, it would not have left Paul in his own hired house in Rome; but would have contained an account of the tragic scenes connected with Paul's death. M. Renan is sure this book was written by Luke, the phy-

* Les Apôtres, p. xxii.

sician, and contains a substantially correct account of the life and travels of Paul, written in the true manner of history, in a calm, a charitable, and truly catholic spirit, and in accordance with the history of the times.

Such is the historic phenomenon that presents itself at the opening of the second century: a wide-spread faith in Jesus, influencing the inner life and outward conduct, and, as is admitted by their enemies, a pure morality on the part of Christians; with certain books, — four histories of the most remarkable man (to say the least) that ever lived; a number of Epistles addressed to Christians, expounding their doctrine and revealing the inner springs of their life; and we have what seems *prima facie* a clear, accurate, and consistent account of the way in which all this was produced. Here there is a phenomenon to be accounted for, what will be acknowledged to be a very wonderful phenomenon, and a very complex phenomenon, — a new life appearing simultaneously in very different countries, among Jews and Gentiles, in Rome and all its diverse provinces, among urban and rural populations, among Greeks and barbarians; in and along with this a series of works, biographies, histories, expositions of doctrine and precept, all tending to one point. How, then, are we to account for this?

There is one way of accounting for it; and that is the simple, the obvious one, that the books speak the truth about Jesus, about Paul and the propagation of the gospel. Adopt this hypothesis, and we can understand the whole, — understand how the new life sprang up, how the faith was propagated, how the doctrine arose, how the precepts came to be so pure. In scientific investigation men form an hypothesis, and then inquire whether facts correspond. Newton supposed that all matter attracted other matter inversely according to the square of the distance; and the hypothesis was found to account for the whole movements of the heavenly bodies, which all became verifications of what Newton supposed to be the law of the solar system. Adopt the hypothesis that Jesus was what he is represented, and the whole of the books and the history becomes a verification.

Any other theory that may be propounded can be shown to be utterly insufficient to explain the phenomenon, to be inconsistent with the body of facts taken as a whole. Let us look at some of these suppositions.

First, the whole is a contrivance, an organized deceit, a cunningly devised fable of designing men. Strange as it may sound, this is the conclusion to which some of the later German infidels have been obliged to come, as finding that all other suppositions, the legendary and the mythic, cannot stand a sifting examination. Some persons known, — say Peter and John, followed by Paul, — or some persons unknown because kept out of sight, deliberately planned a false system and palmed it upon the world. This will be the conclusion to which men will have to come in the end in regard to Mormonism; and this is in fact the last resort to which infidels have been obliged to betake themselves in regard to Christianity, because every other supposition has failed. Even Strauss, though leaning mainly on a vague mythical hypothesis, is obliged to say:* "The narratives of the Fourth Gospel, especially, are for the most part so methodically framed, so carried out into detail, that, if they are not historical, they can apparently only be considered as conscious and intentional fictions." And yet how monstrous the supposition! Scheming men, I admit, have studiously started plans of deceit to gratify their pride or lust or ambition, and have obstinately stood by them when opposed. But what motives could any man have to invent a religion like that of Jesus, which requires us to take up our cross, if we would follow him? But I stand on yet firmer ground, when I maintain that it could not have entered into the heart of any man to conceive a life and a morality like that of Jesus; to picture one of so pure an aim, and to put into his mouth the Sermon on the Mount or the parable of the prodigal son. The great body of sceptics have resorted to more ingenious and plausible suppositions.

It was at one time maintained that the whole phenomenon originated in Legends. There was a foundation of fact it was allowed: there was one named Jesus who exercised a mighty power, first in the obscure province of Galilee, and next in

* New Life of Jesus, p. 208.

Judea; and then there gathered around him a host of stories, which increased as they spread, till now no critic is able to determine what nucleus of truth there may have been in the comet to lead on the nebulous accompanying matter. Now I at once admit that such legends are found in all countries, and that they might have appeared in the Christian Church; in fact they did rise to a most injurious excess in the Middle Ages, and have been incorporated into its faith by the Romish Church. But then such legends have certain marks, and can easily be detected. They are commonly wavering and uncertain, and assume different forms in different districts of country and in different ages. The popular legends of all nations have been full of glaring inconsistencies, — inconsistencies in respect of time, locality, and incident, and of the representation of character, and the embodiment of ethical precept or religious dogma. Who shall be so bold as to attempt to bring any thing like unity out of the legends of the Indians in this country; or of King Arthur in ancient Britain; or of the Argonautic expedition, the hunting of the boar of Calydon, the siege of Thebes, or the siege of Troy, in ancient Greece? If we have these fables related by only one writer, there may be something like a connected narrative; but when they are given us by various narrators, the contradictions become glaring beyond the possibility of even an attempted reconciliation. Now the New Testament bears on the very face of it that it is the work of a number of writers placed in different circumstances, and with different natural tastes, temperaments, and styles of composition; and yet in their writings we have a most wonderful unity, and this in the subjects about which the popular mind is most apt to be confused, — a unity in the ethical system, in the graces of the Christian character, for example; a unity in the grand religious doctrines, as in the view given of the Word becoming flesh, and of sin and salvation; and, above all, a unity in the character of Jesus, who is placed in a great variety of positions, and yet is everywhere one and the same. The wisest opponents of Christianity have come to see this, and have abandoned the Legendary hypothesis as one utterly inapplicable to such connected discourses as the parables of our Lord, and such well-reasoned compositions as those of the Apostle Paul.

But another theory has been devised and elaborated with imposing skill and learning, and has deceived not a few scholars ignorant of the world, though it is not likely to tell with men of good sense, who have had much acquaintance with the motives which sway mankind. It is what is called the Mythic Theory. It is shown that most nations which have risen above barbarism have been in the way of fashioning myths. These differ in many respects from legends. The legend has always a foundation in fact, to which, however, additions have been made in the shape of new, commonly lively incidents likely to strike the popular fancy, and, as being easily remembered, to go down by tradition to future ages.

Myths may, or quite as likely may not, have a foundation of fact. They originate in some popular idea or belief, which has somehow or other come to be very generally entertained; and they are devised to account for it, to justify it, — in one word, to satisfy it. A tribe has grown up with certain predilections, perhaps with a strong vanity in a certain direction, possibly with a very determined ambition to secure certain coveted possessions. To justify all this, a story is devised as to some incident supposed to have occurred at the formation of the tribe; or as to the father of their race, and some feat which he performed, or some promise or blessing or inheritance which he left them. The story at once seizes the popular mind: it so fits into the prevalent prepossession and belief, that it is generally accepted. It needs no evidence: it recommends itself, and passes current from mouth to mouth, and at last may become embodied in verse. German scholars have busily employed themselves in showing how these myths arise; in tracing them in their earliest shape, and following them down to their latest forms: have shown how they have been handed down from one generation to another, and under what modifications they have migrated from country to country, and gone out from the mother country with a colony to a distant region. As might have been expected, there has been an attempt made to apply this Mythic Theory to explain the rise of the gospel faith and the books of the New Testament. But the attempt, while it has taken with some who have spent most of their time in their libraries, is now seen by all men of common sense, who know mankind, to be quite as great a failure as that founded on the Legendary Theory. Give us an idea of any kind widely entertained, and it will very likely generate a myth to vindicate it. Let a people believe that they have a right to a certain stream, temple, or country, or pre-eminence among the nations, and there will be a story to justify it all. With a deep conviction in the truth of Christianity, the mediævals invented and cherished many silly, but also some beautiful tales of the saints. If we could conceive of the rise of Christian faith in the first century by natural means, we could conceive that there might be myths in the second century. According to the Mythical Theory, a religious consciousness of a peculiar character appeared in the first century, beginning at Judea; and by the opening of the second century it had reached every province of the Roman world. This gave rise to myths; and these myths committed to writing are the Four Gospels, the Book of Acts, and some say the Epistles of Paul.

Now, upon this I would remark, in the first place, that the most difficult part of the complicated phenomenon is not explained by this hypothesis; on the contrary, it is assumed. Whence this religious consciousness, this new life so different from any thing that had appeared before, or that has appeared since, — except, indeed, what has been produced indirectly by Christianity? Whence this morality so self-sacrificing, so pure, so tender? Whence this conception of Jesus, — evidently the foundation of the whole, — of his work, his character, his aims? The Jewish mind, so narrow and so sectarian, was utterly incapable of such enlargement; the subtle and sensuous Greek was not susceptible of such simplicity, of such spirituality; and the dreamy Orientalist could not have imparted such definiteness and practical adaptedness to the doctrines and the precepts. The first thing to be explained is this consciousness, not, be it remarked, of one mind, but of multitudes embracing Christianity, in countries widely separated from each other, and gathered out of all grades of society. But, supposing the feeling to have been gendered, the second difficulty is to show how it could produce not myths, but such myths, — the sayings of our Lord, his discourses, his parables, his acts in entire conformity with them; the history of the travels of Paul, and the Epistles attributed to him. There is nothing parallel to this in the history of the world. They tell us that the founder of Buddhism was a sincere man, impressed with the grossness of the Brahminical system, and that he earnestly labored to effect a reformation, and raised up a body of followers who submitted to sufferings as great as the early Christians. Be it so, that the man was seized with a desire to remove evil, and that his comparatively pure but inane system kindled an enthusiasm in himself and his followers, we want entirely the other elements which we have in the early church:

we have no books like the Gospels, no narrative geographically and historically correct like the Book of Acts, no ratiocinations and spiritual appeals like those of Paul.

The Mythic Theory is thus seen to be utterly inadequate to explain the phenomenon. That theory is that an idea gave rise to a story. But the first difficulty is to get such an idea without the story. And the second is to get such a story, so connected, so consistent, out of a floating idea. And the advocates of the theory are not to be allowed to perpetrate the palpable "reasoning in a circle," involved in first creating the idea in order to get the story, and then using the story to get the idea. I am now to call attention to a series of facts and considerations utterly inconsistent both with the Legendary and Mythic theories.

(1) *There is a conformity between these early books and the geography of the countries.* This is a very satisfactory point. Legends and myths pay little or no regard to topographical accuracy. There may be a general reference to some well-known mountain, or river, or fountain, or town, to give verisimilitude to the narrative, but this was reckoned enough in ages when there was no criticism to dispute the popular belief; and as to details, the inventors were not at the trouble to make their story correspond to the actual state of things. Scholars have given us geographies according to Homer, geographies according to the tale of the Argonautic expedition; but they do not attempt to

make these agree with the position of sea and land. Some have been at great pains to discover the places mentioned in the legends of King Arthur, but have found the work hopeless: there are half a dozen places from the south of England on to the middle of Scotland which claim to be the burial-place of Arthur's queen. He would be a bold man who should attempt to sketch the geography of the travels of Hiawatha. But every place visited by our Lord in his tours can be pointed out. Some years ago the little town of Ephraim was discovered by Robinson, and settled a number of difficult points; and now it is thought that we can fix on the precise spot where Capernaum stood, which is identified by certain fish still found in a well, and mentioned as being there by Josephus.

Then we have all seen maps of the travels of St. Paul in strict accordance with the geography of the countries, and also with the narrative of Luke, and the occasional allusions in St. Paul's Epistles. Let us use as a guide-book that able and most accurate work, Conybeare and Howson's St. Paul, and it will enable us to follow the apostle from city to city, from country to country, over land and sea, from the time he enters on his first missionary tour at Antioch in A.D. 48, till he arrives as a prisoner in Rome, in A.D. 61. The unchanging state of things in the East, the sameness of the roads and routes from the earliest date down to the present time, the existence of the old cities,—it may be in a decaying state, or in ruins,—enable us under such a guide to follow Paul, with the fullest assurance that we are treading in his footsteps: and we see that every thing confirms the history of Luke and the allusions in the Epistles. Curious coincidences are ever casting up to verify the whole narrative. At Perga in Pamphylia, John Mark left Paul and Barnabas, not being willing to engage in the work; and no wonder, for Paul and Barnabas as we learn, not from the Acts but otherwise, were about to enter on a very difficult and dangerous journey through a wild mountain country with bold precipices and deep ravines, and infested by robbers and wild marauders, who kept the peaceful inhabitants in a state of terror and often prevented powerful armies from passing through the region. At Lystra the people proposed to offer sacrifice to Barnabas and Paul, supposing them to have been Jupiter and Mercury; and we know from other quarters that this region was inhabited by an ignorant and superstitious people, who had a tradition among them that these two gods had appeared to their forefathers in human form.

We can easily conceive that a legend or a myth might have arisen about Paul journeying to Rome and suffering shipwreck. The persons who invented or propagated it would, however, be at no pains to seek after a minute accuracy. But the whole account given in Acts is minutely accordant with the mode of travelling at that time, with the routes usually pursued, and with the direction of the winds at the season. The centurion takes a passage in a merchant vessel bound for Adramyttum, and this vessel touches at Myra, a seaport in Lycia. There the centurion found a ship which suited his purpose: it was a ship of Alexandria, bound for Italy, being evidently a corn ship carrying provisions to the crowded population in the centre of the Roman Empire. Some years ago Mr. Smith of Jordan Hill, a gentleman well acquainted with nautical affairs, set out in a vessel of his own to verify the account given by Luke; and he found it to correspond in every particular with the prevailing winds and currents, and with the geography of the Isle of Malta. Referring to Mr. Smith's book as giving particular details, I must confine myself to the account which he gives of the wreck thus summarized by Dr. Howson: In the first place, we are told that they became aware of land by the presence of breakers, and yet without striking; and at this point it is certain from the structure of the strand that there must have been violent breakers that night, with a north-easterly wind. At this day the soundings as taken by Mr. Smith were found to be twenty fathoms, and a little farther on fifteen fathoms. It may be said that this in itself is nothing remarkable. But if we add that the fifteen fathoms' depth is the direction of the vessel's drift W. by N. from the twenty fathoms' depth, the coincidence is startling. Again, the character of the coast on the farther side of the bay is such that, though the greater part of it is fronted with rocky precipices, there are one or two indentations which exhibit the appearance of a creek, with a shore described as a sandy or pebbly shore. This spot as seen from the vessel would appear like a place between two seas, and into it they ran. Finally, referring to the fact of the anchors holding during that terrible night, we find in the English Official Sailing Directions that the ground in St. Paul's Bay is so good that, while the cables hold, there is no danger, as the anchors will never start. All these facts seem to prove that this Melita must be the modern Malta, and that the narrative of Luke is in every respect and circumstantially correct.

(2) *There is an accordance between the state of society and the history of the period on the one hand, and the Book of Acts and the Epistles of Paul upon the other.* There is no historical work of ancient times which gives us so clear and faithful a picture of the condition of the world at the time as the Book of Acts; and it is all in congruity with the accounts given otherwise. First, the Jews are brought under our view: both those who were settled in Jerusalem, living on their past glory, and expecting a future earthly grandeur, which was never to be realized by them; and then those who were scattered throughout the Greek cities, carrying on various branches of industry with tenacity and perseverance, but utterly separated, socially and religiously, from the people among whom they sojourned — as they thought only temporarily, and cherishing the idea of returning to their land to share in its coming glories. All

of them are discontented with the condition in which they find themselves, and are looking for a Messiah to bring in a better state of things, but with very different ideas and expectations as to what the character of this Deliverer should be, — some, indeed, expecting such a one as the prophets described to work a moral reformation, but the great body of them longing for a mere temporal prince, or more commonly expecting the Messiah to confirm and consolidate their hard, formal, and self-righteous system of religious beliefs and services. And so we see a number of them expecting Jesus, and waiting anxiously for him; while the people as a whole crucified Christ, and persecuted his followers in the vain thought that they would crush the new evangelical faith on the instant and for ever.

Then we have a picture of the Greek-speaking population in the great cities, as in Antioch, in Paphos, in Ephesus, Athens, and Corinth. In these we see what the Greek civilization, spread by the conquests of Alexander the Great, could accomplish. The great body of the people are degraded, with no attempt made by philosophers or scholars to elevate them: philosophers are spending their intellectual power in sophistic subtleties; the upper classes have a sensuous, and some of them a literary, refinement, but as a whole they give themselves up to pleasures, to games and theatres, and worse indulgences, — paiderastia and association with hetairai being practised without shame and without remorse. Such a people were not fit to resist the advancing power of the Romans, in fact fell under their dominion more easily than the Carthaginians, the Germans, the Gauls, or the Britons did. This Greek people, living in barbarous countries, had no public or patriotic purpose to live for: they felt that it was of no use resisting the Roman dominion, and in fact had no inclination to make the effort. Their old religion had very much lost its hold upon them, and they knew of no better; and having no high aim before them, either for this life or the life to come, they thought that there was nothing for them but to seek and obtain as many of the enjoyments of this world as possible. "Let us eat and drink, for to-morrow we die." A people so situated and so acting must, like the leaves of autumn, so different from the leaves supported by fresh sap in spring, fade and rot and disappear, as in fact all their once famous cities did; so that it is difficult, as to some of them, to find the places where they once were.

Then we have the Romans establishing a strong government, allowing no one to speak or act against the authority of Cæsar or the Roman people, insisting everywhere on obedience and order, arresting lawlessness wherever it appeared, and furnishing facilities for travelling, and thus allowing commerce and knowledge to spread with their civilizing influences; but, we have to add, seeking in no way to improve or to encourage freedom and independence, or the morals or religion of the people. The upper classes in Rome were losing the stern virtues of their fathers, and acquiring the levities of the Greeks without their refinement. In the Herods, — grandfather, fathers, and children, — and in Pontius Pilate, and Festus, and Felix, we have a picture of the sort of men sent out by the emperors to rule the provinces; and there was nothing in the character of the soldiery in a garrison city to improve the morals or refine the manners of the citizens. We perceive the upper classes, both Greeks and Romans, losing their faith in the old superstitions of their nations; and, in their anxiety to have something deeper and better to rest on, betaking themselves to soothsayers and astrologers, who deceived them by pretending to convey supernatural communications, and by the lying wonders which they wrought.

Then we have a picture of the great mass of the people, rude and ignorant, with no systematic attempts to educate or to elevate them, dividing their time between servile work and debasing pleasures, believing in their gross hereditary superstitions, and irritated at all who would disturb them in their beliefs or in their practices; but some of them maintaining an earnestness of belief, an honest industry, and love of independence, such as had very much disappeared among the upper classes.

Now in this book, as well as in general history, we find all these elements, Eastern and Western, meeting, mingling, seething, fermenting. We see, too, a new chemical power thrown into this caldron, meeting with opposition from all, but contending with all, and in a sense conquering them by making them take new forms and dispositions, the result of which is the formation of a soil constituting modern society. For has not the modern European and American world been produced by these four or five causes: first, the Greeks giving refinement; second, the Romans contributing government and order; third, the Hebrews spreading a pure religion; with a popular element derived from those energetic nations which emigrated from Asia, bringing with them their superstitions, but also their love of independence; and finally Christianity working in the midst of them, and seeking to subordinate and sanctify them all, as yet with only partial success, but with such a measure of success as to insure a final triumph? We are here at the point, or rather the time, where the Eastern and Western worlds meet, where the ancient world has reached its limit, and the modern world begins. It is surely interesting, and may be instructive, to stand at such a place, which we are enabled to do by the simple, truth-like narrative of Luke, to discover all these agencies at work, to see the old leaves fallen or falling and putrefying, but dropping in the midst of them a set of undying seeds to germinate into a new and better life.

The instances of correspondence between the Book of Acts and general history might be multiplied indefinitely. Thus, it is in Athens that Paul is met by the Stoics and Epicureans, who strenuously oppose him, as we might expect from the self-righteous character of the one sect, and the pleasure-loving character of the other. It is in Corinth, known as a licentious, commercial city, that impurity breaks forth in the church; and it is in writing to the Christians in that place, so famous for its architecture, that he draws his imagery from the art of building. It is among the Galatians, a Celtic people with all the impulses of their race, that we find so rapid a change in public sentiment, so that, while at first they would have plucked out their own eyes for the good of the apostle (who seems to have been troubled with a weakness of sight), afterwards they turned away from the simplicity of the gospel. The Roman magistrates are represented now as shielding the apostle, and again as subjecting him to penalties, according as they believe that the cause of order will thereby be sustained. The persons who handed down legends or invented myths never troubled themselves to secure such consistencies. But, besides these general correspondences, there are minute coincidences of a still more remarkable character. We can refer only to two.

In his first missionary tour, Paul comes to the town of Paphos, in the Isle of Cyprus. The title given to the Governor by Luke agrees most thoroughly with what we learn from heathen authority. The Romans sent two kinds of governors to their provinces. One set of provinces was under the senate and people, and the governor of these was appointed by lot: he carried with him the lictor and fasces, and he is styled proconsul, in Greek ἀνθύπατος; he had no military power, and he had to resign at the end of the year. Another set of provinces was under the emperor, and the governor was called proprætor or ἀντιστράτηγος, or legatus, πρεσβευτής: he goes with the authority of the emperor, he has full military power, and he remains during the pleasure of the emperor. Now Luke mentions both these kinds of officers, uses the names of both, and he always applies them right; that is, gives to a province the very officer which we find that it had from heathen authority. In our version, he is called simply a deputy; in the original it is ἀνθύπατος. Now Dio Cassius informs us in one passage that the emperor retained Cyprus as a province of his own, in which case the title of the governor should not have been proconsul, but proprætor. But the same historian adds that Augustus restored Cyprus to the senate, thus making the governor proconsul. This is confirmed by a coin found in Curium, in Cyprus, of the date A.D. 52, a few years after the visit of Paul, containing an allusion to Claudius Cæsar as emperor, and representing the governor of the Isle of Cyprus as a proconsul. So minutely accurate is the statement of Luke as shown by these incidental notices which learned research has brought to light.

In his second missionary tour Paul comes to Philippi, "a city of Macedonia and a colony." Augustus, the representative of the highest grandeur of the Roman empire, had bestowed on this city the privileges of a *colonia*. A Roman colony planted in a city was a copy and a sort of representative of Rome itself. The original members of it went out from Rome, and were often veteran soldiers who were thus rewarded for their services. They settled in the city with the pride and all the feelings of Romans. I believe that in the course of years others, not Italians, became amalgamated with them, and sharers in their privileges. But the laws and customs of Rome were there rigidly carried out: they had in their city the Roman insignia, and in the market-place the laws of the XII. Tables were inscribed. The language of the men of office, and indeed of the great body of the people, was Latin. The colony was regulated by its own magistrates named Duumviri, but delighting to call themselves Prætors, in Greek στρατηγὸι. They kept up a direct dependence on Rome, and were not under the governor of the province. The citizens had all the privileges of Roman citizens, such as freedom from arrest, and a right of appeal to the emperor. Such was the city, partly Greek in its people, but eventually Roman in its government, in which Paul now found himself. The treatment which Paul receives in this city is altogether in accordance. He and Silas were dragged into the ἀγορὰν, or Forum, arraigned before the city authorities, ἄρχοντας. The case came officially before the στρατηγὸι, the usual translation of the Roman prætors. The charge was plausibly put: "These men, being Jews, do exceedingly trouble our city, and teach customs which are not lawful for us to receive, neither to observe, being Romans." It was the ancient law and custom of the Romans to admit no foreign religion. The prætors gave the Roman order: "Go, lictors, strip off their garments: let them be scourged." The horrid sentence being executed, they thrust them into the inner prison. But in their passion and hurry they had been guilty of an informality. Paul was a Roman citizen, and they had condemned him without a trial. Afraid of being punished themselves, they gave orders on the following morning for the liberation of the prisoners.

(3) *There are a great many undesigned coincidences between the Book of Acts on the one hand, and the Epistles of Paul on the other.* By observing these, we get a most satisfactory evidence of the authenticity and truthfulness of both, and indeed of the truth of Christianity. This is the point which has been taken up by Paley, in the most original of his works, the "Horæ Paulinæ." He puts the supposition that the two, the fourteen letters and the history, were found for the first time in the Escurial, or some other library, without any collateral evidence in their favor; and he shows that, from a comparison of the two, we could reach the conviction that the letters are authentic, the narrative in the main true, and the persons and transactions real. As a specimen, we may notice the correspondence

between Acts xvii. and xviii. on the one hand, and the two Epistles to the Thessalonians on the other. The history tells us that Paul, before coming to Thessalonica, had been at Philippi, where he was scourged and put in prison (Acts xvi.). In writing to the Thessalonians, Paul says (1 Thess. ii. 2), "After that we had suffered before, and were shamefully entreated, as ye know, at Philippi." The history tells us that when Paul came to Thessalonica (Acts xvii. 5), "the Jews, which believed not, took unto them certain lewd fellows of the baser sort, and gathered a company, and set all the city in an uproar." Paul says (1 Thess. ii. 2): "We were bold in our God to speak unto you the gospel of God with much contention;" and (iii. 7) he speaks of "our affliction and distress." The history says that when Paul left Berea, he left behind him Silas and Timotheus; and that, when he came to Athens, he sent back a message (Acts xvii. 15) that they should "come to him with all speed;" and that, as he was waiting for them, his spirit was stirred within him, when he saw the city given to the worship of idols. Paul (1 Thess. iii. 1) speaks affectingly of his being left in Athens alone, without his usual associates in labor, and with no one to support him. The history implies that, on Paul coming to Corinth, Silas and Timotheus were not with him; and that, seeking for congenial fellowship, he joined himself to Aquila and Priscilla; and he tells us that after a time Silas and Timotheus came to him (Acts xviii. 5): "And when Silas and Timotheus were come from Macedonia." Paul refers (1 Thess. iii. 5) to his being so anxious before Timothy arrived to learn the state of the Thessalonians: "For this cause, when I could no longer forbear, I sent to know your faith, lest by some means the tempter have tempted you, and our labor be in vain. But now, when Timotheus came from you unto us, and brought us good tidings of your faith and charity, and that ye have good remembrance of us always, desiring greatly to see us, as we also to see you." We find Timothy and Silvanus, who have now arrived in Corinth, joining with Paul in writing the Epistle (1 Thess. i.). The history tells us that, so far as Greece was concerned, Paul was most successful in Macedonia and Achaia, and details the cities in which his work was in these countries. The letter-writer says (1 Thess. i. 7, 8), "Ye were ensamples to all that believe in Macedonia and Achaia. For from you sounded out the word of the Lord, not only in Macedonia and Achaia," &c.

But it may be urged that all this might have been done by a forger; that the history might have been written by one who had seen the Epistles, or the Epistles by one who had seen the Book of Acts. To this there is a twofold reply. One is, that the coincidences come out incidentally, and not studiously. A forger would have made the correspondences prominent, certain to be seen by all; whereas, it is clear that neither the historian nor letter-writer is seeking to establish his veracity; and we discover that the one fits into the other, only by collating passages scattered in various places, which passages are all natural in the places in which they are found. Secondly, while we have samenesses, we have also differences between the two, — differences on the surface, and which would never have been allowed to remain by a forger. Thus Paul tells us how he was sustained when he was in Thessalonica (1 Thess. ii. 9), "For ye remember, brethren, our labor and travail: for laboring night and day, because we would not be chargeable unto any of you." And in another Epistle (Phil. iv. 16) he tells us that he got a gift from the Philippians, which, no doubt, helped him in his first residence at Thessalonica. "For even in Thessalonica ye sent once and again unto my necessity." No mention is made of this in the history; and yet this is the very thing which a forger would most likely have fixed to show a forced correspondence. And even at this point there is a general agreement, for the historian tells us (Acts xviii. 3) that Paul did thus labor with his hands at Corinth. And there is a more important difference, amounting at first sight to a discrepancy, but turning out in the end to be a corroboration. Looking to the First Epistle to the Thessalonians, it might seem as if Timothy had joined Paul at Athens (1 Thess. iii, 1): "Wherefore, when we could no longer forbear, we thought it good to be left at Athens alone; and sent Timotheus, our brother, and minister of God, and our fellow-laborer in the gospel of Christ, to establish you, and to comfort you concerning your faith."

From this it seems pretty clear that, while Paul was at Athens, Timothy had left Berea, and come to him; and that, anxious about the Thessalonians, he had sent him back to Thessalonica, with a message of comfort to the persecuted and distracted Christians there. It was after fulfilling this mission that he and Silas joined Paul at Corinth. There is no notice of this in the Book of Acts, which there would certainly have been, if a forger had drawn the history out of the Epistles, with the view of exhibiting an ostentatious consistency. Still the statement in the Epistles does not contradict the history. For the history makes Paul urgently press Timothy to come to Athens; and Paul, who does not seem to have been driven from Athens, remains there till Timothy arrives, and then sends him to Thessalonica, with instructions, no doubt, to join him at Corinth, and bring him a true account of the state of the church at Thessalonica. The two accounts are thus perfectly consistent; but it is not a labored consistency, but a congruity arising from both being genuine and truthful. We might multiply such cases, but it is unnecessary when they are found in so accessible a book as the "Horæ Paulinæ."

Let us view Christianity in its place in the world. The intelligent Hindoo may very reasonably put the question, Has it accomplished what it professes, has it fulfilled its mission? It may be allowed that some of the early Christians expected Jesus and his religion to make an easy conquest of the world.

But the actual history of the church is in entire accordance with the picture presented by our Lord by his inspired apostles. Luke xii. 49: "I am come to send fire on the earth."—"Suppose ye that I am come to give peace on earth? I tell you, Nay; but rather division. From henceforth there shall be five in one house divided, three against two, and two against three." The same lesson is taught in several of the most striking of our Lord's parables, Matt. xiii. 24–30: "The kingdom of heaven is likened unto a man which sowed good seed in his field: but while men slept, his enemy came and sowed tares among the wheat, and went his way. But when the blade was sprung up, and brought forth fruit, then appeared the tares also." It is a picture of what is felt in the heart of the Christian, it is a picture of what is found in the professing church of God. When the Thessalonians misinterpreted the language of Paul's First Epistle, and concluded that Christ was to come in triumph immediately, the apostle hastens to inform them (2 Thess. ii. 3) "that day shall not come, except there come a falling away first, and that man of sin be revealed, the son of perdition." Peter points to scoffers, who shall appear in the latter days, advancing the very objection which we find urged in the present day, from the constancy of nature (2 Pet. iii. 3–5): "Since the fathers fell asleep, all things continue as they were from the beginning of the creation." The last spared of the apostles speaks of it as being well known that Antichrist was to come (1 John ii. 18): "And as ye have heard that Antichrist shall come, even now there are many Antichrists." And in the Book of Revelation there is a prediction of an antichristian power which shall have extensive sway for twelve hundred and sixty days, a day for a year. Every Christian feels how truly our Lord pictures the grace of God in the heart, when he says (Matt. xiii. 33), "The kingdom of heaven is like unto leaven, which a woman took, and hid in three measures of meal, till the whole was leavened." Neander shows, in his "History of the Church," that this is also a picture of the church at large. He thus opens his great work: "The history will show how a little leaven cast into the mass of humanity has been gradually penetrating it. Looking back on the period of eighteen centuries, we would survey a process of development, in which we ourselves are included, — a process moving steadily onward, though not in a direct line, but through various windings, yet in the end furthered by whatever has attempted to arrest its course; a process having its issue in eternity, but constantly following the same laws, so that in the past, as it unfolds itself to our view, we may see the germ of the future which is coming to meet us." We are ever inclined to say, "Why is he so long in coming? Why tarry the wheels of his chariot?" We are made to see that God is not slack concerning his purpose, but at the same time that "with the Lord one day is as a thousand years, and a thousand years as one day." This is a motto which might be placed at the head of every chapter of the history of the geological epochs: it is a truth which we must take along with us, if we would comprehend the solemn and steady march of prophecy. The whole of palæontology is a history of the struggle of life upward from lower to higher forms, the weaker dying out, and the stronger surviving, and prevailing, and propagating its kind. The biography of the individual Christian exhibits a like contest between the mind and the members, with the mind finally gaining the victory. The history of the church in the world is in like manner a record of a struggle between light and darkness, between love and selfishness, between purity and pollution; in which, notwithstanding many reverses, the higher principle is certain to reign in the end. Let us, before closing, take a passing glance at the present missionary work of the church.

For long ages did the Protestant Church decline, like Jonah, the rebellious prophet, to engage in the evangelistic work allotted to it. It is only some seventy years since Protestants — it has to be said, to their disgrace — awoke to the sense and duty of missionary exertion. Some wonder that so little fruit has been gathered, are astonished that the whole world has not been already converted by the efforts made; but the proper wonder is that the churches were so long insensible to their responsibility, and that even yet so little has been done. Of late years our religion has shown that it is as vigorous and fresh for contest as when it first went forth to subdue the world, and as much has been accomplished as in the same period in the early church. Seventy years after the death and resurrection of our Lord, and the outpouring of the Spirit on the day of Pentecost, bring us to the death of the Apostle John and the close of the first century. In the early part of this Lecture we had our attention called to what was done during that period: let us now compare with it what has been done in this century. At home an idea has been created, and a public sentiment been generated and propagated, and organizations have been formed for effective operation. Every congregation has felt the impulse to a greater or less extent, every Sunday school has its missionary box, and contributions come in regularly as the seasons; and from every part of our land young men and women willingly offer themselves as missionaries or teachers, and are ready to go to the forlorn hopes of the warfare, to labor in the most remote islands, and among the most degraded tribes; while prayers rise continually from millions of people and tens of thousands of congregations, who give themselves no rest, and give God no rest, till the promise is fulfilled, and the knowledge of the Lord shall cover the earth as the waters do the channel of the deep. A footing and a settlement have been gained in countries of which the apostles never heard. Rude tongues, without form and void of all elevated and elevating ideas, have been licked into shape, and rendered capable of conveying spiritual truth. A literature of a high and wholesome character has been created in nations which previously had none. The Bible, in whole or in part, has been translated into more than one hundred and fifty languages; millions of tracts, and hundreds of thousands of books, have been distributed. An extensive apparatus for work has been set up in mission-houses, and boarding-houses, and schools, and printing-presses, all radiating a healthy influence around them. We see streaks of light on the mountain-tops in countries on which it cannot be said that the sun has yet risen. The prejudices of ignorance have been removed among many in whom the prejudices of the heart have not given way. Superstitions are being undermined in lands in which they have not yet fallen. In not a few places the prepossessions or the fears of the people are in favor of the missionaries and of the message which they carry. When the children of Israel entered the land, after forty years' sojourn in the adjoining wilderness, there was a fear of them everywhere, which so far helped them in their conquest. When the apostles went forth to proclaim the gospel, there was a feeling abroad among the nations that the old superstitions were about to vanish, and that a new and conquering faith was to come out of these regions; and this prepared men for listening to their message. When the Reformers made their attack on the Romish superstitions, there was an impression that the corruptions had become intolerable; and this removed obstacles out of the way as they advanced. And, at this present time, there is in various countries a widely diffused presentiment that the gods cannot help themselves, and that their reign is drawing to a close.

And we can refer not only to this ploughing and sowing, we can point to precious and substantial fruit gathered in. The gospel has shown itself to be not dead or effete, as some would wish it, but possessed of a living power, quite as much as it had when it rose with Jesus from the tomb, or when it went forth from the upper chamber at Jerusalem to be baptized of the Spirit. In a number of lands, cannibalism and infanticide and human sacrifices have been suppressed for ever. In India, suttee has been abolished, the supporters of caste have been troubled, and the rights of woman asserted, and a beginning made in the way of elevating her. Idols have been thrown down as Dagon was before the Ark of the Covenant; and they preserve as trophies, in missionary museums, idols which no man will now worship. The gods of the land, the gods of the sea, the gods of the woods, the rain gods and the storm gods and disease gods, have been made to give way before the one living and true God, who is now seen to rule so beneficently over the sea and the dry land, and over all the powers and agencies of nature. At hundreds of mission stations there are Christians, many or few, scattered like living seeds among the people, and ready to propagate around them a wholesome influence. These converts may not be perfect, but neither were those of the early church, — for example, those at Corinth; but they make a credible profession, and in honesty and purity and kindness and generosity set as good an example as the members of our churches at home. In parts of India and of Burmah there are communities of Christians numbering tens of thousands. In India there are at least one hundred thousand boys taught in the vernacular schools, and many others studying English in addition to their own tongue; while thirty thousand girls are receiving a Christian education. The planting of Christianity in Madagascar has thrilling incidents, not surpassed for the display of courage or devotedness by any recorded in the early church; and there is a reasonable prospect of the whole inhabitants of that large island professing their faith in Christianity. Mark what is reported of the South Sea Islands: "Sixty-five years ago there was not a solitary native Christian in Polynesia: now it would be difficult to find a professed idolater in those islands of Eastern or Central Polynesia where Christian missionaries have been established. The hideous rites of their forefathers have ceased to be practised. Their heathen legends and war songs are forgotten. Their cruel and desolating tribal wars, which were rapidly destroying the population, appear to be at an end. They are gathered together in peaceful village communities. They live under recognized codes of laws. They are constructing roads, cultivating their fertile lands, and engaging in commerce. On the return of the Sabbath a very large proportion of the population attend the worship of God, and in some instances more than half the adult population are recognized members of Christian Churches. They educate their children, preparing them for usefulness in after life."

In summing up, let us inquire first what account the plain, thoughtful man would give of this world, after having passed through its experience. Perhaps he will be disposed to say, with Robert Burns, that "man was made to mourn;" he will certainly be ready to avow that the dark lines of sorrow run through and through the web of life. Of the four great verities held by Buddhism, which has had such extensive sway, the first two and the fundamental are that the world is full of dissatisfaction and sorrow, and that this arises from sin. Our earth is not what any of us would wish it to be, is not what good men would expect it to be. It is not a scene of confusion, for law is everywhere visible. It is not the product of chance, nor of an unknown power, which may be good, or which may be evil; for we see traces everywhere of wise and beneficent intention. But, on the other hand, it is not such a place as we believe heaven to be. It is a state out of which men may be taken to heaven, but it is not in itself a scene of unbroken beatitude and unstained purity.

Let us now ask of science, of history, and travel, what they make of it. They tell us that they discover in all past ages, and in all countries, traces of a contest. When we look up to the heavenly bodies moving so orderly, shining so beneficently, it might seem as if our world were basking in the light of God, as if it were a scene of beauty and purity like the star-lit sky when not a cloud is resting on it. But when we penetrate deeper, we discover that our Cosmos has been formed in ages past out of warring elements; and we seem to see at this present time broken-up worlds, the débris of dread catastrophes. There is evidence that suffering and death have been in our earth since sentient life appeared, and reigning over those "who had not sinned after the similitude of Adam's transgression." The struggle in the pre-Adamite ages is an anticipation, perhaps a prefiguration, of the more terrible struggle in the post-Adamite period. In the time now present, history and travel disclose ignorance and misery spread over the earth, with destructive wars breaking forth ever and anon even in the most enlightened nations. And if you ask science what it can do to remove the evils, it tells you that there are powerful elements for good in our world, in law, and progressive knowledge and life, and that new and higher agencies have been introduced to contend with and conquer the baser powers; but, if candid, it will add that, while it may so far restrain, it cannot subdue the disease which lies deep down in the depths of the human heart.

Let us come now to Scripture, and ask what it has to say. It announces that, as the works came successively from God's hand, he could proclaim them to be all very good. But it declares at the same time that a disturbing element has been introduced. And have not sincere men felt that in all this Scripture speaks truly, and that a false and flattering picture has been given by rationalism and sentimentalism? In the midst of the struggle, Christianity, under the ministration of the Spirit, appears as the latest power introduced into our world; and we see it repelling the evil, and gathering round it all the better elements—as the magnet attracts the metals. When it is received, it stimulates the faculties, and calls forth new ideas, new motives, and new sentiments. It has been the mother of all modern education. John Knox was the first to introduce the universal education of the people in the eastern hemisphere, and the Puritans established it in the western world. The founders of all the older colleges in Europe and America were men of piety. Our religion has fostered all that is pure and ennobling in the fine arts, in architecture, painting, and sculpture, and has frowned upon the debasing forms which appeared in pagan countries. But, in fulfilling its mission, it meets with opposition, and has to engage in a terrible conflict with the powers of evil. We see the battle raging all around us in this city and in every city, in every dwelling and in every heart. Christianity thus appears in our world in analogy and in accordance with all that has gone before — a new power to contend with the evil, and overcome it. The history of our world is thus a unity from the commencement to the present time. The representation given in the Bible is of a piece with the view given by the latest researches of science and of history.

APPENDIX.

Art. I. Gaps in the Theory of Development.

There is a floating idea among many, and often embodied in a very dogmatic assertion, that, given only bare matter, every thing may be formed out of it by a process of development according to natural law. It may be of importance to show what are the unfilled-up hiatuses in this process. In doing so, I feel that I must bear in mind myself, and ask my opponents to do the same, that it is not easy, or rather it is impossible, for us to determine what are the properties to be found in all matter. It may be assumed that it has mechanical power, the power of motion in accordance with the three laws of Kepler. Has it also essentially a gravitating power inversely according to the square of the distance? This is a point which cannot be settled, for it is not yet determined whether gravitation is a simple power or the result of other powers and collocations. Has it in its very nature the chemical properties? This also is undecided; for we know not whether chemical affinities are original or derivative, — say, derived from other powers and dispositions of matter. As little can it be determined whether the powers of electricity, magnetism, and galvanism, or of emitting light and heat, belong essentially to all matter. The doubts and uncertainties on these points should lay an arrest on those who would dogmatize on the subject of development out of matter. Meanwhile it is certain that, at the present stage of science, there are processes which no man of science can perform, and which we do not see performed in the laboratory of nature, either in the geological or historical ages.

1. Chemical action cannot be produced by mechanical power.

2. Life, even in the lowest forms, cannot be produced from unorganized matter. Since Lecture I. (*supra*, pp. 27, 28) was delivered, Dr. Frankland has published the results of experiments on solutions sealed up in vacuous tubes and exposed to a temperature from 155° to 160° C., great care being taken to exclude organic seeds from the tubes. The liquid in the tubes became more or less turbid; but "there was not the slightest evidence of life in any of the particles." See "Nature," Jan. 19, 1871.

3. Protoplasm can be produced only by living matter.

4. Organized matter is made up of cells, and can be produced only by cells. Whence the first cell?

5. A living being can be produced only from a seed or germ. Whence the first vegetable seed?

6. An animal cannot be produced from a plant. Whence the first animal?

7. Sensation cannot be produced in insentient matter.

8. The genesis of a new species of plant or animal has never come under the cognizance of man, either in pre-human or post-human ages, either in pre-scientific or scientific time. Darwin acknowledges this, and says that, should a new species suddenly arise, we have no means of knowing that it is such. (As to the Darwinian Theory, see Lect. II. and *infra*, Art. II.)

9. Consciousness — that is, a knowledge of self and its operations — cannot be produced out of mere matter or sensation.

10. We have no knowledge of man being generated out of the lower animals. (See *infra*, Art. II.)

11. All human beings, even savages (*supra*, pp. 48, 138; *infra*, Art. II.), are capable of forming certain high ideas, such as those of God and duty. The brute creatures cannot be made to entertain these, by any training.

With such tremendous gaps in the process, the theory which would derive all things out of matter by development is seen to be a very precarious one. I may add that development is in all cases a very complex process, implying a vast variety of agencies, — mechanical, chemical, probably vital, — adjusted to one another and the surrounding medium. The evolution-school ridicule those who would explain the operations of water by "aquosity," comparing it to Martinus Scriblerus' method of accounting for the operation of the meat-jack by its inherent "meat-roasting quality." But this is the very error into which they themselves fall when they account for development by the "development capacity." The present business of physiologists is not to rest satisfied with the power of devolopment, or the law of hereditary descent, but to seek to determine what are the separate powers and collocations involved in the process. In such investigations they need to attend, as Bacon recommended, to the "necessary rejections and exclusions," or, as Whewell expresses it, "to the decomposition of facts."

Some, I find, are now calling in a power of Pangenesis common to all matter. I do not deny, *a priori*, the existence of such a power: some very profound minds, penetrated with religion, such as Leibnitz, have been inclined to believe in it. I am ready to accept it as soon as it can be scientifically shown to exist, and something has been determined as to its nature. Of this I am pretty sure, that, if there be such an endowment, it must be a very complicated one, implying a correlation of properties.

I am inclined to believe that all the phenomena referred to in this article — such as development, production of life — have appeared according to law, in the loose sense of the term; that is, according to an order of some kind. I hold this in analogy with the whole method of Divine procedure in nature. It is very probable that, in many of the operations, there may have been secondary agencies acting as physical causes. But these secondary agencies are, at the present stage of science, unknown: even the agencies which produce development and heredity are very much unknown. In arguing, in these Lectures, for prevailing final cause, my appeal is not to the unknown, but the known, the traces of adaptation in every part of nature; and I cannot allow those who oppose me to appeal to the unknown, when the known is all in my favor. Science may be able to fill up some of the gaps; but when it has done so, I am sure, according to the whole analogy of nature, that, in the process, we will be able to discover final cause, or an adaptation of means to accomplish an end.

Art. II. DARWIN'S DESCENT OF MAN.

WHEN Mr. Darwin published his "Origin of Species," he at once gained as adherents to his theory a large number of young naturalists. His extensive and accurate acquaintance with all departments of Natural History, the pains taken by him in the collection of facts, and the simple and ingenious way in which he stated them, prepared men to listen to him; and, as they did so, they found he was able by Natural Selection to account for a number of phenomena which could not otherwise be explained. But of late there has appeared a disposition, even among those who were at first taken with the theory, carefully to review it. All candid minds admit that it explains much, that it explains modifications which plants and animals undergo from age to age; but many doubt whether it accounts for every thing, whether indeed there is not a profounder set of facts which it does not reach.

Mr. Darwin is candid enough to admit that he cannot account for every thing connected with the appearance of vegetable and animal life. In his fifth edition (1869), he speaks "of life, with its several powers, having been originally breathed by the Creator into a few forms or into one." We have seen (*supra*, p. 80) that he allows: "How a nerve comes to be sensitive to light hardly concerns us more than how life itself first originated." But if Natural Selection cannot explain the origin of life, the origin of nerve-force or sensation, it is clear that there is a power above and beyond it, which operated when life appeared, and when sensation appeared, and which may have operated on other occasions in producing higher and ever higher forms of living beings.

It has been known, since at least the time of Aristotle, that there is a striking analogy between man and the lower animals, between all the tribes of animals, and between animals and plants; and Mr. Darwin has, by an accumulation of facts, first in the "Origin of Species," and now in the "Descent of Man," illustrated this point more fully than was ever done before. But it does not therefore follow that the animal is evolved from the plant, and man from the lower animals. The paintings of Titian have all a certain character, which shows that they are the products of the same great artist. So the correspondences in nature, inanimate and animate, show that the whole proceeds from one grand Designing Mind. We know how the great painter accomplished his aim, by brush and colors and canvas. We see some of the means by which God effects his infinitely grander ends. We see that one of these is the beneficent law of Natural Selection, whereby the weak, after enjoying their brief existence, expire without leaving seed, whereas the strong survive and leave a strong progeny. But the latest science cannot tell how Life arises, or Sensation, or Consciousness, or Intelligence, or Moral Discernment. Even with Mr. Darwin's accumulation of facts bearing on the modification of species, we are made to feel that there are residual phenomena left, which his theory does not explain, and which he does not profess or affect to explain, — in the appearance, for example, of the first plant or the first sentient creature. In the edition of the "Origin of Species" issued in 1869, though he still stands up for Natural Selection as the most important means of producing modification, he allows that it is not the only one. And in his "Animals and Plants under Domestication" (vol. ii. p. 403), he calls in a new theory, that of Pangenesis, according to which every living creature possesses innumerable minute atoms named "gemmules," which are generated in every part of the body, are constantly moving, and have the power of reproduction, and in particular are collected in the generative organs, coming thither from every part of the body. "These almost infinitely numerous and minute gemmules must be included in each bud, ovule, spermatozoon, and pollen grain" (p. 366). It has been generally felt, even by those inclined to follow Mr. Darwin, that this hypothesis is exceedingly vague and confused and complicated. It has certainly no direct evidence in its favor, as these gemmules have never come under the eye of science. The circumstance that Mr. Darwin has been obliged to resort to such hypothesis is a proof that he feels that there is a residuum which his favorite principle of Natural Selection cannot reach.

Whence, then, this element, which we ever come to when we

go far enough back, when we dig sufficiently far down? The older naturalists called it the "vital principle," not thereby meaning to explain it, but to show merely that they had come to an ultimate fact, for which they had to provide a name. Our younger naturalists do not know well what to make of it. Some of the more superficial of them would deny its existence, and explain all by molecular motion. But the profounder investigators feel that they are ever coming to it, and call it by the name of Pangenesis, or (with Herbert Spencer) "physiological units," each with an innate power to build up and reproduce the organism. I do believe that this vital power, whatever it be, has its laws; and science is engaged in its proper work when it is seeking to discover them, and may sooner or later be rewarded with success. And of this we may be assured, that when the discovery is made the wonder of intelligent minds will not be diminished.

Whence this element is still the question? It is at least possible and conceivable that it may have been introduced by an immediate fiat of the Great First Cause, continuing to act as a cause, and producing, as the æons roll on, new germs ready to rise to living beings, or living beings ready to bring forth germs; and we may be sure that what God thus places in our world will fit into all that has gone before, and become intertwined with it, and act in unison with it. But it is quite as possible that all this may be effected by some secondary agency, at present unknown, and which may or may not become known. The whole analogy of the Divine procedure, and the beautiful correspondence between the old and the new, seem to point to some common causation producing the first life and all succeeding life. This agency, which like development is only a mode of the Divine agency, may have produced the first life, the first species, every subsequent species, all according to a Divine plan. It is not the development theory: it goes farther back, and shows that behind the development there is a power which produced the life developed, and is involved in the development, — the powers working in which, naturalists do not profess to be able to explain.

The development theory is largely an appeal to the unknown.

No one supposes that evolution is an evolution from nothing. It is a law of intuitive intelligence, confirmed by all experience, that every production has a cause, and that there must be power in the agents acting as the cause to produce the effect. That which is evolved always implies a potency in that in which it is involved. A plant or animal with the power of development is always a product of previous causes, and is a cause of coming effects. But no one professes to be able to specify what are the powers involved in development. These powers, if we could discover and separate them, might be found, at least one or more of them, to be intimately connected with, and indeed to proceed from, the power, whatever it is, which originates life, — to be a prolongation in fact of that life; the prolongation being implied in the evolution, so that, if there were not a continuance and a transmission of it, there would be no development. There is certainly an element somewhere which gives constant notice of its existence, but has hitherto afforded little insight into its nature, or the laws which it obeys.

It is doubted whether the law of Natural Selection, as unfolded by Darwin, can explain the modifications of plants and animals. Mr. St. George Mivart, in his work on the "Genesis of Species," has endeavored to show: (1) that Natural Selection is incompetent to account for the incipient stages of useful structures; (2) that it does not harmonize with the co-existence of closely similar structures of diverse origin; (3) that there are grounds for thinking that specific differences may be developed suddenly instead of gradually; (4) that the opinion that species have definite though very different limits to their variability is still tenable; (5) that certain fossil transitional forms are absent, which might have been expected to be present; (6) that some facts of geographical distribution supplement other difficulties; (7) that the objection drawn from the physiological difference between species and races still exists unrefuted; (8) that there are many remarkable phenomena in organic forms upon which Natural Selection throws no light whatever, but the explanations of which, if they could be obtained, might throw light upon specific origination. I am far from saying that some of these formidable objections, supported as they are by an array of facts by an accomplished naturalist, may not be answered. But this is certain, that for years, perhaps for ages to come, it will be an unsettled question whether Natural Selection can account for all the ordinary phenomena of the modification of organisms.

In his latest work Mr. Darwin has employed his theory to account for the origin of man. In order to be able to judge of the success of the attempt, it may be proper to state briefly the conclusions which he reaches. Man is descended from the Simiadæ: "This family is divided, by almost all naturalists, into the Catarhine, or Old World monkeys, all of which are characterized (as their name expresses) by the peculiar structure of their nostrils, and by having four premolars in each jaw; and into Platyrhine group, or New World monkeys (including two very distinct sub-groups), all of which are characterized by differently constructed nostrils, and by having six premolars in each jaw. Some other small differences might be mentioned. Now man unquestionably belongs in his dentition, in the structure of his nostrils, and some other respects, to the Catarhine, or Old World division; nor does he resemble the Platyrhines more closely than the Catarhines in any characters, excepting in a few of not much importance, and apparently of an adaptive character. Therefore it would be against all probability to suppose that some ancient New World species had varied, and had thus produced a man-like creature, with all the distinctive characters proper to the Old World division, losing at the same time all its own distinctive characters. There can consequently hardly be a doubt that man is an off-shoot from the Old World Simian stem; and that, under a genealogical point of view, he must be classed with the Catarhine division" (Descent of Man, Part I. c. vi., British edition, 1871). As man agrees with anthropomorphous apes, "not only in those characters which he possesses in common with the whole Catarhine group, but in other peculiar characters, such as the absence of a tail, and of callosities, and in general appearance, we may infer that some ancient member of the anthropomorphous sub-group gave birth to man." "It is probable that Africa was formerly inhabited by extinct apes closely allied to the gorilla and chimpanzee; and as these two species are now man's nearest allies, it is somewhat more probable that our early progenitors lived on the African continent than elsewhere." "We do not know whether man is descended from some comparatively small species like the chimpanzee, or from one as powerful as the gorilla." He can tell us that "the ape-like progenitors of man probably lived in society;" that "the early progenitors of man were no doubt inferior in intellect, and probably in social disposition, to the lowest existing savages;" that "the early progenitors of man were no doubt once covered with hair, both sexes having beards;" that "their ears were pointed and capable of movement;" and that "their bodies were provided with a tail, having the proper muscles."

Mr. Darwin can carry our genealogy still farther back: "Man is descended from a hairy quadruped, furnished with a tail and pointed ears, probably arboreal in its habits, and an inhabitant of the Old World. This creature, if its whole structure had been examined by a naturalist, would have been classed amongst the Quadrumana, as surely as would the common, and still more ancient, progenitor of the Old and New World monkeys. The Quadrumana and all the higher mammals are probably derived from an ancient marsupial animal; and this, through a long line of diversified forms, either from some reptile-like or some amphibian-like creature, and this again from some fish-like animal. In the dim obscurity of the past we can see that the early progenitor of all the vertebrata must have been an aquatic animal, provided with branchiæ, with the two sexes united in the same individual, and with the most important organs of the body (such as the brain and heart) imperfectly developed. This animal seems to have been more like the larvæ of our existing marine Ascidians than any other form known." (Part II. c. xxi.)

I have allowed Mr. Darwin to draw the picture. I confess I shrink from it. I am inclined to urge that the very circumstance that man has a consciousness of a something within, which separates him from the brutes, that he claims to have a higher origin, is a consideration of some value in determining the question. Man's very feeling is a presumption in favor of his having a noble lineage. But it will be necessary to examine the logical connections of the theory.

Mr. Darwin's theory as to man's origin leans very much on his general theory as to the origin of species. Those who doubt of the success of his attempt to explain the origin of animal species will have greater doubts of his being able to account for the origin of man. There are persons favorably disposed towards the theory, as applied to the lower animals, who are not prepared to allow that it can explain the production of a being with a responsible and immortal soul. It is acknowledged on all hands that Natural Selection cannot account for the origin of life; and the power beyond, which produced life, may have found a fitting and worthy occasion for a farther operation in producing man. The difficulty which there is in applying it to man's intellectual and moral nature is making some doubt of the whole theory, as capable of explaining all the phenomena even of vegetable and animal modifications.

Again, there are acknowledged to be wide gaps in the transmission, to be many breaks in the genealogy. Thus Mr. Darwin acknowledges that he cannot account for the appearance of the mental powers in animals. "In what manner the mental powers were first developed in the lowest organisms is as hopeless an inquiry as how life first originated. These are problems for the distant future, if they are ever to be solved by man." (Part I. c. ii.) Some of us wish that he had used the same guarded language as to the origin of man's mental powers as he has used in regard to that of the lower organisms. It is clear that Natural Selection cannot explain every thing, and the production of man may be one of the things which are beyond its reach. We are ever coming in sight of a higher power; we need it to produce life, we need it to produce the instincts of animals, and *a fortiori* we need it to account for the rational and moral endowments. All analogy constrains me to cling to the idea that the same power of God, whether acting directly or by secondary agency, which produced life at first and endowed the lower creatures with psychical properties, has also been employed in creating man and furnishing him with his lofty attributes.

He acknowledges that there are breaks, which he cannot fill up, "between man and the higher apes" (vol. i. p. 187); and he speaks more expressly (p. 200) of "the great break in the organic chain between man and his nearest allies, which cannot be bridged over by any extinct or living species." This means that the animal, which could have given birth to man, has not been found in the geological ages, and has not been seen in historical times, and is not now — so far as is known — on the face of the earth, This is surely a great want in a science which professes to be built on facts. In the lack of facts, he falls back on "the general principle of evolution" (p. 200). I admit the existence of evolution ; but I oppose the theory that would account for every production by evolution, and, in the absence of facts, I cannot allow him to appeal to a principle which, in its exclusiveness, cannot be established without the facts. But he tells us that "we have every reason to believe that breaks in the series are simply the results of so many forms having become extinct" (p. 187). But surely it would only be becoming to be less sure and dogmatic, till these forms cast up, or till we can find a monkey on the earth capable by domestication, or otherwise, of producing a man.

Farther, if we have evidence otherwise of man coming into existence by a special act of God, there is not sufficient scientific strength in the Darwinian theory to overturn it. Now many believe that the Scriptures, while they say little or nothing as to the origin of animal species, settle the question of man's origin. We have seen (*supra*, Lecture II.) that the book of Genesis has anticipated geology by three thousand years, in telling of the successive stages of the production of matter and animated beings ; and it may well be attended to in speaking of the origin of man. Mr. Darwin is obliged to speak of it as being probable that God at first breathed life into two or three forms : there is surely, then, nothing inconceivable or improbable in the Almighty breathing into man the breath of life and making him a living soul. These Scriptures are supported by a body of evidence, external and internal, which those who have weighed it believe to be far stronger than the proof that can be adduced in favor of the hypothesis of man being produced by Natural Selection. Those who have looked most carefully into their own nature will be ready to acknowledge that the Scripture account, which represents man as formed out of the dust, but with a soul formed in the image of God, is far more accordant with our experience than that which would derive both body and soul from the lower animals. To oppose this, we have only a hypothesis which explains a number of facts, but is acknowledged not to explain all the facts, and to fail to explain the facts relating to the appearance of new powers. Every reader of Mr. Darwin's latest book has observed how often he is obliged in his candor to use the epithet "probably," and to say, "it is probable." It is acknowledged that there is no decisive fact to support the theory, nothing of the nature of an *experimentum crucis*. In these circumstances, most men will prefer abiding by the simple Scripture statement, rather than commit themselves to a theory which has so many breaks that cannot be filled up.

The impression left, on reading the account of the creation of man in the book of Genesis, is that while man's higher nature, his νοῦς, which contemplates eternal truth and the infinite God, was produced at once by the breath of the Great Spirit, his lower nature, and especially his body, may have been formed out of existing materials, it may be by secondary causes. And there is nothing unreasonable in the supposition that these secondary agencies may be the same as effect the growth of the young in the womb. "I will praise thee; for I am fearfully and wonderfully made: marvellous are thy works; and that my soul knoweth right well. My substance was not hid from thee, when I was made in secret, and curiously wrought in the lowest parts of the earth. Thine eyes did see my substance, yet being unperfect; and in thy book all my members were written, which in continuance were fashioned, when as yet there was none of them" (Ps. cxxxix. 14–16). The whole school are fond of appealing to the grand generalization of Von Baer, that the growth of the animal in the womb, that the various stages which it reaches, correspond very much to the progress of the animal races in the geological ages. But I have not been able to discover that they have succeeded in detecting the precise agencies which produce each of the effects, and the correspondences between them. There is a mystery here which they have not cleared up, indeed have not attempted to clear up. The analogy seems to me to point to a set of powers above both the processes, and regulating both. And may there not have been a third process analogous to the other two,—the process by which man's body was created, diverse from the animal body and yet in affinity with it? There may be an agency or set of agencies above natural selection, above even hereditary transmission—which may, in fact, be ruled by it—producing, first, each species of animal, and the progressive advance of animals; secondly, the growth of animals in the womb; and finally, the animal part of man. In some such way as this, by the work "made in secret," and "curiously wrought in the lowest parts of the earth," may we get a glimpse of the general causes which produced the organs in living beings, and in certain living beings the rudiments of organs,—such as the mammæ in the male sex,—which have not been developed into utilized organs.

But, coming more closely to Mr. Darwin's arguments, we find them to amount to two: one derived from the resemblances between man and the lower animals, and the other from Sexual Selection.

There is a resemblance in the bodily structure of man and the lower animated creation. Mr. Huxley comes to the conclusion that "man in all parts of his organization differs less from the higher apes than these do from the lower members of the same group." Mr. Darwin declares that, "although man has no just right to form a separate Order for his own reception, he may perhaps claim a distinct Sub-order, or Family" (Part I. c. vi.). The place which man's body—represented in Scripture as formed out of the dust—should hold, is a question for comparative anatomists to settle. If it is determined that man's bodily frame is of a higher order than that of the highest animal, then they will have to account for the superiority. If they prove that it should be placed alongside that of the apes, then they will have to account for his great intellectual pre-eminence, which cannot arise in this case from the body, but must come from some other quarter.

Coming to the soul of man and brute, we find Mr. Darwin on one occasion, when hard pressed with a difficulty, bursting out into the declaration, "We really know little about the mind of the lower animals" (Part II. c. xxi.). We are reminded of the famous saying of the Swiss philosopher, that we will never be able to know what brute instinct is till we are in the dog's head without being the dog. Mr. Darwin candidly acknowledges that he cannot trace the mental faculties from the lower creatures up to man. "Undoubtedly it would have been very interesting to have traced the development of each separate faculty from the state in which it exists in the lower animals to that in which it exists in man; but neither my ability nor knowledge permit the attempt" (Part I. c. v.). Till the attempt is made, and successfully completed, we have no right to assert that man's higher powers are developed out of animal powers; nor, as Mr. Darwin maintains, that "the mental faculties of man and the lower animals do not differ in kind, though immensely in degree."

I agree with Mr. Darwin in thinking that we cannot very well distinguish between what is vaguely called "Instinct," and what with equal vagueness is called "Reason." The fact is, Instinct is merely a loose but convenient name for a set of operations, the nature of which is confessedly very much unknown; and Reason has been used to denote so many different intellectual exercises, that we cannot very well determine what we should understand by it. One thing, however, seems very clear to me: that Instinct is a complex operation, always implying a number of agencies and a concurrence of agencies, and that each of them has its laws or properties, which we will never be able to discover till we can separate the threads that make up the web. It may be farther allowed that Instinct has always more or less of intelligence in it; that is, intelligence is involved as one of the agencies. But it has to be added that intelligence, or Reason, has always more or less of Instinct involved; that is, it knows, believes, and judges, without having or being able to give a mediate reason.

Mr. Darwin has successfully shown that there is a resemblance between the intelligence and instincts of man on the one hand, and those of the lower animals on the other. But in man those operations which we call Instinct become fewer, and occupy a less important position, while intelligence takes a higher place; and human intelligence is found to have an element not exercised by the ant, the horse, the dog, the elephant, the ape, or the most advanced of the brute creation.

I am convinced that in many cases the intellectual powers of man and the lower animals are not identical, but simply analogous; that is, they serve the same end, but do not follow the same laws, or rather do not proceed from precisely the same agencies or properties. What I mean will be understood when I refer to the circumstance, familiar to every naturalist, that the wings of a butterfly and the wings of a bird are represented not as the same organs, but as analogous to each other; that is, both serve the same purposes of flight, but have not the same structure. In like manner there is reason to believe that the same ends are accomplished in man and brute by different mental faculties; or rather there is a discerning or rational power in the operation as performed by man, which is not in the act as performed by the inferior creatures. A rat is not apt to be caught a second time in the same trap. The horse in the carriage is ready to start when the door is audibly closed; and Mr. Darwin refers to a case in which it did so when no whipping would make it start. This may seem reasoning, but it is not: it arises merely from the association of ideas, a very inferior intellectual operation to reasoning. I have remarked elsewhere (Laws of Discursive Thought, iii. § 77), "It is ever to be understood that the train of ideas raised by association, while it aids reasoning, and is the means of enabling us to carry on reasoning so rapidly, is not in itself reasoning. Logicians have shown that, in all proper reasoning, the mind has before it three terms, and perceives the relations between them. I believe that much of what is called reasoning in brutes, and even among children, proceeds from mere association. When the burnt child, and, we may add, the burnt dog, dreads the fire, it is from the mere law of co-existence. All their lives men are more or less under the influence of mere association, when we imagine them to be reasoning. They are led not by a concatenated train of discovered relations, but by mere impulse, as is said; that is, by the suggestion which comes up. Hence the mistakes into which they are ever falling, — mistakes not to be referred to the reasoning power. In all judgment, and in reasoning as implying judgment, there is a perception of the relations of the notions to each other; and it is only thus we can reach a sound and safe conclusion." This is an example of what I believe to be very common, — of a higher mental power being involved in an operation performed by man, which, to the superficial observer, may seem the same as an unreasoning act performed by one of the lower animals.

I have doubts whether the lower animals can abstract, whether they can generalize. That they can perceive resemblances and differences, and remember them, and that they associate things by these, I have no doubt; but that they can form general notions, and abstract notions, such as men entertain, — such as all men, even savages, are capable of entertaining, — there is no reason to believe. For what is involved in a general notion, — say in the general notion, man? Not merely that all the beings put into the class resemble each other, but that the beings possess common properties, and that the notion must embrace all the objects possessing the common properties. In an abstract notion it is involved not merely that we image a part after having perceived a whole, but that we regard the part as a part; that we regard rationality as an attribute of man. Such general and abstract notions are intellectual exercises of a high order, and there is no reason to believe that the lower animals are capable of them. Abstraction as every one knows, is involved in arithmetic. Men low in the scale of intelligence can proceed only a very little way in the employment of numbers. Still, with the use of their digits, they can rise to the number five or ten. But there is no reason to believe that the lower animals can make any enumeration. They miss a person usually associated with others now before them; but there is no proof that they can perform, or be taught to perform, as even savages can, such simple operations as addition and subtraction. The school that I am opposing are accustomed to ascribe man's superiority very much to the power of speech. But many of the lower animals have the power of uttering articulate sounds. "Parrots," says Locke, "will be taught to make articulate sounds enough, which yet are by no means capable of language. Besides articulate sounds, therefore, it was further necessary that man should be able to use these sounds as signs of internal conceptions, and to make them stand as marks of the ideas within his mind." This is the defect of the lower animals, lying not in their vocal organs, but in the mental incapacity to form the "internal conceptions" implied in the intelligent use of speech.

Of this I am sure, that the lower animals cannot form those lofty ideas which constitute the peculiarities, the characteristics, of man: the ideas of necessary truth, of moral good and infinity, culminating in the idea of God. I allow that the ideas of this high kind entertained by savages are of a very vague and meagre character. But they are there (see Lecture V.) in their rudiments, and capable of being brought forth and cultivated, and made to go down by the laws of hereditary descent. Here, then, we have an essential distinction between man and the lower animals. There are ideas which all men, and no brutes, are capable of forming.

It has often been remarked that the lower animals, dogs and horses, act as if they had a conscience. But this arises simply from their having the accompaniments of conscience, the feelings which are associated with conscientious convictions in man. Much of what seems conscience originates in the mere associated hope of reward and fear of penalty. There is no ground for believing that any of the lower animals have a sense of good as good, and of binding obligation, or a sense of evil as evil, and as deserving of disapproval.

Mr. Darwin's theory of the origin of our moral ideas is one of the loosest and most unsatisfactory, — altogether one of the weakest ever propounded. It is clear that he is not at home in philosophical and ethical subjects, as he is in questions of natural history. The following is his summary of his ethical theory: "A moral being is one who is capable of comparing his past and future actions and motives, — of approving of some and disapproving of others; and the fact that man is the one being, who, with certainty, can be thus designated, makes the greatest of all distinctions between him and the lower animals. But in our third chapter I have endeavored to show that the moral sense follows, firstly, from the enduring and always present nature of the social instincts, in which respect man agrees with the lower animals; and, secondly, from his mental faculties being highly active, and his impressions of past events extremely vivid, in which respects he differs from the lower animals. Owing to this condition of mind, man cannot avoid looking backwards and comparing the impressions of past events and actions. He also continually looks forward. Hence, after some temporary desire or passion has mastered his social instincts, he will reflect and compare the now weakened impression of such past impulses with the ever present social instinct; and he will then feel that sense of dissatisfaction which all unsatisfied instincts leave behind them. Consequently he resolves to act differently for the future. And this is conscience. Any instinct which is permanently stronger or more enduring than another gives rise to a feeling which we express by saying that it ought to be obeyed. A pointer dog, if able to reflect on his past conduct, would say to himself, I ought (as, indeed, we say of him) to have pointed at that hare, and not have yielded to the passing temptation of hunting it." (Part II. c. xxi.)

There is an immense number of unfilled-up breaks in this process, far more so than even in his genealogy of man. That the lower animals are social beings, and that this arises from social instincts, is admitted. But social feelings are one thing, and a sense of right and wrong another thing, — quite as different as color is from shape or sound. It is the sense of right and wrong that constitutes man a moral and (taken along with free will and intelligence) a responsible being. It is when man has his social and instinctive qualities under subjection to the moral law revealed by conscience that he becomes a virtuous being. But these higher qualities present in man are wanting in the lower animals, which are, in consequence, not moral or accountable beings. It may even be allowed that our moral nature is intimately connected with our social feelings. Most of our moral perceptions rise on the contemplation of social relations, — our relations to our fellow-men and to God. But they spring up in breasts susceptible of them: they would not come forth in a stock or a stone; there is no evidence that they come forth in the souls of animals. There is no doubt that man is more inclined to look back on the past, and reflect upon it, than the lower creatures, which, I suspect, are not much given to musing or moralizing. But it is one thing to look back on the past, and another to regard it as morally good or evil. Man is led to declare that there is a moral law which "ought to be obeyed," that there are instincts which ought to be restrained; but there is no evidence of such a moral decision being come to by the pointer dog, or any other animal. The reference to the pointer is a clear evidence that Mr. Darwin has not so much as weighed what is involved in our moral perceptions, judgments, and sentiments, how much is involved in the idea of right and wrong, of ought, obligation, merit and demerit.

As the general result of this survey, we see that man has ideas involving principles different from any to be found in the lower creatures. The possession of these puts man in an entirely different order from the brutes that perish: they make him a responsible being, and point to and guarantee an immortality. I believe that man so endowed must have come from the Power which created matter at first, and added life as the ages rolled on, and gave the brutes their instincts or incipient intelligence, and crowned his works by creating a moral and responsible being.

More than one half of the "Descent of Man" is occupied with an investigation of Sexual Selection. The discussion of this question must be left to those who have given attention, as Mr. Darwin has done, to the courtship, the propagation, and domestication of animals. Most of what he says has no bearing on the subjects discussed in these Lectures. The views which he presents are always ingenious, but they seem to me to be wire-drawn and overstretched. When animals have a tame, dull hue, it is because they are thereby less exposed to danger than if they had conspicuous colors. If a male has bright colors, it is to attract the female. He adds, however: "We ought to be cautious in concluding that colors which appear to us dull are not attractive to the females of certain species. We should bear in mind such cases as those of the common house-sparrow, in which the male differs much from the female, but does not exhibit any bright tints." Female birds have commonly a duller color, as bright hues would expose them to beasts of prey in hatching. Some males are white, as thereby they are rendered attractive to the females. But in other cases black seems the favorite color. "It seems at first sight a monstrous supposition that the jet blackness of the negro has been gained through sexual selection; but this view is supported by various analogies, and we know that negroes admire their own blackness" (Part II. c. xx.) A law so flexible may be drawn round a great many phenomena, and seem to bind them. I am sure that in the vegetable kingdom (which I have studied more carefully) there is a beauty of flower which cannot have been produced by selection on the part of man, for I have seen it in remote isles of Scotland, and virgin forests of America never trodden by human footsteps; and this in plants which cannot have been aided by beauty-loving insects carrying the pollen. And if there be beauty in the vegetable kingdom independent of creature-selection, there may surely be the same in the animal kingdom. Here, as in so many other cases, his law explains so much, but not the whole. In all these speculations, — for Mr. Darwin acknowledges that his work is highly speculative, — there are laws and operations implied, of which he can give no account on his theory of Natural Selection. Whence the strong impulses of the males, and the coyness of the females, all implied in the laws which he illustrates, that the male needs gay colors and showy forms to attract the female, who does not require these? Whence the love of the beautiful in the female, the love of certain colors and certain forms, an anticipation of the higher æsthetics among cultivated minds? Whence that love of music appearing in birds, and becoming so cultivated and elevating a taste in advanced humanity? In the way in which all these things have appeared, and in the forms which they have taken, and in the mutual adaptations of all things to one another, and to seasons and circumstances, I delight to trace a presiding Intelligence, foreseeing all things from the beginning, and guiding them towards a grand and beneficent end.

Art. III. On Mr. Herbert Spencer's Philosophy.

Mr. Spencer is acknowledged, on all hands, to be a powerful speculative thinker. Give him a set of facts, and he at once proceeds to generalize them, and devise a theory to account for them. He evidently regards it as his function to unify the metaphysics of the day and the grand discoveries lately made in physical science. He is fond of declaring that a number of the great laws announced in our day as the result of a long course of inductive investigation, such as that of the Conservation of Physical Force, can be discovered by *a priori* cogitation. His strength is his weakness. Instead of proceeding, as Bacon recommends, *gradatim* from lower to higher axioms, and only in the end to the highest of all, he mounts at once to the very loftiest generalizations. My friend Hugh Miller said of an author, that in his argument there was an immense number of *fa'en steeks* (fallen stitches): the language might be applied to Mr. Spencer's philosophy. It may be safely said of some of his high speculations, that they will not be either proven or disproven for ages.

1. He proceeds on the philosophy of Sir William Hamilton and Dr. Mansel, maintaining that all our knowledge is Relative; turning the doctrine to a very different purpose from that contemplated by the Edinburgh and Oxford metaphysicians. Hamilton thought that the doctrine of Relativity, with the consequent ignorance of the nature of things, might be applied to humble the pride of the intellect; Mansel used it to undermine religious rationalism; and Spencer employs it, perhaps more logically than either, to show that God, if there be a God, is unknowable. I have been laboring in these Lectures (see IV., V.), and in my works generally (Meth. of Div. Gov., App. VI.; Intuitions, Part III. B. I. c. iii. § 6), to show that the doctrine, as advocated by these metaphysicians, is not a true one; and I am thus prepared to reject that structure which Mr. Spencer would rear upon it. We know self directly in the state in which it is at the time, and not merely in relation to something else declared to be unknown.

2. It follows that there is nothing inconceivable or contradictory, as the school maintains that there is, in such ideas as Self-Existence and First Cause. We know ourselves as existing, and can thence conceive of others, of God, as existing. We certainly do not know ourselves as self-existing, because we dis-

cover that we are caused; but we can conceive — I mean, think and believe — that God, while he exists, is uncaused. I believe that all causation carries us to a substance with powers. The substances we see on earth are evidently derived; but, as we mount up, we come to an underived substance, — and this without falling even into an apparent contradiction. The whole of these alleged contradictions, so much dwelt on by Hamilton in his "Discussions," and Mansel in his "Bampton Lectures," and Spencer in the opening of his "First Principles," are contradictions simply in the propositions of the metaphysicians, and not at all in the actual laws or beliefs of the human mind.

3. It may be doubted whether he is entitled to say that there is an unknown reality beyond the known phenomena. I have referred to this in Lecture VI. I must leave the farther discussion of it to his school, some of whom will deny that he can on his principles know so certainly that there is an unknown.

4. I have shown, in the same Lecture, that the fundamental verities in the mind, properly interpreted, lead us to a God so far known. He talks of our knowing certain things, and says (First Prin. p. 143), "All things known to us are manifestations of the unknowable;" and (p. 170) that force is "a certain conditioned effect of unconditioned cause;" and (p. 165) "our conception of space is produced by some mode of the unknowable;" and he speaks (p. 168) of "the unknown cause which produces in us the effects called Matter, Space, Time, and Motion." I hold that a cause thus known is so far known.

5. He utterly fails to account on his principles, though he seems to be doing so, for some of the most certain of known phenomena, such as Sensation, Nervous Action, Life, and Consciousness.

Sensation. — Among all the laws mentioned by him, such as the Persistence of Force, Instability of the Homogeneous, no one is in the least degree fitted to produce this common phenomenon, experienced by all of us, in the shape of pleasure and pain. This is one of the most patent of the gaps in his system.

Nervous Action. — He tells us (First Prin. p. 476) that, through the "continuous sorting and grouping together of changes or motions which constitutes nervous function, there is gradually wrought that sorting and grouping together of matter which constitutes nervous structure." Here, as in so many other cases, he misses the differentia of what he would explain. There are everywhere instances of "continuous sorting and grouping together of changes or motions," — we have it, I believe, in the molecular motion of every body, — without those peculiar operations found in the nerves, sensor or motor, afferent or efferent.

Life. — He tells us (Biology, vol. i. pp. 1–3) that organic bodies are composed mainly of ultimate units, having extreme mobility. Three of the elements, oxygen, hydrogen, and nitrogen, are known only in the aëriform state, and defy all efforts to liquefy them. Three of them again, hydrogen, carbon, and nitrogen, have affinities that are narrow in their range and low in their intensity; while oxygen displays a very high chemical energy. Thus these two extreme contrasts — the one between physical mobilities, the other between chemical activities — fulfil, in the highest degree, a certain farther condition of facility of differentiation and integration. He discovers — and I believe he is right — a significance in this. It is part of the means by which organisms fulfil their functions, specially the phenomena of evolution. But while such properties are conditions which enable life to work, they certainly do not constitute life,— still less are they fitted to produce the beauteous and bounteous forms of life which we see around us: they might have been wasted quite as readily in producing ugly or useless products.

Many attempts have been made to define "Life," to show what it consists in. Most of these have been unsuccessful; but the most unsuccessful of them all is Mr. Spencer's. I quote his own account of his efforts, given in his "Psychology," Part III. c. i.: "In Part I. c. iv. of the 'Principles of Biology,' the proximate idea we arrived at was, that Life is 'the definite combination of heterogeneous changes, both simultaneous and successive.' In the next chapter, it was shown that, to develop this proximate idea into a complete idea, it is needful to recognize the connection between these actions going on within an organism, and the actions going on without it. We saw that life is adequately conceived only when we think of it as 'the definite combination of heterogeneous changes, both simultaneous and successive, in correspondences with external co-existences and sequences.' Afterwards, this definition was found to be reducible to the briefer definition. 'The continuous adjustment of internal relations to external relations;' and though, by leaving out the characteristic of heterogeneity, this definition is rendered somewhat too wide, so that it includes a few non-vital phenomena which stimulate vitality, yet practically no error is likely to result from its use." The definition would apply to the appearance of meteors within our atmosphere in autumn, to the simultaneous springing of buds, or the arrival of migrating birds, in spring, to the issuing of bees from the hive when it swarms, or even to the arrival of the elected of the people to the House of Commons in London, or the House of Representatives in Washington. The last form of the definition would apply to a man putting on his clothes and keeping them clean, or the housewife suiting her dwelling to its surroundings. In all of them the essential element of life is omitted; and, in accounting for the things he has defined, he has not accounted for life.

Consciousness.—Still less among all his laws, which are, after all, mere generalized facts of physical nature, has he any means of producing knowledge,—the knowledge which the mind takes of things without it, and of itself and its own operations. Because force persists, it does not follow that we should come to know force, or power, or goodness. If he attribute these, as I believe he does, to a cause beyond sensible phenomena, I agree with him; but then the power which did this is so far known to us.

Intelligence.—In "Psychology," Part III. c. ix., he says that every act of intelligence is "in essence an adjustment of inner to outer relations." Surely the very "essence" of intelligence is lost sight of in such a definition. It is still more vague and unsatisfactory than his definition of Life. It would apply to the adjustment of a letter to its envelope, of a picture to its frame, of a jewel to its casket, of a tree to the climate. In Part IV. c. vi., he says, "Each act of recollection is the establishment of an inner relation, answering to some outer relation." When I recollect that at a certain time I was happy, and at another time I was unhappy, I discover some inner, but I see no outer relations.

6. He cannot account for our higher ideas, such as those of Power and Moral Good. He says (First Prin. p. 22) "that the disciples of Kant and those of Locke have both their views recognized in the theory that organized experiences produce forms of thought." Now I admit that experiences may come to descend in the shape of tendencies, — tendencies to act in a particular way; as, for example, in a disposition to hoard or to spend, to show cunning or courage. But there is no evidence that they can produce what is meant by a "form of thought;" but which might better be denominated a first truth, or first principle, or a fundamental law of belief. First, there is no proof that the brutes have any of those forms of thought which higher metaphysicians discover in man, — as the necessary conviction that every event must have a cause, and the ethical principle that good is meritorious and rewardable, and that sin is of evil desert and punishable. The lower animals nowhere appear with these forms of thought, and man is found everywhere with them. Any tendencies which man may acquire by organized experiences are not of the nature of a fundamental law of thought, belief, or judgment. They are rather tastes and predilections, or tribal and national characteristics, acquired in the first instance by individuals, and going down from one generation to another. They have no reference to beliefs or truths, but are mere inclinations seeking gratification and impelling to action. They do not carry with them self-evidence or necessity of thought. Whereas the forms of thought, in the philosophic use of the term, carry with them their own evidence; are common to all men, are catholic or universal; are found working in children as well as among persons arrived at mature life, among savages as well as civilized men. It is scarcely necessary to explain that, in adult and civilized life, they have higher applications than among children or barbarians; but they are ever operating in the one class as in the other.

7. He places very heterogeneous objects and operations in his wide generalizations. To mention only a few: He is speaking (First Prin., Part II. c. viii.) of the Transformation and Equiva-

lence of Forces, meaning Physical Forces; and he passes on, as if they were the same, to Mental and Moral and Social Forces, which are regulated by mental laws and by motives. He tells us that "a small society, no matter how superior the character of its members, cannot exhibit the same quantity of social action as a large one." As if the Jews, the Athenians, the Dutch, the Scotch, the Puritans, though comparatively small peoples, had not exerted a very powerful social influence. Then he shows, as if it were all done by an accumulation of physical force, that, when there is an unusually abundant harvest, capital seeks investment, labor is expended, and new channels of commerce are opened, while there are more marriages and an increase of population.

In c. ix. he is speaking of the Direction of Motion, and assures us that "volition is itself an incipient discharge along a line which previous experiences have rendered a line of least resistance; and the passing of volition into action is simply a completion of the discharge;" and he goes on to explain, in the same way, a great number of social phenomena, such as "the flow of capital into business yielding the largest returns." That there may be no misapprehension, he says: "By some it may be said that the term force, as here used, is used metaphorically, — that to speak of men as *impelled* in certain directions, by certain desires, is a figure of speech, and not the statement of a physical fact. The reply is, that the foregoing illustrations are to be interpreted literally, and that the processes described are physical ones."

In c. xxi. his subject is Segregation; and he is showing how, in physical operation, there is an advance from the indefinite to the definite, and then accounts on this principle for the separation of races. "Human motions, like all other motions, being determined by the distribution of forces, it follows that such segregations of races as are not produced by incident external forces are produced by forces which the units of the races exercise on each other."

It is by such loose analogies, represented as identities, that he is able so easily to account for the production of the universe by a few wide laws.

8. In his construction of the universe, he fails to discover the need of adjustments, in order that the forces may accomplish beneficent ends. He seems to derive every thing from what he calls the "Persistence of Force," which is the name he adopts to express what is usually called the Conservation of Force; that is, the sum of force in the universe, potential and actual, is one and the same, and when a force disappears in one form, it must appear in another. But every one sees that, but for a regulated channel provided for it, blind force might operate in destructive quite as readily as beneficent modes. The same remark holds good of such laws as that a body follows the path of "Least Resistance," — that is, in which there is least opposing force; the Instability of the Homogeneous, — that is, with the varied operating forces, bodies are not likely to continue in a state of rest; the Rhythm of Motion, — that is, that many bodies liable to be driven or pulled in a number of ways will proceed in curves of various kinds. He shows that from the forces operating there must be such operations, as Segregation, Equilibration, Dissolution. But all these, but for adjustments, are as capable of producing wasting as construction and benignity. That they are made to work as they do, I believe Mr. Spencer would ascribe to the action of the unknown reality. But when I see order, harmony, and happiness everywhere in nature, I argue the reality from which it proceeds must possess wisdom and beneficence.

Cambridge: Press of John Wilson & Son.

UNION THEOLOGICAL SEMINARY,

New York.

THE ELY LECTURESHIP

ON

The Evidences of Christianity.

SECOND SERIES.

BY JAMES McCOSH, D.D., LL.D.

WORKS BY DR. McCOSH

I.

THE METHOD OF THE DIVINE GOVERNMENT, Physical and Moral. 8vo. $2.50.

"It is refreshing to read a work so distinguished for originality and soundness of thinking, especially as coming from an author of our own country." — *Sir William Hamilton.*

"This work is distinguished from other similar ones by its being based upon a thorough study of physical science, and an accurate knowledge of its present condition, and by its entering in a deeper and more unfettered manner than its predecessors upon the discussion of the appropriate psychological, ethical, and theological questions. The author keeps aloof at once from the *a priori* idealism and dreaminess of German speculation since Schelling, and from the one-sidedness and narrowness of the empiricism and positivism which have so prevailed in England. In the provinces of psychology and ethics he follows conscientiously the facts of consciousness, and draws his conclusions of them commonly with penetration and logical certainty." — *Dr. Ulrici, in Zeitschrift für Philosophie.*

II.

TYPICAL FORMS AND SPECIAL ENDS IN CREATION. By James McCosh, LL.D., and Dr. Dickie. 8vo. $2.50.

"It is alike comprehensive in its range, accurate and minute in its details, original in its structure, and devout and spirited in its tone and tendency. It illustrates and carries out the great principle of analogy in the Divine plans and works, far more minutely and satisfactorily than it has been done before; and while it presents the results of the most profound scientific research, it presents them in their higher and spiritual relations." — *Argus.*

III.

THE INTUITIONS OF THE MIND. New and Improved edition. 8vo. $3.00.

"No philosopher, before Dr. McCosh, has clearly brought out the stages by which an original and individual intuition passes first into an articulate but still individual judgment, and then into a universal maxim or principle; and no one has so clearly or completely classified and enumerated our intuitive convictions, or exhibited in detail their relations to the various sciences which repose on them as their foundations The amount of summarized information which it contains is very great; and it is the only work on the very important subject with which it deals. Never was such a work so much needed as in the present day. It is the only scientific work adapted to counteract the school of Mill, Bain, and Herbert Spencer, which is so steadily prevailing among the students of the present generation." — *London Quarterly Review, April* 1865.

IV.

A DEFENCE OF FUNDAMENTAL TRUTH.

Being an Examination of Mr. J. S. MILL's Philosophy. 8vo. $3.00.

"The spirit of these discussions is admirable. Fearless and courteous, McCosh never hesitates to bestow praise when merited, nor to attack a heresy wherever found." — *Cong. Review.*

V.

ACADEMIC TEACHING IN EUROPE: Being

Dr. McCOSH's Address at his Inauguration as President of the College of New Jersey. 50 cents.

VI.

LAWS OF DISCURSIVE THOUGHT: Being a

Text-book of Formal Logic. 12mo. $1.50.

"The position from which Dr. McCosh was called to America was the professorship of Logic and Metaphysics in Queen's College, Belfast; and this volume of two hundred pages is the fruit of his study and experience in the department of logic. It is therefore a condensed but exhaustive exhibition of the principles of the science which he has more thoroughly mastered than perhaps any other living man. He has made that careful inductive investigation of the operations of the human mind which is essential to the constitution of the science, and freely avowing his regard for the old logic, which no modern improvements have overthrown, he is fully in harmony with whatever the greatest thinkers of subsequent ages, even of our own times, have contributed to the subject. The book is admirably adapted to the use of classes in schools and colleges, where it will readily and rapidly find its way." — *N. Y. Observer.*

VII.

CHRISTIANITY AND POSITIVISM. A Series of

Lectures to the Times on Natural Theology and Apologetics. 12mo. $1.75.

ROBERT CARTER AND BROTHERS,

New York.

CPSIA information can be obtained
at www.ICGtesting.com
Printed in the USA
LVHW030120210323
742063LV00002B/460

9 783382 126209